EVENING IS THE
WHOLE DAY

EVENING IS THE
WHOLE DAY

Preeta Samarasan

HOUGHTON MIFFLIN COMPANY
Boston · New York
2008

Library of Congress Cataloguing-in-Publication Data
Samarasan, Preeta.
Evening is the whole day / Preeta Samarasan.
p. cm.
ISBN-13: 978-0-618-87447-7
ISBN-10: 0-618-87447-X
1. East Indians—Malaysia—Fiction. 2. Immigrants—Malaysia—Fiction.
3. Upper class families—Fiction. 4. Malaysia—Fiction. I. Title.
PR9530.9.S26E94 2008
813'.6—dc22   2008004729

Book design by Melissa Lotfy

Printed in the United States of America

QUM 10 9 8 7 6 5 4 3 2 1

The author is grateful for permission to quote from the following:
"Sparrow" by Paul Simon. Copyright © 1963 Paul Simon. Used by
permission of the Publisher: Paul Simon Music.
"Cecilia" by Paul Simon. Copyright © 1969 Paul Simon. Used by permission of the Publisher: Paul Simon Music.
"The Sun Is Burning." Words and music by Ian Campbell. Copyright
© 1964 (Renewed), 1965 (Renewed) TRO Essex Music Ltd., London, England. TRO–Essex Music, Inc., controls all publication rights for the USA
and Canada. Used by permission.
"Mera Juta Hai Japani," by Shailendra Singh. Copyright © 1955 by
Saregama India Ltd. All rights reserved. Used by permission.
"Darling Darling Darling" by Ilaiyaraja. Used by permission of the Indian Record Mfg. Co. Ltd.

For Mom, Pop, and my brothers,
who taught me that words matter

History begins only at the point where things go wrong; history is born only with trouble, with perplexity, with regret. So that hard on the heels of the word Why comes the sly and wistful word If. If it had not been for . . . If only . . . Were it not . . . Those useless Ifs of history. And, constantly impeding, deflecting, distracting the backward searchings of the question why, exists this other form of retrogression: If only we could have it back. A New Beginning. If only we could return . . .

— from *Waterland* by Graham Swift

The sun goes down and the sky reddens, pain grows sharp,
light dwindles. Then is evening
when jasmine flowers open, the deluded say.
But evening is the great brightening dawn
when crested cocks crow all through the tall city
and evening is the whole day
for those without their lovers.

— Kuruntokai 234, translated by George L. Hart

CONTENTS

EVENING IS THE
WHOLE DAY

1

THE IGNOMINIOUS DEPARTURE
OF CHELLAMSERVANT
DAUGHTER‑OF‑MUNIANDY

September 6, 1980

THERE IS, stretching delicate as a bird's head from the thin neck of the Kra Isthmus, a land that makes up half of the country called Malaysia. Where it dips its beak into the South China Sea, Singapore hovers like a bubble escaped from its throat. This bird's head is a springless summerless autumnless winterless land. One day might be a drop wetter or a mite drier than the last, but almost all are hot, damp, bright, bursting with lazy tropical life, conducive to endless tea breaks and mad, jostling, honking rushes through town to get home before the afternoon downpour. These are the most familiar rains, the violent silver ropes that flood the playing fields and force office workers to wade to bus stops in shoes that fill like buckets. Blustering and melodramatic, the afternoon rains cause traffic jams at once terrible — choked with the black smoke of lorries and the screeching brakes of schoolbuses — and beautiful: aglow with winding lines of watery yellow headlights that go on forever, with blue streetlamps reflected in burgeoning puddles, with the fluorescent melancholy of empty roadside stalls. Every day appears to begin with a blaze and end with this deluge, so that past and present and future run together in an infinite, steaming river.

In truth, though, there are days that do not blaze and rains less fierce. Under a certain kind of mild morning drizzle the very earth breathes slow and deep. Mist rises from the dark treetops on the limestone hills outside Ipoh town. Grey mist, glowing green hills: on such mornings it is obvious how sharply parts of this land must have reminded the old British rulers of their faraway country.

To the north of Ipoh, clinging to the outermost hem of the town's not-so-voluminous outskirts, is Kingfisher Lane, a long, narrow line from the "main" road (one corner shop, one bus stop, occasional lorries) to the limestone hills (ancient, inscrutable, riddled with caves and illegal cave dwellers). Here the town's languid throng feels distant even on hot afternoons; on drizzly mornings like this one it is absurd, improbable. The smoke from the cement factories and the sharp odors of the pork van and the fish vendor are washed away before they can settle, but the moist air traps native sounds and smells: the staticky songs of one neighbor's radio, the generous sweet spices of another's simmering mutton curry. The valley feels cloistered and coddled. A quiet benevolence cups the morning in its palm.

In 1980 the era of sale-by-floorplan and overnight housing developments is well under way, but the houses on Kingfisher Lane do not match one another. Some are wide and airy, with verandas in the old Malay fashion. A few weakly evoke the splendor of Chinese towkays' Penang mansions with gate-flanking dragons and red-and-gold trim. Most sit close to the lane, but one or two are set farther back, at the ends of gravel driveways. About halfway down the lane, shielded by its black gates and its robust greenery, is the Big House, number 79, whose bright blue bulk has dominated Kingfisher Lane since it was an unpaved track with nothing else along it but saga trees. Though termites will be discovered, in a few weeks, to have been secretly devouring its foundation for years (and workmen will be summoned to an urgent rescue mission), the Big House stands proud. It has presided over the laying of all the others' foundations. It has witnessed their slow aging, their repaintings and renovations. Departures, deaths, arrivals.

This morning, after only a year at the Big House, Chellam the no-longer-new-servant is leaving. Four people strain to believe that the fresh weather augurs not only neat closure, but a new beginning. Clean slates and cleaner consciences. Surely nothing undertaken today will come to a bad end; surely all's well with the world.

Chellam is eighteen years old, the same age as Uma, the oldest-eldest daughter of the house. Only one week ago today, Uma boarded a Malaysian Airline System aeroplane bound for New York America USA, where it is now autumn. Also known as *fall* in America. She left behind her parents, her eleven-year-old brother Suresh, and little Aasha, only six, whose heart cracked and cried out in protest. Today the four of them thirstily drink the morning's grey damp to soothe their various doubts about the future.

The aeroplane that carried Uma away was enormous and white, with a moonkite on its tail, whereas Chellam is leaving on foot (and then by bus).

She differs from Uma in many other, equally obvious, ways. A growth spurt squandered eating boiled white rice sprinkled — on good days — with salt has left her a full head shorter than Uma; her calves are as thin as chicken wings and her skin is pockmarked from the crawling childhood diseases her late mother medicated with leafy pastes and still-warm piss furtively collected in a tin pail as it streamed from the neighbors' cow. Severe myopia has crumpled her face into a permanent squint, and her shoulders are as narrow as the acute triangle of her world: at one corner the toddy shop from which she dragged her drunken father home nightly as a child; at another the dim, sordid alley in which she stood with other little girls, their eyelids dark with kajal, their toenails bright with Cutex, waiting to be picked up by a lorry driver or a bottle-shop man so that they could earn their two ringgit. At the third and final corner stands Ipoh, the town to which she was brought by some bustling, self-righteous Hindu Sangam society matron eager to rack up good karma by plucking her from prostitution and selling her into a slavery far less white; Ipoh, where, after two-three years (no one could say exactly) of working for friends of Uma's parents, Chellam was handed down to the Big House. "We got her used," Suresh had said with a smirk (dodging his Amma's mouthslap, which had been offhand at best, since Chellam hadn't been there to take offense).

And today they're sending her back. Not just to the Dwivedis', but all the way back. Uma's Appa ordered Chellam's Appa to collect her today; neither of them could have predicted the inconvenient drizzle. Father to father, (rich) man to (poor) man, they have agreed that Chellam will be ready at such-and-such a time to be met by her Appa and led from the Big House all the way up the unpaved, rock-and-clay length of Kingfisher Lane to the bus stop on the main road, and from there onto the bus to Gopeng, and from the Gopeng bus station down more roads and more lanes until she arrives back at square minus one, the one-room hut in the red-earth village whence she emerged just a few years ago.

A year from today, Chellam will be dead. Her father will say she committed suicide after a failed love affair. The villagers will say he beat her to death for bringing shame to her family. Chellam herself will say nothing. She will have cried so much by then that the children will have nicknamed her Filthyface for her permanent tear stains. All the women of the village won't be able to wash those stains off her cold face, and when they cremate her, the air will smell salty from all those tears.

At twenty to ten on this September Saturday morning, she begins to drag her empty suitcase down the stairs from the storeroom where it has lived since she came a year ago. "How long ago did your Appa tell her to start packing?" Amma mutters. "Didn't we give her a month's notice? So much time she had, and now she's bringing her bag down to start!"

But Chellam's suitcase, unlike Uma's, could never have taken a month to pack. Uma had been made to find space for all these: brand-new wool sweaters, panties with the price tags still on, blazers for formal occasions, authentic Malaysian souvenirs for yet-unmade friends, batik sarongs and coffee-table books with which to show off her culture, framed family portraits taken at Ipoh's top studio, extra film for a latest-model camera. Chellam owns, not including what she's wearing today, a single chiffon saree, three T-shirts (one free with Horlicks, one free with Milo; one a hand-me-down from Mr. Dwivedi, her old boss), four long-sleeved men's shirts (all hand-me-downs from Appa), three cotton skirts with frayed hems, one going-out blouse, and one shiny polyester skirt unsuitable for housework because it sticks to her thighs when she sweats. She also has four posters that came free with copies of *Movieland* magazine, but has neither the strength nor the will to take them down. Where she's going, she won't have a place to put them. All in all, it will therefore take her three minutes flat to pack, but even her mostly empty suitcase will be a strain for her weak arms only made weaker by her lack of appetite over the past few months.

Amma will not offer Chellam tea coffee sofdrink before she goes, though she and Suresh and Aasha are just sitting down to their ten o'clock tea, and though one mug of tea sits cooling untouched on the red Formica table as Appa stands at the gate under his enormous black umbrella, speaking with Chellam's father. There wouldn't be time for Chellam to drink anything anyway. There's only one afternoon bus from Gopeng to the bus stop half a mile from their village, and if she and her father miss the eleven o'clock bus to Gopeng, they'll miss that connecting bus and have to walk all the way to their village, pulling the suitcase along behind them on its three working wheels. Chellam will probably have to do most of the pulling, and hold her father by the elbow besides, because he is drunk as usual.

Thud thud thud goes her suitcase down the stairs, its broken wheel bent under it like a sick bird's claw. The suitcase has done nothing but sit empty in the storeroom all year, but its straps and buckles have worn themselves out and it seems now to be held shut only by several long lengths of synthetic pink raffia wound and knotted around it to keep the geckos and cockroaches out. On the uncarpeted landing the sharp edge of the broken wheel scrapes loudly against the floor. Amma flinches and shudders. "Look, look," she whispers urgently to Suresh and Aasha without taking her eyes off Chellam. "Purposely she's doing it. *She* is taking revenge on *us* it seems. For sending her home. As if after all she's done we're supposed to keep her here and feed her it seems."

Suresh and Aasha, wide-eyed, say nothing.

In the past two weeks the many burdens they must share but never discuss have multiplied, and among them is this suddenly effusive, outward-turned Amma who whispers and nudges, who coaxes and threatens, who leans towards them with her face contorted like a villain in an old Tamil movie, desperate for a reaction. It's as if the events of the past two weeks have dissolved the last of her reserve. This is the final victory towards which she's been privately ascending during all those long days of dead silence and tea left to cool, though precisely what the victory is neither Suresh nor Aasha is completely sure. They're sure only that whatever it is, it has come at too high a price.

Mildly discouraged by the children's unresponsiveness, Amma takes a small, exacting sip of her tea. "Chhi! Too much sugar I put," she remarks conversationally.

"For all we know," Amma says, newly galvanized by her too-sweet tea, perhaps, or the mulishness of her children's ears and brows, or the hesitation of Chellam and her empty suitcase on each separate stair, "she's pregnant."

The word, so raw they can almost smell it, contorts Amma's mouth, offering the children an unaccustomed view of her teeth. It makes Suresh drop his eyelids and retreat into the complex patterns he's spent his young life finding in the tabletop Formica. Men in bearskins. Trees with faces. Hook-nosed monks.

"On top of everything she has taken all that raffia from the storeroom without even asking," Amma observes with a sigh and a long, loud slurp of her tea. Even this is out of character: Amma usually drinks her tea in small, silent sips, her lips barely parting at the rim of her mug.

For her journey home, Chellam has dressed herself in a striped men's shirt with a stiff collar and a brown nylon skirt with a zipper in the back. The shirt is a hand-me-down from Appa. The skirt isn't. "Look at her," Amma says again through a mouthful of Marie biscuit, this time to no one in particular. "Just look at her. Dares to wear the shirt I gave her after all the havoc she's caused. Vekkum illai these people. No bloody shame. Month after month I packed up and gave her your Appa's shirts. Courthouse shirts, man, Arrow brand, nice soft cotton, all new-new. In which other house servants wear that type of quality clothes?"

In no other house, thinks Suresh. There aren't any other houses, at least on Kingfisher Lane, staffed with scrawny servant girls dressed in oversized hundred-percent cotton courthouse shirts. If they'd saved Appa's ties they could've had her wear those as well. And a bowler hat and gloves. Then they could've had her answer the door like a butler.

"Hmph," Amma snorts into her teacup, "here I was trying to help her out, giving her clothes and telling her she could save her money for more useful things."

Financial counseling and free shirts: a special Big House–only package deal. It had filled Amma with purpose and consequence, and had indeed impelled Chellam to try to save her money for More Useful Things. That is, until she realized that her father would turn up month after month to collect her wages on payday at the Big House, and that she was therefore saving her money for his daily toddies and samsus. For the back-street arrack that gave him the vision and vigor to beat his wife and children at home, and the cloudy rice wine the toddy shop owner made in a bathroom basin. Still, if you asked Chellam's father (or the toddy shop owner), these were all Useful Things.

"In the end look what she's done with my charity and my advice,"

Amma says, wrapping up her tale with a jerk of the head towards the staircase. "She's taken them and thrown both one shot in my face. Just wait, one by one the others also will be doing the same thing. Why not? After seeing her example they'll also become just as bold. Vellamma can murder me, Letchumi can murder Appa, Mat Din can burn the house down, and Lourdesmary can stand and clap. Happily ever after."

Aasha and Suresh silently note that they themselves are absent from this macabre prophecy. If Amma's words can be taken at face value, the long fingers of fate will clutch at Suresh and Aasha but miss; for this they should probably feel lucky.

But they don't.

Suresh is grateful only that Chellam doesn't understand much English and is slightly hard of hearing (from all the clips her father's fists, heavy with toddy and samsu, visited upon her ears in childhood). He notes that for some reason she's left her suitcase leaning against the banister and hurried back upstairs. *He* isn't going to point this out to Amma.

Aasha rocks back and forth in her chair so that her stretched-out toes, on every forward rocking, brush against Suresh's knees under the table. It makes her feel better that he has knees, even if Uma has disappeared forever and Amma has been strangely transformed. He has knees. And again he has knees. Each time he has knees.

Behind Amma something stirs the curtains. Not wind, it's not that sort of movement — not a gentle billowing, not a filling and unfilling with air, but a sudden jerk, as if someone's hiding behind them, and sure enough, when Aasha checks she sees that her grandmother's transparent ghost feet are peeking out from under the curtains, the broad toes she knows so well curling upward on the cool marble. So. Paati is back again, two weeks after her death, and for the very first time since her rattan chair was burned in the backyard. She's not so easily scared off, is she? While everyone else is otherwise preoccupied, Paati's hand darts out from behind the curtains, helps itself to a stray Marie biscuit crumb on the table beside Suresh's plate, and slips back to its hiding place. And how would the others explain *that?* wonders Aasha in high dudgeon. What would they say, the faithless, doubting blind, who have stubbornly resisted the idea of Paati's continued presence, and rolled their eyes at Aasha whenever she has tried to convey to them the needs and fears of Mr. McDougall's daughter, the Big

House's original ghost and the one who has stuck by Aasha through all her losses and longings? No such thing as ghosts, they've scoffed (all except for Chellam, but other shortcomings mar her record). Now Aasha laps up this moment thirstily, thinks a flurry of I-told-you-so's to herself.

Standing across from each other on either side of the gate, Appa and Chellam's father are reflected in the glass panel of the open front door. Insider and outsider, bigshot lawyer and full-of-snot laborer, toothful and toothless. Chellam's father's dirty white singlet is spattered with rain; Appa holds his umbrella perfectly erect above his impeccably slicked-and-styled hair.

"*Tsk*," Amma says, leaning forward to peer at the glass panel, "your father's tea will be ice cold by the time he comes in. That man is a pain in the neck, I tell you. Normal people will know, isn't it, okay, my daughter has caused so much trouble, better I shut up and go away quietly? But not him. No bloody shame." She takes a biscuit from the biscuit plate. "Of course," she says, and here she shifts her gaze from the glass panel back to the children, looking from one to the other, raising her eyebrows to impart to them the full extent of her inside knowledge, "if you want to talk about shameless men—"

Suresh pulls the biscuit plate towards himself, loudly grating its bottom against the table. "Only Marie biscuits?" he says plaintively. "No more chocolate wafers?"

Amma pauses with her own biscuit halfway to her mouth. She smiles knowingly, leans her head back, exhales, but Suresh, oh brave soldier sister-savior Suresh, does not yield. He holds her gaze, and wordlessly they do battle. For five terrible seconds she sweeps her searchlight eyes over Suresh's face.

"No," says Amma finally, "no more chocolate wafers." Her eyes are still restless. "I'll have to send Mat Din to the shop."

"And Nutella," says Suresh quickly, seizing the advantage. "Marie biscuits are much nicer with Nutella."

"We'll have to make a list," says Amma. "Nutella also finished."

Aasha lets go of the edge of her chair and slips her hands under her bottom on the seat. Under the chair she swings her legs. They will make a list. Tomorrow or next week Amma will give it to Mat Din the driver along with ten ringgit for petrol. He will take the list to a provision shop in town and come back with a carful of groceries: chocolate wafers, Nutella, rice, mustard seeds, star anise for mutton curry, tinned corn and peas to go with chicken chops. Lourdes-mary the cook will put everything away, grumbling about the papaya seeds masquerading among the peppercorns and the staleness of the star anise. And life will go on as it did before Chellam ever arrived, or even better, except there'll be new ghosts in the house: the ghost of dead Paati, growing younger and older and younger again, wrinkles melting into dimples and dimples into hollows, now a toddler, now a bride, now an old lady with a back as curved as a coconut shell; the ghost of Uma Past, suspended in time and forever eighteen years old; and far more terrible than the others, though Aasha doesn't know it yet, will be the ghost of Chellam Future, her eyes wild as she screams to them from her funeral pyre, the ends of her hair already aflame, whole bitter planets orbiting at the back of her gaping mouth.

The two voices at the gate drone on and on. The wheedling dances sorrowfully around the weary voice, now grabbing at it, now stroking it, now tying it lovingly in knots as it falls lower and lower, so low they have to strain to hear it under the gentle fingerwork of raindrops on the metal awning, the whir of the ceiling fan, and the buzzing of a fly that has just entered the dining room. In the glass panel of the front door Amma sees Chellam's father shake his head and wring his wrists like a woman. Then he wipes his cheeks with the heels of his hands, one after the other. He whimpers and moans, and his tremulous voice breaks and bubbles with drink and phlegm. Appa watches wordlessly. From the way he holds his shoulders under his umbrella Suresh can tell that he's waiting for Chellam's father to ask him for something. At best, more tea or a slice of plain bread. At worst, fifty ringgit. Or twenty. Or even two—just enough, he liked to say (as a glorious, con-science-pricking coup before he was given the fifty ringgit he knew he'd get every time), for a handful of amaranth leaves from his neigh-bor's tree to go with his children's lunchtime rice. But this time Chel-lam's father doesn't ask for any of these things; he grovels on behalf of his daughter, who hasn't the shame to do it herself. Useless girl, saar, he says. I should've drowned her when she was born. Appa's shoulders remain stiffly squared two inches below his ears.

Chellam is huffing and puffing once again, dragging her suitcase through the house's endless, haphazard corridors. "Eh! What is this?" Amma whispers, low, urgent, her eyes darting around the room as if the confirmation of her suspicions might lie behind a painting or in-side an urn. "Why she took so long to come down the stairs? Halfway

{9}

down she must've gone back up, you see! And what was she doing up there all this time? Very funny. Very strange."

In the evening Amma will find two ringgit missing from the glass bowl in which she keeps change for the roti man and the newspaper man, and Chellam will be accused in her absence of one last crime, pettier perhaps than the one for which she has been expelled from the Big House, but more shameless given everything that has transpired. Insult to injury, salt to an open wound, another inch taken from the yard of mercy they've already given her. Accused she will remain, until one night Appa happens to mention that the Volvo has been looking quite nice since he gave Mat Din two ringgit from the glass bowl to polish and wax it. (In fact, Chellam went back upstairs in a mostly futile attempt to impose some order on a storeroom thrown into disarray by the hasty extrication of her suitcase from under a pile of old newspapers.)

In the distance, Chellam's suitcase slides and grates on the marble floor, and Chellam herself wheezes and sniffs from the cold that never seems to leave her. Across the dining room she shambles, and into her room under the stairs, where her clothes lie in a heap on her unmade bed. From the walls Kamal Hassan, Jayasudha, Sridevi, and Rajnikanth eye her glossily: Chellam, Chellam, they chide her, all the months you gazed at us while trying to fall asleep, at our forelocks and our nose-rings and our flared nostrils, and today you ignore us like this? But Chellam's mind is elsewhere this morning, and besides, squatting over her suitcase, she's much too far away from their film-star faces to see anything more than the blur of their uniformly wheatish complexions. The suitcase lid swooshes as she drops it and then presses down on it to retie the raffia. She turns the suitcase around and around, pulling the raffia so hard the fibers leave red welts on her palms. She drags the suitcase the few remaining yards to the front door, rubbing her nose with an index finger.

"Chhi!" Amma says, the syllable exploding directly into her mug of tea. "Can't even be bothered to find a tissue! If she'd listened to your Appa and started packing nicely one month ago she wouldn't be in such a mess now, all kacan-mucan running here running there and sniffing and gasping all over the place, isn't it?"

The sniffing, the wheezing, the scraping, and the grating grow fainter and fainter.

Good riddance to bad rubbish, Paati mouths behind the curtain.

Aasha manages to read her lips through the fabric, thanks only to a superhuman feat of concentration.

Through the window on the other side of the dining room, Chellam finally appears in the garden. Aasha and Suresh can see her, but Amma can't. Her determined suitcase-dragging has worked the zipper on her skirt slowly around to her left hip. Her collar has twisted itself to one side, and a button has come undone at her waist. An inch of her stomach shows through the gap, creamy brown, lighter than the rest of her, perhaps pregnant, perhaps not. Unaware she's being watched, she leans her suitcase against the ornamental swing and tugs at her waistband to bring the zipper round to the back again. She buttons the undone button, straightens her collar, and smoothes her frizzy hair. Then, with great difficulty, she drags her suitcase out to the gate, picking it up and kicking it weakly every time a bit of gravel gets caught in its wheels.

"Shall we go, Appa?" she says to her father in Tamil. She doesn't look at Aasha and Suresh's Appa.

He doesn't look at her, either. With his long tongue he worries a desiccated coconut fiber that's been stuck between his molars since lunch. He looks at the ground and scratches his left ankle with the toe of his right slipper, still holding his umbrella perfectly erect.

Chellam's father delivers a quick, blunt blow to the side of her head. "Taking ten years to come with her suitcase," he grunts to Appa. "God knows what she was doing inside there for so long. Bloody useless daughter I have, lawyer saar," he continues, revving up his engine, "you alone know how much shame she has brought upon me, you alone know what a burden a daughter like this can be." He looks from his daughter to Appa and from Appa to his daughter. He hawks and spits into the monsoon drain, and his spittle runs red with betel juice, staining the sides of the culvert as it dribbles. "How, lawyer saar, how will you forgive—"

"That all you don't worry," says Appa. "Forgiving-shorgiving all you don't worry, Muniandy. Just take your daughter and go. Go away and leave us alone."

"Okay, enough of it," says Amma inside the house. "What for all this drama now? Are they waiting for the violin music or what? Why won't he buzz off?"

The latch on the gate clicks shut and Chellam and her father are gone, she pulling the suitcase, her sozzled father swaying behind her.

Till the end of her numbered days the green of the weedy verges she passes on her ignominious retreat will be stamped on the insides of Chellam's eyelids; she will hear the neighbors' whispers in her ears on quiet mornings; whenever it rains she will smell the wet clay and feel her feet sink with each step and her shoulder ache from the weight of her broken suitcase.

Appa stands with one foot on the lowest rung of the gate, watching them as they go. All down the street faces hang behind window curtains like dim bulbs.

"Sure enough," Mrs. Malhotra from across the street mutters to herself, "they're sending the girl home. These days you simply cannot trust servants." She turns from the window and looks at her old father, who sits rocking in his chair and humming urgently like a small child needing to pee. "Arre, Bapuji!" she cries. "You lucky-lucky only that we haven't dumped you into a servant's lap, yah, otherwise you'll also be dead and gone by now!"

The Wongs' retarded son, Baldy, points at them as they pass the house next door, where Amma's parents used to live until they died three years ago. Baldy crows through the branches of the mango tree in which he's perched in the rain, but nobody pays him any attention. His father's at work. His mother's peeling shallots in the kitchen. The neighbors are all used to him.

"Don't say *retarded,*" Amma had scolded the first time Appa had used the word to describe Baldy. "He's just a bit slow, that's all."

"To retard is to slow," Appa had said. "Ecce signum: the inestimable *OED.*" He'd pulled the dictionary off the bookshelf in the sitting room and laid its dusty black cardboard cover on Amma's breakfast plate.

"Okay, enough of it," Amma'd said then, and pushed her chair back so vehemently to leave the table that her tea sloshed onto her saucer. But Uma and Appa had shared a triumphant, twinkling grin, and even Suresh and Aasha had got the joke.

No curtains are stirring at the Manickams' window three doors down: the former Mrs. Manickam is lying in bed in Kampong Kepayang eating peeled and pitted longans from the hand of her new husband, who leaves the office early every day for this very purpose, and Mr. Manickam is at the office though it's a Saturday, burying his sorrows in work as usual.

"Looklooklook," says Mrs. Balakrishnan farther down the street, flicking her husband's sleeve as he sits reading the newspaper. "Sure enough man, they've sent the girl off from the Big House. What for all this drama now? Now only they'll sit and cry. As if it will bring the old lady back. When she was sitting in her corner the whole time they were complaining only. Cannot manage her it seems. Must get another servant it seems. Too grand to look after her themselves. That's what too much money will get you in the end. Just troubles and tears."

With one foot Appa sweeps a few dead leaves and stray pebbles out under the gate. Then he turns and makes his way back to the house, dragging his Japanese slippers on the gravel. For a few seconds he stands looking up at the tops of trees as if he were a visitor admiring the lush foliage, his umbrella turning like a Victorian lady's parasol on his shoulder. *Wah, wah, Mr. Raju, very nice, man, your garden! What kind of fertilizer you use?* "Big-House Uncle!" shouts Baldy from the top of his tree next door. "Uncle, Uncle, Big-House Uncle! Uncle ah! Uncle where? Uncle why?" Appa looks right at Baldy but says nothing. Then, as if he's suddenly remembered something important, he starts and strides briskly into the house.

"What are you two sitting there wasting time for?" he asks Suresh and Aasha as he enters the dining room. "As if the whole family must sit and bid a solemn farewell to the bloody girl like she's the Queen of England on a state visit. Go and do your homework or read a book or do something useful, for heaven's sake."

The children's heads turn towards Amma, and they sit holding their breath and biting their lips, waiting for her permission. To go and do their homework (although Aasha doesn't really have any). To read a book. To do unnamed useful things. To scamper off and live children's lives (or to discover that such a thing has become impossible for them, even after the morning's promise of a new beginning) and leave Amma bereft at a crumb-scattered table, with no audience.

"What? What are you looking at me for?" says Amma. "As if *I* wanted you to sit here. Both of you sitting with your busybody backsides glued to your chairs as if this whole tamasha is a Saturday morning cartoon, and now looking at me as if I'm the one who wouldn't let you go."

A tiny gust of air escapes Appa's nostrils. A laugh, a snip of surprise, a puff of fear. *Good grief,* Appa thinks, it's true: she's kept them here to witness her righteous fury at Chellam the Ingrate. And not just to witness it — to share it, to catch the whole rolling mass of rage with nowhere else to go, to parcel it out for future use. Lesson One: how some people turn against you even After Everything you've done for them.

He unfolds the two-color map of his wife in his head and adds to it another little landmark, a white dot before the border. Call it Shamelessness. Call it Stopping-at-Nothing, a triple-barreled name for a quaint English village. From the pit of his belly his own ravaging shamelessnesses threaten to rise in twos and threes and fours into his chest, waiting to accuse him in their discordant voices of calling the kettle black, waiting for him to acknowledge that the children have been caught between his old shamelessnesses and her new ones. He blinks and swallows, and thinks instead of the children's pause for permission. That's what has really jolted him, not this sudden change in his wife. That's what has sent cold air spiraling out his nostrils in two swift exclamation points. *She's kept them here,* he thinks, *and they know it.* For some reason he can't put his finger on, this frightens him. His head swims a little, as if he's just woken from a dream in which chickens talked and suns turned into moons.

He shakes his head and strides past them to calm his nerves with a cool shower in a bathroom humming with the ghost of his dead mother, before driving off the screen into an alternate universe in which he can forget the intransigent truths of this one.

In the kitchen Amma puts the dishes in the sink, and says, without turning around, "Next time why don't you just go with your father on Lourdesmary's days off? You want me to plan each Saturday night dinner one week in advance or what? Write out a full dinner menu with a fountain pen? Wear white gloves to serve you from silver trays?" Then she goes up to her room and stays there until Suresh and Aasha have made and eaten a dinner composed of Emergency Rations: golden syrup on Jacob's Cream Crackers, Milo powder straight from the tin, raw Maggi noodles broken into pieces and sprinkled with their grey (chicken-flavored) seasoning powder. At eight o'clock, Amma comes downstairs to eat her own dinner while listening to the kitchen radio in the half-dark. The radio's still set to the Tamil station to which Chellam used to listen while combing Paati's hair in the mornings. The theme song for the ten o'clock film-music program would always come on just as she pulled Paati's hair into a silky white knot barely big enough for two hairpins. Now, though, there's only a man with a gravelly, black-mustachioed voice interviewing a young lady doctor about the health benefits of almonds.

Suresh ceremoniously lays out his books and pencils, then takes his HB pencil and ruler out of their metal tin and starts his mathematics homework. "Please can I have just —" Aasha begins, and Suresh tears her a sheet of foolscap from his scrap paper pad and gives her a blue rollerball pen with a fat nib. On this cadged piece of paper Aasha draws an elaborate picture indecipherable to everyone but herself, a picture of Chellam the ex–servant girl, once beloved (but hated) and hated (but beloved) by Suresh and Aasha, now in ex-ile in her faraway village of red earth and tin roofs.

Ex-ile is an island for people who aren't what they used to be. On that lonely island in Aasha's picture Chellam wanders, tripping on blunt rocks in barren valleys, scaling sharp, windblown slopes on her hands and knees, minding starved cows that graze on rubbish heaps as if they're mounds of fresh clover. Blindly arranging and rearranging clouds of dust and dirt and bloodstained bathroom buckets with a ragged broom. Inside her head a dozen snakes lie coiled around one another in a heavy mass. Inside her belly stands a tiny matchstick figure, a smaller version of herself, pushing against the round walls of its dwelling with its tiny hands.

This matchstick representation of Chellam is accurate in at least one respect: there is indeed a terrible colubrine knot of bad memories and black questions inside Chellam's head that will die with her, unhatched. Aasha outlines the snakes again and then colors and colors them till the ink spreads down into Chellam's heavy-lobed, oversized ears.

"*Tsk,* Aasha," grumbles Suresh, "wasting my good pen only. For nonsense like that can't you use a pencil?"

Aasha caps the pen and rolls it across the table to Suresh with a pout. She climbs down from her chair and goes upstairs to sit in Uma's empty room. Around her the night sings with crickets and cicadas, with creaky ceiling fans and the theme songs of all the television programs being watched all the way down Kingfisher Lane. *Hawaii Five-O. B.J. and the Bear. Little House on the Prairie.* Aasha's quivering ears make out each one, separating them like threads on a loom, but downstairs she hears only silence. The silence, too, can be teased apart like threads: the silence of Amma staring out the kitchen window into the falling darkness. The silence of Appa's empty study, from which there are no rustlings of papers or whistlings of tunes. The silence of Suresh doing his homework all alone, feeling guilty for grumbling about his wasted pen. The silence of Paati, whose weightless, see-through body bumps noiselessly into furniture and walls, looking for the unraveling rattan chair on which she once sat all day in her mosquito-thronged corner. Merciful flames have freed the chair's spirit just as Paati's cremation freed hers, but the chair hasn't reappeared to sit transparently in its corner, and Paati is inconsolable. Her clear-glass joints creak silently as she settles onto the floor where her chair used to be.

A small voice outside the window says: "That's how Paati knows she's dead. Her chair isn't there anymore." Aasha turns to see her oldest (yet very young) ghost friend perched on the wide windowsill, tilting her head as she sometimes does. If Aasha were tall enough and strong enough to open this window on her own she would, though Mr. McDougall's daughter's not asking to be let in this time.

"You remember how *I* knew I was dead, don't you?" She doesn't look at Aasha as she asks the question, but off into the distance, so as to hide her great yearning for the correct answer.

"Yes," says Aasha, "of course I do. But tell me again anyway."

"When I couldn't see the sunlight and the birds. Before that I was alive, the whole time my Ma and I were sinking down through the pond — there were no fish in it at all, it was silent and dark like a big empty church — but I could see the light far away at the top, above the water. When I couldn't see it anymore, that's when I was dead."

Aasha lays her head on Uma's pillow, curls up, and closes her eyes to meditate once more upon this familiar confidence.

The following afternoon Amma finds Aasha's abandoned drawing of Chellam under the dining table. She squints briefly at the drawing, and then, deciding it must be a character from one of Aasha's storybooks, makes her list for Mat Din on the back. Chocolate wafers, Nutella, star anise for mutton curry, tinned corn and peas to go with chicken chops.

2

BIG HOUSE BEGINNINGS

I N 1899, Appa's grandfather sailed across the Bay of Bengal to seek his fortune under familiar masters in a strange land, leaving behind an emerald of a village on the east coast of India. Barely had he shuffled off the boat with the rest of that vast herd in Penang when a fellow offered him a job on the docks, and there he toiled, sleeping four or five hours a night in a miserable dormitory, sending the bulk of his wages home, wanting nothing more for himself than to be able to pay his passage back home someday.

What changed his dreams in twenty years? All Appa's father, Tata, knew of it was that by the time he was old enough to stand before his father in knee-length khakis for morning inspections before school, his father was saying: "Study hard. Study hard and you won't have to be a coolie like me." Every single goddamn morning he said it, the milky coffee frothing in his mustache. Study hard and the world will be yours. You could be a rich man. With a bungalow and servants.

And so Tata studied hard enough to get himself a clerk's position with the Cowan & Maugham Steamship Company when he left school at sixteen, and somewhere in all that hoping and studying and preparing, something else changed: India ceased to be home. Sometimes it glimmered green and gold in Tata's father's tales of riverbank games and ten-day weddings and unbreakable blood bonds. At other times it was a threat, a nightmare, a morass in which those who hadn't been lucky enough to escape still flailed. But Tata had no pictures of his own to attach to his father's word for India: *Ur*, the country. This, this flourishing, mixed-up, polyglot place to which they had found their way almost by accident, this was his country now. Malays Chinese Indians, motley countrymen they might be, but countrymen they were, for better or for worse. What was coming was coming to them all. It would be theirs to share.

This was what Tata, eyes shining in the dark, told his pretty wife. *It's our country, not the white man's.* And when she said, *But they've only been good to us,* he insisted: *You don't know. You don't know their dirty hearts. But you'll see what this country can become without them. You'll see.*

To his five children — Raju the good-for-everything, Balu the good-for-nothing, and their three inconsequential sisters — Tata regularly said: *We're lucky to live here. It's the best place on earth, none of India's problems. Peace and quiet and perfect weather. Just work hard and the world could belong to you here.* Then he'd ruffle the hair on Raju's attentive head and box distracted Balu's ear.

By the time Tata retired, in 1956, he owned a shipping company that rivaled his old employer's. A wry sun was setting with a vengeance on the British Empire. Tata decided to buy himself a house that would declare his family's stake in the new country. A great house, a grand house, a dynastic seat. He would leave Penang and look for such a house in Ipoh, far away from the dockyards, hilly, verdant, the perfect place to retire.

The house of Tata's dreams belonged to one Mr. McDougall, a dyspeptic Scotsman who had owned two of the scores of mines that had sprouted up in and around Ipoh in the 1850s to tap the Kinta Valley's rich veins of tin. He had already sold the mines to a Chinese towkay; now he had only to get rid of his house.

Mr. McDougall had three teenage children who'd been born and bred among the Chinese miners' offspring in Ipoh, running around in Japanese slippers and eating char siu pau for breakfast. He also had a mistress and a bastard child, whom he kept in relative luxury in a bungalow in Tambun. Mr. McDougall's life had meandered pleasantly along its course for years — mornings visiting the mines, afternoons with the mistress, evenings at the club — when he decided to leave the country, for two reasons. The first was that Her Majesty's government was preparing to withdraw. The second was that his mistress, sniffing Mr. McDougall's own flight in the air, had begun to demand a bigger house, a chauffeured car, and a wedding ring. *If you don't leave your family,* she told him, *I'll come and pull you away myself. I'll drag you off with my hands and my teeth, and your wife can watch.*

In response, Mr. McDougall had whisked his wife — Elizabeth McDougall, née Fitzwilliam, a colonel's daughter and in her time a great beauty whose attentions all the British bachelors of Malaya had coveted — and their three children off to a home they'd never known in the Scottish Highlands. And the mistress? For attention, for revenge, or out of simple, untainted despair, she had drowned herself and her six-year-old daughter in a mining pond. If Mr. McDougall had learned of her demise, he had never given any sign of it.

"I'm not sure his legitimate children fared any better," Appa would say whenever he told the story of the house. "Wonder what happened to them. The father simply uprooted them just like that and packed them all off lock stock and barrel."

> *Lock, Stock and Barrel, three men in a tub.*
> *One said roll over and another said rub.*

It was Suresh who penned these two inspired lines on the inside cover of his science textbook. He was nine years old at the time, and he entertained the idea of sharing the couplet with Appa, who would surely roar with laughter and pat him on the shoulder (if they were standing up) or the knee (if they were sitting down), the way he laughed and patted Uma whenever she displayed a wit worthy of her genes. But in the days after Suresh composed the verse Appa was hardly ever at home, and when he was his mood was so uneven that after three weeks of waiting, Suresh scratched the lines out with a marker pen to avoid trouble in case of a spot check by the school prefects.

"Going home it seems," Appa would snort, recalling Mr. McDougall's final words to Tata. "That's what McDougall told them. What nonsense! *His* home, maybe, not theirs. Their skin may have been white but they were Chinks through and through, let me tell you." *Chink* was a small, sharp sound that made Amma suck her teeth and shake her head, but this only encouraged Appa. "Probably wandering the moors looking for pork-entrail porridge," he'd go on. "Wiping their backsides with the *Nanyang Siang Pau's* business pages. Shipped specially to them by courier service."

Then Uma would giggle, and Suresh, watching her, would giggle with equal intensity, a number of giggles empirically guaranteed to flatter Appa without risking a mouthslap or a thighpinch from Amma. Only Aasha never joined in, for amusing as she found Appa's portraits of the McDougall children, her heart was with the little drowned girl, who wore her hair in pigtails; who had eyes like longan seeds and lychee-colored cheeks; who sometimes, on close, moonless nights, begged to be let in at the dining room window. *Please,* she mouthed to Aasha, *can't I sit at the table in my father's house?*

Don't talk rubbish, Appa and Amma and Uma and Suresh said when Aasha told them. And when once she opened that window, she got a slap on the wrist for letting in a cicada.

WHEN MR. MCDOUGALL fled to the Scottish Highlands, it had been nine years since King George VI had relinquished the cherished jewel of his crown. To be more precise: he'd dropped it as if it were a hot potato, towards the outstretched hands of a little brown man in a loincloth and granny glasses; a taller, hook-nosed chap in a still-unnamed jacket; and three hundred and fifty million anonymous Natives who'd fiercely stayed up until, by midnight, they'd been watery-eyed, delirious with exhaustion, and willing to see nearly anything as a precious gift from His Majesty. Down, down, down it had fallen, this crown jewel, this hot potato, this quivering, unhatched egg, none of them knowing what would emerge from it and yet most of them sure — oh blessed, blissful certainty! — that it was just what they wanted. Alas, the rest, too, is history: in their hand-clapping delight they'd dropped it, and it had broken in two, and out of the two halves had scurried not the propitious golden chick they'd imagined, but a thousand bloodthirsty monsters multiplying before their eyes, and scrabble as they might to unscramble the mess, it was too late, all too late even for them to make a last-minute omelet with their broken egg.

Now, in 1956, a slip of a nation just across the water prepared to lower the Union Jack forever, convinced (and correct, in a way) that here things would be different. This land awakened, shook out its hair, and readied itself for a decade of casting off and putting on names as if they were festive raiments. The Federation of Malay States. Malaya. Malaysia. Before another crowd of breathless, bright-eyed Natives, another Father of another Nation cleared his throat. Tunku Abdul Rahman, Oxbridge-educated, like so many new Fathers. Fond of his Yorkshire pudding and his steak and kidney pie with lashings of gravy. But bravely he cast these from his mind (or tried to), exchanged his morning coat for a baju melayu whose rich gold threads chafed his skin, and rose, adjusting his tengkolok on his head, to lead his people from their paddy fields, their family plantations, and their one-room school-huts to a new age of glory. They'd never had Yorkshire pudding or steak and kidney pie, but they trusted him: in his veins ran good Malay blood, and that, they believed, could not be diluted by any amount of bad English food.

Mr. McDougall knew the people of Malaya all too well; he'd helped to create them, after all, he and his fellow settlers. They'd brought the Chinese and the Indians out here on lurching boats for their brains and their brawn, for the raking in of taxable tin profits and the slaving under the midday sun. Like God, Mr. McDougall and his compatriots had watched their word take miraculous material form, Malay and Chinese and Indian stepping up unquestioningly to fill the roles invented for them. The Malay peasant sloshing about halfheartedly for a few hours a morning in the rice paddies of his divinely ordained destiny, content the rest of the day to squat in the shade under his hut-on-stilts. The Chinese coolie sniffing his diligent way to tin and opium. The indentured Indian, so high on betel juice that he could dig ditches for twelve hours, happy as a water buffalo in mud, burning his brown skin black under the sun and shuffling home at night to drink cheap toddy and beat his wife. For seventy years they'd all lived in harmony with the white men who ran the country, but for a few isolated incidents: a governor stabbed while he bathed, a ragtag protest. On the whole, things had gone according to plan.

Mr. McDougall couldn't say with any certainty when it had all begun to change, but he'd taken notice when the Chosen Few had started to get too big for their boots. That's what he and his chums at the miners' club had called the boys His Majesty's government had been specially grooming for the Malay Administrative Service and God only knew what else. Those scrubbed little weasels, schooled at the Malay College or the Victoria Institution or the Penang Free School and shipped off to Oxford and Cambridge to keep the Natives happy. For a while a pat on the head here and a promotion there had been enough to keep them going when they got home, but even then he had smelled trouble coming, seeing them return in their robes and powdered wigs. This Tunku chap was the worst of that lot. Before Mr. McDougall had time to say I told you so, the boys from the Malay College had begun to rouse the rabble. Them on one side, and on the other the bloody Chinese communists, wretched turncoats: the very weapons the British had given them to fight the Japanese were now being used to murder Briton and Native alike.

King George was gone. His daughter now wore his plucked crown: above her solid English face it sat, with a large hen's egg of a hole smack above her forehead, a pair of smaller round holes to the left, and to the right a row of tiny emeralds and rubies, loose as a seven-year-old's milk teeth, waiting to be knocked out.

It was precisely because Mr. McDougall knew the Tunku's people so well that he saw what would hatch from this latest little jewel-egg: nothing but the same old kind of trouble that had swamped India and Burma and the Sudan. Shifting their weight from foot to worried foot, their eyes glittering like wolves' in the dark, the Chinese and the Indians were already waiting on the sidelines. That was to say, those who hadn't already joined the communists, whose "insurgency" — Mr. McDougall chuckled bitterly every time he heard this namby-pamby word — they'd be lucky to put down before they left. Oh yes, no doubt about it, this was going to be a circus, a zoo, and a Christmas panto-mime all rolled into one.

What with his mistress raving and raging at his heels, threatening to bring the outside world's insanity into his high-ceilinged house, Mr. McDougall wasn't wasting any time. On the fifteenth of December 1956 he had his lawyer draw up the bill of sale for the house and its ad-joining acres, coconut trees and all; on the eighteenth he broke camp and headed home to Scotland, resigned to the prospect of spending a puking Yuletide on the high seas. He'd sold the house at a loss, but he didn't care, not even when he saw the self-satisfied glint in the eyes of the wog who bought it. This man was a walking symptom of the soft-ening of the empire. When a dockyard coolie could send his son to Oxford, thought Mr. McDougall as he signed his half of the unevenly typewritten, smudgily cyclostyled contract, that's when you knew it was time to cut your losses and flee. *The Rise of the Middle Bloody Class all right. That's all we need.*

"So!" he said aloud to the fellow, looking at him from head to toe and back. He was all spiffed up, this chap, decked out in a spotless white shirt and a bow tie just to come and sign an agreement in the back room of the miners' club. "Got yourself a deal, eh?"

"Yes, yes," said Tata. "Thank you very much, and good luck on your return to Scotland, Mr. McDougall." He held out his hand, and Mr.

McDougall took it with distaste, unable to shake the feeling that the fellow was having the last laugh.

He was right, of course, that Tata was pleased with himself for one-upping a vellakaran, for making off so effortlessly with such a bargain. "This," he said, holding the deed out to Paati where she stood peeling onions for the day's chicken perital, "this is the beginning of a new age. For us and for Malaya."

Paati, her hair still black, her hands still soft, nodded uncertainly. "Maybe," she said, "maybe so. But when the British are really gone for good, we'll miss them." And under cover of her onion-peeling, real tears, earnest and round, ran down her face. She wept for the Englishmen who would be booted out unceremoniously for the supposed sins of their fathers, sins she had never known, for she had known nothing but a glorious, sturdy contentment in her childhood. She wept for old times, for her missionary schoolmistresses and her red-bound Royal Readers, for "God Save the Queen" and the King's Christmas Message on the radio. She wept for old, lazy-eyed Mr. Maxwell, the overseer at the Cowan & Maugham Steamship Company; for Mr. Scotts-Hornby, the late manager whose position Tata had filled; for Lieutenant Colonel Phillips and his wife, who had rented the bungalow behind the house to which Tata had brought her when they were newly married. And she wept for one Englishman in particular, whose name she did not speak, even to herself.

"*Tsk,*" said Tata now. "How many times have I told you to peel the onions under water and wear your glasses while doing it? Aadiyappa, how you women let vanity rule your lives!"

Obediently Paati dropped each onion with a plop into a large ever-silver bowl of water, and no more was said of the British on that day.

BY THE TIME Mr. McDougall packed away his coconut-frond fans and his tropical-weather Wellingtons for good, Ipoh, never the cultural hub of British Malaya, had begun to split her thin colonial skin, and a new town peered out from under it, its pavements wet with phlegmy spittle. Bustling kopitiams sprouted around derelict whiskey bars like toadstools around rotting logs. Inside them flocks of old Chinamen squatted at marble-topped tables, dipping fluffy white bread in their morning coffee, slurping their midday bak kut teh. The Cold Storage, with its gleaming, chrome-stooled milk bar, closed forever on a quiet Saturday afternoon. In its place arose an establishment shifting uneasily between supermarket and wet market, alive with flies, slick with the sanguine juices of fish and fowl. The University Bookstore folded, and all over town, small, disreputable-looking bookstalls, with Chinese names and Indian film magazines strung across dark doorways, popped up. The raucous revelry of Chinese businessmen and Indian doctors expelled the last ghosts of Englishmen's subdued scotch-and-cigar evenings from the richly paneled rooms of the Ipoh Club.

Having selected an auspicious moving day from their Tamil calendar, Tata and Paati packed up their house in Butterworth and drove to Ipoh with her rosewood trunk on the back seat and his wiry old bicycle strapped to the roof of their maroon Bentley. Tata's pleated khaki trousers bulged with assets and liabilities: a hefty balance at Lloyd's Bank, various and sundry investments in the industries of the inchoate nation (so that when he died the obituary writer at the *Straits Times* fanned out for his readers the entire pack of catchy double-barreled monikers Tata had amassed: Rubber Baron, Cement King, Duke of Durians, Tapioca Tycoon, Import-Export Godfather), a wife still fresh and dimpled at fifty-eight, and three unmarried daughters. His two sons were away: Raju had got a job with a law firm in Singapore after coming down from Oxford, and Balu, newly married, was winning ballroom-dancing competitions all over Europe.

"Useless bloody fool," Appa was to growl years later, pointing out Uncle Ballroom to Uma and Suresh and Aasha in old family albums with moldering construction-paper pages. And, jabbing with an index finger the pictures of Uncle Ballroom's doomed garden-party wedding: "Tangoing and foxtrotting his way to penury. Foxtrotting only he found his fox. Too bad she could trot faster than him. He was cha-chaing this side, she was choo-chooing that side. Bloody idiot got outfoxed by his own fox. Hah!" "And probably eating steek," Suresh would whisper to Aasha when they were out of earshot, "with a knife and fork. And sleeping with no shirt on. Like J. R. Ewing only."

But in 1956, Tata was untroubled by visions of his profligate son's future. As the country charged towards birth and impetuous youth, he embraced his twilight years with a grateful sigh and a settling-in sense. Hiring servants only to cook and clean, he busied himself with his rose bushes and his vegetable garden. He harvested ripe chilies and twined tender tomato plants around stakes. He pruned, he weeded, he mowed twice a week. He planted trees: guava, mango, tamarind. He put up garden walls and trellises and came in for tea at ten past four, sweating but radiant, smiling around his kitchen at the rightness, the in-placeness of it all.

In a shed hastily erected in the garden, he spread mail-order instructions out on a workbench and built and varnished strange pieces of furniture he had previously only read about in books: secretaries, hall trees, cane stands.

He ordered a chandelier from France and, when it arrived, spent six days sitting in front of the opened crate, turning each part around and around in his hands. On the seventh day, a sudden fire roaring in his belly, he stayed up well past his usual bedtime to assemble the chandelier by the light of a kerosene lamp, frowning and muttering at the poorly translated directions, struggling, struggling, lipchewing, jawgrinding, squinting at the diagrams, until finally, at one minute to midnight, he dragged Paati from her bed in breathless triumph. They raised their faces towards the hanging chandelier in numinous expectation. Tata put the index finger of his right hand to the switch, took a deep breath, and flicked it on. At exactly midnight on the thirty-first of August 1957, there was Light . . .

. . . at precisely the same moment as, two hundred hopeful miles away, Tunku Abdul Rahman raised his right arm high on a colonial cricket ground and saluted the country's new freedom to the accompaniment of an aroused-and-rousing cheer of "Merdeka!" — Freedom! — and the eager choreography of the flag boys: in perfect synchrony, the Union Jack was lowered and the new flag raised. There, too, was Light. The blazing Light of a dozen fluorescent streetlamps, the crackling Light of a hundred flashing cameras, the (metaphorical, now, but no less real) inner Light of pride and ambition that shone in a million patriotic breasts just as it had shone in other breasts at other midnights.

Convinced that the Big House should grow and glow and celebrate sympathetically, Tata consulted a firm of architects about several extensions. An extra guest room. Two extra bathrooms (one with a claw-foot bathtub). An orchid conservatory. A music room–cum–smoking room (although there was but one gramophone, and no one smoked). An English kitchen equipped with a gleaming Aga range, in which the cook refused to set foot, preferring her outdoor Indian kitchen with its squealing tap and its gaping drains ready to receive fish guts, vegetable peelings, and leftover curries. And finally a servant's room under the back staircase, although neither Tata nor Paati got around to hiring a live-in servant to occupy it. Paying no heed to Mr. McDougall's conservative taste, Tata had the new wings built in a proud local style: solid wooden slats on a concrete base, patched willy-nilly onto the austere symmetry of the original grey stone structure, so that in less than two years the house metamorphosed into something out of an Enid Blyton bedtime story. Unnecessary corridors met each other at oblique angles. Additions, partitions, and covered porches seemed to rise out of nowhere before the eye. Green mosquito netting thumbed its nose at the Battenburg lace curtains in the next room. Sweat and steam and coal smoke from the hot Indian kitchen invaded the immaculate English kitchen and smeared its shiny surfaces. And above it all, the house's bold features — the quick, damning eyelids of the shutters, the sharp gable noses so different from the flat roofs around them — shuddered with a Scotsman's thin-lipped rancor. *These bloody Nati'es. That's whit ye gie when ye gie a boorichie ay wogs 'eh reit tae rule.*

Tata's last home-improvement venture before he died was to paint the outside of the house an unapologetic peacock blue, as if to stamp upon the building his ownership, his nation's liberty and his own. It was a color Tata's neighbors were accustomed to seeing only in wedding sarees and Mughal miniature paintings. Now the house practically glowed in the dark. The Big House. 79 Kingfisher Lane. You can't miss it, people took to saying when giving directions. It's nothing like the others. Appa's one concession to the mawkish sentimentality of the Indian son, as far as his children were ever able to tell, was to select the same blinding color every five years when he had the house repainted. "Any other color just wouldn't be the same," he'd say with a regretful headshake. "Got to honor the old man's magnificent jasmine-and-marigolds curdrice-and-pickle Madras-masala aesthetic sensibilities."

WHEN TATA keeled over in his vegetable garden one luminous May morning in 1958, Paati ordered her daughters to summon their oldest brother. Then she settled herself on the south-facing porch (noncovered, alas) to wait, squinting at the horizon as if she could see the hump of Singapore rising like a turtle's back through the blue water three hundred miles away, and astride that hump, like the Colossus of Rhodes, her fearless firstborn, ready to clear the Tebrau Strait in a single leap and come lumbering across the land into this manless garden, law degree in one hand and hoe in the other. At dusk her daughters begged her to come indoors; at eight, despairing, they brought her mosquito coils and a pillow for her back. But she barked her questions without looking at them. At what time had the telegram been sent? Had a response been received? At what time was Raju to start from Singapore? In the morning she was still there in her rattan chair, covered in red bites the size of grapes, her voice hoarse from the smoke of the useless mosquito coils. Scratching furiously, she got up to greet Appa as his pea-green Morris Minor pulled into the driveway.

"I dropped everything and sped straight home, *foof!*" he was to tell his children years later. "Just like that I had to tender my resignation. Tup-tup-tup and I was standing here consoling the old lady and taking charge of everything." Tup-tup-tup and three snaps of his fingers. So magical had been his haste, so uncanny the lightning progress of the Morris Minor on the old backcountry byways. "Just imagine," Appa would say, "just try and imagine if you can. Zipped home just like that." And dutifully the children would feel the wind of that speed in their faces, and see unanimously the image each one had purloined without a word from the thoughts of the other: a young Appa zooming through the brightening air with one arm stuck straight out before him like some undersized, chicken-chested superhero.

After Tata's funeral, Appa bagged a coveted associateship in the venerable law firm of Rackham Fields & Company. Though his bosses were all British for now, they'd be throwing up their jobs and leaving one by one, and whom would they choose to fill their shoes if not a fellow who'd come down from Oxford with first-class honors? Both precedent and informed speculation suggested that such a job would provide the perfect sparkling counterpoint to the meteoric political career Appa envisioned for himself. He had inherited — oh, most precious of legacies! — his father's uncompromising ambition. With a bit of work everything would be his: a Mercedes in the driveway, a Datukship on the King's birthday, the country itself. The whole country, his for the taking, his generation's. What an inheritance! They would not squander it. They would make this country the envy of all Asia, even of the bloody British themselves.

As part of the understanding that he would see his sisters well settled, Appa had also inherited an ancillary tripartite legacy: 1) the Big House, that twisted, hulking setting of his father's twilight years; 2) half of the shipping company; 3) the lion's share of Tata's wisely invested nest egg.

The house welcomed its new lord with wide-open doors and a garland of vermilioned mango leaves strung across the top of the front doorway. But the shipping company, managed these past two years by a loyal secretary, could no longer be kept. "I'm a barrister, not a bloody boatman," Appa declared to anyone who would listen. "And my brother is a fool. Amateur and professional. You think sambaing and rumbaing will keep the boats afloat or what?" So the company was sold, the rubber, cement, durian, and tapioca investments divided, and Uncle Ballroom's share grudgingly forwarded to him in Europe per his instructions. Appa gave the boy five months (in the end it took seven) to spend it all before he began dashing off desperate pleas for more. Ah, well. The luckiest of men had thorns in their sides, and unlike some, he, at least, didn't have to worry about a younger brother who would stumble into an unsuitable match with a dimwitted troglodyte, spawn six snotty brats, and ensconce himself and his family in a spare room upstairs whence they would all descend in a cavalcade for free idli sambar at each mealtime. No, such burdens would almost certainly never be his: on the shelf in the dining room sat his brother's latest All-Round Ballroom Champion trophy and a framed photograph of him and his partner in some obscenely gilded ballroom in Vienna, in exactly the same pose as the faceless gold-trophy couple. Thus freed of the firstborn's burden, Appa invested his half of the nest egg twice-wisely and pondered his place in the newborn nation.

3

THE NECESSARY SACRIFICE OF
THE BURDENSOME RELIC

August 26, 1980

ONE EVENING a week after Paati's death, Aasha follows Uma down the stairs and to the back door of the Big House, her heart hammering like a wedding drum, elemental words blistering her tongue like beads of hot oil: *What, Uma? Why?* But her mouth will not spit these words out, and her legs refuse to shorten her customary following distance of three yards. What is it about Uma that frightens her this evening? Her purposeful step, the resolute look in her eye, the way her arms are folded tightly over her stomach? Or is it something greater than the sum of these signals, yet unnameable? Certainly it could be no threat or suggestion Uma herself has made: she has neither uttered a word nor done anything else unusual all day. She has remained behind the locked door of her bedroom; she has ignored Aasha just as she has been ignoring her for so long that you might mistakenly believe this icy, silent Uma had obliterated the memory of that other Uma, the laughing, teasing, bicycle-pushing Uma who had inherited Paati's dimples and smelled (close up) of Pear's soap.

But when Aasha trails the new Uma around the house, the old one walks behind them both, soft-footed, humming under her breath. When Aasha swivels around on the balls of her feet, hoping to catch her, she is gone. What else can Aasha do but follow the new Uma around, hoping, wishing, willing her thoughts to fly across the three yards between them and settle, dove-winged, on Uma's impregnable heart? From the back door, she watches as Uma strides through the garden.

It is dusk, that aching, violet dusk that has come to seem the permanent state of this whole year. Just as Uma reaches the garden shed the streetlights come on, and clouds of moths and beetles appear from nowhere, as if they've been waiting for this moment all day. They divide themselves into equal clusters, even around the one streetlight that flickers on and off and on and off all night but refuses to die.

In front of the shed, Uma stops and stares at Paati's worn rattan chair, in which the old lady sat every day from eight in the morning till nine at night (except during her fever this year, when she didn't get out of bed for weeks). For as long as Aasha can remember, this chair has belonged to Paati, though In The Beginning she sat in it only to relax after lunch. Then one day she made an official announcement that she was Old and Tired. With that, all the air seemed to leak from her at an alarming rate. Her after-lunch rests grew longer; then before-lunch eye-closings preceded them. And finally, after-breakfast catnaps ran into those, until Paati simply ceased to stir from the chair all day. During all that time the chair never budged from its original spot next to the crockery cabinet at the end of the long corridor outside the English kitchen, in a sleepy, dark corner where shadows drift and settle like feathers, and where the mosquitoes fly in slow motion and hum an octave lower than they do anywhere else in the Big House.

Never budged, that is, until Amma threw it out. From the afternoon Paati died, Amma was forced to repeat regularly for five days: "Aasha, please stop staring at that chair. Come away. Never mind, it was better for Paati this way, don't you know? Too old already she was. At least she went quickly." The first time he heard these words, Suresh ran upstairs to lie down on his bed and think: *Quicklyquicklyquicklyquickly. Quickly is merciful and merciful is quick and it's true no matter what that everything is better this way and anyway I don't know anything and I don't remember anything.* After that he made sure never again to be in the room to hear Amma coax Aasha away from the chair, which was easy enough, for an eleven-year-old boy goes to Boy Scout meetings, trots off to the corner shop with twenty cents and a plan in hand, sequesters himself in his room to read *Dandy* and *Beano* comics, and no one thinks anything of it. Boys at that age. You know how they are.

But Aasha, trapped at home, jabbered and chattered and spewed the fruits of her tortured mind at Amma's feet.

"Look how Paati curled up in her chair," she squealed the morning after Paati died. "Look, she pulled up her feet also, look at her curled up small-small round-round like a cat! Then after she'll be complaining only, knees paining legs paining joints paining. Silly Paati!"

"*Tsk*, come and drink your Milo, Aasha. Paati passed away. Paati is not there."

But *passed away* was what the soapy black water from afternoon bucket baths did, gurgling and burping into the bathroom drain, sweeping a hair clump and a stray sliver of soap with it.

That was not, in fact, how Paati had gone. Her departure had been much messier—oh, so much more than water into the bathroom drain!—and more dramatic (incorporating all the elements of a first-rate thriller: gasps, footsteps rushing hither and thither, impulsions and compulsions). Also far less final, for Paati was not yet all gone. She was transparent now, and each day since she died she'd been missing another small part of herself: first one of her dangly, distended earlobes, then a knobby big toe, then a little finger. But the important parts—fierce head, fired-up chest, burning belly—made their piss-and-vinegar presence felt.

Later that morning, Aasha returned to Paati's shadowy, mosquito-saturated corner and gripped her rattan chair by its armrests.

"Eh Paati Paati, don't pull your hair like that, don't shout and scream, your throat will pain! Chellam cannot come and comb your hair lah. Chellam all the time sleeping only now. Wait I ask Amma to come, don't scream, don't scream!"

Amma dragged Aasha off by the strap of her Buster Brown overalls. "Come," she said. "Come and read a book or draw a picture or something. I'll ask Suresh to lend you his color pencils. You want F&N orange squash? You want ginger beer? I'll send Mat Din to buy for you."

For five afternoons Aasha went to the chair at teatime, with a jelebi or two bondas or a handful of omapoddi in her sweaty hand.

"Here, Paati," she whispered, depositing her clandestine offerings on the chair. "Amma threw away your bowl already, what to do? Eat faster-faster, don't tell anybody." She stood and stared. Mosquitoes landed on her arms and legs ten fifteen twenty at a time like tiny aeroplanes, and she slapped and scratched but did not move away. "Nice or not, Paati?" she asked, leaning forward, her hands clasped behind her back. "Bondas hot-hot. No need to eat dry rice from our plates. Nice or not? Careful, don't burn your mouth, what Paati, so hungry ah? So long didn't eat, is it?"

These displays were nothing new; the whole family was familiar with that other nonsense concerning Mr. McDougall's dead daughter. "Maybe," Chellam had often whispered to Suresh, "your sister can see ghost, what. Maybe she got special chance from God."

The family had sought explanations less metaphysical.

"You people," Amma said, "you people tell her funny-funny stories, who tells a child this age those kinds of stories? Of course she's going to make up all these rubbish stories. Trying to make herself interesting, that's all."

"Well, it's not working, is it?" said Suresh.

Yet for reasons best known to them — and each of them had different reasons — they could not dismiss Aasha's sightings of Paati quite so easily. "This is getting a bit too much," said Amma. "Some ghost story character is one thing. Talking to her own dead grandmother is another. People are going to think she's a Disturbed Child."

Appa said, "What I want to know is, since when did she and the old lady become such soul mates?" A fair question, for Aasha had hardly spoken to Paati when Paati was alive. She'd been born too late to know the Paati who'd sung Uma to sleep and picked the peas out of her fried rice, and in any case Uma had always been Paati's favorite; there'd hardly been room for Suresh and Aasha in her heart.

The day Amma found a pile of disintegrating bondas, rock-hard jelebis, dusty omapoddi, and limp curry puffs on the rattan chair, she picked it up by its armrests and made off with it.

"Chhi!" Amma said to Aasha on her way out the front door with the chair. "Just because we're feeling sorry for you you're climbing on our head now. Taking advantage of everybody's sympathy."

Defying this last assertion, Aasha threw herself down on the marble floor and loosed a wordless series of ascending wails that floated like bright scarves — purple, fuchsia, puce — towards the ceiling, to be blown into the street by the fan as Amma set the chair down by the dustbin and shook her head.

"That girl is having fits or what," said Mrs. Balakrishnan to Kooky Rooky, her boarder. "I'm not surprised. What a terrible thing she saw, no joke, isn't it?"

"Aieeee! Aieeee! Aieeee!" shrieked Baldy Wong. "I also can scream what! I can scream louder! AIEEEEEEEEE!"

Mrs. Malhotra's barrel-shaped dog began to howl.

"Chhi!" said Amma, slamming the front door shut. "The whole world is going mad. Aasha, you want one tight slap? Hanh?"

Aasha swallowed her viscous, salty saliva and sat hiccupping on the floor for an hour until she fell asleep. At dinnertime Suresh came and poked her in the ribs with a foot and then sidled off to his own rice and rasam.

"Why you threw away Paati's chair, Amma?" he asked. He knew the answer; his question was nothing but a thinly disguised accusation. He'd had to muster up all his courage to ask it, and the mustering had left his ears sticking out farther than ever. Under the table his knees were cold. *You threw it away,* he thought, *because you couldn't bear to look at it anymore, isn't it? Maybe you're scared Paati's really sitting in that chair and you can't see her.*

Amma only said breezily, "Oh, why should we selfishly hang on to things we can't use? The dustbin men will probably want it. It's still usable, after all. Some families would kill for a chair like that."

Suresh considered this. Some families killed for lesser reasons, but poor chairless families, needing the chair-ity of rich families, were driven to violence only by their desperation. The thought was terrible and wonderful: skinny men in open-chested shirts with red bandanas around their heads, wrestling for an old rattan chair while the women and children gasped and shrieked in the background. Then one of them would pull out a gleaming knife. He'd pick up the chair in one arm and his beauty-marked, melon-breasted village belle in the other; he'd hoist the chair on his back, slip his bloody knife back under his belt, and before you knew it he'd be leaping across the moonlit rooftops, leaving the others to moan in their spreading pools of blood.

On Monday morning, when the dustbin men came to collect the rubbish, they picked up the chair and tossed it playfully between them. "This one's for you, Ayappan," one of them chortled, "you can sit in it and eat your thairsadham and scratch your armpits." "Ei, maddayan!" Ayappan shot back, as the other demonstrated the armpit-scratching part of the deal. "The family personally told me it was for you, special-special only, for you to sit on the porch and comb your lovely locks." When they exhausted the chair's possibilities they dropped it, dumped the rubbish into their lorry and drove away. It lay on the grassy verge by the culvert, where Aasha could hear its labored breathing. In the evening Amma dragged it into the backyard and left it by the shed. "Oo wah, style-style only these dustbin men nowadays," she said. "Those days they used to grab whatever we left for them. Broken also they would fight for it. Now even we would lose to them in taste and class, lah!" she grumbled, as if she'd paid for the old kind of dustbin man and received the new kind in the post.

And there by the shed the chair has remained since last night, upside down, the watery stains of Paati's numerous failed attempts to make it to the bathroom in time visible even on the underside of its sagging seat. One stain shaped like a one-eared bunny, another like a fat frog, a third like a butterfly. Three of Paati's silver hairs, relics of a particularly savage combing by Chellam, are caught between two loose strips of rattan on the back of the chair. Its unraveling legs stick up in the air like the limbs of some dead mouse awaiting the ant armies.

As Aasha watches from the back door, Uma drags the chair to the hump by the garden wall and sets it right-side up. Then she walks back to the shed, opens the door, and goes in.

While she's inside, Paati's ghost slips out from behind the tamarind tree and takes her rightful place in the chair, regal and disdainful as a queen. Is that where she's been hiding all these days, behind the tamarind tree, since Amma first put the chair out for the dustbin men? No one knows, and before Aasha has a chance to ask her, Uma comes back. She's carrying a big tin with both hands, her shoulders hunched in such a way Aasha can tell it's heavy.

Then, in a shattering surge of memory, Aasha realizes what it is: a tin of kerosene. She's seen Mat Din the gardener pour kerosene on his piles of branches and weeds before he lights his bonfires, huge, roaring, smoky flame-towers that darken the sky and make the birds disappear for hours.

Uma sets the tin down by her feet and folds her arms once more. There are permanent bags under her eyes because she hasn't slept in a week. Oh, she's caught forty winks here and a catnap there, but the winks are carefully rationed, thirty-eight thirty-nine forty okay enough, and the catnaps are not the cozy indulgences of the happy housepet but the vigilant sleep of the one-eye-open one-ear-missing stray. In the past week, the loose weave of her occasional slumber has let in many undesirable objects: old promises issued and received; the inexplicable scent of Yardley English Lavender talcum powder; a long sigh that revealed itself, when she opened her eyes, to have been nothing more than a sheet of paper blown by the ceiling fan from her desk to the floor.

The children call this grassy mound the ceremonial hump, for it was here that Amma burned her hand-embroidered, Kanchipuram silk wedding saree one long-ago morning after Appa didn't come home all night. Uma had watched from the back door, and Paati had reminded her once again how much cleverer, how much worldlier and tougher and classier she was than her Amma, because she had her father's blood in her and would therefore never do something as crass as throwing a fit in the backyard for all the neighbors to see.

And two years after the saree-burning, Uma and Suresh and Aasha buried Sassy the cat by the hump after Mr. Balakrishnan from across the street ran her over in his car in the middle of the night. If you're not careful, Suresh has warned Aasha ever since, if you accidentally step on that hump or even brush against it carelessly, Sassy's clawed foot — just white-white bones only, no more flesh — will burst through and grab your ankle.

In the old days, before Uma stopped speaking, she and Suresh used to take turns pushing Aasha around the hump on her tricycle, chanting:

> *Sassyhump*
> *Dead cat bump*
> *Smelly wormy rotty lump!*

Once Aasha flew head-first off the tricycle into the African daisies, her foot grazing the hump. Her full-throated wail had brought Lourdesmary hurtling out into the backyard like a bumblebee launched from a cannon. "A big monkey like you, pushing your sister until she falls!" she scolded Uma. "You should have known better."

Surely, surely, Aasha thinks now, watching Uma from the back door, Uma should also know better than to do whatever terrible thing she is going to do.

Except that Uma doesn't think what she's about to do is so terrible; in fact, she has deemed it necessary. One should never forget that all things pass: hopes, cats, chairs, life itself, each a spun-glass rose in a monkey's hand. In the twinkling of an eye everything can change, and there's never any going back. You can't bring a dead cat back to life. You can't resurrect a saree or a marriage from two charred tassels. You most certainly can't uncrack the cracked skull of a cantankerous grandmother by imagining her back in her unraveling rattan chair.

Only Aasha sees the ghosts arrive from all directions, united by their unhealthy fascination with tragedy, with unfinishable business and lingering discontent. All the bloodsucking pontianaks about whom Chellam once warned the children; all the red-eyed, fleet-footed toyols; all the polongs and pelesits; and among them, almost unnoticed (but for Aasha's extra-sharp eyes), Mr. McDougall's petal-pretty daughter, a little afraid, a little unsure, but curious nevertheless. And though her bubble of a heart skips a beat at the sight of Uma — those dark, unblinking eyes, those impetuous movements, all these recall her mother's most dangerous days — she's resolved to provide her customary moral support to Aasha in lonely and troubled times.

The ghosts converge on the backyard like crows, long tresses streaming, red eyes glowing. They look at Paati in her chair and whisper to each other. They settle on tree branches and on the rims of flowerpots. They bear Aasha no ill will, yet she knows they would not be here if some ghastly spectacle were not about to unfold. She also knows that no one — not she herself, not Mr. McDougall's fervent daughter, not any of the other ghosts with their hot breath and their portentous mouths — can reach Uma now. Uma's stepped behind her invisible glass door and locked it; Aasha recognizes the signs.

On the garden wall, swinging his skinny legs, sits Suresh. He tilts his head back and pours into his mouth, while keeping a vigilant eye on Uma, an entire box of Chiclets he found on the school bus this afternoon. (You never know when someone might catch you and confiscate the Chiclets you've been saving so wisely and with so much restraint — and then where will you be? Better to relish life wholeheartedly while you can.) In his mouth the Chiclets form a fat, minty wad, smooth in some places but still surprisingly grainy in others. He bites down and bursts a hidden bubble with a snap. He watches Uma douse Paati's chair in kerosene and draw a matchbox from under the waistband of her skirt, as if it were a sword for fighting off anyone else who wants the chair. He rests his chin on his hands and knows he's not getting involved. No way, no fear, not even if the police come.

None of this is his problem. Not even if Uma is flagrantly breaking a rule she herself made up at a long-ago feline funeral: no bonfires in the backyard, she'd said when he'd suggested cremating Sassy. Well, look at her now. Rules, too, were fragile.

Aasha steps out into the backyard and makes her way, holding her breath, clenching her fists, past the teeming ghosts. At the tamarind tree, directly across from Uma, she stops and kneels. The ground here is covered with tough, brown tamarind pods, and because Aasha's helpless hands itch to do something, she gathers them up in familiar fistfuls and pulls them apart for the seeds. She fills her pockets with these, as if they were insurance against future catastrophe.

"Don't you wish we could do something?" Mr. McDougall's daughter whispers to her. She's sidled past the others to come and kneel beside Aasha. "But maybe we've no choice. Nobody really cares what we want. My ma," she begins, and for once Aasha doesn't want to hear her story—*not now,* she thinks, *not now, I have to keep both eyes and both ears on Uma*—"you know how my ma wouldn't let go of my hand that day? So tight she held it. Nobody ever held my hand like that before so I was a little bit happy. A little bit happy and a big bit frightened. It was all mixed up. When my ma jumped, at first I didn't realize we'd jumped, that's how mixed up I was."

"Wait a minute," says Aasha, because Uma's lighting the match. But Mr. McDougall's daughter, trapped as always in the net of her last memory, goes on:

"The whole time we were falling through the air, my ma held on to my hand. I could feel her fingers with my eyes closed, and I could hear her breathing, and I could feel her long hair on my neck. The air wasn't hot anymore while we were falling. But now I know she only held my hand to comfort herself. And to make sure I didn't get away."

Uma flings her match onto the chair and steps back.

"It was a long way down to the water," Mr. McDougall's daughter remembers, "a long long time between jumping and swallowing water. I counted to twenty and I wasn't even counting fast. Even when we hit the water my ma didn't let go of my hand. And all the while we were sinking, she still didn't let go of it."

There's a brief burst of flame as the kerosene burns. Paati clutches the armrests and pulls her feet up onto the seat.

Mr. McDougall's daughter turns a terror-stricken, fire-lit face to Aasha. For a long moment they stare at each other, two old friends marooned together on the uncertain island of adult whims. At least they have each other. In Mr. McDougall's daughter's grey eyes the fire glows amber.

Undeterred, pitiless, Uma licks her dry lips and waits. Aasha drops a handful of tamarind seeds. Click, clack, click, they slip through her fingers and fall onto other seeds already under the tree. She stands up. She takes one step forward, no more. She thinks of Uma in *The Three Sisters* in July, emoting onstage as she never does at home; of Uma reciting long, winding lines in funny English before her mirror; of Uma standing on the rug outside the bathroom, wrapped in one towel and drying her hair with another, smiling, singing Simon and Garfunkel songs under her breath. That is the real Uma; this is a different Uma, blind, unforgiving, a dangerous shapeshifter.

On the wall Suresh snaps his gum again. And again. Snap! The sound cracks like a whip in Aasha's face. She flinches and sniffs. She rubs her nose with an index finger. The air is full of smoke and frying pork from the Wongs' kitchen. She waits, balanced on her heels.

Paati's chair braces itself for a difficult battle. It stiffens its arms and hunkers down, while on the seat, tight and tiny as a coiled pangolin now, Paati cowers.

Oh, Uma should know better, she should. A big monkey like her, trying to set fire to a chair that's been sitting outside in the damp for days. What's left of the flame singes the three silver hairs, chars the chair's thick legs on the outside, and begins to subside. So Uma adds more kerosene. Then she folds her arms across her chest and hugs herself as if she's cold, as if the weather is different where she stands.

Slowly, gleefully, sensuously, the flames finally begin to creep up the legs of Paati's chair. Paati trembles and covers her face. The heat of the fire lays its gold-flecked wings across Aasha's face, and a drop of sweat traces a searching trail down the misted glass of Uma's invisible door. From someone's television set the Muslim call to prayer lifts off into the air like a man in a billowy white robe tiptoeing lightly off a roof.

Allah-u akhbar! Allaaaaaah-u akhbar! The man's sleeves fill like sails. There he hangs, not rising or falling, looking up and down and left and right for some thoughts to think.

The man turns into a dove.

The chair crumples and kneels, weeping, gathering its skirts of flame about itself.

It's just a scrap of a chair with a scrap of a ghost in it, a skin-and-bones ghost whose feet don't touch the ground. What an unbearable indignity it is that Paati must summon her few remaining shreds of will to outwit these new flames that tastelessly echo the funereal flames of just-last-week. It's entirely possible that this time, weakened by those first flames, deprived of days of teatime omapoddi and curry puffs, Paati will not make it.

Aasha opens her mouth to scream. Suresh snaps his gum, three times in a row, each louder than the last, because that's all he can do without sticking his own neck out. But it's too late. The scream rolls roundly out of Aasha's mouth, like a bubble escaping from an underwater balloon, and shoots up to the leafy top of the tamarind tree. On its way it pops against a sharp, low branch and spills its words onto the rain-dark earth.

"Uma, Uma, please don't burn Paati, *please!* Pull her out! Pull her out! *Pleeeease!*" The last *please* quivers, turns to liquid, and seeps into the damp soil, suffusing the roots of the tamarind tree in its desperate grief. Next week Lourdesmary will complain that its fruit is becoming less succulent, drying out and turning too fibrous in the pod.

Transparent Paati lies amid the flames, limp as an empty plastic bag, her eyes slightly surprised, her head and chest and belly growing smaller and smaller as they melt. Stunned and saddened, the other ghosts drift off down the driveway in twos and threes, like mourners going home after a small child's funeral. Unsure how to arrange their faces or hold their heads.

At the last possible minute, just as the fire begins to lick at her chin, Paati spirits herself out of the flames with a final burst of her posthumous strength. She's put everything she had into this effort, and now she spirals up to the sky in a puff of smoke, a decrepit little genie with no wishes to grant. Her deflated head and chest and belly refill like balloons. Aasha holds her breath and hopes Uma hasn't noticed; she would close her eyes, too, but then she wouldn't be able to make sure Uma doesn't leap up and grab Paati by a foot and hurl her back into the flames. But Uma's flame eyes are glued to the crackling chair. Paati is safe, after all; she's lost nothing but the ends of her hair to the fire. All the same, she's had a good scare. Now she drifts off towards the Wongs' house, and after a moment Aasha hears Baldy start to whimper at nothing on his porch swing.

After the bonfire dies, Uma goes indoors to finish packing. Aasha climbs the stairs behind her, a woeful pull-along toy on an invisible string. With silent wheels instead of squeaky ones, and cracks in hidden places.

Yellow light spills out of Uma's open door, setting the dark wood of the floor agleam. Almost as if she were inviting Aasha in, Uma leaves her door open tonight. But on the landing, Aasha stops, unsure. She studies Paati's wedding picture, an old black-and-white photograph with blurred outlines, hairlines bleeding into faces, noses melting into mouths. Grave, handlebar-mustachioed men in suspenders and bow ties. Women with accusing eyes, necks and wrists heavy with gold. And, seated cross-legged on the grass, a little girl with ringlets, in a frothy white frock and sturdy dark boots ridiculous in the Madras heat. No one seems to know her name, though Aasha once offered Paati suggestion after suggestion. Meenakshi? Malathi? Madavi? Radhika? If they knew then, the mustachioed men sweating under their collars or their aching-necked wives, no one knows now. Probably the little girl grew up to be a spinster aunt, sending out tins of murukku and thattai to her nieces and nephews every Deepavali. Probably she died in her bathroom and no one found out for a week. Aasha settles down on a stair and waits, chin in hands, for nothing in particular.

It's obvious, even from Paati's wedding photograph, that she will not share the unfortunate imagined fate of the little girl in ringlets. Eighteen years old and not a month more, Paati stands with her twenty-five-year-old groom in the front row, erect, unsmiling, feet and hands red with henna. You can see in her eyes, blurry as they are, the thousand guests that have been invited for the month-long celebration, the five canopies erected on her father's land, the special photographer from Singapore. (*Watch the birdie, Mr. and Missusssssss,* he'd said over and over, grinning and winking, *watch the birdie, later on you can look at each other, Mr. and Missussssss!* though they hadn't been looking at each other, not then and not for days afterward.)

Future, present, and past do brave battle in the bride's kajaled eyes, and the photograph refuses to reveal which Paati will win.

These are the Paatis competing for supremacy, in reverse chronological order:

6) The eagle-nosed matriarch, widow of Thambusamy the Rubber Baron, Cement King, Durian Duke, etc., etc., determined to rule in her son's house as she did in her husband's;

5) The beautiful maddam, powdered and painted, who feels the stares of white men follow her in town;

4) The good Indian wife adept at fading, in public, into the background behind her men;

3) The young mother of a newborn bigshot lawyer, glowing with the achievement of a boy-on-first-try;

2) The shy-smiling newlywed (with feet and hands still faintly red but fading), mismeasuring the sugar for her husband's tea and mourning the life she was used to in her father's house;

1) The spoiled little girl who has simply to hold out her hands for extra kolukattai and jelebi, secure in the knowledge that her parents, having lost three babies before her, are wrapped around her little finger.

Or will none of these prevail? In the end, has 7) the bag of aching bones in the rattan chair staked out the surest claim in the fertile territory of other people's memories? Or is it — no turning back now, because now that we've come this far we have to set a foot, however hesitant, onto the precarious ground before us — 8) an even later incarnation that will stay with Paati's survivors? A little brown heap of bones turning cold as death rattles and gurgles in its throat?

A little brown seeping heap. It trickles into drains and dark wood floors, into the white sheets of a deathbed, into Aasha's head. She shakes her head like a wet dog. Be gone, brown heap; be gone, blood droplets; be gone, flailing hands and uncurling toes. But new waters rush in to fill Aasha's head, bearing their own flotsam and jetsam, because once, yes, Paati was as young as Amma, and before that she was as young as Uma (and Chellam), and before that, she was as young as Aasha. Younger, even. A toddler. A baby, soft and swaddled. Not for the first time, as Aasha's mind strains to accommodate this incredible, uncomfortable truth, something in her chest sinks and settles like silt in a slow river. She swallows and takes a deep breath; then, heavy-footed, she climbs the remaining five stairs up to Uma's room. The door's still open, but Uma's at the window and doesn't turn around when she walks in. Not that she expects Uma to comfort her; she's grateful enough for the tender offering she knows the open door to be. And the yellow light out of which she's been locked for years, and the view from Uma's window, and the clean smell of her pillow. All these are Uma's way of saying *Sorry for everything.*

To answer *It's okay I forgive you*, she clambers onto Uma's bed and folds her thin legs under her tartan skirt. Uma backs away from the window and returns to her packing, pulling from the shopping bags under her bed clothes stiff with newness, their tags turning like mobiles in the fan breeze: a hooded cotton sweatshirt that won't be warm enough even on the plane; a stack of practical skin-tone panties that come up to her waist, specially picked out by Amma; a white blazer that will soon reveal itself to be comically unfashionable in New York. She lays these things on top of the clothes already in the red suitcase and smoothes them down with her hands. The suitcase smells of oil-cloth on the outside, mothballs on the inside, and everywhere, inside and outside, of the cold, sterile rush of foreign airports, the rubber of conveyor belts, the suspense and rewards of Appa's trips abroad back when the courts of young Malaysia took their appeals to their ex-Queen. Once there'd been a hand-embroidered dress for Uma in the bottom of that suitcase, once a model aeroplane kit for Suresh. Now floury mothball dust clogs the ridges of its grey lining. Uma's eyes are too bright, her hands too quick, her nails bled white and bitten ragged.

"Uma," whispers Aasha.

Uma looks up, and it's only now that Aasha notices a tear hanging off her chin, round and heavy as quicksilver. The more Aasha looks at it, the more it doesn't fall. Pictures move inside it, swirling, melting into each other like palm sugar syrup stirred into coconut milk.

Afternoon sunlight on bathroom tiles.

An eversilver tumbler of water.

A blackened chair with swirling skirts of flame.

Now there's a tiny body (brown, with a cracked hip and a cracked-er skull) in the flames instead of a chair.

Then only the flames are left.

"Uma!" Aasha gasps, and her breath makes the tear fall. Uma reaches out and touches Aasha's cheek lightly with one cool finger, and underneath that fingertip the blood blooms hot in Aasha's cheek. Can it be, can it really be that all is forgiven? That Aasha's atonement for her sins of the past has been noted and accepted? Because Aasha is overcome with the surprise and thrill of being noticed at last, because she is bowled over by her own hereness and nowness, by the solid warmth of her cheek under Uma's finger, by the volcanic joy of being not Aasha-alone-and-invisible, but Aasha-with-Uma, taking up space on Uma's bed and in her life, she offers up all her hope in a single, shameless rush:

"Promise you'll write to me, Uma," she says. "Promise you'll send me stamps and maps. And stickers for my birthday."

Uma blinks, slow as a cow. Then she says, "Promise me you'll never again ask for a promise or make one yourself."

And because this is an impossible conundrum — how can she promise if she's no longer supposed to make promises? — Aasha can do nothing but watch Uma turn back to her suitcase and stuff into it the six pairs of footwear she has wrapped in twelve plastic bags, each shoe in its own bag so that the sole of one will not besmirch the upper of its mate. Curled up on Uma's bed for the last time, Aasha thinks about packing, about what people take and what they leave behind, about how much room there is in a suitcase, and how you can take everything you want with you wherever you go, your packed-up life, no stopping no promises. She hugs her knees to her chest and holds perfectly still, a small heap of tinder, ardent, waiting, ready.

4

AN OLD-FASHIONED COURTSHIP

I N 1959, when his father had been dead a full year, Appa set out to find himself a bride. Marriage was part of his first five-year plan, which was itself every bit as determined, purposeful, and specific as the nation's own. Marriage, children, two cars, servants, a job with prospects, hard-earned fame by forty: these would be the accoutrements of his climb to real power, to earning a generous piece of the national pie-in-the-oven. The climb itself had begun while he was still in Singapore, where he'd joined the Party, the only party that mattered, the party that believed in a Malaya for all Malayans, Chinese Indians Eurasians included, no matter what contrary chauvinist castles the Malays were building in the air. To Malaya, the Party would bring prosperity and peace, and to Appa, great glory both public and private.

Appa had no wish to settle down and procreate with any of the worldly women with whom he dallied. Lily Rozells, long-legged and sharp-tongued, smelled of brandy and had a preternatural eye for a winning horse; Claudine Koh had read English at Cambridge and Adorno and Benjamin in her spare time; Nalini Dorai entertained dreams of producing avant-garde political plays in Kuala Lumpur. These women were his equals, and they knew it. They looked him in the eye. They asked him to spell out his dreams for them: How, Raju? How will you convince the Party you're the best man for the job? What'll your platform be? Why would your average Ah Chong and Ramasamy vote for you? They flirted with him, viewed him with curiosity, fondness, and, yes, it had to be said, indulgence. *Oh, that Raju. Such a darling. Such big-big dreams for our half-past-six country. Ah, but what would we do without angry young men like him to hope, yeah? Every nation needs them.* Appa knew full well what they said about him behind his back; it was not what he wanted his wife saying. His wife would be admiring, respectful, adoring, but more than that — what was it he imagined? What was the quality so clearly lacking in Lily and Claudine and Nalini, who did, however grudgingly, admire him and his grand vision? Appa could not put his finger on it, but he knew he'd recognize it when he found it.

NEXT DOOR to the Big House, in the squat bungalow one day to be occupied by Baldy Wong and his harried parents, lived Amma, her six siblings, her father, and her mother. The house was barely visible from the street, situated as it was at the bottom of a narrow, dark garden thick with mango trees and hanging parasitic vines. Appa's parents had never entered that house or any of the others in the neighborhood, nor invited any of their neighbors into the Big House; they had never even discussed such social adventuring. The Big House had stood aloof from its neighbors in Mr. McDougall's time, and Tata and Paati had seen no reason to change the established order of the street. Among the other neighbors, Amma's father was known to be the sort of man who kept to himself, who held his family to a life of quiet decorum and high principles. He'd been a bookkeeper for a cement factory; when the business had foundered and his British bosses had talked about retrenching their staff, he'd taken an early retirement to allow a younger colleague to keep his job. Word had spread. He was a decent man, a good man, a man who was vegetarian twice a week and didn't let his daughters wear above-the-knee skirts. He spent his days listening to the wireless radio he'd bought after his retirement and watching the four angelfish he kept in a small tank. Once a month he allowed himself a solitary treat of the latest Tamil film at the Grand Theatre in Jubilee Park (choice of two masalvadai or one bottle Fanta Grape as intermission refreshment).

Behind his bland grey doors he regularly beat his modestly clad daughters with his leather belt, and had once held a meat cleaver to his wife's neck when she'd gone into town to post a letter without his knowledge. None of his neighbors ever discovered his belt-and-cleaver tactics, which was somewhat of a pity, if only because several of them would have admired this ultimate show of mastery from a man they'd pegged as a phlegmatic, fish-feeding teetotaler.

The year that Appa came home from Singapore, Amma was twenty years old and still fit into her box-pleated Convent of the Holy Infant Jesus pinafore. No one, least of all Amma herself, had ever noticed her unpolished beauty: the reedy figure Uma would inherit from her; the impossibly straight teeth in her rare smile; the glossy skin all her negligence could not tarnish; the suggestion of concealed intelligence and unrelieved concentration in her eyes. To her siblings and schoolmates she was an unfortunate exemplum of all the worst physical characteristics of Tamil stock: skinny, shapeless legs, almost-black skin, frizzy hair. To her father her eyes betrayed nothing but impudence, stubbornness, and a secretly mutinous spirit. She was the eldest child, already careworn, slouching a little to hide her height. Her voice had a grainy edge. She'd struggled but never been a star at school, faithfully attended miserable, muddy practices but never been good at games. She'd disappointed her father's belt-mourned dreams of an oldest son with a straight back and shiny shoes, who would be captain of the hockey team and study medicine in England. She'd watched helplessly as her mother, Ammachi, receded into an austere life of the spirit once she judged her children to be old enough to fend for themselves. "I've done my worldly duty as a wife and mother," Ammachi had declared on her youngest child's sixth birthday. "Vasanthi is already fifteen years old; she can run the house as well as I can. It's time I went on to the third stage of life."

"Ohoho," her husband had proclaimed to the fidgeting relatives and neighbors who had, for the first time anyone could remember, been invited to a party at their house, "look at that, my Eighth Standard–educated wife is suddenly turning into a great Hindu scholar it seems! What all does this third stage involve, may I ask? Wandering naked from temple to temple? Begging for food with a wooden bowl?"

"Illaiyai," Ammachi had demurred softly, frowning to herself as though her husband's questions had been born of honest curiosity. "No, all that is the fourth stage, yaar," she said, neatly placing slices of cake on saucers and handing them to Amma to pass around the table. "Fourth stage only is sannyasa, complete and total renunciation.

Third stage is the stage of the forest dweller," she said enigmatically, licking a blob of butter icing off one finger. "Vanaprastya."

But it had been decades since the last forests around Ipoh had given way to housing estates and cement factories, so Ammachi devised her own makeshift vanaprastya, comprising several non-negotiable elements: fasting three times a week, reading the Upanishads alone in her fanless white-curtained room, shunning meat, and sleeping on a wooden board. In just a few months she grew oblivious to the daily domestic struggles going on outside her door. She lay on her board chanting endless, booming mantras, humming bhajans, blind to the loneliness of a daydreaming oldest daughter being driven slowly to the brink of a terrible womanhood by her brood of needy, bickering siblings.

After a year, deciding perhaps that worldliness adhered to her sweaty skin like dust whenever she crossed the threshold of her room, she stopped leaving it altogether (with one unfortunate exception). When her meals were brought to her she ate only the rice or chapattis and drank all the water; the rest of the food, dhals and curries and bhajis, she pushed to the rim of her eversilver plate and arranged in neat little mounds with her spoon. After a week of this she left a note for Amma under the water tumbler on her tray. "Please: only rice or chapattis once a day," it read, and after that when Amma brought in the tray and tried to coax her to eat two spoons of dhal or three French beans she'd shake her head, hold up one index finger, and pause in the chanting of the day's mantra to repeat only that first word, *please,* inflected upwards as if it were a mnemonic device meant to call forth, from the recesses of Amma's faulty memory, a profusion of words.

By far the most egregious result of her mother's sequestration was the chamber pot, which was in fact not a chamber pot at all but an earthenware cooking vessel that Ammachi had taken from the kitchen on one of her last forays outside her room. It had its own earthenware lid and sat covered under her mattressless bed, but when Amma brought in her meal each afternoon the stench did brave battle with the smells of the family's dinner simmering on the kitchen stove, so that when Amma stood in that bleak room, her blindsided faculties perceived the contents of the pots on the stove and those of the pot under the bed to be essentially interchangeable. Simmering shit, festering dhal, sizzling turds, it was all the same to her. Astonishing that excrement composed entirely of rice or bread — and that only one at a time — could pack such a punch. Amma's head swam as if she'd lost a pint of blood, and as soon as she was out the door each afternoon she gagged, she swooned, she lay down on the settee with the back of her wrist on her forehead and dreamed ugly, malodorous dreams. It was true that Ammachi let no one else touch the pot; it was part of her humble new deal with the universe that she reject no task as being beneath her, that she welcome the lowliest, most odious of burdens as an opportunity to asphyxiate the id. Every night Ammachi waited until the family was asleep, and then, barefoot and squinting in the dark, stole out to an abandoned outhouse that no one had used since the Japanese occupation, to empty the pot into its narrow black hole. But her humility, as far as Amma was concerned, was all for nothing; Amma's imagination, fertilized by her mother's rich effluvia and flourishing as rapidly as the rest of her was withering, needed only to hear the click of her mother's door and the shuffled footsteps across the corridor to conjure up unanswerable questions — why did she have to use the outhouse? why not empty the pot in the bathroom, where no risk of tripping on a pebble, of missing the dark hole in the night, of blindly splashing her own saree with its seething contents, presented itself? — and unbearable pictures.

As the weeks went on Amma ate less and less, grew thinner and thinner, and began to tie a man's handkerchief over her nose and mouth to keep out the food smells as she cooked the family's meals. Her principal fear in these last few years before she left her childhood home for the house next door was that one of her few acquaintances from school might unexpectedly pop in with a question about the day's homework, or a new record or film star poster, or an invitation to an outing, and would then hear the chanting, smell the pot, and spread the ghastly word. She concentrated her efforts on keeping such encounters at bay, avoiding the casual advances of other girls, taking care to mention that she never listened to music or watched the latest films (both true), and rushing to and from school with her eyes lowered and her shoulders hunched around a soft center she knew people were waiting to poke at with sticks.

Motherless, waning, weak at the knees, she beat a shaky path through the duties she'd inherited, cooking and cleaning, ironing her father's shirts and her sisters' box-pleated pinafores, tying her brothers' striped school ties, packing the family's lunches, and bringing home, at the end of every month, report cards limp with C's. Every report card day her father had the children line up in a row before him in reverse order, youngest first, Amma last. One after the other they'd sit on the ottoman in front of his armchair and hold out their report cards to him. Some bursting with pride. Some trembling with unspilled tears. Some indifferent to it all, waiting to get it over with so that they could resume the game of marbles, hopscotch, or five stones they'd abandoned for the ritual. Amma had the misfortune of coming right after her brother Shankar, captain of the boys' hockey team, Best Speaker on the debate team, Assistant Head Prefect, straight-A student, teacher's pet. Their father would take one look at Shankar's report card, chuckle, and dismiss him with a "Not bad, not bad" and an admiring whack on the right shoulder. Then he'd look up at Amma and lick his lips like a wolf before a kill. "And what special treat have *you* brought us this time, Vasanthi?" he'd say. "No doubt about it, you're the genius of the family, no?" Amma would sit on the ottoman with her head bowed, cleaning her nails with a hairpin, dreaming of her escape. Over the years she learned to concentrate on the world outside and bear her father's cruel words like a chained dog in the rain. Hungry. Vigilant. Ready to grab her share when it showed up. "What?" her father would press on. "Hanh? Suddenly-suddenly this manicure is oh-so-urgent, yes? A girl with zero brains and zeroer prospects must of course have tip-top nails for all those high-flying job interviews and society tea parties just around the corner, what?" Then, just as she was starting to feel herself crumple under his gaze, just as the first tears began to sting her eyes, he'd pull his pen out of his pocket without warning, sign her report card, and throw it in her face. "Okay," he'd say. "Go. Go and sit in front of your books and sleep."

And sleep she did, though inexpertly, uncomfortably, and joylessly, just as she did everything else: exhausted from cooking and ironing, from trying to help her siblings with trigonometry problems she'd never understood how to do herself, from wading against the life-sapping current of her mother's unsplendid isolation, she slept, one arm folded under her cheek, on geography textbooks, on history flash cards, on rulers and protractors and compasses. "Pah, pah, I can't wait till you bring home the results from *this* exam," her father said the year she finally sat her Senior Cambridge Certificate. He rubbed his belly under his cotton singlet, like a peasant sitting down to a hot midday meal of dosais and sambar. "Whatta whatta treat that will be for us all. Straightaway they will accept you for post of Head Drain Sweeper. No questions asked. Or maybe better I start buying cows for your dowry now itself, hanh?" Then he'd give her head a sudden shove with the flat of his palm, grunt, and pronounce, "Fifty sixty cows also won't convince anyone to take this numbskull off my hands, I tell you."

His apprehensions were justified. Amma got C's in all her papers except geography, which she failed because of a panic attack at the last minute. "Syabas, Vasanthi!" her father exclaimed after glancing at the slip of paper she'd held out wordlessly. "Con-gra-chu-laaaaaa-tions. You've really outdone yourself this time. Surpassed even my expectations, man!" He whacked her heartily on the right shoulder, then walked away whistling. "Start drafting your career plans now it-self," he called over his shoulder. "U.N. Secretary-General or editor in chief of the London *Times*? What'll it be?"

For a few months she halfheartedly combed the classifieds for job vacancies. Clerk, cashier, receptionist. She circled them all with her leaky red pen, made phone calls, set up interviews. She dressed for each interview in the same navy blue skirt, white blouse, and sensible leather pumps she'd bought with the money relatives had given her for passing her senior Cambridge exam. In between interviews she washed, ironed, and starched the skirt and the blouse. She took the town bus to each interview, thrilled but terrified to be out on her own, convinced it was all useless. They were going to snort with laughter the minute she walked in. They were going to shake their heads at her failing grade in geography and send her home. As it happened, they never asked to see her results. One after another, they took one look at her trembling hands, heard a single stuttering answer to the sim-plest question, and sent her home with a promise to call. She busied herself while she waited, scrubbing the sink three times a day, scrap-ing the grout between the bathroom tiles, polishing the linoleum on all fours, her ugly cotton housedress tied in a knot around her knees. At the back of her mind a tiny black seed began to sprout: the fright-ening thought that this was what the rest of her life would be. Wait-ing and scrubbing. Polishing and dreaming. Its terrible tendrils threat-ened to cut her breath short, to clog her veins if she gave it free rein. So she stuffed her head full of unyielding, ready-made pictures that left no room for her seedling of doubt. She choked it to death with lurid love scenes from Indian films she'd seen on family outings in her childhood. With richly embroidered wedding sarees and a loving hand feeding her sweetmeats before a hairy-chested, chanting priest. With handsome, blurry men in fedoras and Italian suits. Smoking imported cigars. Peppering their Tamil with English declarations of love and defiance.

That was the year Appa came home from Singapore in his pea-green Morris Minor with beige leather seats. Amma was cleaning the shutters in her father's bedroom as it pulled into the driveway next door one Sunday afternoon. Had she been standing there two days before, she would have seen Appa's father keel over in his beautiful garden. Now, rag in hand, she peered through the shutters and watched Appa unload three matching leather suitcases, a black briefcase, and a small trunk. Sunlight spilled in between the wooden slats of the shutters and fanned out in neat swaths on the spotless floor of the bedroom. "Vasanthi!" her father called from the foot of the stairs. "What is this, taking three days just to wipe the shutters? If you have no brains can't you at least make your hands useful?"

When she and her father went to pay their last respects to Tata, she sat with her navy interview skirt pulled carefully over her knees and watched Appa curiously out of the corner of her eye. So this was what someone with a law degree from England looked like. This was how one moved and talked when one had matching monogrammed luggage. With an air of subdued authority. She watched him make his rounds of the shady sitting room, full of drooping potted palms and women's sorrow. When he got to Amma's father he shook his hand wordlessly. "Very sorry, my wife simply couldn't make it," Amma's father lied with a mournful shake of the head. "Not feeling well. We ourselves are getting old, what to do?" Amma thought of her mother, erect and white-lipped that morning when her father had gone to ask her to come next door for a few hours. "For God's sake," he'd said, "stop this nonsense for one day. All the neighbors will be wondering whether I've killed you and hidden the body. At least just come for a few minutes to pay your last respects to the old man."

"Let the dead bury their dead," Ammachi had said, momentarily switching from the Bhagavad-Gita to the Bible. Amma, who'd had twelve years of Scripture Knowledge at her convent school, noted the inappropriateness of the quotation's coming from a woman who'd renounced the world and refused to budge from her room. "Why mourn?" her mother had continued, her philosophizing growing stubbornly expansive in the face of her husband's intransigent scorn. "The old man has come one step closer to escaping the chains of rebirth. In fact we should all be rejoicing for him. Why all this fuss? Why two hundred three hundred people should crowd their house? All simply coming for free food only. Shameless. Why not let his family quietly remember him and celebrate his passing?"

In the end they'd had to go without her. Now, face-to-face with the dead man's oldest son, Amma's father hastened to compensate for his wife's disrespectful absence by gesturing a little too eagerly towards Amma. "My eldest," he said, lowering his eyes as if fully conscious that the replacement offering was inadequate. "Vasanthi." Appa looked at this thin, dark girl, several inches taller than he, too awkward to meet his eyes as she mumbled her pleasedtomeetyou, and saw, with considerable surprise, that she was beautiful. Excruciatingly gauche, yes, and quite dark, but the first oddly underscored her beauty, and the second was a matter of taste in which he took some pride. He liked obscure Continental writers, game, and dark women; among his friends he had a reputation as a man of rarefied appetites. And so he stored her away for future use, this girl whose loveliness could not be suppressed by her unfashionable oiled braids or by the probably unshaven legs beneath her drab ankle-length skirt; for now, he had other matters to see to. A father to cremate, three sisters to marry off.

It was a whole year before Amma met her new neighbor again. Between the slats of the shutters she saw him come and go in his pea-green Morris Minor every day, getting out of the car to open and close the high iron gates of the Big House. She knew in which pocket he kept his house keys (left), which way he ran the chain around the gate (always clockwise) before he padlocked it, and how many pairs of dress shoes he owned (three, two black and one brown). She learned to recognize the days when he was going to court by the black coat he carried on a hanger. She noticed when he came home with a new pair of glasses, in stylish horn-rimmed frames. One Saturday afternoon she saw him come out to the gate to pay the newspaper boy, wearing a cotton singlet and a checkered sarong, still sucking his lunch out of his teeth. She smiled to herself, and the wan light of her smile seeped out through the shutter slats and pooled in a patient, watery circle on the top of Appa's Brylcreemed head.

When his sisters were married, one after the other, Amma watched from the upstairs windows as men put up marquees in the compound and strung colored bulbs from the awnings. The smell of sweetmeats frying in ghee wafted up to her, and every now and then a voice would detach itself from the general murmur: the shrill, nasal scolding of a fat old matron, a child's whine, a man's sozzled laughter. Her father attended all three weddings alone, the envelope of money for the newlyweds crisp in the front pocket of the batik shirt she'd ironed. The morning after each of these weddings there was a crumbling laddoo in a serviette on the dining table for whichever of her brothers was first to rise that day.

After the third wedding had been successfully executed and his youngest sister packed off to make her new home with her country-doctor husband in Padang Rengas, Appa went to call at the pale green bungalow next door. He sat in the sitting room and talked to Amma's father, man to man; Ammachi stayed in her room reading the Gita, and whether Appa had heard tell of her odd habits, or merely thought it natural that she should leave them to their business, he didn't inquire that day after the lady of the house. "Vasanthi!" Amma's father called after Appa had been greeted and seated. "Can't you see we have a guest? Our own next-door neighbor and you're taking one hour to bring a cup of tea and some titbits, what is this?" Amma made the tea and laid out half a dozen ginger snaps and a plate of murukku on a bamboo tray. She looked in the mirror above the kitchen sink, wet her palms, and smoothed down her housework hair. Then she stepped through the bead curtain in the entryway and took the tea tray into the sitting room. Behind her the curtain drizzled quietly back into place. "Bleddi fool of a girl!" her father grumbled to his guest as she left the room. "First time you are coming to the house and she puts the murukku on a chipped plate. Useless bleddi girl, I tell you." "It's okay, Uncle," she heard Appa say with his mouth full, "the murukku will still taste just as good." At that visit Appa asked Amma's father's permission to have a brick wall built between their houses. "No offense, Uncle," he said. "The hedge breeds mosquitoes, that is all. Without it it'll be one job less for the gardener I'll be hiring." When that was settled he asked Amma's father's permission to take his daughter out.

Every Saturday for a year after that visit, while he was scrambling up the steep slopes of his career, Appa took Amma out with only her two youngest brothers as chaperones.

Brushing her hair, dabbing eau de toilette on her wrists, ironing her cotton skirts before these outings, what did Amma imagine lay at the Technicolor conclusion of her courtship?

Certainly not the crumbling white shell her parents called a marriage.

Nor would there be anything seamy about their marital bliss. It would have nothing in common with the vulgar cavortings of Tamil-film couples or the school gardener's leer whenever a girl's petticoat had shown under the hem of her skirt. No, their joy would be cool and pure and exalted. On the weekends she would bake cakes; when she had a baby they would have family portraits taken at a studio.

In Appa's eyes, her lack of experience added to her allure. He would introduce her to the wonders of eros; she would bloom under his expert tutelage. Already he relished the prospect.

"That girl?" Paati said when she found out who was occupying his Saturday afternoons. "That clerk's daughter? After all your foreign education? Why not look for a girl of your own standing?" This, as far as Paati was concerned, had been the purpose of all her husband's hard work: that his sons should have the pick of the country's marriageable Indian maidens. "She's not even nice-looking also," Paati reasoned. "As shapeless as a coconut tree, and so black."

"Oh, come off it," Appa said. "As if I'm marrying the girl tomorrow. Just a way to pass the weekends, that's all."

She believed him; hadn't he always been the good son, the one who'd followed his father's advice, taken a sensible degree, and written home every week? *It's true,* she thought, *he's not serious about that girl. Well, let him have his fun. He's young. Already saddled with so much responsibility, poor thing.*

What she couldn't have guessed: spice the satisfaction he already derived from his unusual tastes with a dash of the forbidden and a soupçon of public disapproval, and Appa was well and truly hooked. After all the years he'd been away, she hardly knew him. He'd left a boy and come back a half-foreign man, and every detail of that transformation startled her. The smell of cologne in the bathroom in the mornings; the plummy accent he couldn't turn off even for her or the servants; the lordly, masculine way he spread himself out and drank whiskey after dinner, one arm thrown over the back of the chair next to him, shirtsleeves rolled up, tie loosened.

And so Appa's casual lie about the tenor of his association with Amma slid smoothly down Paati's throat as, away from Kingfisher

Lane but still under the eagle eyes of Amma's young brothers, he closed suavely in on his quarry.

"Ah, I look forward to this all week," he told her every Saturday when he picked her and her brothers up for the matinee show at the Lido Theatre. "The thought that on Saturday I shall get to take the most beautiful girl in town to the pictures keeps me going from Monday to Friday." And, when she averted her eyes in response and tucked her hair behind her ears: "I'm sure a girl like you must be inured to all these compliments by now, eh?" He knew it wasn't true; he knew no one had ever paid this girl a compliment in all her mean, miserable life. One Saturday as she came out into the sitting room where Appa waited for her, her father stuck his head out from behind his newspaper, grunted with mild amusement, and said, "Who you trying to fool, Vasanthi? I think so Raju here still has his eyesight. Each week doing some fancy-fancy new thing with your hair, as if it makes any difference to your donkey face." He looked at Appa with a "Hah!" that was more an order to laugh than an invitation. But Appa did not comply. He stood up, opened the door for Amma, and said, without taking his eyes off her, "I do indeed still have my eyesight, Uncle, and it's yours I'm worried about. Either you're blind, or you come from a land of supernally beautiful donkeys."

"Hah!" Amma's father said again. But his defeat was evident; he had not sufficiently understood Appa's retort to attempt one of his own. Out of the corner of his eye Appa saw the pinched look on his face as he retreated behind his newspaper, but directly in front of him he saw Amma's hungry, luminous eyes meet his own, and in them he recognized at once what he had longed for all this time, what had been lacking in the attentions of Lily and Claudine and Nalini: gratitude. This girl was grateful to him, had been grateful from the day he'd first rescued her from her father's house for four hours, and would, if he played his cards right, be forever grateful. He swallowed, and the knowledge warmed him like whiskey as it went down. Outside, the whole street—windows and leaves, bicycles, the Saturday smiles of Amma's two brothers—glittered in the sunlight.

Every Saturday evening upon her return to her father's house, he made her stand before him and deliver a thorough account of the film she'd seen. "Stand straight," he'd say, "stand straight and talk properly." When she'd fidget he'd reach out with one equine leg and hook a foot around her ankle to jerk her closer. "What's the matter?" he'd say. "All this high-class gallivanting around town and still you behave like a goat." But now she knew he was doing all this just to humiliate her, because he knew she was winning, slipping from his grasp as he watched; he was in a hurry to grind her down before she got away. She'd show him, all right. *Old devil. Syaitan. Think you'll be able to bully me like this when I'm the lady of the Big House?*

Of her rise in the world's esteem she was deliciously conscious, for each week some small incident reminded her of it. One afternoon they were sitting in the FMS Bar & Restaurant, their customary teatime haunt, when Amma struck up a wordless, effervescent friendship with a child at an adjacent table. She'd caught the child's eyes and smiled at him deliberately, wanting Appa to witness this interaction, and sure enough, just as the child began to play peekaboo with her through the bars of his chair, Appa said, "I see you're a natural with children, after all these years mothering your brothers and sisters."

Her brother Nitya snorted loudly at this, and his shoulders shivered with laughter over his F&N orange squash.

"*Pfft!*" her brother Krishen smirked.

"Nitya, Krishen," said Appa, cuffing them one after the other on the head, "show a little respect for your Akka, please. After all she's done for you. Bringing you up single-handedly because of your poor mother's frail health."

She looked up at Appa. His eyes were invisible behind the glare of his glasses, but she felt *seen* then, more seen than ever, her sacrifices noted, appreciated, and put into words; her sufferings keenly felt; her many weaknesses — her report card C's, her failed geography paper, the chipped murukku bowl — forgiven.

"You want to buy comics on the way home or not?" Appa barked at the boys' downcast faces. "Hanh?"

"Yes," said Nitya.

"Yes, Raju Anneh," said Krishen.

"Then hurry up and say sorry to your Akka and let's go."

"Sorry," said Nitya.

"Sorry, Akka," said Krishen.

It was, as far as she could remember, the first time anyone had ever apologized to her for anything. Never again were Nitya or Krishen offhandedly rude to her, in Appa's presence or otherwise.

One Saturday eleven months after Appa had first picked Amma up for a matinee, they were reaching the end of their pot of tea at the

FMS Bar when he announced his intention to bring dinner home to her family.

"Mee goreng and char kuay teow," he said. "Half and half. That way there'll be something for everyone."

"I don't think . . ." she began. "Actually there's plenty of food in the house, I — we've — cooked all week, so many leftovers there are —"

"Oh yesyes, that of course," he said hastily, "that I understand. It's not that you don't have food. No doubt they are not sitting and starving and waiting for my two measly bowls of noodles. But just for a change, no? It'll be a treat for your brothers and sisters. Eh? Why always Nitya and Krishen only should be the ones nicely-nicely enjoying?" He gave Nitya an affectionate rap on the head with his knuckles. "How about it, boy?"

"Can also," said Nitya. The more he looked at his sister, the more his misgivings encroached on his appetite. When she caught him alone he was probably going to get a few good ones. Thighpinches, mouthslaps, earboxes. Assorted hot-and-spicy treats. But mee goreng was mee goreng, and in the grand scheme of things it would be worth a few good ones.

In the car there were two enormous eversilver dishes Appa had brought for the mee goreng and char kuay teow. He parked on Anderson Road and crossed the busy street alone, holding first one dish and then the other out to a hawker as Amma and her brothers watched from the car. Krishen licking his lips. Nitya patting his rumbling belly and hoping he'd get to pick out at least six prawns before his siblings helped themselves. Amma reacquainting herself with the smoky flavor of certain doom. If Appa came to dinner at her father's house, she knew, her friable fairy tale would crumble. Her mother's room was just off the dining room, three steps up the corridor. He would not sit at the table for two hours without piecing together — from her mother's conspicuous absence, from the odor that would steal into the room, from her siblings' indiscretions and unfunny jokes — the startling truth of her mother's illness. For that was how Amma thought of it: an illness, a sad and irreparable snapping in the head, a condition to be whispered about within the immediate family.

After tonight, nothing would put her façade back together again, no radiant hint of her motherly potential, no searingly romantic American film theme shared silently in those plush red seats in the darkness of the rolling credits. Her five senses closed shop one by one, and all things faded away: the creaking of overloaded trishaws, the mingling smells of street food and exhaust fumes, the slap-slapping of rickshaw men's slippered feet, the whizzing of cars and ringing of bicycle bells outside her open window, until she found herself looking as if through a tunnel at the terrible scene unfolding in her head: Appa crossing the threshold of her father's house, bearing his eversilver bowls aloft like a hotel waiter. Left toe to right heel, right toe to left heel, shiny leather shoes slid effortlessly off on the doorstep, no hands needed. Man and bowls sailing into dining room, man in finest-gauge black socks, whistling "Bengawan Solo," bowls laden with fragrant noodles. Then the chanting that could no longer be ignored, the small befuddled smile with which she'd grown so familiar. And finally, most horrendously of all, the depredatory bouquet of the chamber pot (brimming as it always was at this late hour), sneaking through the keyhole and the crack under the door. The painfully polite meal, the reddening of Appa's eyes as he tried manfully to hold his breath for an hour. And at the end of it, the retreat: No no, it's okay, keep the bowls, don't worry, see you next week. Only of course there would be no next week. She would stand at the front door and watch the pea-green Morris Minor reverse carefully down her father's driveway. Next Saturday would come and go, and she would return to watching a stranger — shoes keys black coat for court cases — through the upstairs shutters.

But there was, at first, no chanting to be heard when they got out of the Morris Minor. In the sitting room Amma's father was ensconced in his armchair, peering intently at his angelfish, tapping the glass of the aquarium with a fingernail. He looked up when Amma and the boys came in.

"So?" he grunted. "Today what grand-grand flim did you see? Hanh?"

"I've brought —" said Amma.

"Raju Anneh came home with us," said Krishen. "Brought dinner also. Mee goreng. Char kuay teow."

"Ohoho," said his father. "Ohoho, I see. Very nice. Very nice. Not always we get company in this house. Go and ask your brothers and sisters to wash their hands and come down and say hello." He stood up and shut the fish food canister with a click.

Now that every wriggling cell in Amma's nose was tuned to the shitpot station, she had to admit to herself that the keyhole and door-crack were not so easily overcome by its noxious emanations as she'd remembered. Perhaps she'd confused her own mephitic dreams with this milder reality; perhaps her judgment had been warped by her years of shame and resentment of all that the chamber pot stood for, because this smallest of earthenware pots, sooty-bottomed and unassuming, hardly big enough for one day's dhal back when it had been in kitchen use, had been so much more for so many years. The selfish piety of a mother who thought she sat and shat at the right hand of God. The pitiful, caged life she'd blithely inflicted on her abandoned daughter. The odious nighttime clicks of the door latch on her unnecessary outhouse missions. The ceaseless bhajan-singing and chanting that provided the ridiculous background to the beatings and beltings and sobs of her children.

Amma stood outside all this and considered it. These things were invisible now; humiliation had no odor, and the sounds of this afternoon's beatings, as far as she could tell, had dissipated into the still, grey air. If luck remained on her side—just this once—Appa need never know about their secret lives.

Wordlessly, her ears buzzing with anxiety, she stepped through the bead curtain into the dining room. In the far corner of the room was a glass-doored cabinet lined with *Straits Times* pages from June 1950 and filled with the remnants of her parents' senescent marriage. A tarnished pewter kris and moon kite, still in the box in which they'd arrived as wedding presents. Frayed baskets and a brass plate etched with the Dutch Fort, from their honeymoon in Malacca. Faded formal photographs of their children at various ages in cracked leather frames. Miniature models of the Taj Mahal, the Eiffel Tower, the Empire State Building, and Buckingham Palace lined up conveniently in a row, courtesy of their better-traveled relatives, a majestic but garbled package deal for the miniature tourist in a hurry. The bottom two shelves of the cabinet were taken up by a set of dishes and glasses that hadn't been used since the birthday party at which Ammachi had announced her withdrawal from the world.

Amma knelt and drew these things out, noting as she did so the disintegrating bodies of flies and beetles in the grooves of the sliding doors. With a clean, wet dishcloth she wiped the plates off one by one. She poured ice water into the clear blue glasses and saw Appa slip cleanly into the beginning of the scene she'd spun out in her head. It was like watching a master diver: one minute he was outside, standing in the harsh light of the low-slung sun, and the next minute he'd slid sharp as a knife into the soft dim of the sitting room, a larger-than-life five-foot-five magnet with a field too powerful for this little house. Already his ample, energetic gestures seemed to overwhelm it. He slid his shoes off with his dexterous toes, just as she'd imagined, and as he strode in with his eversilver bowls, arrogant and unapologetic, a small-minded, prudish shiver seemed to run through the walls.

"Ah, good, good," he said when he caught sight of Amma with her bottle of ice water. "Put out plates for everyone. Nitya, Krishen, call all your brothers and sisters." His booming voice ricocheted off every unyielding, dusty surface. The old mahogany sideboard rattled its stores of cutlery as Amma opened its top drawer. The dining table shook under its oilcloth cover. The angelfish darted in marble-eyed alarm from corner to corner of the fingerprint-smeared fish tank. Under Appa's cool, commanding gaze Nitya and Krishen turned sniggering and pigeon-toed.

"What?" said Appa. "What's the problem? Want to eat but don't want to help, is that it?"

They turned and scuttled up the stairs.

Appa laid his bowls on the two wooden trivets Amma had put on the table and strode off to the kitchen to wash his oily hands.

Amma set the table with the newly wiped plates and the forks and spoons she'd found in the sideboard drawer. Stained stainless steel; she hadn't thought it was possible. To compensate, she rummaged in another drawer and found an unopened packet of serviettes in a pretty cerise, also left over from that fateful birthday party seven years ago. She pulled out nine and began to fold them meticulously into fans, running over each crease with a thumbnail.

"Oo wah," said Appa, coming back into the kitchen with his hands in his pockets, "getting rather fancy for a couple of bowls of roadside noodles, aren't we?"

She smiled but said nothing, and he stood and watched her with arms akimbo.

Her father came in through the bead curtain. "Well, well, well," he said. "Not bad, not bad." But he didn't give Appa a friendly shoulderwhack. He pulled out the chair at the head of the table and took his seat, drumming his fingers on the tabletop. One by one the other children trudged down the stairs, the hair around their faces damp from quick splashings at the bathroom sink. One sister's eyes still red-rimmed from an afternoon beating or punishment Amma had missed. Again the thought struck her that if luck stayed on her side everything that happened in this brutalizing house, even if it remained stolidly next door, may as well be taking place in some terrible faraway dictatorship she read about in the newspapers.

The children took their seats, shuffling, lipbiting, sniffing diffidently, each one vaguely aware of the momentousness of this occasion and its import for their trembling, serviette-folding sister.

"Wah," said Valli, the oldest girl after Amma and her special favorite, "thanks for bringing all this, Raju Anneh. So nice of you." But she avoided Appa's eyes, and smiled instead at the eversilver bowls.

"Sit, sit," said Appa. "Come, let's eat before everything gets cold. What about your mother? Not joining us?"

"Oh, she doesn't take Chinese food," said Amma casually. "And anyway she only takes a midday meal, not dinner." She took another serviette from the pile and began to pleat it.

"Maybe she'd like to come out and have a cup of tea with us?"

"She's resting," said Amma. "She retires very early for the night."

"I see, I see. Well, that's all right then, let her rest, yesyesyes, my own mother is the same. No appetite, she says. Getting older, what to do, she says."

No one else said anything. No repressed giggles from the boys. No muttered invective from her father. Amma looked up and saw her father's eyes on her busy hands, his lips thin and tight, his nostrils flared. Like a cold gust in her face it dawned on her: not only was he in on the game, he was, for once, on her side, slavering at the prospect of its many benefits: the rich son-in-law, the numskull daughter taken off his hands forever, the stamped and sealed reputation as just another nice, old-fashioned Indian family. Gingerly she put each finished serviette fan next to the others. There were six of them in two rows now, bright on the dark wood of the table.

"Come, Uncle," said Appa with a clap of his hands, "why don't you do the honors?"

But Amma's father, unfamiliar with the invitation, served only himself, and with a grunt began to shovel the mountain of noodles on his plate into his mouth. "What're you all waiting for?" he said to the children between mouthfuls. "You heard what Raju Anneh said.

Serve yourselves and eat before it all gets cold. No need to wait for your sister to finish her handicraft project. By the time she's done the food will have gone moldy also."

"Oh, nonono, not to worry, Uncle," said Appa, "see, all ready." He picked up the fans in both hands and with a flourish deposited one at each place setting. "Sit," he said to Amma, gesturing at the empty chair beside him. Lifting the plates one by one, he heaped food onto them.

The dining room clock ticked loudly. The fish tank pump hummed and whirred. On either side of their father Nitya and Krishen fought noiselessly over the prawns and cockles. Appa sat opposite Amma's father, and to his right sat Amma, bent low over her plate, her skin raw with embarrassment at her father's manners, at her own awkwardness with noodles and fork, at Appa's eyes on her. After every mouthful she dabbed at her lips and chin with her serviette. But Appa, watching her, saw not her awkwardness but her simplicity: the anxious table manners, the missionary-school daintiness. A pang of nostalgia for his own childhood rose up through him; what had he been doing with women who smoked and quoted Marx and Engels? They would dismiss this girl as bourgeois, of course, but no matter; this was what he wanted to come home to. They would roll their eyes behind his back, accuse him of paying lip service to revolutionary notions while in private he kept a wife who fluttered her lashes and left the thinking to him. And yet—Appa realized now, watching Amma's father scrape his fork determinedly against his plate, belch, and go on to his second helping—weren't these the sort of people true socialism would have them all embrace? Somewhere along the way, hadn't they confused idealism with elitism in choosing to consort only with fellow intellectuals? Let them believe, then, that he'd made the cowardly choice of a woman unsullied by inconvenient aspirations of her own; in fact, he would be the bravest of them by taking on the real work of nation-building.

Had Appa not been blinded by two equally powerful strains of romanticism, he might have noticed that Amma's father showed little sign of sharing his optimism. That the man seemed to breathe only while drinking, behind the shield of his water glass. His face was drawn; his lips were pinched. His eyes darted around the table, accusing all his children of having sold their souls. Oh, he wasn't exempting himself either: he may have been sitting at the head of the table, but with this bowl of char kuay teow he'd ceased to be the head of the household, and he knew it. Two bloody plates of noodles and he'd nicely wrapped his own balls up with a red ribbon and offered them to this bow-tied fop. He belched again, more loudly than before, and gulped down the rest of his water. "Well, well," he said. "Thanks, man. This is a first-class meal. I'm sure you know we mostly eat simple home-cooked food only. All this flim-watching FMS-Barring all where I can afford?"

"Heh-heh," said Appa, wiping his mouth with his unfolded serviette-fan, "no problem, Uncle, all this is nothing much—"

But before he could belittle himself in proper munificent style, the door to Ammachi's room opened with a distinct creak, and Ammachi emerged, bony feet first, then the rest of her, gaunt, pasty, her hair bun flat from the plywood board on which she slept. She shuffled towards the table, the stench of her cramped quarters coming off her white saree in puffs as she moved. All around the table there was a unanimous sucking in of breath so deep the house turned for three seconds into a vacuum, still and voracious, and a sparrow flying past an open window was pulled against the mosquito netting and held fast for those three long seconds. Then everyone exhaled, the sparrow fled in a bewildered flurry of feathers, and Amma's father dropped his fork onto his plate with a clatter. Grunting, he pushed the plate sharply away from him so that it slid a foot down the table and collided with one of Appa's half-empty eversilver bowls. All around the table there was a stiffening of shoulders, with one cheery exception.

"Oh, hellohellohello, Auntie," said Appa, "how nice to see you. So sorry to interrupt your rest. Too-too loud we must have been—my fault—"

"Foof!" said Shankar the favorite son, burying his nose in his cupped hands. Through the open door of Ammachi's room the fumes of the chamber pot, every bit as powerful as Amma had remembered them, slithered forth in a thousand black dragontails. Nitya picked up his water glass and pressed it to his face, his desperate breath misting its bottom. Krishen broke out in a fit of consumptive coughing, the tip of his pink tongue sticking out of his greasy mouth. Even sweet, sympathetic Valli picked up her crumpled serviette and began to pat her nose with it.

"Please join us, Auntie," said Appa imperturbably, "there's still so much left."

"Oh, no," said Ammachi quietly, pulling the pallu of her saree over her disheveled head. From under this hood she peered narrowly out at each one of them, her eyes slowly going around the table. "No thank you. I don't take Chinese food." She looked pointedly at the golden pool of pork fat on her husband's plate. "Simply came out to see who came. Many many years we have not had any visitors, you see."

Under the table Amma's knees quivered. She curled her long toes and dug her heels into the cool cement floor.

"Oho, yesyes," said Appa, "so sorry to intrude but I just thought —"

"No problem," said Ammachi, "not intruding at all. All this is no longer my business, after all. Who comes and goes, who eats what. I've taken a vow to withdraw from this world, you see. All my mundane duties I've carried out. Simply only today I came out, I thought first time someone coming to the house after so long, maybe something was wrong or what."

"Actually," said Appa, "it's not the first time. I live next door, you see. I came first to ask for Uncle's kind permission to build that new wall. And now I drop in every Saturday to pick up Vasanthi and Nitya and Krishen for a film."

Amma kept her eyes lowered, avoiding her mother's inscrutable gaze. Yet she felt that gaze sweep across her face, and she knew the thoughts behind it: *So that is what my daughter has become. A glorified call girl. Going out with men in exchange for a free meal. Giving in to all of her base instincts at once.*

But Ammachi only said: "Ah. I see. Well all that is not my concern. Carry on. Please carry on. Time already for my evening puja." Then she turned and shuffled back to her room. A fresh whiff of excrement-spiced air wafted out from the folds of her saree and draped itself around Amma like an octopus tentacle. Ammachi's door shut with another loud creak. Amma looked down at her plate, her tongue suddenly thick and salty, her throat clotted with viscous tears. She felt herself rise and strain, suspended in time like a wave ready to crash against a rocky shore.

"Better I turn up the fan," exclaimed Valli, ever the resourceful one. "I think so somebody's septic tank must be broken again. So sorry Raju Anneh, you see that Malay family on the other side of the road is always having this problem and always it happens at dinnertime." She jumped up and turned the ceiling fan up to its highest setting. "Let me open the windows also. *Tsk tsk,* whatta whatta terrible stink, no?"

"Stink?" said Appa, pausing with a forkful of noodles an inch from his mouth. "What stink? Must be I'm sitting in the best bloody seat in the house because I can't smell anything."

It was the first Amma knew of his missing sense of smell. She looked up, blinked disbelievingly, and then felt the blood drain from her burning cheeks to see him chewing peaceably on a tough cockle. In the heavens a chorus of angels with clothespegs on their ethereal noses began to sing, the nasal strains of their joy filling the skies just as Ammachi's praise rose in concurrence:

> *Om Trayambakam*
> *Yajaamahe*
> *Sugandhim Pushtivardhanam . . .*

THREE WEEKS after that miracle, on one of those balmy Malayan evenings when the light turns milky before dying, Appa asked Nitya and Krishen to wait in the Morris Minor while he and Amma crossed the street to buy the now-customary dinner. "I need a bit of help today," he said. He handed her a third bowl and turned to the boys in the back seat. "How about a little after-dinner something for an extra-special treat?" he said with a wink. "Ice kacang? Or would you prefer cendol?"

They decided on ice kacang (with dollops of vanilla ice cream for the boys), and as Amma and Appa stood before the char kuay teow stall in the smoky dusk, the boys rolled down a window and leaned out like two eager young dogs, nudging and smirking, whistling too quietly for Appa or their sister to hear them, and enjoying the exhaust-fumed, lard-spiked air in their faces.

Across the street, Appa leaned towards Amma and gripped her elbow as if to steer her along the right path. Towards respectability and comfort, ladies' tea parties and sturdy furniture, nest eggs and new clothes for the children every Deepavali. The wild flames under the hawker's cast-iron wok burned blue in Appa's horn-rimmed glasses. Sweat circles darkened the underarms of his wilting pinstriped shirt, and his nascent bald spot gleamed like a baby moon. Like a dancer's jewels, perfect round beads of sweat studded the dip between Amma's nose and lip.

"I want to marry you," he said, "even if *I* have to pay *your* father a dowry. I can't wait any longer. You know I will make you happy. You know you'll have a first-class life. No cooking no cleaning. Whatever jewelry you want. Chauffeur-driven car."

"*Tsk*. What is this, talking about private matters all here on the roadside."

But she smiled and giggled and shrugged, as if reading from a script. As if she'd already read the play and picked a part in advance. Across the street, two little extras in a Morris Minor sniggered and demonstrated the mechanics of copulation with their hands. A Chinese grandmother pushing a pram along the five-foot-ways of the shophouses caught sight of them, averted her offended eyes, and hissed imprecations about bad Indian boys to her drowsy grandchild.

"What's wrong?" Appa said half indignantly to Amma's shy, shrugging shoulders. To himself he noted that the hair at the nape of her neck was soft and almost straight, most unlike the coarse frizzy mane she'd pulled into a loose knot today. "Nothing to be ashamed of," he persevered. "Bloody Chinaman can't understand a word anyway."

He held out his hands for the dish of noodles, slick with grease from the hawker's stovetop.

Afterwards she was never sure what it was that had won her over: the simple eloquence of his pared-down proposal or the promise of prosperity in that brimming eversilver dish.

When she told her father the news, he smiled his acrid smile for a while before saying, "Not bad, Vasanthi. For an idiot you haven't done too badly for yourself. Syabas!"

Next door in the Big House, Paati held her son by his shoulders and shook him. "You're mad," she said. "You're going to regret this decision all your life. They're not our kind of people. How can you bring a girl like that into this house?"

"Amma," he said, freeing himself from her grip, "come off it. Enough of this nineteenth-century mentality. Not our kind of people? Well, last I looked they all had two eyes and a nose and a mouth, just like us. It's thinking like yours that's going to hold this country back."

Paati drew back, folded her arms, and narrowed her eyes at him. "Now I see," she said. "I see what that girl has done. Shameless gold-digger has poured out some sob story on your shoulder, and you've fallen for it. Good. Do what you want and suffer. Just don't come crying to me, and don't expect me to treat her like a queen in my own house."

"Actually, it's my house," said Appa, "and you will treat her with the same respect you owe any human being."

5

THE RECONDITE RETURN OF
PAATI THE DISSATISFIED

August 21, 1980

ON THE AFTERNOON of Paati's cremation, Uma makes a ham-and-cheese omelet to feed those members of the household who are not attending the funeral — to wit, herself, Suresh, Aasha, and Chellam.

This four-person omelet, Aasha reasons, means that Uma does not *hate* them. Its edges are a little burned; there is so much cheese in it that it clogs Suresh's throat, and he makes a great show of choking to death, rolling his eyes back in his head, thumping frantically at his chest. "Death by cheese," he gasps between coughs. "A Krafty murder. Tomorrow's headline: St. Michael's Boy Asphyxiated by Overstuffed Omelet." Aasha would like to imagine that Uma smiles at this, just the breath of a smile before she turns the page of her book, but it's simply not true. Uma doesn't even look up; she only turns the page and spears a stray cube of ham with her fork.

Nevertheless, and notwithstanding its obvious imperfections, the omelet is proof that Uma harbors a new glimmer of fondness for them, perhaps especially for Aasha, because she served Aasha first, and then left Suresh to cut his own piece. Though Aasha can count on one hand the occasions on which Uma has spoken to her in the past year, it's clear that Uma loves her once again, in some secret place.

This evening Uma might invite them outside to wait for the roti man with her; then she might let Aasha sit on her bed and listen to Simon and Garfunkel. Tomorrow she might tell Appa and Amma she doesn't want to go to New York after all. Return the plane ticket, she'll say. Put away the brown airport suit in the rosewood chest. I'll put the suitcase back in the storeroom.

The thought of it — the fragile possibility, thin as the air on a mountaintop — turns the air in Aasha's nostrils cold and chills her throat and chest.

You goondu, Suresh would say if he were privy to Aasha's deductions. You stoopit idiot. Uma made the omelet because Amma ordered her to, and Amma ordered her to because Chellam wouldn't make it. Simple as that. Easy to see.

It's true, Chellam wouldn't have made the omelet, though Amma didn't even ask her; since Paati died two days ago, Chellam's been tossing and turning and burning in that bed in which she has suffered two fevers since coming to the Big House. Spread-eagled, fetus-curled, face-down, in all these positions and more she waits for her father's final visit, when he will collect his unwanted daughter instead of the money that has kept him smacking his chops and rubbing his palms together every month for a year. When he comes, he will spit at her feet and knock her head with his knuckles. On the bus ride home he will not look at her. She's squandered his toddy shop account, his still-novel popularity among the men of the village, his lazy afternoons, all his happy stupor. Each time she thinks of that imminent bus ride home, Chellam buries her face in her pillow and sees how long she can go without breathing.

"Uma," Amma said before she left for the funeral, "you'll have to do something about lunch. There's bread, there are eggs, there are yesterday's leftovers. After what Chellam did I don't want her making your food."

Amma shook her head as she said this, as if she'd made a difficult-but-firm decision, as if Chellam had been begging for the chance to make their lunch. But Suresh wasn't fooled by Amma's frowning and head-shaking; he knew she simply didn't dare ask Chellam to rouse herself. He saw the fear in her fluttering hands; he wondered what she thought Chellam would say if asked to make an omelet. And what *would* Chellam say? They were all terrified of her now, because she knew their secrets, because she was a wounded, cornered beast — but sometimes a wounded beast just licks its wounds and slinks away. No, Suresh can't quite imagine Chellam rising like a fury from her bed to point a bony finger at Amma and denounce her:

You! How dare you ask me to feed your lying children! What-what evil you can do, but you can't break your own bloody eggs, is it?

It's almost funny to picture: shrimpy Chellam, suddenly turned into a pontianak ghost from an Indonesian horror film. Chellam, who for months has barely been able to look Amma in the face to tell her someone's on the telephone, who seems to want nothing more than to disappear so that they can all pretend she never existed, whose very farts and toilet flushings, these days, are afraid, ashamed, damaged.

The Simon and Garfunkel cassette tape that Uma has had in her cassette player all morning has reached its end once again; the hiss of its static fills their ears. Uma puts her book and her fork down, gets up, and flips over the tape.

Hello darkness, my old friend, sings Paul Simon for the fifth time that day.

Uma resumes her seat, and the ceiling fan casts its regular shadows on her book-reading face above her omelet plate. And while Paul Simon warns his audience of fools that silence like a cancer grows, Suresh counts the seconds between the fan shadows on Uma's face, and Aasha shovels gooey forkfuls of omelet into her mouth without swallowing, until she, too, gags. Hers is not a pretend gag for comic relief, so Suresh sucks his teeth, kicks her under the table, and says, "Ee yer, so disgusting you. Cannot take smaller mouthfuls, is it? If you want to be disgusting I also can be disgusting." Then he burps long and loud, a mouth-open burp that echoes in the silence before the next song on Uma's cassette.

Which one of them is right about the crucial question of Why Uma Made the Omelet? Aasha, in her terrified state of infinite and illogical hope, or Suresh, in his uncompromising realism?

Both, actually. It's true that Uma made the omelet primarily because the process took far less time, effort, and thought than resisting Amma. She could've said, Let them all make their own omelet. Or, Let them starve for an afternoon. But then there would've been more words, more drama, more questions and accusations, and Uma has had enough of these, she feels, to last her the rest of her life. She wanted peace and quiet, no noise but the Simon and Garfunkel and the whir of the ceiling fan, and the easiest path to that was to make the bloody omelet.

And yet.

She will neither return the plane ticket nor put the suitcase back in the storeroom, but even as she keeps her eyes riveted to her book, she's keenly aware of Aasha's eyes on her. Today — unlike all the other days on which they have enacted this scene — this awareness brings a rush of tears to the very top of her throat. She swallows to keep them down.

Little Aasha. Uma wishes she could put down her book and look at Aasha, properly look at her and pull her onto her lap. In this impossible alternate world, Uma would find a way to express all the wrenching thoughts for which *sorry* and *thank you* were inadequate. Then they would both cry, for many of the same reasons.

She won't do this. She can't. It's too late and too dangerous. Uma is an all-or-nothing sort of girl, and she must be what she's chosen to be until the end. Until she boards that aeroplane in five days. If she makes an exception — even a brief one, even now, *especially* now — the walls will come tumbling down around all their ears. Chaos. Questions. Drama. Everything she doesn't want, and none of it will do anyone a bit of good.

The alternative, much like the omelet, is easier and better for all concerned, even if some can't accept that.

Soon Paati's ghost will make its first appearance at the Big House. This is a certainty in Aasha's world of doubts and questions and moral dilemmas: nothing can stop the dead from crossing the thin line that separates them from the living if they want to. And Paati will want to. She wasn't done with life; she'll be back to clamor for more tea-time treats, more respect, more attention, more of everything her arthritis cheated her out of by confining her to a rattan chair in a dim corridor. At this very minute she is probably limping away from the flames, muttering darkly about ash-in-the-nostrils and smoke-in-the-lungs, scolding Appa for being God only knows where when she met her undignified end in the bathroom.

Sometimes Aasha's heart races at the thought of Paati's return. Will she punish them all for their many sins against her? Will she suck blood, break glass, overturn furniture, like the pontianaks and the hantu kumkums about which Chellam once warned them?

But at other times, Aasha is at peace. She knows, somehow, that Paati has forgiven them; liberated of her old bones, she's seen and heard everything at once, the whole truth, past present future, and she's understood it all. Why they did what they did. Why they had to. How they were sorry, even if they would never say so aloud, for their mistakes and their weaknesses. For leaping before looking. For being cowards. Now that she has no more aches and pains and cataracts, Paati's turned into something like an angel or a fairy godmother. She floats above them like a kite. She forgives them afresh every day.

When she comes back to the Big House, she'll be able to walk around on her own (which is a good thing, since Chellam is in her bed with her sarong-blanket over her head). *SH-sh-SH-sh,* her silky soles will slide on the marble downstairs floors, just as they did fifteen or twenty times a day when Chellam led her to and from the big bathroom. She'd been a dense little bundle of bones and calluses enclosing a perpetually full bladder: Chellam has one bulging Popeye-the-Sailor-Man arm and one skinny-servant arm, from a whole year of these daily journeys.

In the dining room, Uma and Suresh and Aasha can hear Chellam sniffing and creaking the bedsprings every time she turns, which is often. Uma tries to shut out these small noises. *She'd be in the same situation whatever had happened,* Uma tells herself. *Her job ended once Paati was gone.* Suresh wishes Chellam would just go to sleep. Drink a whole bottle of whiskey if she has to. Eat a whole goat. Whatever it takes.

Aasha wonders if Chellam, too, awaits Paati's return. If she fears it, or welcomes it, or simply can't be bothered anymore. Does she think Paati will come back to help her?

But you were nasty to Paati all the time, thinks Aasha. *When she comes back she'll be on our side. Because we're family.*

Over the curtainless window of her room under the stairs, Chellam draped a thin cotton saree when she first arrived at the Big House, a saree she must have brought with her for yard work, or for sleeping in, or for precisely such a use as this — substitute curtain, or dustcloth, or source of reusable sanitary pads — because it's so thin, and so full of holes, that it surely could not have been used for anything else. It barely keeps the afternoon sun out today: Chellam sees bright red behind her shut eyelids, solid, bright red. Bright green bile froths at the back of her throat. She reaches under her pillow for her diminishing supply of Chinese red ginger (purchased from the corner shop with Uncle Ballroom's generous rewards for miscellaneous favors) and shoves a piece between her parched lips. She hasn't had a complete thought since she took to her bed. Her head is a jumble of snatches and shards, familiar smells, nauseating colors, unspoken fears that set her joints twitching. She's been reduced to some dim, pre-sentient state, so that some of those who stop at her door to make sure she's still alive feel the occasional pang of pity, or an uncomplicated tenderness, or an anodyne curiosity, but nothing more, because there she is, twitching and breathing her shallow, uneven breaths in her smelly room, and what can one do but shrug and turn away? What can one do but leave one's trays of Jacob's Cream Crackers and Maggi instant noodles and hurry back to the real world, where everything raw can be concealed behind words?

Today Uma cut Chellam her own slice of omelet for lunch. "No matter what they do to us," Amma said before she left for the crematorium, "we don't let our servants go hungry. That is not the kind of people we are." And then, even though Uma had said nothing to contradict her, she'd added, "Let her sins sit on her head alone. All that is between her and God. We don't need to sink to her level and starve her."

Uma knew Chellam would not eat her part of the omelet. Appa, who was preparing to lift the casket into the hearse with the help of three old men and a good heave-ho, knew it. Amma herself knew it, Suresh knew it, Aasha knew it, and yet Uma cut that slice and Suresh carried it upstairs on its tray, so that it now sits, cold as a jelly, on the table outside Chellam's door. A lost daytime moth is drowning in the glass beside the omelet, its wings spread against the water's tough surface.

At five o'clock Appa and Amma come home, stopping at the outside tap to cleanse themselves of the crematorium's unsalutary vapors. They splash, they gargle, they rub cool water on their scorched arms. There's still no sign of Paati, who, as far as Aasha can tell from the sitting room window, is not perched on the roof of the car, or lying supine on the hood, or crouched in the back seat. (And yet she is, indisputably, not far away: Aasha is still so sure of this that she stares out the window for a minute without blinking, until her eyeballs dry out.)

"Bloody hell!" Appa says in the dining room. "It's a furnace out there." He takes off his glasses and runs the palms of his hands over his face. The edges of his hair are still damp from his post-funeral ablutions. The circles under his eyes are darker than ever; he's been staying up every night for weeks working on his latest case, the notorious Angela Lim murder trial. The nights have lately been noiseless and stuffy, as if someone turns off the flame under the earth every evening but forgets to lift the lid. In that steamer-pot silence, Appa has been bending over his desk, poring over the facts of the case. Which are:

Angela Lim, ten years old, raped and murdered and found stuffed down a manhole near the Tarcisian Convent School.

Shamsuddin bin Yusof, an office boy accused of the rape, and the murder, and the stuffing.

On the front page of Appa's newspaper (which now lies at his feet, its pages fluttering in the fanbreeze like the wings of a hurt bird), the Minister of Internal Security has urged the public not to turn the case into a Racial Issue. (But on the letters to the editor page, that public continues to sneak their subtle defiance past the tea-break-heavy eyes of the censors: in pointed comparisons to past murder trials, in disingenuously philosophical nature-versus-nurture meditations, in dry discussions of urban demographics.)

Tonight, as on many previous nights, Aasha's wide-open eyes beam two bright spots on the ceiling above her bed. In addition to the facts of the case, which have been on TV and on the radio and on the lips of the Ladies at Amma's tea parties, Aasha knows all sorts of other things without knowing how she knows them: the number of parts Angela Lim was in when they pulled her out of that manhole; the colors of the bruises on her thighs; the splintery feel of the stick with which Shamsuddin (a tongue twister, that name: not Shamshuddin, not Samsuddin, but Shamsuddin, a drill for those aspiring to she-sells-seashells) clubbed her before tightening the just-in-case rope around her neck; the type of white canvas Bata shoes (mud-spattered from a recent game of rounders) Angela was wearing when Shamsuddin lured her into his red Datsun. But it's not what she knows that keeps Aasha awake at night; it's what she doesn't. The exact meaning of *rape,* a word that suggests scrape and grate and rake, all sharp and painful things not nice to do to a soft human body. The tricks of timing by which a man can stuff a girl in five parts into a manhole on a street where people drive and cycle and walk day and night. What *kind* of man this Shamsuddin is, because the question of *kind* rises to the surface of every conversation, and yet, once there at the surface, stays just beneath, refusing to show itself, slipping away from her hands when she reaches for it. *You know what, their kind of people. The only reason they pray five times a day is to cover up the havoc they do. Hah! Even five times a day is not enough for them. Rape, incest, drugs, you name it it's their kind who's responsible for ninety-five percent of it.*

As far as Aasha can tell, Shamsuddin is a skinny kind of a man in a cheaply made bush jacket. His hair is already thinning. He looks as if he might have bad teeth, but she can't be sure because he isn't smiling in any of the newspaper pictures.

"Sick bastard," Appa has said every day since he took on the case. "Doing a thing like that to a child that age."

"Suresh, bring me a glass of ice water," Appa says now, just back from Paati's cremation, even though Suresh is in the middle of his maths homework, his face a ball of concentration over the square-lined pages of his exercise book, while Uma is reading what is technically (however much she, too, must concentrate to squeeze meaning out of it) a storybook. Even though Uma has no homework whatsoever and will no longer have any for her remaining five days in the Big House, because she's home and dry now, she's scored the ultimate goal, college in America, just waiting to leave, sitting on laurels that leave welts on her bum and make her shift constantly in her chair. Even so. Appa does not look at Uma; Suresh sees to his ice water. *Thunk-thunk-thunk*, it pours heavily out of the already-sweating Johnnie Walker Black Label bottle into Appa's glass, and Suresh wonders if he should whistle, just to make a sound, any sound to which meaning cannot be attached, anything other than Appa breathing hard in his chair, and Chellam twitching and sniffing behind her too-thin door, and Paul Simon's successive songs about suicides. Still wondering, he refills the Johnnie Walker bottle at the kitchen sink, caps it, and puts it back in its place inside the fridge door.

All things considered, he's decided against whistling, luckily for him, because Amma presses the Stop button on the cassette player and says, "For heaven's sake, Uma, even today you must play your eerie music ah? At least today have some respect. Your own grandmother's funeral today. Poor woman, what a terrible death. Hai hai"—she sits down across from Appa and rubs her temples with the tips of her fingers—"what is the use of dwelling on all that now anyway? Let go, let go and move on. What has happened has happened." No response from Uma. A melancholy trinity of smells—camphor, wood smoke, sandalwood — wafts from Amma's hair and the folds of her sa-ree. Frosty glass in hand, Suresh studies the back of her head: droop-ing curls, three drops of sweat on the nape of her neck. What has happened *has* happened, he thinks, and perhaps it doesn't really mat-ter who made it happen. Time to let go, move on, or just *move,* but suddenly he can't; he grips the glass ever more tightly, until he can feel it on the brink of shattering in his fingers. A drop of condensation wanders down one side at exactly — *exactly,* it seems to Suresh — the same pace as one of Amma's sweat drops trickling down the top of her spine. He wonders why she doesn't seem to feel it.

"Suresh," says Appa, "what is this? Are you having a catatonic fit? Are you pretending to be a broken robot? By the time you bring me that water it'll be hot enough to make tea with."

Suresh tears his gaze away from the back of Amma's neck, but on his way across the room he sees, out of the corner of his eye, red run-ning down Amma's face, bright red, liquid, sprung from somewhere on her scalp, making its way down her forehead, and he shudders, not a shudder that everyone can see — there's much about Suresh that no one sees — but a single mouse-shudder deep inside his chest, some-where between his rib cage and his stomach.

"Suresh," says Appa again, "what is wrong with you? Spilling here there everywhere — do I have to tell you to hold the glass with both hands, as if you're a bloody two-year-old?"

Of course. The rivulet of red on Amma's face is just the vermil-ion she smeared on her center parting before the funeral, of course of course of course — Suresh has never seen Amma sweat like this, but that's what it is, of course, the dastardly results of funeral heat. Vermilioned sweat, nothing to do with her skull, nothing whatsoever to do with skulls in general and how they crack and bleed. This isn't some supernatural revenge, just a trick of the heat and his jittery eyes. Poor Paati will never have a chance at revenge, whether or not she deserves one. Suresh puts the glass down before Appa and clears his mind with a forced blast of cool relief.

But Aasha, whose belief in ghosts has never wavered, is baffled. Appa and Amma are back from the funeral; where is Paati? Why is she taking so long to get here? From where she sits, Aasha can see that her chair remains empty. But then again, why would she sit qui-etly in that chair once she's back? What a way that would be to cel-ebrate her new freedom. She's spent more than enough time in that chair, none of it happy; in that chair she's received slaps and knocks and pinches, all of them quick, some of them deserved. Because it's true that there were times when Paati was Too Much, when her questions and her badgering and her fret-fret-fretting went Too Far, when she was asking for trouble from whoever gave it to her. That is to say, from Amma and Chellam.

Amma because she was a clockwork toy someone had wound up all the way and left unattended; she couldn't help herself. She sat sipping tea at the Formica table, and threw tea parties, and gave Paati headknocks and thighpinches, because these were the only things she knew how to do.

And Chellam because she was just that *kind*. Whatever *kind* Shamsuddin was, Chellam was almost as bad. She was the kind who was nasty when other people weren't looking. A very bad person. A terrible person who deserved everything she was going to get. Once she had fooled them; once they had loved her. Now they knew they'd been wrong.

"Did you all eat your lunch?" Amma is asking in the dining room. "Did you take Chellam a tray?"

Uma turns a page and Suresh says yes, yes, we ate our lunch.

"Eggs?" Amma asks. "For Chellam also?"

"Not nice also," Suresh says. "Uma put too much cheese." Clever Suresh, wise Suresh, quick-on-his-feet Suresh, always able to steer conversations around potholes.

"Aaah," says Appa, smacking his lips after a long drag from his icewater glass, "that is because Uma's head is already in America. Yes or not? Her body is here, but her mind is at Columbia University, within the ivy-covered walls, not on our omelets-bomelets my boy, oh yes sure enough, already Joyce is her choice, hi-funda stuff beyond the rest of us, yes or not?"

Uma raises her eyes from her book and blinks in Appa's direction several times in quick succession, as if she's thinking of something else and wishes he would move out of the way.

Appa chuckles three colorless chuckles, his mouth stretched tight in a grin that doesn't reach his eyes. It doesn't go away; his face won't ungrin itself now. Suresh watches a weariness creep from those aching face muscles into Appa's eyes, then give way to panic when Appa realizes his face is stuck fast. Then, just when Suresh has stopped breathing, Appa's face breaks free. He closes his eyes and presses his thumbs hard into their inside corners. "One more, please," he says when he opens them, holding his empty glass out to Suresh, and Suresh repeats the steps with only minor modifications: brisk walk to fridge, open door, grab *second* Johnnie Walker bottle (because the first, so recently refilled, isn't cold enough yet), fill glass with a *thunk-thunk-thunk* and a private *should I whistle?* This time he notes, as he stands there by the fridge, that Aasha has made her meandering way (stopping here and there to sniff and listen and retrace, he's sure, like the lost ant she's been for the past few days) to Paati's old rattan chair.

"*Psst!*" he hisses. "Oi! What stupid thing are you doing now?" Not as though he can't see: Aasha is running her hands (still oily with butter from her omelet) down the thin arms of Paati's chair, patting the seat, pulling on each loose bit of rattan, and even—this is when he knows she is irredeemably crazy—putting her nose to the backrest and breathing deeply, as if the chair were a bloody jasmine garland.

"Nothing," Aasha says, and when she turns to look at him her eyes are as wide as Sassy the cat's were on the afternoon Amma caught her with a whole fish in her mouth. "Not doing anything also."

"Stooooopid," Suresh offers pleasantly, and returns to the dining room with Appa's glass of ice water.

"Thanks, my boy, heartfelt thanks," says Appa. "I better take this into my study. Hell of a lot of work to do. This case is giving me bad dreams and making my hair fall out." Chair legs grate on the marble floor, and Appa is gone, into his den with a sweating water glass and a head full of troubling facts.

There's a Paati-bum-sized trough in the chair's sunken seat, and it smells funny, different from the backrest. The piss of a thousand accidents has infiltrated the very fibers of the seat, never to be completely got out, not with all the Dettol-scrubbing and Clorox-splashing in the world, and God knows Chellam tried, because Amma made her. With great difficulty, Aasha clambers up onto the chair and scoots her bottom back, cheek by cheek. In the afternoon lull she begins to nod, just as Paati used to, and her chin, just as Paati's used to, drops to her chest, and finally she surrenders to the great grey blanket of sleep, leans her head on the arm of the chair, and dozes, just as Paati used to . . .

. . . until Amma—who has gone upstairs and showered and changed, put her funeral saree to soak in a pail in the outdoor kitchen, and attempted to assuage her crematorium headache with repeated sniffs of a handkerchief doused in Axe Brand Camphorated Oil—comes swishing, caftan-clad, past the rattan chair, catches sight of Aasha, and wakes her with a hearty smack on the knee.

"Aasha! Go and sleep properly on your bed, please!" she snaps. "Sleeping like a dog in the kitchen. When your neck is paining who will you go crying to?"

Whom, indeed? To whom would Aasha go crying with a crick in her neck? Not to Amma, certainly. Not to Appa, who will be either locked in his study with the quinquepartite ghost of Angela Lim or out (in town, at the club, or on other adventures). Not to Suresh, who will laugh and call her stoooopid for falling asleep in an uncomfortable chair. Not to Chellam, who might once have sympathized but who now has greater worries of her own. And not to Uma, who might also once — longer ago — have sympathized, but that was so very long ago that Aasha must make a conscious effort to hold on to the memory.

The logic of Amma's argument being thus unassailable, Aasha goes upstairs to sleep in her bed, with its pink gingham sheets and its peeling stickers of the Seven Dwarves.

Through her window Aasha sees a tour bus parked across the street, outside the Balakrishnans' front gate. She knows this bus well: it belongs to the (so-called) husband of Kooky Rooky, who rents a room in the Balakrishnans' house. The bright green lettering on the side of the bus sings in an operatic voice: *Sri Puspajaya Tours*. And in a softer, breathier, dewier voice, the smaller words sing the familiar tune from the TV ads: *To Know* (know, know) *Malaysia Is to Love* (love, love) *Malaysia*. Twilight begins to fall; the streetlights come on (even the one that will only flicker all night); downstairs, neither Amma nor Appa nor Uma says anything about dinner, so Suresh opens the fridge and lifts two small, bony morsels out of yesterday's chicken curry, the fat clinging to them in translucent white gobs studded with coriander leaves. He takes them upstairs — Aasha hears his steps on the stairs, the lightest, steadiest steps in the house, light and steady past her door, light and steady down the corridor, light and steady into his room with nary a sound from the screen door — and eats them sitting on his bed in the dark, collecting the clean bones in one closed fist.

Downstairs in his study Appa considers the evidence against Shamsuddin bin Yusof: his identity card was found, along with a rope and a big stick and a bloodied Kwong Fatt Textiles plastic bag, stuffed in a culvert near the manhole that housed all of Angela Lim's parts; an eyewitness saw Angela (or at any rate a Chinese schoolgirl with a ponytail) being lured away by a skinny Malay man near the Tarcisian Convent School gates; later that afternoon the owner of a mini-market in the area noted that a small, fair-skinned (yes, yes, probably Chinese, the mini-market man agreed when asked to clarify), anxious-seeming girl came into the shop with a young Malay man in a bush jacket to buy a packet of Kandos chocolates. Shamsuddin, of course, says he's innocent, says the truth shall soon surface to set him free, says he was at home having dinner with his seven-months-pregnant wife. And she agrees, and rattles off that night's menu (it's a short menu, for Shamsuddin and his wife are not well off: plain rice, soy sauce, fried kembung fish), and makes dire predictions of curses to befall those who have framed her husband, and cries in court and wipes her tears with the ends of her headscarf.

Crocodile tears, the spectators say, shaking their heads. She knows he did it. She's covering up for him.

And yet, paradoxically and obediently, they imagine the framers: fat men, rich men, men wearing dark glasses in the back seats of Mercedes Benzes, with thick curly hair on their forearms. Sultans' sons, ministers' brothers, industrialists with cushy government contracts. They know the types. In school the good people of Malaysia have been taught: *The heights by great men reached and kept / Were not attained by sudden flight . . .* That part, at least, is true. Not by sudden flight, but by hiring thugs to slit the tender throats of their rivals' children, by strangling whores who threaten to talk and commissioning generals to blow up their bodies in the jungle, by paying off the police to ignore the drunken indiscretions of their children.

Appa alone cannot allow the framers to swagger around inside his head the way they want to, chuckling and thumping each other on the back. He puts them firmly out of his mind and concentrates on the face of the dismal little man he must convict: the flat nose, the overbite, the weak chin, all conjured up as clearly as if Shamsuddin were sitting across from him in this silent study.

Sick bastard, Appa repeats to himself. To do a thing like that to a —how old, how old now?—ten-year-old girl. Ten! Ten is a *child!* Ten is no breasts, no hips, no nothing. His job is to believe in guilt where guilt is assigned. He clicks the top of his rollerball pen five times in quick succession. It's hot in the study, boiling hot; once again, the day's furnace heat doesn't seem to be retreating with the daylight. Appa rises and turns the fan all the way up to speed five so that it whips around dangerously, *hwoop hwoop hwoop*, its joints creaking as if at any minute it might work itself loose from the ceiling and launch itself through the mosquito screen and into the falling night, spinning like a flying saucer, like the chakra of some demented modern-day avatar of Krishna, slicing off the heads of homebound sparrows and others who have done no wrong, for this modern-day Krishna is interested less in justice than in diversion. It's been a dizzying day — the white heat of the sun, the grand pantomime of Paati's last rites, the chanting singing weeping wailing, the black heat of the hearse, the red heat of the incinerator. Appa feels slightly ill and wonders if he should venture out to the kitchen for more sustenance than a glass of ice water, but decides against it. The house expands with accusatory female breath.

Suresh throws the chicken bones into his wastepaper basket and washes his hands in the upstairs bathroom. He studies his face in the mirror without switching on the light, and then squeezes the skin of his nose hard between his index fingers to extrude the margariney grease the way Chellam taught them to. The whites of his eyes are very white in the dark, and the black of his Brylcreemed hair very black. He whistles, finally, all the whistles he's been holding back all afternoon, released in a single, too-full-to-be-tuneful burst of blown air. He whistles a snippet of Boney M and a snatch of a Boy Scout song, a phrase of Barry Manilow and five notes of *A Night on Bald Mountain*.

In the dark, after even Amma and Uma have gone upstairs to bed, after Suresh has stolen down and up the stairs two more times for two more pairs of bony chicken pieces, after Chellam's sniffing and tossing has slowed somewhat for the night, after Appa has fallen asleep over Angela Lim's glowing moonface in the leather armchair in his study (to whom will *he* go crying with the crick in his neck? Amma doesn't ask, because she knows the answer), Kooky Rooky's husband revs up his tour bus with an ear-splitting roar and takes off at top speed, a Tupperware of bhajia and chutney on the passenger seat beside him.

Of course, he's only a So-Called Husband. A bluff one. He and Kooky Rooky aren't really married. He has to talk like her husband and act like her husband when they're playing house, which is still better than being a bluff baby, but he probably got tired of it anyway. It was only a matter of time before he left like this, in the dark, at full speed. Now perhaps the make-believe will be over, and they will all stop calling him her husband in her presence. Or will they?

· · ·

"THE FELLOW'S TOUR BUS has disappeared," Amma says in the morning. "Left late at night in a big hurry. I thought Kooky Rooky said he was on leave for a week or so? Then what so fast gone already?"

They are having breakfast in the dining room, Appa (trying to ignore the crick in his neck), Amma, Uma, Suresh, and Aasha. No one attempts an answer to Amma's questions, though Aasha remembers quite vividly the dream she had in the hour or so of sleep she snatched in the night: a dark figure at the wheel of the tour bus, crazed, teeth bared, veins sticking out everywhere, driving straight off a cliff. But when people went to tell Kooky Rooky the awful news, they found her husband upstairs in their rented room, eating green grapes and watching TV. And that was when they realized it'd been Kooky Rooky in the bus, Kooky Rooky who'd driven off the cliff with her eyes closed.

What woke Aasha from her dream: toes tickling her forehead. She looked up to see Mr. McDougall's daughter perched on the headboard of her bed. Mr. McDougall's daughter smiled at her, a don't-be-scared smile, small and warm and quiet.

"Something must have happened between him and Kooky Rooky," Amma goes on now, at the breakfast table. "Or suddenly he must have been overcome with love for his first wife. Couldn't wait another minute to see her."

"Kooky Rooky died," Aasha says flatly. She notes that even Uma looks up for a moment before turning back to the comics page of the newspaper. Let them all see that Aasha has her own sources. So what if they hide their secrets from her with words and voices designed to keep her out of their adult world? She knows things they don't, even if she doesn't yet understand what kind of a man Shamsuddin bin Yusof is.

But Appa only chuckles at her revelation. "If only," he says. "It would make things so much easier for that poor bloke. And for the noble cause of truth in this dishonest world. Without Kooky Rooky, there'd be five hundred fewer lies told per day, worldwide. Here, Suresh, pass me the butter, would you?"

"*Tsk,* don't simply-simply make everything into a joke," Amma says. "Your daughter talks rubbish as usual and you turn it into a grand comedy. Living and dying is not a joke, Aasha. Kooky Rooky might be sitting at home crying, but she's not *dead*. Please."

Aasha knows very well that living and dying isn't a joke; it infuriates her to be told. She frowns at her toast and falls into silence.

Suresh looks at Amma and thinks, *You, of all people, telling her that dying is no joke!* Aloud, he says, "Can I have the butter back, Appa?"

This morning Suresh replaced yesterday's omelet-bearing tray with a fresh one on the table outside Chellam's door: this one holds a plastic plate with two buttered-and-jammed slices of Sunshine bread on it and a cup of Milo that has already acquired a thin skin. Amma has made Quaker Oats for the rest of them, but — "No no no, not for Chellam," she said when Suresh approached the pot with Chellam's bowl, "give her bread and jam — oats is so disgusting when it gets cold, you know?" So even Amma understands the futility of these many trays; even she acknowledges that this apparent kindness is a mere formality. Chellam didn't stir when Suresh left the tray on the table, but now, as the rest of them sit in the dining room eating their oats, she rises and stumbles, *eyes* — Suresh can almost swear it though he catches only the quickest glimpse of her — *still closed,* down the corridor along which she led Paati fifteen-twenty times a day until two days ago, and into the big downstairs bathroom where she allegedly put a definitive end to Paati's dwindling days.

And there in that bathroom, as Appa and Amma and Uma and Suresh and Aasha try valiantly to eat their porridge, Chellam has a thundering, volcanic attack of diarrhea, all rapid-fire bangs and squeaks and liquescent bursts, all orchestral-class hooting and tooting and blasting and rolling, an attack so explosive and so importunate that despite Amma's attempts to drown it out by blowing energetically on every spoonful of her oats (because yes, the one thing about Amma that hasn't changed after all these years is her continued mortification at eating shitting sweating fucking and at any hint of others' participation in said activities), it continues to command their attention, so that eventually Suresh snorts ever so lightly, and Aasha giggles despite her persistent secret worries, and Uma concedes an ephemeral half-smile. "Goodness gracious," says Appa, "how on earth can she have so much to shit out when she hasn't eaten for more than a week?" This new question supersedes all prevailing inner monologues on life and death, truth and untruth.

"Who knows?" Amma says, her lower lip still curled. "Maybe she *is* expecting after all. That can play havoc with one's digestion."

They put down their spoons and ponder Appa's question and Amma's hypothesis, because oats porridge is a very difficult thing indeed to eat within earshot of a diarrhea attack: five bowls of it are left to cool into lumpy beige sludge that is dumped, later that morning, into the kitchen rubbish by a still-revolted Amma.

This morning, Appa and a small band of die-hard funeral enthusiasts will return to the crematorium to collect Paati's ashes and unburned bones, all of which they will set free at the seaside in Lumut. After breakfast, Appa pulls on a pair of non-courthouse trousers (because he must wade into the sea for this final sendoff) and is gone, with a jingle and a jangle of his car keys, with a slam of the grille that brings a small shower of paint flakes down onto the front steps. Amma is left to clean up the breakfast things and do the dishes, something she hasn't done since she reinvented herself in the image of a tea-party-throwing bigshot-lawyer's wife. But clean up she must, because Lourdesmary and Letchumi and Vellamma have been given two days' leave, and Chellam has subsided into her bed after ejecting the last contents of her bowels. And not only must she clean up today, but she must do it alone, because:

1) Uma has beaten a hasty retreat to sit on her bed and read and think about what she will put in the battered red suitcase that was once a brand-new, going-to-university gift from her grandfather to her father.

2) Suresh has also hurried upstairs, for upon waking this morning he noticed a fat black trail leading to his wastepaper basket, and in the basket a velvety black blanket over the six chicken bones he so mindlessly discarded there last night. Drawing closer, rubbing the sleep from his eyes, he affirmed that the blanket was indeed of the minutely milling, moiling, swarming sort, a blanket of juicy-bodied black ants, an ecstatic, feasting blanket. So he returns after his non-breakfast to embark upon a quick recovery mission: he stamps his bare feet on the trail of ants, leaving juiceless black bodies crusted on feet and floorboards (and a few ant legs still stirring, feeble and futile, in the air); he dumps the contents of the wastebasket onto three sheets of newspaper surreptitiously filched from the storeroom; he balls up the newspaper into a snug bundle and saunters, light and steady, down the stairs and out the back door to deposit it in the outside dustbin.

3) Aasha has stationed herself in her favorite spot in the house: behind the green PVC settee at the end of the corridor leading to the downstairs bathroom. She waits, her faith undented, although a day has passed since the funeral, and even now Appa is gathering Paati's ashes and her unburned bones into two clay pots; Aasha suspects

Paati will show up first either in her chair, where she spent most of her days, or in the bathroom, where her life ended.

At the crematorium, under the hawk eyes of three old men who are somehow, surely, related to him, Appa sprinkles water and milk on Paati's ashes and gingerly picks out seven unburned bones: big-toe bone, bit-of-kneecap, hip scraps number one and two, fourth rib, collarbone tips.

On his way out to the dustbin with his own bundle of bones, Suresh nearly collides with Kooky Rooky, who has run barefoot across the street, everything about her coming loose: hair bun, sarong, face, blouse buttons. Aasha sees her too, from the landing upstairs. A most unghostly Kooky Rooky. Shaking, and full of tears waiting to come out, but not dead yet. Aasha doesn't care that she misinterpreted her dream very slightly, as past rather than prediction. *Watch out, Kooky Rooky,* she thinks. *You better be careful.*

Kooky Rooky looks at the bundle in Suresh's left hand as if it might contain something she's been yearning for all her life, and he wants to say, Here, take, take, please take and go away and leave us alone, and don't come crying and sniffing and spilling in here because we've had enough of that recently.

But before he can speak, she looks from the bundle to Suresh's unyielding face, and she says, "Where your Amma?"

"Inside the house only."

The briefest of exchanges; he proceeds on his errand, and she trips, light but not so steady, towards the back door and into the kitchen, where she finds Amma scrubbing out the porridge pot with a firm wrist and a clenched jaw.

In an attempt to pick a particularly stubborn crusted bit off the bottom of the pot, Amma chips one manicured fingernail, mutters "Chhi!" under her breath, turns off the tap, and senses someone behind her. Does she hear Kooky Rooky inhale before speaking, or glimpse a desperate, trapped-bird movement in the corner of her eye, or smell the sleepless night of devastation that rises off Kooky Rooky's skin? Whichever it is, she turns just in time to hear her speak:

"Vasanthi Akka!"

Amma takes one look at Kooky Rooky and knows that what's coming is more than just a routine display of kookiness. She's not here to tell Amma about the time she went to England and met the Queen in a supermarket, or about her father's two condominiums in Hollywood, or about the seventeen kinds of pullao served at her wedding; no, she wants something large and impossible. Amma's back and shoulders ache from all her pot-scrubbing, and her head still throbs faintly from funeral fumes trapped somewhere in the back of her throat. Whatever Kooky Rooky wants, it's too heavy for Amma to lift alone, and she's seized by an urge to sit down and lay her head on one outstretched arm and pretend to sleep, as children do at nap time in nursery school. But she only dries her hands on her caftan and says:

"What is it, Rukumani? Come, come, sit down" — Amma pulls out a chair, all briskness and bustle — "you want hot drink or cold drink?" Instead of waiting for an answer, she fills the kettle, far fuller than it needs to be for two mugs of tea or coffee or Milo.

"Akka," Kooky Rooky says, still standing in the doorway, "he gone away. He not coming back."

"What nonsense, why shouldn't he come back?" Amma lights the stove under the kettle. "He has to give his tours, isn't it, to pay the bills? He'll give his tour and come home as usual, don't worry. Next week he'll come home as usual, bringing five-six packets of nutmeg from Penang or dodol from Kelantan or whatever it is, you know how he is, isn't it?"

"No, Akka, this time he not coming back."

Amma puts her hand on her hip and ponders this. "Why?" she says. "What happened this time?"

"He told me, Akka, he only told me. He said enough of this, he got not enough money not enough time to have two family." Kooky Rooky says this matter-of-factly, as if her husband's real family has never been a secret, as if she's always discussed the subject openly with anyone who cared to listen. For the briefest of moments Amma considers keeping up her end of the appearances, considers saying, What two families, Rukumani, what are you talking about? But exhaustion overcomes her again, a leaden weight in her head and chest. She can't summon the will to speak, let alone play her part in a farce that seems to have ended.

"I was all the time asking him," Kooky Rooky is saying, "when will we move to our own place, because I tired of staying in other people's house, Akka, that Mrs. Balakrishnan everything also she counting, how much water I using in the bathroom, how long I bathe, how much electricity I using at night, everything—"

"That you have to understand," says Amma, "Mr. Balakrishnan is nicely-nicely drinking up all their money every night, so of course she wants to be careful. That you mustn't—"

"Of course, yes I know, Akka, but one side I must understand Mrs. Balakrishnan's problem, the other side I must understand my husband's problem, in the end who is going to understand my problem? I got nowhere to go. I understand, yes, my husband got another family, so many small-small children all that, he got no choice, yes I know, but what about me?" Kooky Rooky's voice cracks, and she comes forward and sits, finally, in the chair that Amma pulled out for her when she first appeared. She folds her thin hands in her lap and hangs her head.

Amma measures out heaping teaspoons of Milo into two mugs, then sugar, and then, as she turns to get the condensed milk out of the fridge, sucks her teeth and says, "Rukumani, you just got to learn not to expect so much from men. After all, you knew what type of man he was from the beginning, isn't it? If he could do that to his wife, how reliable could he be?"

Kooky Rooky looks up at Amma with enormous, wet eyes. "Reliable?" she repeats. "How reliable?"

"I mean," says Amma, pouring hot water into the two mugs and stirring so furiously that the teaspoon chimes through the house like an alarm, "if he could play her out, why shouldn't he turn around and play you out?" She holds the condensed milk tin over the first mug and watches the pale yellow milk stream down in a thin, viscous line.

"Yes," says Kooky Rooky slowly. "Yes, that is also there. I only didn't realize . . ."

And perhaps because she's still tired from yesterday's funereal exertions, tired and dried out like something smoked over a slow fire, or perhaps because she's never liked Kooky Rooky all that much anyway, something goes off inside Amma's head—with a crack-and-flash like an old-fashioned camera—and she finds herself thinking thoughts so clear that they seem to scroll in thin letters across a blinding white screen behind her eyes. Needlethoughts. Knifethoughts. Sour-as-green-mangothoughts: they make her eyes narrow and her mouth pucker. *Why should I, of all people, feel sorry for you? You deserve what you're getting, Rukumani. What goes around comes around.*

She puts the condensed milk tin down on the counter and turns to face Kooky Rooky. "Of course you didn't realize," she says. "Of course as long as everything is working for us we don't realize what's happening in other people's lives. But it's time to realize now. You can live with him and call him your husband, but the truth is, that is still his real wife, isn't it? His first duty is to her. Those are his children, and that is his wife, not you."

Kooky Rooky nods like a punished child being asked if she's learned her lesson. As if every nod hurts her, but she knows she'll be dismissed if she can nod just a few more times. She sniffs, wipes her nose with the knuckle of an index finger. As Amma puts the two mugs down on the table, Kooky Rooky sobs a single sob, gets up, and hurries out the door, half running, half walking.

Amma watches her from the kitchen window. Down the garden path she goes, barefoot, apparently unconcerned about ringworm, and then back across the street. The screen behind Amma's eyes flickers, dims, goes dark, and she's left with herself and two mugs of Milo, not one of which she wishes to drink, because, truth be told, she's still feeling a little ill from her diarrhea-disrupted breakfast. She pours the still-steaming Milo down the drain, one mug after the other, and thinks, *Not my fault. Not my fault. I've got enough problems of my own.* She's tired, so tired she feels she could go to bed and sleep for days, just like Chellam. She's tired of life and death and truths and lies, of betrayals and loyalties, of youth and age. Of blame and blamelessness and the long, winding road in between them; of those three feeble words themselves: *not my fault.*

Not until appa arranges her seven unburned bones in their original configuration on a layer of raw rice on the beach in Lumut is Paati's spirit resurrected. Appa is willfully unaware of his role in this metaphysical transaction; he has banished all macabre thoughts from his head by concentrating on the anatomical fact of these seven bones. His task is purely mundane, the solving of a brainteaser, the taking of a biology test. At the top the charred collarbone tips gracefully bracketing the unmistakable absence of neck and head; below them the rib, like one bar of a dismantled birdcage; below those—here Appa pauses, but the three old funeral die-hards do not offer any assistance in this case. They wait, silent as cold gulls, as Appa watches the hairs on his forearms stir in the sea breeze. Finally he places one scrap on the left and the other on the right, and about a foot below these, the bit-of-kneecap, curved like a piece of a rice bowl. And last of all, down at the bottom, the big-toe bone, perfectly flat on the rice. Appa vaguely wishes that he could make it hover in the air where it really belongs, or at least stand upright.

But he needn't worry that this pitiful connect-the-dots puzzle with insufficient dots is a mockery of his mother's spirit, because as soon as he lays the big-toe bone down, Paati rises from her remains. Of course neither Appa nor his three spavined sidekicks recognize her, but rise she does, the scrappiest of vapors, buffeting the fringes of one old man's tonsure, lifting the other's dhoti. "Very windy today," one of them says as he holds his dhoti down girlishly. "Rain coming or what."

Appa rubs his forearms.

In the Big House, Uma is packing her suitcase. Aasha is squatting in the doorway, watching her, when two feathers from some mysterious source — a hole in Uma's mattress? a pigeon on the awning outside? a neighbor's illegal chicken? — spiral down right in front of her face, almost brushing her eyelashes.

The feathers land unnoticed on the bottom of Uma's suitcase.

A puff of Yardley English Lavender talcum powder teases Aasha's nose, but she can tell, in the split second before she sneezes — a godlike, seismic sneeze that rattles the windows and shakes Uma's bed frame — that Uma doesn't smell it.

So Paati is back. Aasha wanders out to the landing to look for her, and there she is: she must've slipped in between the bars of the front grille. She's acquired an odd new gait, a no-gravity shuffle, a geriatric astronaut's glide. At the foot of the stairs she sees Chellam's uneaten food on its tray outside her door.

Today it's rice and sambar, with ladies' fingers pacchadi on the side. The food has turned into a hard cake; it looks like a plastic toy meal.

If you let your plate dry out like that, Chellam once told Suresh and Aasha, hungry ghosts will come and eat from it. And sure enough, right before Aasha's eyes, peckish, transparent Paati clutches the edge of the little table with her permanently turmeric-stained fingers, unfurling her tongue, lizard-like, towards a particularly tempting grain on the rim of Chellam's untouched plate. Her jowls spread on the Formica tabletop. The white whiskers on her upper lip twitch and bristle. A flick and a lick of that deft tongue and the coveted grain shoots down her gossamer throat into the glass bowl of her belly. The rest she eats with her right hand as usual, making neat balls of the dried-out rice, popping them into her ready mouth. She soils only her finger-tips; Paati was always a neat eater, not one of the palm-licking, curry-dripping ilk. When she's had enough—she's hardly made a dent in even Chellam's meager portion, but ghosts have small stomachs—she belches, a small, translucent sound like steam hissing in a pipe. Then she moves on through the house, towards her rattan chair. The gentle breeze of her trailing, transparent saree floats up to Aasha's face on the landing. It smells slightly musty, a little damp with seawater perhaps, but on the whole rather comforting. Aasha hears her settle soft as a feather into the chair to wait for teatime. *Don't worry, Paati,* she thinks. *I'll bring you a handful of omapoddi and two murukkus. Now I can take care of you. Now that you're a ghost, I can make sure that no one is ever mean to you again.*

Aasha goes back up to Uma's room, and this time she walks right in. She picks a *Mad* magazine up off the floor and riffles through it, and a sheaf of stamp-shaped *Alfred E. Neuman for President* stickers (free with a year's subscription) flutters out. The rashes on the insides of her elbows feel hot and itchy.

"Look, Uma!" she says, the words a single gust of need. "You can stick these free stickers on the suitcase. That way you won't lose it at the airport." She holds the stickers out to Uma, her arm so straight it bends the wrong way at the elbow. Her fingers clutch the sheaf; her eyes are as bright as disco balls. *I'll take care of you too, Uma,* she wants to say. *I'll take care of you and everything will be all right.*

She hopes the stickers convey at least part of this message.

Uma takes them with a soft smile at the floor. She drops the lid of her suitcase and begins to stick them all over it: first along the sides in neat rows and then haphazardly on the top, her hands working as though the task were somehow urgent. Aasha counts the stickers, fourteen fifteen sixteen just on top, and imagines Uma unpacking in a New York room with a carpet, humming, lifting out her scratchy sweaters three by three. At the bottom of the suitcase, underneath all those sweaters, will be those two (goose? pigeon? chicken?) feath-ers, refreshed from their long across-the-sea slumber. When Uma lifts out the last three sweaters they will float up and tickle her nose, and she will sneeze such a sneeze that they will be blown clear across the room and behind a bookshelf, where they will remain forever, a secret link to the Big House and Paati, and to Aasha, who is close to tears at this moment with her failure to prevent Uma's departure.

All Aasha's strategies have been imperfect. Uma will leave, never to return; Chellam is sniffing and whimpering in her bed. As for Paati, well, neither sticks and stones (or slaps and knocks) nor words will hurt her now, but she's a lonely, restless, hungry spirit. It will be all Aasha can do to see to her needs.

6

AFTER GREAT EXPECTATIONS

DISAPPOINTMENT BLOOMED everywhere in the first days of Appa and Amma's marriage. It sprouted under Amma's feet, sick yellow, smelling of ammonia and new paint, as she stepped into the Big House on the night after their wedding reception at the Ipoh Club. She'd had too many crab rangoons, drunk alcohol for the first time in her life. Like a passenger fresh off the boat in a foreign land, she stood at attention in the sitting room, squinting at the oil paintings and running her fingers along the upholstery of the settee on which she'd sat only thrice before. Three times before the wedding Appa had invited her to tea. The first time, his mother had run her eyes up and down Amma, said hello with a smile that made Amma wonder if her blouse might be conspicuously stained or missing a button, and then retreated into the depths of the house. The second time, Paati had sat with them for two minutes, during which she'd asked Amma questions about her father's education and career and met each answer with a perfectly still face, no nod, no smile, no acknowledgment whatsoever that she'd received the information she'd sought. And the third time, she had greeted Amma at the front door with a curve to her lips that Amma had almost interpreted as a smile—perhaps she'd passed the old lady's tests after all?—until she spoke: "My goodness," she said, "red really doesn't suit a girl of your color, Vasanthi."

Now a sudden fear stole Amma's breath like a draft of cold air. What had she done? In the dim light the Big House felt vast and unyielding. Her father's house was just next door, but she could not run there for solace. If all she'd done was to jump out of her father's lovingly tended fire into her mother-in-law's sizzling frying pan, they would never know it. She would, she *would* make a new life here, whatever the odds against her. She would etiolate the miserable green house next door by keeping the curtains on that side of the Big House closed, by never speaking about it, by giving it no space in her mind, no air, no offhand concern.

Appa unknowingly interrupted her vision of the future: "What do you think? I got the place spruced up a bit. New paint and new curtains for the sitting room and dining room. Not bad, eh?"

Of course he could not smell the new paint, or the ammonia with which the maid had been mopping the floors as they'd sipped champagne at the club.

"Yes," Amma said weakly. "Quite nice."

This tepid approval was far removed from the praise Appa had expected — surely she could've at least been impressed with his choice of curtain fabric — so far removed that it seemed to come from a different girl than the one who'd been awestruck by a simple treat of popcorn at the cinema.

"Well," said Appa, "I thought that daffodil-colored fabric went very nicely with the blue upholstery in here." Then he took Amma's suitcase and led her up the grand staircase.

Just this morning in the master bedroom of the Big House one of Appa's officious aunts, her heavy hips swathed in a gaudy sarong, had maneuvered her breathy way around the double bed, pulling the clean white sheets a little too tight, folding the thin blue wool blanket and placing it demurely at the foot of the bed. Appa had walked down the corridor while she'd been making the bed and happened to catch her eye; he'd avoided her for the rest of the day, even at the wedding, more out of consideration for her shaken sensibilities than any embarrassment of his own. Now he sat down on the bed, lowering his bottom carefully onto one corner as if he wished to take up no room on it, to mar its creaseless perfection as little as possible with the twin dents of his buttocks. He pulled off his shoes and then the black sport jacket, already sweat-soaked on the inside of its collar from the half hour since he'd left the air-conditioned banquet hall of the Ipoh

Club. He tugged off his bow tie, unbuttoned his shirt, and sat watching Amma, elbows on knees, casual as a man in a cigarette advertisement, desperate to convince himself that it was proper and natural for his cotton singlet to be showing in front of a girl who had probably learned only that morning — if, dear God, some stoic and self-sacrificing aunt had filled in for the duties that should've been her mother's — what was to happen in this bed tonight.

Out of her suitcase Amma delicately extracted a white eyelet cotton nightgown.

As Appa heard the bathroom lock click into place, the bolt follow it, the tap gush, he thought of a girl he'd known in Singapore who'd slipped off her panties and peed in front of him as he'd stood talking to her in the doorway of her tiny bathroom. Afterwards, in her bed, they'd eaten a whole roast chicken with their hands. Wooden blinds, the kind that usually hung outside Chinese shophouses, covered her windows. A ceiling fan grey with dust stirred the webs of two spiders in a corner of the room. The roast chicken had been fatty and salty, and three quarters of the way through it the girl — what was her name? Mei Ying? Mei Yin? Su Yin? — had run downstairs and out into the street in nothing but a batik housedress pulled over her naked body to buy them two packets of iced sugarcane water, sweet and sticky and sweating on the outsides when she brought them into the bedroom.

But he had decided to leave all that behind: the women who slurped noodles in their underwear, the women who smoked skinny cigarettes and swore like bottle-shop men, the women who compared him to former lovers or speculated out loud about future ones. He had chosen this instead, not for the sake of novelty, nor merely to defy the consternation of his colleagues and his mother, although that gave him private satisfaction. He had chosen this — *this life that begins tonight,* he thought, and his whiskey-slowed heart stirred and soared — because he believed in goodness and simplicity, in the value of a blank slate, in his own power to exalt and educate.

The unfamiliar path stretched before him. Doubt, regret, a sudden reluctance to make the sacrifices he had pledged — all these were normal, he told himself. All these would pass. Tonight he must set himself the most modest of goals: only to try not to turn up the heat of Vasanthi's already stifling discomfort.

So Appa, who had once (and not so long ago) walked stark naked and nonchalant, cock flopping, balls swinging like two mangosteens in a net bag, around that Singapore girl's room, and around other girls' rooms in other shophouses, and, further, around the larger and more impressive rooms and flats and houses of still more girls and some women too, now seized these minutes of Amma's private preparations to undress himself in a flash and slip into his silk pajamas. Then he spread the wool blanket and arranged himself in a suitably patient, unconcerned attitude under it.

The bathroom tap ceased its gushing; the bolt slid back. Very quietly, faint as the tapping of a fingernail in a dream, the lock clicked open. For a moment Amma stood in the bathroom doorway, her thin legs showing under the nightgown in the bright light. Then she switched off the light and walked, silent except for her breath, towards the bed. In the moonlight he saw her put out a hand and pat the pillow as if to make sure it was there, then lay down and stretch out her legs on top of the blanket instead of under it. "Nice big window," she said, looking out the window.

"You must be tired. Quite early you must have had to wake up for them to dress you." He waited, half hoping she would grab this rope, agree that she was exhausted, turn away, and curl up on her side. Stray jasmine buds clung to her loosened hair in places, recalling the strings of flowers that had been braided into it for the chaste scent that was wasted on him. He reached out and plucked a single bud from her hair; then, unsure what to do with it, he let it fall to the floor.

"Oh, not too early," she said. If she'd noticed him touch her hair, she gave no sign of it. "Six-thirty seven something like that. I'm okay."

Should he invite her to tuck herself under the blanket? If he contrived to pull it out from under her and spread it over her himself, would the gesture come off more brutish than chivalric? Should he simply climb out from under it? In the end he went with the third option, to avoid either verbal or mechanical awkwardness.

On that England-imported blanket Tata had purchased for the house during his emphatically domestic retirement, Appa and Amma had pungent, painful sex for the first time. He didn't know what else to say, and so said nothing more — he, a man of words if of nothing else, consummate spinner of sweet nothings in all four major Malaysian languages, whisperer of naughty suggestions into the ears of giggling waitresses. The moonlight seeped stubbornly in through the lace curtains, and he wished she could switch this last light off just as she'd switched off all the others.

He wished several other things besides: that Amma would close her eyes, or at least turn her head, so that he would not be faced with her mildly puzzled frown; that his own senses, save his mercifully impotent nose, were not so uncannily, distressingly heightened (for every creak of the bedframe echoed in his ears, and each one of Amma's meek twitches shook his consciousness gale-like); that he had pressed upon her the option of delaying the deed until tomorrow. Tomorrow, her wedding nerves subsided, she would not have been quivering before the mythical hurdle of The Wedding Night. *Let's get some sleep,* he could've said. Kindly, lightly, after paying her some reassuring compliment or other. *We're both exhausted.*

He fished around for fantasies, but this moment — the creaks, the twitches, the knees knocking shins, the elbows driving into ribs, Amma's eyes huge and incandescent in the moonlight — permitted none. He wondered idly why his penis had never felt quite so much like a battering ram although one or two of his girlfriends had been virgins.

Maybe it's just as well to get it over with tonight, he told himself. *Maybe this way tomorrow will be better.*

In the end there had been no need for the subtlety of the blanket, since Amma never moved to take off her steadily-less-virginal nightgown, and Appa, when he thought of it, was stopped by a vague sense that this would be cruel in some petty way, like forcing a cat to walk through a puddle.

Amma, too, reasoned with herself: *Every married woman has to go through this, isn't it? Nobody enjoys it. Anyway it won't be every night. He's always so busy and preoccupied with his work. After staying late at the office he'll be too tired. It's okay, I'm okay, look at the moon outside, how low it has come, like it's hanging from the guava tree by a string only!* For ten minutes she concentrated all her desperate energies on that large yellow moon; when this became an insufficient distraction from what was going on Down There, she shut her eyes and ears like windows and slipped effortlessly out of her skin to hover just below the ceiling. Rapt, incredulous, she watched the bodies on the bed until the sight shamed her. She drew her breath in until she could hold no more air, then disappeared in a quiet puff of smoke.

On the main road a cement lorry swerved, its brakes screeching, to avoid a stray dog out on a nocturnal hunt. A cicada fell silent, exhausted by its hours of ecstatic song.

When once more she found herself on that wide bed, Appa lay beside her with his eyes closed, his pajama bottoms pulled up and re-knotted at the waist. She slid her legs off the bed and shuffled back to the bathroom, shutting and locking and bolting the door behind her before switching on the light.

Before Appa fell asleep he saw her feet in the sliver of light under the bathroom door, immobile, probably rooted to the floor in front of the mirror, probably cold. It was minutes before she stepped away towards the toilet.

Appa could not easily concede defeat or a failure of judgment: when Tomorrow Night was no better, he put his faith in the next night, and the next, and the one after that, until, a month and a half after their wedding, he found himself once more — and this time with unmitigated longing — thinking of the girl with whom he'd shared a roast chicken in bed. He still could not remember her name, but this time the vision of her slipping on her batik housedress and wooden clogs turned on a tap inside him, turned it so very slightly that it only dripped at first: one night he caught himself staring at Lily Rozells's panty line under her silk trousers, the next night he noticed how long and hard Nalini Dorai laughed at even the worst of his jokes, and about two weeks afterwards he realized with a jolt that the droll angle of Claudine Koh's eyebrows whenever she looked at him was nothing but an invitation cloaked in irony. He made no move to confirm or accept this invitation, but the tap continued to drip, and then to trickle, and finally to run steadily, sapping his hope that his nights and days with Amma would improve. Two months into their marriage, Amma still sat at attention at the dining table, knees pressed together, dabbing nervously at her mouth between bites whether or not Paati was present. Beads of sweat still broke out on her brow whenever either one of them had to use the bathroom while the other was in the room; when once he'd left the door open a crack while urinating, he came out to find her practically trembling at her dressing table, the damp hair at her temples curled into tight corkscrews from the shame. Her terror was as inconvenient as a small child's fear of its own shadow, for it was as impossible for her to shake off what made her hair stand on end: the human body, its varicolored viscous and runny fluids, its gradual absorptions and sudden expulsions, all the unconcealable noises of its flawed workings.

It wouldn't have mattered, Appa was to reflect later. *None of that*

{ 96 }

would've mattered if she hadn't been so stupid. He'd be lying to himself, of course. Had she been a genius, she would still have driven him to lascivious despair. That despair merely arrived more quickly because there was nothing behind her innocence after all, no raw proletarian wisdom for him to draw out and sculpt. When he brought her with him to official and social gatherings—for now that she was his wife, there was no hiding her from the likes of Lily and Nalini and Claudine—she stood around holding her drink in both hands, rewarding their ferocious curiosity with one-word answers. It was true these miniskirted, cigarette-puffing women and all their lushly sideburned firebrand boyfriends were daunting at first; Appa did his best to protect Amma from their clutches, answering for her, keeping his arm around her shoulder, steering her towards safer clusters of people whenever possible. She'd get used to his friends eventually, he thought. Even if she couldn't match their ideas, she'd think of questions to ask. But when, after half a dozen gatherings, she still hadn't thought of questions, he found his pity shifting, sliding slowly towards his old friends. He'd never thought he'd *pity* them, of all things, and yet how awkward it was for them to find this prudish, Form Five–educated girl planted in their midst.

He tried to summon up the old exhilaration of taking her out into the world: she'd been like a kitten let outdoors for the first time, running her hands over the plush velvet seats in the Lido Theatre, eating her popcorn kernel by kernel. When he'd asked her for her opinions about the films they saw together in those days, she'd tucked stray wisps of hair behind her ears, smoothed down her skirt, and hazarded halting sentences that trailed off: "Funny names they all have, no? Toothpick and Spats and whatnot . . . Aiyo, not nice lah to see men dressed as women . . . Must be a frightening place, America, don't you think?"

He'd found her tentativeness charming then; now, not having heard a complete, worthwhile thought from her in months, he felt himself turning to dust every time he looked at her across the dining table. Nothing, no joke he could tell or treat he could offer her rekindled the old exhilaration in him. He brought her ice kacang, cendol, char kuay teow from the same stall in front of which he'd proposed to her. She ate two or three bites, rolling each one doubtfully around in her mouth as if these were all foreign foods. "So stingy they are with the coconut milk nowadays," she said about the cendol. And, pushing away the plate of char kuay teow: "I can count the prawns with one hand. You got nicely cheated."

Appa concluded that his plunging affections were not his memory's fault; he could remember the old Vasanthi quite well and still muster a fierce fondness for that vanished creature. But that girl was not the one opposite whom he found himself sitting every day at the dining table. Some spiteful black magic had left this soured wife in place of the girl whose cool hand he'd held in the Lido, that woman-child haloed in delight and gratitude. He did not entertain the possibility that he had done anything to deserve these disagreeable moods, or he might have pored over the record of their days more thoroughly and thereby guessed what she was thinking: *Now you can sit there and try to be nice to me, but at the club it's all "Let me get you a drink Lily, oh Claudine you're too much," while I stand like a coconut tree in the corner. Think you can still buy me with a plate of char kuay teow? Well, those days are over. Outside you treat them all to oysters and lamb chops and who knows what else you eat, and then very nicely you come home with one packet of char kuay teow for me.*

He began to let her wander off on her own at parties and club nights and open houses, to think her own thoughts and make her own friends. The first time he saw who these friends would be, his single-malt scotch turned brackish on his tongue. He was holding some sort of fussy hors d'oeuvre on a toothpick; when he glimpsed Amma's misguided overtures from across the room, the task of eating it suddenly seemed insurmountable. He put the topheavy toothpick in his empty glass and, still watching Amma, surreptitiously abandoned the glass on top of the piano. They were at the Tambun mansion of Dr. Surgeon Jeganathan, whose Chinese wife, Daisy, Amma was questioning about her tailor's rates. "I must ask that Daisy which tailor she goes to," she'd said to him the previous week. "Her husband is one famous topdoctor, isn't it?" And now, watching them, Appa saw Daisy's thoughts flutter above her head, a crown of vivid butterflies: *Yes, I suppose this girl can afford my tailor, husband a toplawyer after all.* "So reasonable!" Amma squealed. "Not bad at all, man! I mean I'm prepared to pay *quite* a bit more for workmanship like that, you know?" Daisy Jeganathan narrowed her eyes at Amma, half appreciative, half disdainful. "So reasonable," Amma insisted. "I'm delighted to hear it."

I bet she's had nothing but ice cream soda, Appa told himself as he watched Amma finish with a series of overly sincere nods. *She's drunk* on something else entirely. So that's the only way she wishes to improve herself, eh? Learning from the equally stupid wives of my equally unfortunate colleagues. Fancy that. She's capable of learning, after all, when it suits her. For among the rich wives of Ipoh, Amma's face took on an alert, cat-like cast; he could see her mind's gleaming wheels turning more smoothly than they ever had as she absorbed all those women's rules and rituals. The preferred makeup brands, the favored hairdressers, the fashionable saree colors. Did she realize they weren't even friends with each other? Did she understand the reptilian dynamics at play in their every interaction? And finally—most important of all—was she really as enthralled as she seemed to be by their non-conversation, their Ha-ha-hee-hee-I-paid-four-hundred-for-this-saree-even-on-sale-you-know, their tetchy flattery and undeclared tests?

He made a few final valiant efforts to take charge of her intellectual development at home. Surely she wanted to become one of those women only because she'd so little faith in anything else. But he was accustomed to cynical women; he knew how to stir them into a contrarian passion. Perhaps if he could make her understand how the nation's fate would affect her, Lawyer Rajasekharan's wife, even sitting at home doing nothing, gadding about town eating curry puffs, even so, yes indeed—"The problem with their racial politics," he began, "is that—"

"Aiyo, all this politics all I don't know lah," she said. "Whatever they want to do as long as they leave us alone it's okay isn't it?"

"Leave us alone? *Leave us alone?* You call this leaving us alone? Their bloody Article 153 and their ketuanan Melayu, yes yes I know you'll insist you can't understand a word of Malay, so let me explain it to you, let me tell you what it means: it means Malays are the masters of this land, do you understand? Our *masters!* With that kind of language—"

"*Tsk,* after all it's their country, what, so why shouldn't they be the masters? Just because you cannot sit at home and keep quiet means—"

"But it's our country just as much as the bloody Malays'! Do you realize some of our families have been here longer than theirs? Ask the Straits Chinese—"

"*Tsk,* all these grand ideas . . ."

Grand ideas. The sin of which he'd always stood accused, by Lily and Nalini and Claudine, by others before and after them. The difference was that Amma's own ideas really did stop there. Her very thoughts trailed off into nothingness, not just her sentences.

Appa tried to conceal his disenchantment from his mother, but her eager eyes saw the signs. "What did you expect?" she asked him every other day, not quite out of Amma's earshot. And one afternoon: "Now you and I are stuck with her for good. Satisfied?"

"For heaven's sake," said Appa, doing his best to bristle. "Stuck with her for good! You talk about human beings as if they were furniture. I knew what sort of woman I was marrying, thank you very much." All three of them could hear the desperation in his voice, and yet he went on: "If I'd wanted a wife like Marie Curie I'd have found one. Please keep your narrow-mindedness to yourself. Just because she's not like *you* doesn't mean—" He stopped, as though startled by his own sentence.

After a pause Paati said, "Lourdesmary bought some lovely pisang raja to fry for tea."

But Amma could not let Paati's deft *you and I* go. As soon as she had spoken those words, flesh sheathed their white skeleton, blood filled the ready webbing of their veins, and the dull throb of their heart beat all day in Amma's head. He and she, she and he, mother and son: it was them against her. She was still the interloper, the bloody clerk's daughter from next door.

All she could do against the intransigent order of the universe was to concentrate on her transformation into rich man's wife, which she had begun promptly upon her arrival at the Big House. Just a week after her wedding—even before she'd had examples to follow—her father had seen her emerge, kajaled and clad in bright, streaming silks, from her gilt cocoon. She had climbed into the Morris Minor, given her orders to the driver, and returned an hour later with her hair cut short.

Now that she'd stored copious mental notes from her evenings in the presence of Ipoh's wealthy wives, she lay in bed till ten-thirty every morning, reading *Woman's Own* and eating cling peaches from a crystal bowl. *At least I don't have to get up,* she kept reminding herself. *I don't have to go downstairs and face that witch. I could stay in bed all day if I wanted, there are servants to do all the work.* Nevertheless, she rose at noon and went out saree-shopping, then to a beauty salon for a manicure or pedicure or facial. Anything to escape Paati's supercilious shadow.

Paati was not one of the dreaded mothers-in-law of Tamil films and newspaper reports, whose insufficiently dowried daughters-in-law died in mysterious fires or disappeared suddenly. She had no problem with her daughter-in-law's life of leisure: it was only fitting that Amma should sleep in and leave her plate on the table after lunch, for these were markers of Appa's status. Amma could not be berated for bad cooking; neither Paati nor Amma had any need to set foot in the kitchen. No, Paati reserved her bile for immutable truths: for Amma's origins rather than her destination, for who she was rather than what she did.

"You seem to like these bright-bright colors," Paati remarked offhandedly one afternoon, glancing at the marigold silk saree in which Amma had arrayed herself for a garden party at the club. "I think so I'm just behind the times when it comes to fashion. In my day those were the colors laborer women would wear for Deepavali, you know? So in my silly old fuddy-duddy head I still think of them as rubber-estate colors."

And another time, picking up the latest issue of *Woman's Own* where Amma had left it lying on the coffee table: "So this is what you bury your nose in all day, is it? Quite entertaining it seems. Lots of nice colored pictures. Romantic stories too. It's good you can find reading material for your level. After all Raju has his own friends with whom he can discuss his philosophy and politics and whatnot."

Amma's only response to these comments was to add twice-weekly Ladies' Coffee Mornings to her schedule, as well as a solitary tea at the FMS Bar and Restaurant. Braving the men's furtive glances, she made her way to the same table every time and spent exactly sixty seconds studying the menu — turning its pages so steadily she could've been using an under-the-table metronome — before ordering two curry puffs and a pot of tea. *Isn't that Lawyer Rajasekharan's wife?* some fellow would always murmur. *Yah, that's the one,* another, in the know, would reply. *Don't know why she comes here every day to sit and watch us drinking our beer.*

She'd answer silently: *Don't know means I'll tell you: I come here because I've nowhere else to go. What do you think of that? Lawyer Rajasekharan's wife has to seek refuge at the FMS Bar.* But she never did tell them. She covered her mouth so that they could not see her chew her curry puff, and at some point every afternoon, despite the late mornings and the cling peaches and the servants, she found herself thinking: *I'm even worse off than before. At least in my father's house no one was watching me like this.*

They were waiting for her to show her low-class roots; she would do nothing of the sort. She acquired a servant-addressing voice, somehow both crisp and languid, at once high and muted. She learned to call Mat Din *Driver* instead of by his name. As long as she could avoid Paati's eyes, even she was convinced by her metamorphosis.

Six months after her wedding, she threw her first tea party for the Ladies. She knew they came only because their husbands wished to curry favor with Appa. In their fluttering false lashes, in their feverish enthusiasm for every cushion cover in her house, every photo frame, every finger sandwich she served, she saw what an unnatural strain they were under. "Our husbands," they said to her that first afternoon, "our husbands are all sure Raju will be a minister one day." They spoke in this way — each sentence delivered in that breezy first-person plural by a spokeswoman who appeared to have been selected in advance, or mysteriously agreed upon with no need for discussion — to mark the separation between themselves and Amma, for all of them resented her, and yet each one wanted to be her special favorite. Amma persevered: she covered herself in custom-made jewelry, bought an authentic Persian rug for the sitting room, and commissioned original artwork for the entryway. *Why shouldn't I?* she thought. *Doesn't he give me his checkbook to distract me from everything he can't give me? I'm just doing what he wants. This way he doesn't have to feel guilty about anything.* At the parties she threw and the ones to which she was — grudgingly at first — invited, she made passing references to Appa's golf games with party members and club nights with ministers. She met all flattery with a serene smile and did not reciprocate.

Sure enough, the acid undertone of the women's admiration was gone within a few months, leaving behind nothing but a velvet envy. She'd become the gold standard against which they measured their own lives. *I've fooled them all,* she thought. *Even better than I fooled myself. How easily they've forgotten where I came from. We only pretend history matters; in the end all that matters is money.*

All that mattered to the world at large, at least. It was not what mattered at home; she could not expect Appa and his mother to be impressed by her flaunting of their own money. At the dinner table every evening, an immense melancholy choked her; it was all she could do to swallow Lourdesmary's exquisite peritals and kurmas without gagging. When she looked straight ahead she saw Appa's deepening listlessness, his fish-darting eyes and eight o'clock yawns. When she turned to her right, there was Paati, chewing with the dignity and precision of a thoroughbred mare, contempt glinting in her eyes. So she trained her gaze on the portrait of Tata to her left. *Old man*, she thought, *if you hadn't kicked the bucket you also would be sitting here looking down on me, yes or not?*

At bedtime, Appa yawned still more and pleaded exhaustion. She'd wished for such respite from the beginning, but now she was torn between relief and anxiety. When Appa began to stay out until two, three, four in the morning, even the old blessing of his missing sense of smell turned into a curse. He would climb into bed without having tried to conceal the scents of whiskey and women's perfume on his skin, and Amma, keeping her eyes closed and her breath slow to feign deep sleep, would turn slightly to bury her nostrils in her pillow.

Never mind, she tried to reassure herself. *It's not important anymore. I've got better things to do. It's not as if I'm sitting around all day pining for him. I'm a different person now.* But the more complete Amma's transformation — for, after a point, all that was left was fine-tuning, the substitution of one brand of tea for another at her parties, the favoring of certain cakes above others — the sharper grew the pain of the few details she could not change. Each of her father's teatime visits — once a week while Appa was at work — was a swallowed thumbtack, pricking tiny holes in corners she'd forgotten she had.

As soon as her father walked through the front door, Paati sent Lourdesmary out with a tray. Occasionally she graced him with a vague greeting before retiring to her room. But Amma's father seemed not to notice these pointed snubs; he cracked groundnut shells between his teeth and began the conversation, each week, with the same airy question: "So tell me, Vasanthi, what is it like being a rich lady?" Amma, confused by all the unfamiliar feelings doing battle in her chest — embarrassment, pity for this old man who waited for these visits all week because he was too cheap to buy his own groundnuts, hatred for Paati for making her feel sorry for her father, and mingling freely with all these, an illogical nostalgia for her childhood — always had to take a nap after he left. "Well, Vasanthi, how are your parents?" Paati inquired sweetly each week as soon as the front grille had closed behind her father, but Amma was already climbing the stairs, murmuring "Fine, all okay" over her shoulder before getting into bed and pulling her blue blanket up to her chin.

With a little effort and some unprecedented honesty, Amma could have answered her father's favorite question. She could have told him that even in the privacy of her own home, months after her promotion to Rich Lady, she felt like the first-time star of a primary-school play, her skin burning under the greasepaint, the bright lights stinging her eyes. That hiding in bed until noon or sitting alone in the FMS Bar and Restaurant, she missed his house, where at least she'd had a purpose; here she spent her days building toy castles with blocks too big for her hands.

My mother-in-law, she could have told him, does not wield a leather belt or knock my head with her knuckles. But that's because she's a high-class lady: her belly secretes just as much scorn as yours, but her tongue is a thousand times subtler.

IN THE DIM VACUUM of their days, what a miracle Uma's conception seemed to Appa and Amma! To Appa it was a suspension of the laws of logic: not a virgin birth, but close enough. A life created out of the striking together of their bodies like two cold rocks. A sapling sprouting in a desert, in a body that shriveled like a salt-sprinkled snail when you touched it.

A thin stream of hope trickled through Amma: *At least now I won't be all alone. I can keep busy with a baby. And I'll have one person on my side in this house. One person who won't think I'm a useless numskull.*

And Uma's fittingly spectacular arrival fed Appa's pride and Amma's dreams. At four in the morning, as the hospital groundskeeper's roosters roused themselves, stretched their necks, and heralded the dawn, Uma somersaulted out into the harsh fluorescent light. In Amma's arms she snuffled and squirmed, fat, wide-eyed, alert as a seven-year-old. Her newborn face teetered playfully on the edge of a smile. "Foof!" yelped Dr. Sharma after performing the customary series of tests. "Weight in the ninetieth percentile, length and reaction times in the ninety-eighth, a real Superwoman baby you've got yourselves, man!" In a fit of uncharacteristic humor he held Uma aloft and trumpeted a superhero fanfare: "Ta-ra-ra-*RA!* Here comes Superbaby!" The nurses giggled and covered their mouths with their hands, all except the matron, who bustled forward, gasping, to seize Uma. "*Tsk tsk tsk!* Careful, careful, Doctor! What's got into you? Tired is it? Working too much is it? Better you go and sit down and rest, go!" And it was true: this unprecedented jollity was a bad omen, for Uma was the last baby Dr. Sharma would deliver. Two days later, he was in one of his own hospital beds slurping pureed chicken from a plastic spoon, paralyzed from the neck down by a massive stroke.

"That Dr. Sharma himself, with all his years and years of experience, couldn't handle the shock of seeing such an amazing baby as you," Appa would tell Uma as she grew up. "Your magnificence made his heart race like the Lone Ranger, *pa-ra-rum, pa-ra-rum, pa-ra-rum-tum-tum,* and his brain short-circuited, *phut-phut-phut-phut* just like that, what to do?"

"What, Appa? What did his heart and his brain do again?" Uma would ask over and over, giggling, tugging at his trousers.

"Chhi-chhi," Amma would scold, "don't make fun of the poor man. Like a vegetable he is, no joke no joke. Uma, don't listen to your Appa."

"*Phut-phut-phut-phut!*" Appa would repeat, rolling his eyes back in his head and flailing his arms. "*Phut-phut-phut-phut!*" And Amma, excluded from this bond of mirth and mockery, would wander off to her *Woman's Day* and her toenail polish.

Should Amma have taken heed, learned then that Uma was and would always be her father's daughter, resigned herself to being forever an outsider in her husband's house? Should she have fought for Uma's adulation with tricks of her own? Perhaps. But in those first few years of her childhood, Uma's supernal brilliance held all their attention. They fed her Scott's Emulsion in the morning and barley malt before bed. They bought her Fisher-Price toys and Ladybird clothes. They watched her grow as if she were a hero-child in a folktale; they could not look away.

At two, Uma could ride her red tricycle all the way down the driveway to the wrought-iron gate and back again in two minutes flat.

"Can you believe it?" Mrs. Balakrishnan marveled from her front window, knife in one hand, half-peeled potato in the other. "Now itself she should enter Olympics. That age our children couldn't walk properly also, man! Don't know what-what black magic they do in that house."

At three, Uma swung from the branches of the mango tree, singing Hindi film songs perfectly in tune at the top of her voice:

> *Mera juta hai japani*
> *Ye pat lun inglishtani*
> *Sar pe lal topi rusi*
> *Phir bhi dil hai Hindustani.*

(My shoes are Japanese
These trousers are English
The red hat on my head is Russian
But still my heart is Indian.)

By her fourth birthday she could read the *New Straits Times* from front page to sports page, and the Ladies Amma invited to her tea parties gasped and gurgled and cooed as she read the headlines out loud for them: "Malay Privilege a Birthright, PM Reminds Nation"; "PM Warns Opposition Against Racial Politics"; "Police Say Chinese Gangs Responsible for Recent Spate of Violent Crimes."

United by their pride in Uma, distracted from their hard lessons or strategies, Appa and Amma wondered if they might now be an almost normal family. For Uma's fifth birthday they decided to celebrate this possibility almost as lavishly as the nation, just turned ten, had feted its impressive progress since independence in 1957. They could not have fireworks on the lawn or a military parade, but Amma put her entertaining experience to good use: she had one hundred and fifty invitations printed at a local press, drew up sample menus for Lourdesmary weeks in advance, and taught Letchumi to fold serviettes into swans and water lilies.

In years to come, Amma and Appa and Uma would remember this period of hopeful arcing towards contentment as if it existed forever in a tiny bubble. On the eve of the party, after Appa and Uma had picked up the pink Cinderella birthday cake from the cake shop, all three of them had stood around the table contemplating it. Appa had taken pictures of it; Uma had leaned against him and inhaled deeply to savor the smell of his bestquality trouser cloth. When she'd reached up and pulled his ironed handkerchief out of his pocket, he'd chuckled and called her the Artful Dodger. And Amma — if they were imagining this, they all imagined exactly the same thing — even Amma had given them a laugh instead of her usual tight smile that stretched the skin thin over her cheekbones.

"We heard your daughter's a genius," the birthday guests said to Appa. "Last year itself could read newspapers, it seems, now she must be reading, what? *War and Peace,* is it? *Moby Dick*? Show us, little girl, come on!"

So Uma showed them. In the center of a canapé-munching circle she declaimed Tennyson and Shakespeare, followed this with her fourteen-times tables, and rounded off her performance with an up-to-date listing of African capital cities in alphabetical order.

The party was an unqualified success (according to all but Lourdesmary, who the following morning had to wash six crystal punch bowls and a great quantity of fine china, scrub out the cake icing crusted on the Persian carpet, and take the thirty empty champagne bottles out to the rubbish bin), yet its afterglow, just like the nation's, was short-lived. Uma was growing up: each week she laughed a little harder at Appa's jokes and yawned a little more at the entertainments Amma offered her. But I don't want to make paper dolls, she would say. I'm tired of playing masak-masak and beauty saloon. Why do we have to play these silly games just because we're girls? Why can't we make up more interesting stories?

"She may take after you in her looks, Vasanthi," said Paati one day later that year, after Uma had rattled off the Gettysburg Address at the tea table, "but up here" — she tapped a finger on her temple — "up here she's all Raju, isn't it? Too bad for us poor duds. Already she's left us in the dust."

Thus flayed, the truth squirmed before Amma's eyes. Her daughter, her five-year-old daughter, intimidated her. Already she could answer few of Uma's questions: she didn't know what a bare bodkin was, or how to find the Seychelles on Appa's globe. "Amma," Uma blurted out in frustration one day, upon catching her reading her horoscope while Uma recited "The Lobster Quadrille" for her, "you don't care about *anything*. You don't know anything and you don't read any interesting books."

For a little while, Amma stood around drawing patterns in this dust in which she'd been left behind. Then, blowing it out of her eyes, she moved on. The garden parties and coffee mornings were still there. The jumble sales, the hotel high teas.

And if silk sarees and custom-made jewelry could not ensure true gratitude, Appa was now willing to settle for its appearance. He was hardly home these days. The Party, thrashing like a speared tiger after the secession of Singapore in 1965, devoured everything he had. They had to marshal their resources; they had to keep fighting. Malaysia for all Malaysians: the Party would not rest until it could do for Malaysia what Lee Kuan Yew would do for that single pearl he'd yanked off the string.

Alone at home (not counting the servants — but then, in those days, who counted servants?), Paati and Uma amused and edified each other. Paati taught Uma English proverbs and Tamil poems; Uma threaded Paati's needles for her. Paati washed Uma's hair; Uma massaged Paati's pre-arthritic legs. Uma wove soaring fictions for Paati; Paati fed Uma peeled facts.

"Why Appa got no time to eat also?" Uma asked one evening when Appa, showered and changed, rushed past the dinner table and out the door.

"Your Appa has a big brain and a big heart," Paati said, "and people like that always have big-big dreams to match. Your Appa wants to make the world a better place for everyone else, but he forgets to think of himself. What to do?"

"Does Amma also forget to think of herself?"

"No," said Paati, "your Amma is having dinner at the club, after her cocktail hour."

"What's a cocktail hour?"

"It's just something for people to do when they're bored."

"But why is Amma bored? We're not bored. We can read books and sew dolls and make funny hairstyles and—"

"You see," said Paati, "people who are boring get bored very easily. Inside their own head they got nothing to look at and nothing to think about. They can't come up with their own games and stories, so they must go out to clubs-shubs all to hear other people's stories."

One evening Appa did not come home at all. In the darkness before dawn, Uma's eyes sprang open. The streetlamps' pale blue light poured in her open window, along with the scent of night-blooming jasmine and the songs of crickets. But none of these had woken her up. There'd been something else, a voice, voices — yes, there they were. Voices in Appa and Amma's bedroom: short words bouncing off the walls like drops of water on a hot griddle, long sentences that draped themselves over that fury like fox furs, flashy and arrogant. Then something heavier than a word hit the wall and fell with a metal clatter.

Uma got up, tiptoed across the corridor to Paati's room, and opened her door without knocking.

"Paati!" she whispered.

"Come, come and sleep in Paati's bed tonight."

"Paati, why are Appa and Amma shouting?"

"Don't worry about all that. I'll take care of you."

"But why are they so angry?"

"*Tsk,* your Amma cannot understand anything, that's all. But it's also your Appa's fault."

"Why?"

"It's his own fault for marrying the wrong woman. This is what happens when people marry beneath themselves."

"What you mean beneath themselves?"

"I just mean, when people get married to those who are not as clever as them, not as educated, not as classy, not as wise."

"Not wise like how?"

"Aiyo, Uma, Uma, at four o'clock in the morning you're asking me all these questions. Just look at your Amma's father and mother only and you know they're not people like us. Yes or not? One as cheap and crude as a bottle-shop man, the other one gone bonkers with her praying. That's what your Amma came from, so what did your Appa expect when he married her? He made a mistake, that's all."

"But what are we going to do now if Appa made a mistake? What will happen to me?"

"Nothing will happen to you, maa. Paati is here for you. Promise me you'll sleep quietly until morning and tomorrow I'll ask Lourdes-mary to make laddoos for tea."

So Uma screwed her whole face shut, burrowed into Paati, and tried not to think of poor Appa's unsolvable problem, or of almost-as-poor Amma, who didn't have any games and stories of her own to occupy herself when Appa had to work all night. In the dark, Paati was a soft bundle of smells: Yardley English Lavender talcum powder, starched cotton, Tiger Balm. Even if Appa and Amma broke everything in their room and shouted until morning, she would be safe behind Paati's door, and tomorrow there would be laddoos for tea.

"Okay I promise," she said. But not ten seconds later she had another question. "Paati?"

"What, Uma?"

"Will you always, always take care of me? You promise or not?"

"Promise, promise. And you also promise you'll take care of me?"

Uma's giggles at this truncated bedtime game — now *she* was the Paati, and Paati was the baby! — were muffled by the crisp cotton of Paati's nightgown, but her reply was still audible: "Okay I promise, Paati."

That night Uma dreamt she was eating laddoos under a ceiling fan, in a nest she'd built herself of indigo-washed bedsheets and gingham pillows.

7

POWER STRUGGLES

ON A MAY MORNING in 1969, Amma, eight months pregnant, feet swollen as large as loaves of bread, announced her intention to visit her sister Valli in Kuala Lumpur.

"But you hardly went to see Valli when she lived next door," said Appa. "I didn't know you were all that close."

"That's no concern of yours," said Amma. "She asked me to go and help. She's finding it very difficult to manage with the baby. It's her first child, after all."

"But in your condition —"

"Oh, for heaven's sake. Suddenly so worried about my condition, is it? Then where have you been for the past eight months? The Party this, the Party that —"

"Vasanthi, there are elections next week. General elections. Do you realize what these elections mean for our country? This might be the last chance we have to challenge the bloody supremacists. You want our children growing up in a Malaysia just for the Malays? Is that it?"

Amma flared her nostrils at this and took three quick sips of her tea before replying: "Well, if that's the case, don't you want to be left in peace to work on your all-important elections? You can eat and bathe and sleep at the Party headquarters, no need to worry about anything. I'll take Uma with me also."

"Don't be ridiculous. Eight months pregnant and you're going to take care of yourself and your sister *and* Uma?"

"I'll do what I want," said Amma. "You do what you want, so why shouldn't I?"

When Paati learned of Amma's plan, she laughed and bobbed her head. "Of course," she said. "Doesn't surprise me one bit. Anything stupid to make you feel bad, she'll do. Perfect timing also. She waits until the most hectic period for you, and then suddenly her sister needs help it seems. Anyway, you tell her she can't take Uma. Nothing doing. If she wants to do stupid-stupid things, that's fine, but she won't be using my granddaughter just to seek attention for herself."

Would Uma go or stay? The conflict sucked up all the air in the Big House and hung, hot and bloated, over the vacuum it had left. Appa slicked back his hair, tied his necktie, and dashed off to the Party headquarters, leaving the women to settle the matter.

"Well," said Paati, smiling patiently at Amma, "why don't we just ask Uma what she wants to do?"

So Uma was summoned, and the various wonders she would encounter on this adventure were enumerated for her. "You'll get to go on the train with me," Amma said. "You've never been on the train. And you can see K.L. Such a big, busy town, not like Ipoh. We can go shopping in air-conditioned emporiums and have lunch at A&W. Root beer, hamburgers all they have. And your Valli Chinnamma will be so happy to see you, you know or not?"

"Is Appa also coming?" asked Uma.

"No," said Amma. "Appa has to stay and do his politics."

"And Paati? Is Paati coming?"

"No, maa," said Paati, "I'm afraid I can't sit on the train for so long with my arthritis and all."

Uma looked from Paati to Amma and back again. She thought of the trains she'd seen in books, of air conditioning and root beer and new dresses and shoes. Then she contemplated experiencing all these with Amma, and the longer she considered this prospect, the lonelier she felt. Lonely and hollow and tired. Tired and wrong and out of place. Inside her head she couldn't wait to go home, already, even before she'd left. And all that time, while she drank root beer and ate restaurant chicken chops with Amma, Paati would be all alone, squinting to thread her own needles, ineffectually massaging her own aching legs.

"I don't want to go," Uma said. "I want to stay at home with Paati."

But now Amma, surprising herself—for what did she care, really?

She wasn't among those mothers who lived for their spoiled brats, and wasn't half the reason for the trip to get away from all this, Uma included? — turned into a cheater, a liar, a no-fair playground crook. She'd agreed that Uma's word should resolve the conflict, but now she said: "No, I don't think so. Paati can't look after you all by herself. You come with me."

"For me it's no problem looking after Uma," Paati said. "Uma is not the type who needs looking after and constant attention. I've always said she takes after her father. She'll happily find a book and sit by herself. She'll play her own games quietly. And she's a big help to me, isn't it, Uma? Aren't you a big help?"

Chewing on her lip, Uma nodded very slightly, for though she'd understood the words of Paati's question, she felt quite certain that a small but significant part of it swung beyond her grasp. She loved Paati, wanted nothing more than to be on her side, to defend her in this obscure battle. But what were the rules? What would the winner get? Much as she desired Paati's victory, it seemed cruel to gang up on Amma, who wasn't as clever as Appa, who didn't know how to make up her own games and stories, who, despite all her pretty clothes and expensive necklaces, cried like a small child in the night when no one was supposed to be listening.

Amma saw this seed of doubt, seized it, and held it up in triumph. "She's just saying what you want her to say," she said to Paati. "Of course she wants to come to K.L. I'll buy you your own little suitcase, Uma. We'll go and choose it today."

When Paati exercised her motherly right of appeal to Appa, he shook his head over and over like a wet dog and said, "You women can fight this one out. I haven't even had the time to eat or sleep or shit in the last two weeks. If you ask me, the easiest thing would be to just let Vasanthi have her way. It's not like she's taking Uma into the jungle." And so Paati surrendered, though only to herself. To everyone else, she feigned a gracious yielding to an inferior. "All right then," she said, "if such a small thing is sooo important to Vasanthi. If that's the only way she can make herself feel important." If Paati felt her feet slipping on her rung of the household hierarchy, if she saw herself languishing, in years to come, in an out-of-the-way corner under her daughter-in-law's ineffective reign, she said nothing of it to anyone.

On a Saturday morning, Mat Din drove Amma and Uma to the railway station and unloaded their bags on the pavement. They were an hour early for the train, though Amma had scolded Uma and twisted her ear for dawdling over her breakfast. "Don't you do that," Paati had growled, wagging a finger. "Don't you bully the child just because you're angry about Other Things." Uma had worried, yet again, about the many injustices Amma might perpetrate on this trip, far from Paati's watchful eye.

But now that they'd left the Big House behind, Amma's mood had lifted perceptibly. "Come," she said, taking Uma by the hand, "come we go and have a soft drink or something."

A bellboy in a red jacket pulled the creaking accordion gate of the lift shut behind them. On his breast pocket, just under a nametag that said "Lim," the words *Historic Station Hotel* were embroidered in gold cursive.

"Going outstation, Madam?" he said to Amma. He grinned at their bags.

"Yes, going outstation," repeated Amma, adjusting her saree on her shoulder, drawing a little farther into her corner of the lift. When they got out she said under her breath, without turning to look at Uma, "Trying to be funny only this Chinese boy. As if he can't see for himself we're going outstation. What, he thinks we're bringing two three suitcases just to ta-pau our lunch or what?"

At the Station Hotel's restaurant they sat in wicker chairs on the balcony, amid the elegant remnants of empire: a scuffed and stained checkerboard floor, rolled-up bamboo blinds creaking gently in the breeze, a potted fern wilting genteelly onto the edge of their table. A fine dust coated the ledge under the blinds. Uma, fancy-frocked, sashed-and-stockinged, a thousand pins holding her hair up in a precarious, juvenile bouffant, extended one index finger and—because the dust was dark yet silver, because it was soft and inviting and gave off that quiet, wise dust smell—ran that finger along the balcony ledge, up, up, up towards Amma, over bumps and cracks, leaving a dustless swath in her trailblazing finger's wake. When she could reach no farther she lifted the finger and examined, close up, the whorled fingerprint grooves highlighted by the coating of dust they had acquired. "Only Uma Rajasekharan has these fingerprints," Paati had told her once when she'd run her fingers along a dusty upstairs windowsill at the Big House. And, kissing her dirty fingertips one by one: "Uma alone, Uma and no other. Even your brotherorsister will have different fingerprints."

But Amma displayed no such enthusiasm for this evidence of an inviolable Umaness-without-end. "Chhi!" she snapped. "There also you must put your hands, is it? Cannot keep quiet ah?" She folded her arms and crossed her legs. "Whatta-whatta grand place this Station Hotel used to be back in the British days, you know or not?" she went on. "Since they took over they've kept it like their face only. Dust everywhere. Taking two hours to come and take our order."

Now that Amma was expecting a brotherorsister, everything disgusted her even more than before. Her lower lip was permanently curled, at smells, at colors, at hot weather and slow fans and jaunty radio jingles.

BrotheROARsister, brotheROARsister.

That was the noise that echoed in the baby's little red ears as it swam around in Amma's belly, fingers and toes splayed like a frog's.

Three beads of sweat gleamed above Amma's upper lip whenever Uma looked at her. Rashes appeared and disappeared on her skin as Uma watched, and she smelled of fish curry in the mornings.

Below the railway station balcony, cars constantly pulled into and out of the long driveway. People milled about the kacang puteh stall across the street, buying treats to bring on their trips. A man at the back of the crowd hawked and spat into a nearby flowerbed. "Chhi!" Amma said again and flared her nostrils. "Don't feel like eating also now."

Nevertheless, when a stingy-whiskered, sniffling waiter came and stood by their table, Amma opened the laminated lunch menu and pondered its columns. Cheese toasties, chicken chop, mutton cutlets. The waiter's coat had seen whiter days; his cuffs were, plainly speaking, grey. Suspicions of stains lingered around the pockets and under the arms, though one couldn't be sure. Perhaps they were shadows or tricks of the light. And one stamp of empire had been permanent: the obsequious curve of the man's shoulders, a half slouch that sent his thin neck bobbling out like a turkey's. "Yes?" he ventured. "You are ready to order, Madam?"

Amma was: one inche kabin, two freshlime, the first to be pushed aside for being too oily after a single bite, the second to be rejected (with an evocative screwing shut of the eyes and a twisting of the mouth into a tiny pink knot) for being too sour after a single sip. "Don't know what kind of chicken they use these days also," Amma added when she had recovered from her sip of freshlime. "All skin and fat. Enough for me. You also don't drink too much of this terrible freshlime, Uma, otherwise you'll be asking to go to bathroom every two-three minutes. Please."

A please from Amma was the opposite of a please from Paati. A please from Amma didn't mean that Uma was being a big help.

Amma paid the bill with exact change, counting out the coins from the embroidered coinpurse she kept in her cream-colored handbag. She clicked the clasp of the handbag shut. Then she got up and took Uma once more by the hand.

Downstairs on the platform the heat hit them in the face, abloom with all its food smells, its industrial fumes, its faint human odors. Fried bananas from the goreng pisang stall. Thick black grease and fresh paint. Someone's sly, lingering fart. Glossy election posters plastered the walls and columns, their smooth, confident faces and bold letters shining in the sun. VOTE NATIONAL ALLIANCE FOR UNITY AND SECURITY. DEMOCRATIC ACTION PARTY, PROTECTING YOUR INTERESTS. UNDILAH GERAKAN RAKYAT MALAYSIA! On the back of a bench someone had pasted one poster on top of another, and a third person had come along to cover both with a DAP poster, then pasted two more on either side of it for good measure. Under its torn corner the first two layers were still fresh and bright.

Amma looked at the posters and smiled a sour smile. She opened her handbag and withdrew a small, knotted handkerchief she'd doused in Axe Brand Camphorated Oil. "Oo wah," she said, pressing the handkerchief to her nose and her sweaty temples, "your Appa's cronies are all over the station, man! Whichever way you turn also you see their faces only."

The train drew in, giving a great metallic shudder at its own whistle. People put their fingers to their ears. "Only twenty minutes late," Amma said. "Almost nothing at all. Too-too efficient our great country is becoming, just like they promised us. Charging into the modern age."

The inside of the train was all green. Green curtains, green seats, green doors leading to other cars. An antimacassar embroidered with the words *Keretapi Tanah Melayu* lay delicately on each headrest.

"What does it mean, Amma?" Uma asked. "Carry-tuppy Tanah Me-lay-oo?"

"Uma, don't start," snapped Amma. "You know I don't know all that. I didn't study their wonderful Malay language in school. Anyway

I think it's something to do with the train only. Nothing so great."

But someone demurred, someone who wished at least to qualify this dismissive verdict of *train only* and *nothing so great,* and at most to . . . well, what that someone wanted at most, in the best of all possible worlds, is not yet relevant. Not quite yet. For now he, a Malay man seated across the aisle and behind Uma and Amma, concentrated on correcting certain misconceptions. "Eh thanggachi!" he called out softly, leaning sideways in his seat, his teeth yellow under the black velvet of his songkok. "Thanggachi!"

Thanggachi meant little sister in Tamil, but Uma, six years old, in stockings and a smocked dress with a sash, knew two things without having to think about them: 1) the Malay man didn't really speak Tamil; and 2) she wasn't anyone's little sister.

"I'm not thanggachi," she said, and, by way of honest-but-friendly introduction: "I'm Uma Rajasekharan." Only implied, but keenly felt by all present: And who are *you,* audacious songkok wearer with yellow teeth?

"*Tsk,*" said Amma, one hand flicking Uma's knee, "don't be rude." She shut her eyes against the green glare streaming through the curtains and leaned against the headrest.

"Oh oh, so sorry lah thanggachi," said the Malay man, "but I tell you something, okay?"

Uma blinked at the man. Just above his left eyebrow the velvet of his songkok had worn off to leave a pale, mangy spot.

"You asking-asking your poor mummy so many questions, I answer for you can or not?"

A vendor was making his way through the train, his voice barely audible in the distance. "Naaas'lemak naaas'lemak naaas'lemak kari-PAP! Nasi lemak nasi lemak nasi lemak kariPAP!"

"Keretapi Tanah Melayu means railway lah thanggachi," the man went on. "Means Malay Land Railway. Malay Land that means Malaysia lah, thanggachi, that also you don't know ah? Looking at me with eyes so big, your own country also you don't know the name is it? Aiyo-yo thanggachi, your own Na-tio-nal Language also tak tahu ke? No shame ah you, living in Malay Land but cannot speak Malay? Your mummy and daddy also no shame ah, living in Malay Land and never teach their chirren Malay?"

Malay Land! But this was magical and impossible, a mountainous land for giants and monsters and brave, sarong-clad heroes. Malay

Land was like Disneyland or Never-Never Land, not a place where people spat into flowerbeds and farted in crowded railway stations and served too-oily inche kabin. To hear about Malay Land, a land obviously hidden from the naked eye of the uninitiated, might be almost worth forgiving the songkok wearer for saying thanggachi, for appropriating words to which he had no blood-given right and which, moreover, were inaccurate. Perhaps even for his audacious no-shaming, which creased Uma's brow and burned her cheeks. *My Appa,* she wished to inform the yellow-toothed man, *is much cleverer than you, and he can talk proper English, not like you.* But one did not say such things to grown-up strangers.

"Naaas'lemak naaas'lemak naaas'lemak kariPAP!" insisted the vendor, his voice drawing closer and closer.

"Uma," said Amma, "please stop disturbing the other passengers."

"But Amma —"

"Uma. You heard what I said."

Uma leaned back in her seat and studied the antimacassar in front of her. Across the aisle the Malay man subsided with a sharp chuckle, as if someone had just delivered a terrific punch line. The vendor burst in through the door behind them and bustled through the car, trailing a diaphanous tail of smells behind him. Coconut rice and spicy sambal ikan bilis. Curry puffs made with just enough flour to bind the Planta margarine, and fried in palm oil.

The man across the aisle bought a packet of nasi lemak and two curry puffs, talking to the vendor in Malay. To Uma, who didn't speak the Na-tio-nal Language, their conversation was impenetrable, but after the vendor moved out of the way she peered around the back of her seat to see what the man had bought. Sedap dimakan. Good to eat. It was one of two phrases in the Na-tio-nal Language she'd learned from an instant-noodle advertisement on TV, the other being cepat dimasak, quick to cook, patently less applicable to the songkok-wearing man's snack. Sedap dimakan. Se dapdi makan. Sedapdima kan. She went over it again and again, ruthlessly tearing apart and putting together syllables, waiting to see if the words would say themselves out loud in her mouth, but they didn't, and she didn't ask Amma to buy her anything. The vendor strode up the aisle and out the green doors into the next car.

"Naaas'lemak naaas'lemak naaas'lemak kariPAP!"

Amma unwrapped a cucumber sandwich and handed it to Uma.

"Here," she said quietly, "stop staring at other people's food." But the cucumber had turned the thin white bread soggy, and the sandwich wasn't salty enough or buttery enough. Uma fell asleep with it in her hand, and after a few minutes Amma lifted it out of her fingers and threw it into the paper bag she'd brought for rubbish, taking care not to touch the neat C that Uma had bitten out of it.

AMMA'S SISTER VALLI never turned off the radio in her kitchen. From morn till night it blared its Tamil film songs, interrupted only by the news in English three times a day. Sometimes she left the radio on when she went to bed, and it crackled on like a dying fire into the dawn, after the last news had been read and the last chord of the national anthem had trumpeted through the house. During the day Valli's baby wailed his own slightly more than two cents under and over the solemn news reader, the soaring jingles for Teijin Tetron fabric, and Lata Mangesh-kar's mosquito voice. Tears ran down his red face. Gas and fatigue and a fulminating nappy rash drenched his tiny brow in sweat and made his lips tremble. Amma's camphorated handkerchief hadn't left her fist since she and Uma had walked into Valli's kitchen.

Valli didn't have a maid to keep her kitchen clean: a thin film of oil coated the floor, so that Amma's Japanese slippers slid dangerously on the tiles. The tinfoil Valli had tacked above and around the gas stove had turned black with soot. On each sheet of foil the secret messages of a thousand layers of turmeric-yellow and tomato-red curry were as plain as daylight:

The times they are a-changing.

The baby isn't really colicky. He sees the future, that's all.

Valli's husband misses his mother's cooking.

In other kitchens people will soon be sharpening their knives, and not because they'll have chickens to carve.

Valli loves Amma a wee bit less than she did back when she could feel sorry for her.

"Chhi, what is this, Valli," Amma blurted out on the second day of their visit, overcome by the heat of the stove and the ceaseless ra-dio noises. "At least mop once a week, for goodness' sake. My feet are slipping and sliding all over the place." As soon as she said it she knew what was coming.

"Sorry lah Akka," Valli said, pouting playfully. "What to do? My husband is only a poor gomen clerk, not a high-fi lawyer. If I had three-four servants my kitchen also would be sparkling clean."

In the silence that followed, Lata Mangeshkar soared towards her highest note yet.

Outside in the hot sun, all over the country, people were out voting today. Appa had driven himself to the Party offices after two hours of sleep, giving Mat Din the driver the day off to vote. Mat Din had ridden his bicycle to cast his vote, alone among the servants at the Big House. Lourdesmary the cook, Vellamma the washerwoman, and Letchumi the sweep weren't voting. Lourdesmary didn't think any gomen would move her family out of their cave dwelling and into a house, and Vellamma and Letchumi had been born in India and couldn't vote. "Red IC, saar," they'd said in unison when Appa had offered to give them a lift to the polling station. Letchumi had pulled her red identity card out of her paper-bag handbag and thrust it under Appa's nose.

"Chari, paruvalai," Appa said, "next time all that will have changed. You vote for my party, new gomen will come, new gomen will change your IC for you. Then next election you can vote."

"Aaaaaman," Vellamma said to Letchumi as Appa went outside to start the car. "As if. Gomen going to hand out blue ICs left and right. Lawyer-saar dreaming big-big dreams."

"Even the Indians born and bred in the country they still call foreigners, immigrants, intruders," Letchumi agreed. "You mean to say some new government like magic is going to make us citizens?"

Amma and Valli hadn't even discussed voting. They'd come downstairs this morning to find the news reader already going onandonandon about the election in his dry monotone. Latest polls. Favored candidates. Estimated turnout according to district. Amma laid the baby on the dining table and began to undress him for his morning oil massage, her arms stretched straight out to reach him in front of her pregnant belly. If she'd been able to bend over or sit or squat or kneel she would've put him on a mat on the floor; because she could only stand he had to have his massage and bath on the table, like a chicken being dressed for the stove.

"For goodness' sake, Valli," Amma said, "can't you switch that thing off once in a while? Cannot hear myself think also." On the vinyl tablecloth the baby screamed and writhed and waved his clenched fists in the air.

Valli switched the radio off.

In his voting booth in Ipoh, Appa put a series of confident check marks in a column of boxes, including one next to his own name. Lawyer-saar still young and hopeful for his young country. Lawyer-saar dreaming, according to Vellamma and Letchumi, big-big useless dreams.

In another voting booth, five miles down the road from Appa's, Mat Din carefully traced his check marks in different boxes.

In unseen rooms all over the country, men sat at long tables tallying votes on ballots emptied out of full ballot boxes. These rooms were silent but for a few faint sounds: ceiling fans clicking like tricky joints, papers rustling, dry fingers rasping on paper, tongues licking thumbs. Was it in these rooms that Rumor began her scrabblings? Its nudgings, its sneaky nibblings at the hopeful hearts of men, at their big-big dreams of peace and compromise? Or was it outside on the traffic-choked streets, where its *psst-pssts* and its pesky squeaks were at first indistinguishable from the creaking of the unoiled chains on the rattletrap bicycles of Mat Din and a million others like him? Did Rumor steal shamefaced into the wet markets and the kopitiams for her clandestine assignations with Fact? Did Appa, high-fiving his hungry, unshaven fellow dreamers as the results were announced, notice them stealing hand in hand past the grimy windows of the Party offices? The day after the election, did Rumor and Fact attend the unofficial victory rallies together in disguise? Did they help to lift Appa onto the shoulders of his rejoicing supporters and then slip away to mourn with the gomen losers?

Impossible to say, but three days after the election, Rumor and Fact burst forth into the noonday Kuala Lumpur heat, Rumor in a red dress, Fact in coat and tails, and together they began a salacious tango in the streets. Their hair was suspiciously rumpled, their eyelids heavy, their skins slick with sweet afternoon bed-sweat. People pointed and whispered. Schoolchildren leaned out of bus windows and gaped. Good Muslims averted their eyes and wondered what would become of the country if such public immodesty were condoned. But their dance was mesmerizing, and soon crowds — even the good Muslims — began to gather despite themselves. Then Rumor and Fact picked up the pace of their dance, as if somewhere an orchestra played only for their ears. Faster and faster they twirled, Rumor in her red dress, Fact in his coat and tails, until their feet were such a blur that the most intent of the spectators could no longer keep track of whose feet were whose, and people caught their breath as the pair swept past their noses, stirring the air like a speeding car.

The stories that Rumor and Fact spun together poured like lava through the city: fourteen non-Malay opposition members had been elected in the state of Selangor alone; these Gerakan and Democratic Action Party victors were going to strip the Malays of their God-given scholarships and housing loans and job quotas, overturning Article 153, undoing the social contract, just as they'd been threatening to; Selangor was going to fall to the Chinese, just as Singapore and Penang had fallen before it; the Chinese were going to grab Selangor for themselves, just as they'd grabbed Singapore, as if their pockets weren't bulging enough already; the Chinese were going to force Maoist communism on everyone; the frightened gomen had gunned down a Chinese Labor Party activist for no reason. And the Indians? They'd staged a drunken midnight demonstration, an excuse for a brawl, really, so typical of those bloody booze-guzzling estate coolies. Chinese and Indians, Indians and Chinese: their yellow and brown faces loomed large in the electrified Malay imagination, their gloating laughter, their bloodcurdling cries of victory, their eyes like embers ready for stoking by Malay politicians desperate for scapegoats and simple stories. And every man, Chinese, Indian, and Malay, forgot his contempt for the views of the departed British and savored the taste of his old masters' stereotypes. *Coolie*, they hissed. *Village idiot fed on sambal petai. Slit-eyed pig eater.* They'd been given a vocabulary, and now, like all star pupils, they were putting it to use, relying on the old, familiar combinations, patting each other on the back to applaud their own initiative, encouraging the back rows of the classroom to rise to the challenge.

Was it Rumor or Fact that ragged crowds of Indians and Chinese had trailed through Malay settlements with promises and suggestions? *Your turn to lick our boots! Talk about ketuanan Melayu, now we'll see who's whose tuan! Kuala Lumpur belongs to the Chinese! Balek Kampong!* Go back to your backwater villages. Go home. Go back where you came from. A sarong-clad Pandora with a hibiscus bloom behind one ear opened her box: these words fluttered blackly out, and in no time it ceased to matter whether they had really been spoken or not. They were real and here to stay. They burst into flames; they blazed in plain view and brought tears to unprotected eyes. Anyone could say those words now. A could spit them to B, B to C, and C could turn around and spit them right back to A. Because really, in this country, that *go home* cry could be directed—delicately or not so delicately—at just about anyone. The people who had (allegedly) said it would have the farthest to travel to get back to where they'd come from.

As the rioters tore apart the shining capital, Appa and his fellow dreamers shook their heads and buried their faces in their hands.

"That's racial harmony for you," sneered Lily and Claudine and Nalini. They'd come to the Big House to commiserate with Appa, but faced with his childlike disillusionment had found commiseration beyond them. "Our miracle nation has surpassed herself this time. Goes to show, doesn't it? Even the most well-trained dog will maul the other feller for a bigger piece of meat. Human nature. Nothing we can do about it." And Appa, who would once have quoted Lee Kuan Yew at them, only shook his head some more. "I suppose we won't be seeing you at the club," Lily said.

They wouldn't, and that sober, sobering night in the deserted Bengal Room was to be their last for a week, for even Lily and Claudine and Nalini would lack the spirit to break the curfew that was to be declared.

Two DAYS AFTER the election, Amma noticed the date on Valli's Swami Vivekananda wall calendar and wondered idly how Appa's golden vision had fared, whether his women were fawning over him at the club for some petty victory that would change nothing, or cradling his head in their laps as he drowned his sorrows. But the kitchen radio had not been turned back on since Amma's complaint on Election Day. *Who knows?* she thought. *Who cares?* Then she went weightily about her duties, dragging her Japanese slippers on the oily floor, sighing and *tsk-tsk*ing to herself while Valli sulked and brooded and the baby wailed.

Upstairs, in the bedroom she was sharing with Amma, Uma was reading. She'd already been through all the books Amma had packed in her suitcase twice and was now reading them a third time.

> "Consider your verdict," the King said to the jury.
>
> "Not yet, not yet!" the Rabbit hastily interrupted. "There's a great deal to come before that!"
>
> "Call the first witness," said the King; and the White Rabbit blew three blasts on the trumpet, and called out "First witness!"

Uma picked a mosquito bite scab off her knee and turned the page.

At six o'clock Valli's husband, Subru, charged wild-eyed into the kitchen, not stopping to take his shoes off, his panting louder than the baby's fussing. Amma looked up sharply, bouncing the baby in her arms. Valli, who was stirring the evening's dosai batter in the far corner, paused mid-stir and opened her mouth to say something. Two geckos, absorbing the tension in the air, charged at each other and began a noisy, inappropriate fight on the ceiling.

"There's trouble," Subru said before she could speak. "Going to get even worse it seems."

"Ennathu?" Valli said irritably. "Running in like a madman and simply-simply talking like this, as if we know what you're talking about? What trouble? Heng Kiat's dogs got into Ranggama's back yard again, is it?"

"Dogs!" Subru said. "You think I'm talking about dogs and cats and donkeys? Turn on the bloody radio, man, then you'll know what-what terrible things are going on out there. Sitting here staring at each other's faces only, what is going on in your own back yard also how can you know?"

"No need to shout at me," said Valli. "Akka had a headache, it's because of her only I switched off the radio. Now what?"

And it was only then, when Valli's husband marched to the radio and switched it on, that the news reader's sharp, clipped voice delivered the turbulence of the outside world to their waiting ears, although it was not yet time for the news: *In response to yesterday's victory rallies, about three hundred supporters of the United Malays National Organisation have gathered at the Selangor Chief Minister's official residence to urge him to organize a counterdemonstration . . .*

But what did they care about demonstrations and counterdemonstrations by people with too much time on their hands? "Ithu ennathu," Valli grumbled, "you think what, you're an Englishman, is it? Walking all over the house in your filthy shoes, and then I only will have to scrub and—"

"Chumma irru!" Her husband leaned forward on his elbows, his ear up against the radio. "For you shoes and slippers are the whole world, I tell you. Shaddup your mouth and listen."

The Malay leaders, the news reader went on, *have voiced concerns about the tone and content of the Gerakan and DAP rallies earlier today. According to one UMNO official . . .*

As if he alone shared his father's alarm, the baby took a deep breath, reddening as his lungs filled with air, and screamed with all his might. Under that scarlet scream the reader's voice droned on: *Threats . . . Kampong Baru neighborhood . . . Gerakan . . . DAP . . . demonstrations . . .* Amma pulled out a chair and sat down suddenly, bouncing the baby so vigorously his scream vibrated in his throat.

Uma stole down the stairs and sat on the landing. Through the stair rails she watched Amma's hair bun bounce along with the baby in her arms.

"Enough!" cried Valli. "You think what, I am sitting and shaking my legs all day, is it, like my millionaire sister here? What, you've given me fifteen-sixteen servants, is it, that I can lie in bed and listen to the news all day? Read two different newspapers and keep up with current events? *Hanh?*"

At the present time, said the radio voice, *it appears that Dato Harun has given his permission for a peaceful demonstration.*

"You people," said Amma, "such a small thing also must fight ah? I think I better leave you and go upstairs to see —"

"Small thing!" Valli threw back her head and, laughing like a car that wouldn't start, upended the bowl of dosai batter over the sink, slopslopslop. "Oh, for you of course it is a small thing, you with your cook driver washerwoman bellboy footman butler, what problems —"

"Please, for heaven's sake," Valli's husband said. "Both of you please. There is going to be enough fighting out there, no need for us to start our own fight in here. I'm telling you. I heard the Malay fellas talking at the office. Finish for the Chinamen in this country. Finish. The bastards are quietly-quietly sharpening their parangs. Lock the front gate and don't go out tomorrow. I mean it. Don't even step outside the front door."

"Hanh?" said Amma, pressing the screaming baby against her chest. Over his muffled cries she laughed the high-pitched, wondering laugh of a small child watching a magic trick. "What is sooooo terrible outside there," she said after a moment, "that we cannot even go out to buy a few vegetables from the vegetable van?"

"I don't think so your vegetable man will be coming tomorrow," said Valli's husband. "If he has anything at all upstairs," he continued, tapping his temple with a forefinger, "he'll sit at home and keep quiet."

Dato Harun, said the news reader, callously unruffled by all these theatrics—*his* dosais were crisping nicely on his wife's griddle at home, after all—*has reassured the crowd that there is no danger that the state will fall into DAP hands, despite the opposition's claims to the contrary. He has promised to reveal*—

Here, having dumped out the dhal she had soaked for the evening's *sambhar,* Valli switched off the radio and retrieved her hiccupping baby from Amma. "I can take care of him," she said stiffly. "If you all want dinner you can find something at the Chinese stalls."

But when her husband came back downstairs, showered and buzzing with Boy Scout be-preparedness, he snorted at the idea of venturing out to the stalls. "You are deaf on top of everything else, is it?" he said to Valli. "Cannot understand what I said? Or you think I'm joking? There's nothing to joke about. We're not leaving this house tonight."

So they ate sliced Chinese white bread for dinner, toasted over the flame of Valli's sooty stove and spread with sweet brown kaya. Then they drank coffee (for the adults) and Milo (for Uma) and went upstairs. Amma's belly made a great, dark shadow on the wall beside her bed. BrotheROARsister, brotheROARsister, that shadow growled. One of those was coming soon, its eyes shut tight in concentration, its tiny fists clenched in preparation for battle. The brotheROARsister would be round and red, toothless and flat-nosed, louder and more hiccupy than Valli's baby. Of this Uma was certain.

VALLI'S HUSBAND had been right: on the following morning, three days after the election, the vegetable man was nowhere to be seen. There was a strange silence, broken only by the thin chirping of sparrows. The pork vendor's robust cry, the crunch-crunch of his cleaver cutting bone, the quack of the vegetable man's squeeze horn, the newspaper boy's thick bundles crashing onto porch after cement porch (narrowly missing dogs cats porch lights grandfathers dozing in creaking rattan chairs): it was as if some celestial conductor held all these parts at bay with a raised hand.

Valli's husband sat unshaven at the kitchen table, eating more toasted Chinese bread with kaya for breakfast. No one had put the bread away last night after dinner: it had dried out on the kitchen counter and now tasted like sweetened sawdust in his mouth.

The baby was taking his morning nap, snuffling and whimpering now and then to keep his mother and aunt from slacking off and attending to other, less important matters.

Valli sat at the table with her chin in her hands and her eyes closed.

Amma stood at the kitchen window with her arms folded, watching nothing happen.

Uma was upstairs reading, lying on her cot bed, stomach down, feet in the air, elbows aching from the weight of her head, ears alert because something, somewhere, was amiss, and not just the absent vegetable man and pork vendor and newspaper boy.

What Valli's husband suspected, Valli could not have cared less about, Amma feared, and Uma and the baby felt in their soft bones: civilization as they knew it was crumbling.

In Ipoh, Appa and his fellow ex-dreamers had locked up the Party offices and gone home. Appa had barricaded himself in his study with two bottles of whiskey. When Lily and Claudine and Nalini arrived, it was Paati—simultaneously bristling at the indignity, eager to please her son's fine-feathered friends, and disdainful of their unsubtle wares—who went out to open the gate for them. *Women these days,* she thought as she smiled her greetings at each of them. *So much makeup, skirts that practically show their panties, and still cannot get husbands. Throwing themselves at Raju like this, don't they realize he's got better things to do?* Out loud she said, "Come in come in, Raju is in his study. Can I get you all a drink?" The servants had not come to the Big House today. Vellamma and Letchumi and Lourdesmary had heard the general advice to stay at home and lock all doors (even the merely metaphorical doors of Lourdesmary's cave dwelling) just in case the trouble spread from Kuala Lumpur to Ipoh; Mat Din was hoping it would, so that he might have a chance to join the struggle with his countrymen. He, Mat Din bin Mat Ghani, would gladly answer the first call to arms. He would fight for Malay honor and throw off the yoke of the oppressors; he would never again have to take a lowly job working for a glorified foreigner who talked like he owned this country.

In settlements all around Kuala Lumpur, other Mat Dins were getting ready for the evening's march, with rag strips and tins of kerosene, with knives and machetes. Permission had been granted for a peaceful demonstration, but no one had expressly forbidden a bit of melodrama here and a smidgen of symbolism there. So the would-be marchers donned white bands of mourning around arm and songkok, nifty accessories that both expressed their wearers' feelings on the outcome of the election and concealed mangy spots on their songkoks. Just as they and their neighbors had found themselves flinging the old British epithets at each other, now they resurrected a symbol they'd first leveled against the white man. Multipurpose mourning white. May be worn whenever the wearer feels his place has been usurped by interlopers and his country overrun by outsiders.

At four o'clock the city began to shut down. Chinese shop owners pulled the iron grilles over their storefronts with long poles, nervous sweat bathing their bare arms. Government workers cut short their last tea break of the day and hurried home. In the suburbs and outlying areas wives waited for their men by front gates.

At five o'clock Amma, feeling restive, began to pace around the kitchen on her heavy feet. Valli considered telling her to stop it but didn't.

By six-thirty the peaceful march had seen its first victims, two Chinese fellows on motor scooters. No one could say what had really happened, or how, or least of all why. Rumor and Fact fornicated openly in the empty streets. The march had taken an inexplicably scenic route through Chinese parts of town. There were words, then blows, then blood, lots of it, and flaming torches for good measure. Someone had produced these last on short notice from God only knew where. Amazing what people could do when they were willing to improvise.

Money-minded ancestor worshipers! Wipers of bottoms with paper!

News of the battle spread. Mini-mobs sprouted in magic circles around Chinese cars and scooters, wherever invisible droplets of blood from across the city had sprayed the waiting pavements.

The wise among the Chinese had summoned reinforcements: uncles in gangs (for those lucky enough to have such uncles), cousins with illegal guns, brothers-in-law who'd acquired valuable experience during the communist insurgency. Now they burst onto the streets as one, shouting unimaginative slogans of their own.

Balek kampong! Go home to your villages and your paddy fields! We're going to finish off all the Malays! They brandished brooms — an easy, ready symbol, for which house doesn't own a broom? — to illustrate their imminent sweeping-out of the Malays from the city.

In Valli's kitchen Amma tried, to no avail, to stretch her back and relax.

Rumor daintily hiked up her red dress, held her dancing shoes in one hand, and waded through the rivers of blood. The march tore down Batu Road as one, like the parts of a prancing Chinese New Year lion. Here was the head, here the lithe waist, here the tail, and the whole thing had somehow, by an enormous concentration of will and coordination, to be kept writhing and dancing in the right direction, devouring screaming children, spitting them out, belching fumes in their parents' faces. Killing and burning and howling the fury it had been saving up since men and women of Paati's generation had shown themselves to be nothing but sycophants of the British, fattening themselves on their filthy colonial system and secretly (or not so secretly) hoping the rulers would stay forever.

No one but Rumor stopped to remark upon the exaggerated beauty of the scene, the reflection of sunset's bloody colors in the bloody ballet below, the golden light glancing off parang and cleaver and glinting in pools of blood. No artist could have imagined a more lavish union of movement and feeling and sound and smell; in every corner there was something to freeze the senses. The lion roared and shook its terrible head from side to side. Hatred and bloodlust tainted each fresh sorrow. Wails and sobs filled the gaps between war whoops. The earthiness of smoke consorted with the salty sting of spilled blood.

The brotheROARsister hammered the inside of Amma's belly with its tiny fists, took a deep breath, and dove head-first towards freedom. "Aaaah!" Amma cried out. Valli's eyes sprang open. Her baby stopped whimpering to listen. "Sit down, sit down," Subru said helplessly, his heart shriveling to the size of a chicken liver. Water leaked out of Amma and down her thighs. "Don't tell me," Valli said.

Amma didn't need to tell her. She doubled over, she grabbed the windowsill, she gasped and turned red in the face. Through a blue haze of pain she saw Uma standing in the doorway, tugging at the hem of her Buster Brown pinafore. She heard Uma's heart flutter in her chest, *ptrr-ptrr-ptrr-ptrr,* a fluttering that grew deeper with each breath Uma took, that grew into a thumping, then a thudding, then a gong-boom that drowned out all the other sounds of the living world and forced everyone to move to its beat.

"Go, go," said Valli at once, shoving her stultified husband out of his seat, "go and find a bloody taxi, man."

Valli's baby summoned a never-to-be-duplicated super strength and sat up in his cot for three full seconds before toppling backwards. (After this miraculous, sadly unnoticed feat, he was to lag forever behind the average ages for the various developmental milestones listed in the free pamphlet his mother had received from the hospital on the day of his birth.)

Amma clung to the windowsill with one white-knuckled hand and matched Uma's short, shallow breaths with her own. "Aiyo!" she cried. "Aiyo, what are we going to do?"

Subru pulled on a shirt, unlocked the deadbolt on the back door and the three padlocks on the iron grille, and scurried out the side gate into the violet twilight, toast crumbs still dotting his whiskers.

"Don't worry," Valli said to Uma, "we'll take your Amma to hospital and everything will be okay."

But everything-will-be-okay was, as it so often is, a premature verdict, wishful thinking, for in the falling night Subru ran from locked gate to locked gate, peered into dark windows, was barked at by jittery dogs. A Chinese taxi driver lived three doors down — his taxi stood on his cement porch, flaunting its glossy paint in the light of the streetlamp — but no one answered Valli's husband's hollering at his gate.

"We have to go home to Ipoh," Uma declared, solemn and unshakable, in Valli's kitchen. "We have to go home *now*, on the Malay Land train."

"No, no, don't be silly," Amma shot back between gasps, "no no no no all that cannot."

Valli, panic rendering her unreasonable enough to try to reason with a six-year-old, explained, "No time for all that, Uma, you know how long the train takes, isn't it? Chittappa has gone to find a taxi."

Finally, as Amma sank onto all fours on the greasy kitchen floor that had so repulsed her, Subru came rocketing in through the back door he'd (with uncharacteristic laxity) left open, trailing an elderly, bowlegged Indian man with two days of stubble on his cheeks. This was Ratnam, a onetime taxi driver who still owned his vehicle and drove it distractedly around the neighborhood on weekends, shuttling the prettier housewives to and from the wet market for a nominal charge and refusing all lengthier assignments. Ratnam preferred to pass his time drinking Anchor beer and cracking groundnut shells with his bad teeth in his dusty sitting room, his radio turned up loud enough to compete with his wife's scolding. Look at the Chinese, she said every day. Look at that Chinese taxi man two streets away. Look how hard they work, look how rich they get, and here you sit on your fat arse, man, and spend money you don't have on Anchor beer and Thumb groundnuts. That is why we Indians are in this state.

Today, for once, Ratnam's wife had been keeping to herself. She'd been crouching like a mouse in her favorite armchair, sewing a pajama set for their grandchild and secretly reflecting that she'd never thought the day would come when she'd be glad not to be Chinese, when Subru had jumped over their front gate and come pounding on their door. "Please," he'd panted. "My wife's sister is giving birth now itself." He'd invoked Rule Number One in the survival handbook of the wet-behind-the-ears, would-be Multiethnic Paradise that was Malaysia: We have to help our own kind, man. We Indians have to stick up for each other, otherwise we'll all sink together.

Rule Number Two was that anyone who said no to such appeals was officially a selfish bastard and a traitor to the blood in his veins. Ratnam had *tsk-tsk*ed and repeated relevant phrases both Rumor and Fact had whispered in his waxy ears during the night. He'd offered his considered opinion that they'd never reach the hospital. But now his taxi was idling outside Valli's gate, coughing and sputtering, sending worrisome puffs of black smoke into the already smoky night. Valli helped Amma to her feet, Subru and Ratnam stretched their arms out under her, and together the two men lifted her sedan-chair style, Ratnam's bowlegs bowing even more, caving in like melting wax under Amma's weight, curving irremediably into two opposed C's, so that Uma, hot on their heels, felt compelled to cry out, "Taxi Uncle, don't drop my Amma, careful Uncle careful!"

They loaded Amma into the back seat of the taxi; Valli climbed into the front seat. "No room for anyone else, don't you worry Uma, you stay here with Chittappa and the baby," each of them said in turn, Amma, Valli, Subru, Ratnam the taximan. "Everything will be okay."

Everything is not okay, Uma retorted in her head. *You're all lying, just like you always lie. I should've stayed with Paati.*

Ratnam sucked his teeth and drove off down the road. At the traffic light he opened the glove compartment — "What is this, Uncle," fretted Valli, "light changed already and you are sitting there searching for what I don't know?" — and impassively extracted a box of toothpicks. He stuck one between his two chipped bottom incisors before driving on. "You thee maa," he lisped, turning to look Valli in the eye, the toothpick wiggling as he spoke, "the big problem ith going to be getting into town."

They'd turned onto the main road before it became clear that Ratnam's prediction had been accurate. Before them a Chinese provision shop was burning grandiosely to the ground. Screams flew through the air and spattered the windscreen of the taxi. A little boy blood-drenched from a gaping head wound ran across the road. Thicker, darker blood, shining under the flames, was coagulating on the asphalt. "Better you roll up the windowth on your thide, maa," Ratnam said.

Amma began to whimper. Valli began to pray.

"Open your bloody eyes and help me," growled Amma, "who do you think you are, our bloody mother or what? Chanting-banting while the world comes to an end!"

"Taxi Uncle," said Valli, coming to her senses, "can't you take another route?"

"Other route ellam illai maa," explained Ratnam peaceably, leaning back against the headrest. "All the roadth around here are going to be like thith only."

"Then drive, Uncle, drive, maybe they'll let us through, isn't it?"

"Not to worry, Uncle can drive"—he shifted gears, bobbing his head from side to side—"but if we get ththuck then the big problem will come."

And the big problem, invoked with such faith, did come. As Ratnam drove on, the crowd thickened around the taxi; people poured out of burning buildings; faces loomed large and bright through the windshield and windows, twisted and glistening, full of teeth and eyes. Something small and hard grazed the roof of the taxi.

A man's face pressed itself against Ratnam's window, white headband, greying hair, fat mole between crevice of nose and left cheek, sweat spraying the glass as the man's hand slapped the window hard.

"Uncle!" cried Valli, but it was too late, Ratnam was rolling down the window, his toothpick jutting insolently into the man's face, his right hand trembling on the gearshift. The thick, smoky air rushed in, the groans and screams and sobs, the heat of a dozen hate-fueled fires. "Aiyo, aiyo," Amma cried. "Cannot even breathe!"

Though Ratnam took care to withdraw his toothpick before speaking, his market Malay, already tyrannized by his Tamil tongue, now tripped on his panic, stumbled, stopped and started, searched for words that would not come, lost itself in a labyrinth of prefixes and honorifics and useless, invented tenses. "Sorry lah, Encik," he said over and over. "This woman, you see this woman. Baby coming. Sorry Encik, sorry sorry sorry," and what he really wanted to say was not just Sorry for driving blithely through your streets in these turbulent times, Sorry for appearing so oblivious to your far more important cause, but also: Sorry for being outsiders, for failing to master your language with its many subtleties and its splendid tradition of pastoral poetry, Sorry for having skin just a shade too brown, Sorry for being a blatant worshiper of wood and stone idols, Sorry, most of all, for voting for those who would wrest control of this fecund Malay Land from your deserving hands. But since Ratnam could barely have articulated these sentiments in Tamil, he did not, under the extreme conditions of that night, come close to saying them in Malay.

Whether the mole-in-crevice man nevertheless understood all these various apologies from Ratnam's ham-fisted *Sorry Enciks*, no one, least of all Ratnam and the man himself, could say for sure, but after ninety seconds of Ratnam's blithering, the man straightened up, yelled "Orang Keling!" to the amassed forces, and, turning back to Ratnam, pointed unambiguously down the road they had come. "Go home, get a midwife," he said. "Are you crazy, trying to go to the hospital on a night like this? The hospital," he added grimly, "has better things to do tonight." Keling Bodoh. Keling mabuk todi. Duduk Malaysia, tak tahu cakap Bahasa Melayu. Words, words, only words — what were these compared to the sticks and stones (and parangs and cangkuls and flaming torches and gleaming knives) out there? Pure, childlike gratitude rushed to Ratnam's waxy ears, to Valli's hot cheeks, to Amma's tortured womb. Ratnam shifted gears and began a laborious, exultant U-turn on that burning road, his heart beating sweet relief in his mouth because O, thank all his inferior gods, they were Orang Keling, mere bloody Indians and nothing more, deserving only of all the harmless qualifiers the mole-man had heaped upon their innocent heads: stupid Indians, drunk-on-toddy Indians good for nothing else, Indians who lived in Malaysia but could not speak the Na-tio-nal Language, but still just Indians, O yesyesyes, thank all the gods, because look at the Chinese. Look at the Chinese tonight.

But Ratnam had neither the time nor the heart to look too closely. Relief powered his taxi's homeward journey, and what a different journey it was: charged with urgency, full speed, toothpickless, brimming with brisk assurances and unlisped sibilants. "Sh-sh-sh, we'll go home, my children," he told Valli and Amma, "and there my wife knows a lady a few doors away, an old lady, a kind lady, delivers her own grandchildren by the dozens every year like batches of idlis only, that's how easy it is for her, nicely-nicely they pop out, perfect and unharmed and healthy. Sh-sh, don't worry."

That was how, on that night of bloodshed and bedlam, of dreams sent up in flames and ideals abandoned in dirty back alleys, Suresh was born in Ratnam the taxi man's back room, where Salachi, the grandchild-popper-outer from three doors down, had set up a makeshift bed and Ratnam's wife had filled the metal basin normally used for washing greens with boiling water. Out Suresh tumbled, wet with the brave blood of life and hope, while so near and yet so far away the heroes of Malay Land soared through the skies, soaked with a seamier blood. Tonight was one of those rare nights terrible enough to force these storied heroes out of their hibernation, and when they emerged, clad in sarongs, in regal tengkoloks, in songkoks with no mangy spots whatsoever, their Chinese foes blinked in disbelief and prepared for the worst. Bullets could not pierce the hearts of these heroes; knives could not break their skin. They flew into burning houses and came out unscathed. They slipped into locked houses through keyholes and under doors, and appeared, whole and glowing, before people cowering behind sacks of rice in dark storerooms.

Their invincibility, their foolproof strategies for survival, their thick skin: Suresh breathed all these in as he was born, and as he slippery-fished his way into Salachi's knobby hands, they were seeping into his bloodstream (along with soot particles, molecules of burned flesh, dying whispers, and Amma's beginnings-of-a-cold).

There would never be another night like this in Malay Land. Yes, there'd always be the cracks under the skin, the whispered cautions, the weak spots. But hands would be slapped and acts would be passed. After the state of emergency had been lifted and parliament had resumed, after the blood had been cleaned from the streets and only the faintest haze lingered in the sky—barely odorous, indistinguishable, really, from the haze of hawker fires and lorry fumes—the gomen would introduce the New Economic Policy. Stated goal: the eradication of poverty, regardless of race. But come on let's face it (said the gomen, suddenly pally, arms around shoulders, ready to stand everyone a round of teh tarik): talking about poverty without talking about race, mana boleh, in this country? Not possible. A little redistribution of wealth, ala sikit-sikit aje, and a few small guarantees, you Chinese are so rich you won't even notice the difference, and the Indians, never mind the Indians, they hardly know how to make a real fuss. Thirty percent of national wealth for the Malays, that should make everyone happy, no?

No? No means please shaddup your mouth and go away. Go back where you came from, otherwise sit here and keep quiet, because questioning this, or Article 153, our master status—which makes you all what? If we're the masters, you're the—go and fill in the blanks yourselves in the corner, over there, like good boys and girls, but above all please be quiet, because we've got news for you: questioning any of this is sedition. No more pontificating, no more Malaysian Malaysia campaigns, no more talking about race (unless you made the laws, in which case you are free to mention the R word as and when necessary).

Thus would the heroes and Everymen of Malay Land be lulled into sugared bliss, with the abundant, buttery, magical cake of these pocket-filling policies (Eat all you want, the cake grows no smaller! Every missing slice reappears in its place!), with the stern warnings to Chongs-come-lately, and with the deftly piped icing: Malay would be enshrined as the one and only Na-tio-nal Language, so that henceforth all thanggachis and ah mois would have to learn it in school, speak and read and write it to get anywhere in life, and never, never have to ask their ignorant colonial throwback parents what a simple thing like Keretapi Tanah Melayu meant.

And the firebrands, the dreamers and campaigners, the heroes of the other side? They would learn to sit on their hands to keep from moving while Fact watched them reproachfully with his earnest eyes and Rumor winked provocatively, because man-made disasters, in this magnificent land where everyone was to get along in vaunted harmony, would be strictly against the law.

If Appa had been a different sort of man—braver or more cowardly, more principled or less principled, more happy-go-lucky—he might have chosen any of a number of options available to him. He might have risked jail or emigrated to Australia. He might have switched parties and gone nonchalantly on in politics with the if-you-can't-beat-'em pragmatism of some of his former cronies. He might have released his dreams through the nearest window, brushed off his hands, and turned to the easier goals of his nondreaming peers: making what pots of money you could without (overtly) breaking the rules. Finding clever, tortuous paths around the new limitations on non-Malay wealth.

But from his uncomfortable, in-between spot, Appa viewed all these possibilities with distaste. Jail scared him; wealth bored him. He was already rich, and the thought of devoting his energies to the acquisition of more wealth kept him in his bed in the mornings, blinking at the ceiling, wondering if his life was over. His life as he'd planned it, dreamt it, and loved it, at least. When a prestigious job opened up in the deputy public prosecutor's office, Appa sacrificed the last of his ideals to personal glory, applied, and was, to his great surprise, hired. Did they not know who he was and what he'd been fighting for in his recent past? Or was hiring him their last dig, a victory gesture calculated to show the public who was at whose mercy now? *Look how your hero has come crawling to us for a pat on the head.* Why should he care? What was so wrong with a little vanity when he had so little else left to him? Maybe the illusion of power was better than nothing. The grand pretense, the grinning page 2 photos people would mock in between the headlines and the sports page. And yes, on the King's birthday, maybe, someday, if he behaved himself, a Datukship. *You should've stayed far, far away from the bloody boat that brought you here*, he said to his grandfather silently. *In India I would've had a real chance.*

8

WHAT AASHA SAW

August 19, 1980

O N T H E D A Y Paati dies, a black butterfly finds its way into the Big House. It's the biggest butterfly Aasha has ever seen: each wing is the size of Amma's palm, with trailing teardrop tails. Around the edges of its wings are tiny flashes of cobalt blue, easy to miss because the butterfly moves so haphazardly, alighting for half a second on a bookshelf and two seconds on the coffee table, but Aasha nevertheless notices the blue and thinks of a certain sapphire pendant once belonging to Amma, and of how that, too, turned and twirled and trapped the morning light. As she ponders this memory, the butterfly's panic drips blackly from its teardrop tails into her wide eyes and open mouth, so that all of a sudden the spectacle of Suresh trying to shoo the butterfly out the window with one of Paati's coconut-frond fans makes her heart pound. She breathes so fast and hard that each breath sweeps hurricane-like through the house, blowing the lace curtains ceiling-high, sending pages of the *New Straits Times* flying from coffee table to dining room and kitchen floor and back yard, rotating the blades of the turned-off ceiling fans. "*Tsk,* Aasha," says Suresh, opening another window, "what you behaving like there's a tiger in the house? It's just a butterfly, for heaven's sake. Calm down."

But the more Aasha looks at that butterfly, the more her eyes search for those elusive flashes of blue, and the more panic suffuses her face ears neck shoulders, until it seems that there are fever hands touching her everywhere, and all she can think, though the words make no sense to her at this moment, is *too late too late too late.* Is someone else too late to save Aasha, or is she too late for some unknown but crucial engagement? She doesn't know, she cannot know, and not knowing is the worst part of it—how is she supposed to do anything to remedy the situation? Just when she's about to burst into tears with the unbearable weight of this realization, the butterfly seems to fall through the air towards her burning face, and then there it is, just above her nose, the size of a bat the size of a crow the size of an owl, only now it's all blue, though it still casts a black shadow on her face, a black owl-shaped shadow, and the tears hanging round and ready in her throat bloom into a ragged scream.

"Aasha! Ish! Go, go away. Go and read a book," says Suresh, fanning at the butterfly where it hovers above her face.

But Aasha's feet are frozen; she slumps down onto an ottoman and continues to watch. By the time one of Suresh's fan-swipes sends the butterfly flitting out an open window, her ribs ache from all that battering her heart has inflicted on them, and her eyeballs are so dry she can't blink. She moves to the settee, lies face-down, and sleeps until almost noon.

When Aasha wakes up she hears Chellam stirring sugar into Paati's pre-bath coffee.

"Chhi!" she hears Paati scold; she can tell by the pitch and timbre of Paati's voice that Paati thinks no one's listening. This is her low-heat, just-barely-bubbling, complaining-to-herself voice. "Every day," she continues, "*every day* I have to remind her about the coffee. If I don't tell her nicely-nicely she pretends to forget, just to get out of it. When it comes to taking my son's money every month she doesn't forget; only the work she's being paid for she forgets. How many times does she have to be told, if I don't have a hot drink before my bath just like that I'll get sick again. Choom, choom, choom all day, I'll be sneezing till my head hurts. Haven't I just been sick? Did she learn nothing from that? She thinks I'm sixteen years old, that I can take a bath without a hot drink first."

Chellam's still stirring that eversilver tumbler of coffee, though the sugar must be long dissolved by now, stirring stirring stirring, more and more vigorously, that teaspoon chiming like an alarm bell.

Aasha yawns, stretches, and—finally ready to take Suresh's advice

—wanders upstairs to find a book. She chooses the book she took out of the public library on the one and only trip she made there with Uma in June. "Come and put on your shoes," Uma had said. "I can't be waiting all morning." Aasha had put on her shoes, and they had set off. As simple as that. For that is what miracles are like sometimes: quiet, unheralded, unglamorous to all but the beneficiary.

Uma long ago returned the book she checked out for herself that day, but Aasha, uninvited on subsequent trips to the library, has held on to *The Wind in the Willows,* and it is now shockingly overdue. She has dipped into it solely while waiting and watching, hoping and listening for greater things. One eye on Uma or Chellam, one eye on the book. By this method alone she has reached page 98, an achievement that would have been recognized as exceptional had not the novelty of genius worn off, within the family, after the golden age of Uma's childhood. Appa and Amma and Uma and Suresh barely notice what Aasha reads these days.

Book in hand, Aasha goes back downstairs and takes her place behind the green PVC settee in the corridor, from which vantage point she keeps track of Paati's many Chellam-assisted comings and goings from the bathroom.

Two years ago, Paati submitted to a magnificent decline. Almost overnight, as if some evil spirit had snatched away her old body for itself, her pinhead cataracts fattened into coins. The arthritis that had been nibbling at her knees for years sank its fangs right in. Soon after, it cauliflowered her hands, then coconut-shell-curved her back. Now she sits all day in her rattan chair, counting weeks and months, money and grudges, on her fingers. She rises only to be led to the bathroom or to bed by Chellam, who was hired for precisely these tasks (plus a few more). Behind her execrations of the obvious targets — Chellam, Amma — boil unregistered complaints against those she once trusted.

The arthritis and cataracts are minor woes compared to the devastation of her bladder and bowels. Her bladder and bowels, of all things — oh, for shame, for shame. She tries in vain to subdue them by sheer force of will. There have been accidents, increasingly frequent in recent months. Could she have expected better from her daughter-in-law than the slaps and knocks she's received? In the old days, children cleaned up their old parents' messes and kept quiet about it; they understood that the shame was chastening enough. Not today, and certainly not a woman of Vasanthi's class. The pettiness, the lack of scruples, the waiting for twenty years to get even—it's all in her blood, after all. People like that can paint their faces and style their hair, but their true colors always come through. The only way they can feel tall is to step on others' heads. No, no surprises there. But the servant girl, the girl Raju pays to see to her needs—from a mere servant she would never have anticipated such bold disrespect. It only goes to show what's become of society since the British left. The order and decency of the old Malaya, each man grateful for his place in life, everyone clean and scrubbed and ready to work, all that has been tossed to the birds.

There's a hole in the upholstery on the back of the green settee. Aasha finds it without having to search at all, sticks her finger into it, finds a mote of comfort in the lumpy stuffing and the rickety rigging underneath it.

Soon Paati and Chellam will be coming up the corridor. Fresh water is running into the water tank in the bathroom: Chellam has turned it on in preparation for Paati's bath. The bathroom door is wide open; the sunlight streaming in the high window in the back wall stipples the floor in front of the tank with fluid, glinting spots like fish scales.

No one knows Aasha is behind the settee, though only Suresh, who is putting together an Airfix Scammel Tank Transporter in his room, is even remotely wondering where she is.

Uma's in the sitting room, looking at photographs of the production she was in last month, Chekhov's *Three Sisters*. Uma played Masha, the middle sister. At the curtain call a St. Michael's boy she'd never seen named Gerald Capel came up to the edge of the stage to give her a bouquet of tea roses, and it's this picture, of Gerald shyly handing this offering up to her, that she's studying now: as she bends over in her patched-pinned-tucked, mothball-scented nineteenth-century costume, her cleavage tantalizes, but gentleman-Gerald appears to have his eyes steadfastly fixed on her face.

She hums along with Simon and Garfunkel while she turns the plastic pages of the complimentary-with-your-proofs album: *Who will love a little sparrow / And who will speak a kindly word?*

Amma is in the kitchen, browsing through a *Ladies' Home Journal* cookery book with a view to selecting three guaranteed-to-impress recipes for the Ladies' next tea party. Will it be salmon mousse or jellied prawns? Lobster Newburg or crab canapés? Bombe Alaska or lemon soufflé?

Appa is at the office, preparing to go to court for day three of the Angela Lim case, where he will look Shamsuddin bin Yusof squarely in the eye, fix his mind on Angela's ravaged body, and dazzle everyone once again with his wit.

Chellam is in Paati's dim, mosquito-thronged corner, combing the knots out of Paati's hair because today, Tuesday, is the day for Paati's weekly hairwashing.

"Ei," Paati says, and then again more loudly, *"Ei!* You're being too rough." In Tamil, and not just because Chellam's English is like a child's or a clown's, but because the language is another layer flaking off Paati with time. Underneath are all the old words, not only the words for thoughts too big and dark or too small and twisted for English, but also for the basic materials of a life being lived out in a rattan chair: sweetmeats, vegetables, colors, days of the week, calls of nature, chicken parts, public and private parts of the human body, types of fish, denominations of currency, breakfast beverages, balms and unguents. "You're pulling my hair," Paati says. "It hurts my head."

Chellam holds her tongue. Her silence creeps icily past Amma's ears and Aasha's, tickling Uma's earlobes in the sitting room.

The sun is out today, but what a thin, watery sun! It keeps Aasha's very skin wide awake with its suggestion of timid newness, of just beginning.

> The Rat [she reads in her book] let his egg-spoon fall on the table-cloth, and sat open-mouthed.
> "The hour has come!" said the Badger at last with great solemnity.
> "What hour?" asked the Rat uneasily, glancing at the clock on the mantelpiece.

Out of nowhere, the fresh, hopeful feeling of the day notwithstanding, that teardropped butterfly flits frantic into Aasha's head: *Too late!*

Chellam has finished combing Paati's hair, and they're making their way to the bathroom for Paati's bath-cum-hairwashing. Aasha hears the *slap-slap-slap* of Chellam's Japanese slippers on the marble floor, and the *sh-sh-sh-sh* of Paati's bare soles. *Sh-SH, sh-SH, sh-SH.* Paati favors her left leg, such as it is: as bowed at the knee as the right leg, but somehow, invisibly, more trustworthy. *Sh-SH, sh-SH, sh-SH.*

They hobble and shuffle into view, an incongruous pair in everything but their equal bitterness, and begin their laborious journey up the corridor. Paati's a little slower, a little more wobbly at the knees than she was only a few months ago: she's just recovered from a nasty bout of flu brought on by Chellam's neglect (according to her) or by exposure to Chellam's own, prior fever.

Chellam herself is as good as new, as far as Aasha can see, though new was never all that good. Her skin is as sallow as ever, flabby on her chicken-wing arms, scarred tight and shiny on her brow, worn to a high shine on her knees and elbows. But at least her hair's oiled and freshly plaited, and the curdy smell that never left her during her illness has been scrubbed away in the shower. There's that hard lump in the corner of her jaw, bitter as a langsat seed. Aasha looks for it every time, and every time she finds it.

A quarter of the way up the corridor, Chellam fizzes over with the words she's been bottling up in her belly. "What is this?" she says. "Are you trying to walk as slow as possible on purpose so that I'll have to clean up after you? Just this once why don't you try to make it to the bathroom on time? Why?"

Paati's the only person to whom Chellam says more than a few words at a time these days, and then only when she thinks no one else can hear her. At these paroxysms, Paati flinches or sniffs or rears her head weakly like a hot-and-bothered turtle. Aasha notes every word uttered but never repeats a single one to anyone else.

Paati stiffens her shoulders and does not answer Chellam's *why;* it's obvious to all present that Chellam isn't expecting an answer.

"Just this once!" Chellam repeats. Putting her own recommendation into practice, she hurries forward, her thin arm dragging Paati's loose-skinned one along with it, and the *sh-SH-sh-SH* of Paati's soles turns spastic, going faster faster faster and then stopping short, starting and stopping, stopping and starting, so that Paati's arm-skin flaps like a luffing sail. Aasha can't see Paati's face, but doesn't need to: she's seen it before, that cowed yet bullish face, flinching at unspoken threats but preparing to bite.

Not a yard from the bathroom door, Paati comes to a dead stop, and her hips and thighs begin to shake visibly under her thin cotton saree, and there's a squelchy, bubbling sound that she and Chellam (and Aasha) know only too well: the sound of defeated bowels.

"Don't tell me!" Chellam mutters under her breath. The lump in her jaw comes to life now, throbs like the throat of a tree lizard. "You're a noose around my neck! Coming to this house must've been my punishment for all the sins I committed in my previous lives!"

A stream of brown dribbles onto the marble floor between Paati's broad, bony ankles.

Aasha counts the tiny slaps Chellam delivers to Paati's shoulders: one two three four in a row. They're only small, light finger-blows, but Paati's shaking with rage, and not just from the exertion of her battle with her bowels. She screws up her whole face and sniffs wetly and indignantly. Soon she'll wipe her nose on the sleeve of a saree blouse with a snotful sound to match the squelchy ones her bottom continues to make, but though all this is very disgusting indeed, Aasha is sure Chellam's the one who'd be in trouble now if she were found out. It's because Chellam's paid (or not paid, but Aasha's logic is too black-and-white for these subtleties) to perform her duties with a smile that she is so sneaky with these slaps, these quick-as-a-flash pinches, these under-the-breath threats and curses. *Who do you think you are, Chellam?* Aasha asks silently. *Who do you think you are?* Then, because Chellam won't be answering the question, Aasha does so for her: *You're a sly, sneaky Chellam. You're a lazy, useless Chellam for not wanting to do what you're paid for. You're a big-bully Chellam for hitting and pinching the only person in the house more helpless than you are yourself.*

The crowning grievance: Chellam snubs Suresh and Aasha now, acts as if they were never friends, as if she'd never taught them a hundred lessons they'd needed to be taught. All the things no one else could be bothered to teach them: the habits of ghosts, the shameful tricks of human and animal bodies, the names and defining characteristics of the ten most popular Tamil film actresses (this one had a curly forelock, that one a prominent chin-mole, the third eerily light-colored eyes). Why, now, did she refuse even to look at them? They hadn't done her any wrong; they were just the same as they'd always been. It was the rest of the world that was tilting and shifting under them, so that someone could be friending you before teatime and not-friending you after. These were strange times indeed, and Aasha didn't know when they'd begun, but the change in Chellam she could pinpoint exactly: it was after Chellam had had her fortune told. "Just ignore her," Amma had said when Chellam took to her bed and stopped eating or talking. "She's seeking attention only. All this drama, as if Uma's acting-shacting is not enough, now we have another flim star in the house."

So they'd ignored her, but she'd ignored them back. She'd no right. She was just some rubber-estate girl who put coconut oil in her hair. Who did she think she was?

Who, who, who do you think you are, Chellam?

"Intha veeduku vanthu maaraddikirain," Chellam is saying now, rising slowly to her feet after kneeling to mop up parts of Paati's accident with a rag (other parts, she's missed, because to her weak eyes Paati's brown spots blend into the floor's brown marbling). Halfway up, her knees still bent, she stops to pinch the fleshiest part of Paati's hip (which isn't so fleshy after all). Intha veeduku vanthu maaraddikirain: Here in this house I'm . . . I'm . . . Aasha doesn't know what those last words mean, but she memorizes the sounds. She prizes each new Tamil word she learns from Chellam while spying on her; she keeps them all in the pockets of her skirts, like evil little jewels, like saved-up nose pickings, and when she's alone she takes them out to admire them and wonder what she'll do with them.

Now Chellam and Paati are in the big bathroom. There's a brown smearsmudgestreak on the marble that Chellam will have to attend to on her second round of peering and wiping, before anyone walks in it and spreads it all over the house on the soles of their feet, before Amma sees it and threatens to dock Chellam's wages (which threat would have her father wailing and showering ear-splitting curses upon her the next time he came to collect those wages). But first, before attending to Paati's shit-wake, Chellam undresses her: she unwinds the thin blue saree, all six yards of it, and drapes it on the towel bar; she unhooks the four hooks fastening the front of the saree blouse; she tugs on the drawstring of the white cotton petticoat so that it puddles around Paati's feet. And all that time, Paati looks straight ahead, marmoreal and bitterly dignified even when, finally liberated of saree blouse and petticoat, she stands stark naked. Her feet are planted exactly two tiles apart. She's a monument to dignity — no, more than that, a warrior for the cause, ready to fight tooth and nail for what time is grabbing and pinching and picking from her. Certainly her plucked-pigeon body has little to fight for; it's nothing but skin flaps everywhere, sagging back, stretched-out-sack bottom. In each of those empty bottom sacks there's room for at least three coconuts. Her hair hangs down her shoulders in dry wisps so fine her scalp glows through them. No, her dignity comes from some other, deeper place: a walnut-sized gland in the center of her brain, a fifth chamber of the heart, two extra inches on her tough tongue. Whatever the anomaly, it will escape Dr. Kurian's gimlet eye, and no postmortem will introduce it to science.

The bathroom in which Paati waits to be watered and soaped hasn't changed much since the house was built in 1932. In the heat of his home-improvement fever Tata had it retiled, gave the walls above the tiles a fresh lick of paint, and put in a new medicine cabinet, but other than these sprucings-up, he left it in the local style Mr. McDougall had preferred: a water tank in one corner, a drain hole in the floor for the water from bucket baths and bottom washing. As far as Tata was concerned, Mr. McDougall had gone too far native, a tendency unbecoming in British expatriates, who should—so Tata considered—have preserved their dignity with bathtubs, powder rooms, and, most important of all, toilet paper. Tata himself had installed a clawfoot tub in the master bathroom upstairs, but whether he'd preserved the downstairs bathroom in its original state purely out of nostalgia, or as a testament to the addling effects of heat on the tastes of respectable white men, or simply because he'd died before he'd had a chance to renovate it, here it remained in 1980, four times repainted in the original pale green, twice retiled in the same color. Two tiles away from the main water pipe is a chipped tile, the only one in the whole bathroom, for Aasha has looked thoroughly on several afternoons—always with a deep sense of applying herself to a crucial task—and never found another. Only the toilet bowl is a different color now than it was in Tata's time: a delicate robin's-egg blue that looks like an egregious mismatch because it's so close to the pale green of everything else and yet not quite the same.

A foolish spider's web stretches from the main water pipe to the wall behind it. This, too, catches the sunlight, though Aasha can't see it from where she stands, Paati's too blind to see it even from three feet away, and Chellam isn't looking. In a few minutes Chellam will splash water on that web and wreck it, and the spider will scurry up the wall to nurse its disappointment in a corner of the ceiling. The space between the water pipe and the wall is thick with cobwebs, but those are mere uninspired strings and tangles of dust; only this soon-to-be-destroyed web bears the marks of instinctive genius and blind persistence.

Chellam turns the taps off, and for a few moments, while the water settles, sunlight dances on its surface like suddenly scattered beads.

"Aah-pah! Mmm, mmm, mmm, Aah-mah!" Paati exclaims when Chellam pours the first bucketful of lukewarm water on her head, just as she exclaims every afternoon. She sucks her gums and smacks her lips; she opens her purblind eyes wide and blinks and blinks and blinks, forgetting the slings and arrows of the past few minutes, forgetting the late-as-usual coffee, the scalp-stinging combing, the slaps the pinches the scoldings the insults. That perfect water brings her such joy that Aasha's bat ears pick up those blissful blinks from yards away though her owl eyes can't see them: *slup* after soft *slup* of wet grey lashes on slack cheeks.

"Aah-pah! Mmm, mmm, mmm, Aah-mah!" Paati exclaims again after each new bucketful of water.

Half of the third bucketful spills on its way from the water tank to Paati's head: that's the end of the spiderweb, and there goes the unlucky spider.

Paati's sag-kneed legs still shake, now with pleasure.

But then Chellam puts down the bucket and slings a good-morning towel over her shoulder. "Stay here," she says. "Hold on to the edge of the water tank and wait. I have to go and clean up your mess properly."

She bustles out of the bathroom, but Paati hasn't heard her; as soon as her back is turned Paati blinks three quick, surprised blinks and asks, "Enna?" What? What're you saying? When Chellam doesn't answer, Paati raises her voice a notch: "Eh, Enna?" Then two notches: "Engga porei?" Where're you off to? And then, because this interruption of her bath is so very rude, and also because her selective memory has allowed her to forget how recently she was in trouble, she's off like a train, unstoppable: "Where're you going without even telling me? Why're you leaving me here like this in the middle of my bath? Don't you know I've just recovered? Now I'll catch a chill again, I'll get a chest cold even worse than the last one, choom choom choom I'll be sneezing all day till my head hurts, I'll get pneumonia like that Malhotra woman's father got last year." Here she pauses, cocks her head like a bird to ascertain if her tirade has had any effect. It hasn't. "Eh!" she calls, real vitriol creeping into her voice now. "Eh, eh, where in

God's name is everybody? Where are all you good-for-nothing, think-only-of-yourselves donkeys?" No one answers; Chellam has made her way down the corridor and into the kitchen to fill a pail with soapy water.

For a moment Aasha considers going up to Paati to tell her that she isn't alone, that she, Aasha, is here, that Chellam will be back after cleaning the floor. Something stops her, though: the length of the corridor? her indefatigable desire to be neither seen nor heard? Aasha's days are an endless game of hide-and-seek in which she is both hider and seeker: hiding to see what she can see, but seeking only Uma and Chellam, who refuse to be sought, who pretend not to have been found even when they have been, who never, no matter how many times Aasha finds them, look up and laugh and say "You win!" Though no one else is playing now—no one knows or cares (yet) that she's hiding—she's as loath to reveal herself as if it were a real game with a prize at the end of it. And what prize would she choose? A packet of Cheezels? A walking-talking doll? A box of thirty-six color pencils in shades she can't pronounce? No, none of these; Aasha's prize, though she's never named it to herself, is her sister. Uma as she used to be, walking-talking Uma, laughing Uma, Uma who drew her maps and taught her the names of African capitals and improbable diseases. Scurvy. Kwashiorkor. Beriberi. And if she can't have that Uma, then Chellam as she used to be. Consolation-prize Chellam.

Peace and shade reign in the space above Paati's fear and Chellam's anger. Aasha leans her chin on the headrest of the green settee and hangs her arms down the back. The PVC fabric is cool against her skin.

"Look!" Paati shouts. "Look at this! Look how they've all left me! What would my son say if he knew how they treat me behind his back! Nicely-nicely they all take his money, wife, servant, everybody, but then when it comes to taking care of his mother they make like it's not their job! Where would any of them be if not for me? Where?"

Aasha hears footsteps coming this way from the kitchen, and she knows they're not Chellam's. They're too brisk, too determined, none of Chellam's shuffle-and-drag. Amma appears around the corner to confirm Aasha's hypothesis. She swoops up the corridor in the blink of an eye and stands at the open bathroom door with her hands on her hips.

"What is it?" she barks. "Why all this noise?"

"Who's that?" asks Paati.

"It's me, Vasanthi. What's the matter?"

"Oh, you." A five-second silence, during which Amma and Paati reflect, as they have done dozens of times a day for the past two or so years, upon the nonchalance with which time is trying to reverse their roles in the household. Once Amma was the outsider, gauche and gaudy, struggling to reinvent herself with hairspray and silk caftans. *Your mother's people,* Paati would say to Uma, *are not like us,* which devastating diagnosis was meant to include their parochial morals, their choice of toothpaste and hair-oil brands, and certain rumors about a chamber pot under a bed. How small and cold and naked Amma felt then, hearing these words, and now what a literal revenge time seems to have chosen for her: standing at the bathroom doorway, she could (if she were so inclined) count the moles on Paati's old back and follow the course of a half-dried stream of shit down the back of her right thigh. It's Paati who's not like the rest of them now, Paati who's a shriveled extra limb hanging off the family's robust torso, waiting to fall off.

But there's more to this realignment of their stars than meets the eye: face-to-face (and even face-to-back), Paati and Amma share too much history to accept their new positions without some misgivings (on Amma's part) and much righteous disdain (on Paati's). *Twenty years ago she was dressing like a rubber-estate worker and picking her teeth with her fingernails when she thought no one was looking,* thinks Paati, *and now she tries to act like she owns this place. She might have everyone else fooled, but not me. Oh, no.* And Amma has more to occupy her than mole-counting: *What's the old wretch plotting now?* she wonders. *Not enough that she turned my own daughter against me, she's still cooking things up inside that balding head of hers. I can see her evil brain working away. Acts all pitiful and helpless, but she's not fooling me.*

Aloud, Amma says: "Chellam's coming. No need to shout until your throat dries out." Without waiting for a response, she swoops back down the corridor, her caftan sleeves filling with forced importance like a magician's cloak. Back to her *Ladies' Home Journal* cookery book and her shopping list for Mat Din. (So far the list reads: two pounds prawns from Cold Storage, twenty-four eggs, a dozen lemons, icing sugar. Amma seems to be leaning towards the jellied prawns and the lemon soufflé.)

On her way down the corridor she passes Chellam, who's heading back this way with a full bucket in one hand and two fresh rags in the other. Aasha hears both sets of footsteps stop as they cross each other.

"Are you mad?" Amma says. "What are you doing, leaving Paati dripping wet in the bathroom while you do your sweeping mopping dusting?"

Chellam blinks and breathes.

"Hmm?" Amma says. To her unanswerable questions, Amma does expect answers. "What? Answer me! Don't stand there staring like a goat."

Still Chellam says nothing.

"If you need to do all this," Amma continues, "can't you do it before undressing her and pouring water on her head? If she catches a cold it'll only be more trouble for all of us, for you especially! Are you a six-year-old child that you can't think of these things for yourself? Go, go, stop standing there like a fool. The more I look at your face the angrier I get."

The footsteps resume: brisk ones receding, shuffling-dragging ones approaching. In the distance Aasha hears Amma mutter something to herself, but can't make out the words (Chellam can: "Feel like slapping her only").

In the bathroom, Paati's still as an old, hungry tiger. Waiting in the shadows, storing something up. Out it comes, as soon as she hears noises in the corridor (the bucket being set down, and Chellam's dragging, Japanese-slippered feet): "Chellam! Is that you? What do you think, leaving me here to shiver? It's not funny. You wait till Master hears. You just wait. Nobody in this house cares about me but him, but I've been taking pity on all of you and keeping quiet. All I have to do is tell him what really goes on —"

Chellam rises from all fours, rag still in hand, and goes to the bathroom door. She leans on the doorjamb, and when she speaks her voice is a little hoarse: "What now? Singing your same song? I've got some cleaning to do out here, have you forgotten? Let's see if you can close your mouth for two minutes. Two minutes and I'll clean up your mess and empty the bucket and come back to wait on you. Okay? Satisfied?"

Stillness again, quiet. Only Paati's knees move this time: a tiny movement, a not quite buckling, a hint of a wobble. She might be getting tired from the combined exertions of standing and vituperating, or she might actually be cold. She's eighty-one years old, after all. She wobbles a more definitive wobble, grabs the edge of the water tank.

Aasha watches the second hand on the red-and-cream clock on the wall. When that hand has gone twice around the clock face it will have been two minutes, and Chellam will have lied about how long cleaning the floor would take.

Lying, tricking Chellam, telling a cold old lady tall stories just to shut her up.

The second hand comes back to seven, where it was when Aasha started watching it, for the first time.

And the second time.

It's all the way up at two again before Chellam rises to her feet and picks up the bucket. That, already, is much longer than two minutes. Chellam must know this, because she stops once more at the bathroom door before going back out to the kitchen. "Just wait a bit," she says, "I have to go outside to empty this pail, I can't just leave the dirty water sitting here. I'll come back fast."

Then she is gone. Water drips off the ends of Paati's hair and down the wide crack between her bottom sacks, but Paati doesn't try to squeeze her hair out or sweep the water off her skin with one hand. She's not letting go of that water tank; perhaps she sees what's coming.

"Raju," she growls, "why have you left me here with them? Don't you know what happens while you're there at your office? Raju, O Raju, my child, my son, my eye, look at them! Look at your useless family!" She pauses, as though she's trying to think of what to say next, of what entreaty might be most likely to reach Appa's distant ears and bring him speeding back to the Big House in his silver Volvo —but in fact this song, too, is a familiar one, and she shouldn't need to pause to remember what comes next, because Aasha does. Aasha has said the words three times in her head before Paati joins in, her out-loud rendition exactly in time with Aasha's silent one:

"Rajooooo, Rajooooo! My throat will dry out from calling and calling before anyone comes! After all I did for my children, all that hard work all my life, and now look, it's freezing in here, *chhi*, what you're paying that girl for I don't know Raju, nicely she's cheating you, she and her low-caste drunkard father!"

This time Paati's so loud that Aasha hasn't heard Amma's footsteps when, suddenly, she appears in the corridor. She doesn't stop at the bathroom door this time. She goes right inside, her bare feet making squelchy sounds on the wet floor. (Wet squelchy sounds! Still more wet squelchy sounds! They are everywhere this morning, and no longer able to bear them, Aasha presses first one ear down onto the headrest of the green settee and then the other. She knows she should cover her ears with her hands, it would be easier and more effective, but somehow she can't, can't move her hands, her hands won't move, only her neck turns to protect each ear in turn.)

There's another sound, a wet thump, a flat slap, but because Aasha's left ear is pressed to the headrest, she doesn't see the source of this sound, and only her right ear hears it. She knows what it is, though, because she's witnessed its production before: a hand on a back. Thump, slap, ouch. Paati growls some more, and snarls a little, just like a tiger, but because she's an old tiger, riddled with aches and lumps, her growls and snarls are not just worse than her bite, they're all she's got. No literal bite at all: dentures replaced her teeth years ago, and she's not wearing them now. And hardly any metaphorical bite: how could her tiny, crumbling body stand up to any of them? Even Aasha could knock her over with one hand. Her body's the least fearsome part of her, the only part Amma's brave enough to attack.

"Shut up!" Amma says, very softly, after her hand has done her mind's dirty work.

Very softly is worse than very loudly. Amma folds her arms quickly, as if to deny to herself that that hand, not a minute ago, was slicing ruthlessly through the air and towards an arthritic shoulder. Still very softly, so that her words are barely discernible in the low hum that reaches Aasha's ears, she goes on: "Shut up now! That's enough. We don't need to hear about your wonderful son, okay? He's not here now. He's nicely fled for the day, leaving you on our heads. So no need to call him. Understand?"

A brief silence. Paati pulls her shoulders up to her earlobes and frowns at the water tank. Then she says, just under her breath, "Chhi! Can't even ask for a small thing in this house without everyone behaving like junglees."

"What? What's this small thing you want?" Amma asks.

"Never mind. It doesn't matter. I'm sure all of you have much more important things to do. No need to bother yourselves on my account."

"What do you need?" Amma asks again.

So Paati racks her brains for a plausible necessity and, clearing her throat, announces: "Very nicely that girl gave me my coffee before my bath, to keep me warm it seems, but now I've to stand here for two hours without a cloth around my loins while she does I don't know what. But one small tumbler of hot water would be too much trouble it seems."

Amma steps out into the corridor. "Chellam!" she calls. "Chellam! Please bring Paati a tumbler of hot water! Now, please!"

But Chellam is emptying her pail and putting her rags to soak in the outdoor kitchen, well out of earshot. Above the squealing of the outside tap she thinks she hears her name, carried on the wind like a song from a neighbor's radio. She pauses mid-scrub, looks up, then shakes her head and goes on with her task. She'll be done in thirty seconds (forty-five, to be precise, but Aasha isn't here to count), then she'll go in and see if someone is indeed wanting something urgent. It's probably just Paati, yelling her frustrations to the gods as usual.

In the corridor Amma's getting impatient. "Where the bloody hell is that girl?" she says to herself. She wanders into the middle of the corridor, looks around, sees only the empty settee, behind which Aasha is now crouching, her book open on her lap.

"This very morning," continued the Badger, taking an armchair, "as I learned last night from a trustworthy source, another new and exceptionally powerful motorcar will arrive at Toad Hall on approval or return."

Amma's in the empty dining room now, and then the sitting room. "Uma," she says, and her voice is like a small stone thrown with perfect aim into the blue pool of Paul Simon's gentle invitation:

Come a-runnin' down the stairs, pretty Peggy-o
Come a-runnin' down the stairs, pretty Peggy-o . . .

Uma looks up, her thumb and forefinger still holding one plastic page of the album (it's the picture of Gerald Capel with his laudatory bouquet again; she's come back to it, after reaching the album's end). She says nothing.

"Uma," Amma says again, "what are you doing here, anyway?"

"Looking at pictures."

"Pictures? What pictures?"

"From the play."

"Oho! From the play! Very nice. Here your own grandmother is shouting until she chokes, and you can't even get up to see what she wants, so busy looking at pictures, is it? Reliving the moment when you took that boy's flowers like a cheap prostitute? Can you please get up and bring your grandmother a tumbler of hot water, please?"

Please once is bad enough. Please twice, in the same sentence, is terrifying.

"Fine," Uma says, "I'll get her a glass of water." Her chair falls backwards as she stands up, but before Amma can say anything about that, she's strode past Amma and across the dining room. Her heels drive themselves into the marble floor as she walks, so hard Aasha can feel the vibrations all the way down the corridor.

At this moment, Chellam makes two decisions she will regret for the rest of her life: she goes out to hang up the rags on the clothesline in the sun, instead of draping them quickly over the garden wall. This takes her an extra minute, so that when she comes back into the house, Uma has already left the kitchen, water glass in hand. *I'd better put the kettle on for the old lady's post-bath Milo,* Chellam thinks. *She'll claim she's freezing to death; she'll want her drink practically before she's sat down in her chair. All she knows how to do is fill her bladder all day to give me more work. Coffee Milo tea water, coffee Milo tea water . . .* She picks up the kettle and goes to the sink to fill it.

"Hanh!" Amma says with a dry laugh in the empty sitting room. Only Simon and Garfunkel are listening; enthusiastically Simon suggests that she go tell it on the mountain, but she dismisses this advice. "I've had enough of it, man!" she says, turning her back to the cassette player. "Enough! Everyone knows how to sulk and whine as if *their* life alone is hell. Hanh!" Then she climbs the stairs, faster than Aasha has ever heard her climb them, practically running.

Perhaps Paati's deaf ears somehow latch on to the sound of Amma's leaving, or perhaps her paper-thin short-term memory has failed her again: she takes up her litany once more, first a low rumble in her throat, a toad-crooning—"Rajoooo, Rajoooo," every *oooo* rising a little as if struggling to become a howl, "Rajoooo, oh this feckless family of yours, you don't know, you don't know what's going on behind your back" — then louder and louder, until, as Uma approaches with the glass of water, her hollering is drowning out everything: the whistling of the teakettle in the kitchen, the go-tell-it-on-the-mountaining of two fired-up New York boys, the chiming of the pendulum clock in the dining room (one chime: the half hour, twelve-thirty).

Abruptly — because her throat has worn itself out without the desired lubrication of the tumbler of water — Paati pulls in the heavy nets of her dirge and begins to whisper: "Raju, Raju, such a good boy you are, such a good son, if only you could see what consequences your one mistake in life has had, if only you could see the kind of blood you married into. Useless! Useless! Not one of them deserves you!"

What is it that freezes Uma just two feet behind Paati, within arm's reach? Holding the tumbler of mildly steaming water out to Paati's back, as if she and Paati are playing A-E-I-O-U and Paati might swing round at any minute? Is it the sudden drop in volume of Paati's voice (for Paati seems not to be playing the same game: on and on she whispers, shaking her head, rocking back and forth like some ecstatic worshiper), so that Uma has to keep still to hear her words? Is it the sunlight in Uma's eyes, streaming in from that high window (because Uma's tall, after all, taller than anyone else who's been in this bathroom today)? The startling sight of Paati's nakedness, on which Uma — unlike Aasha — has not laid eyes in years? The ruddy palm-and-five-fingers mark on Paati's back (which will, very shortly, begin turning blue in some spots and purple in others as Paati's blood thickens and slows)?

Yes, all of these, but also a familiar weariness, heated now to searing point. Each of Paati's words is a red-hot, almost last straw on Uma's young and straight back, each one a stab to her eardrums. Hotter and hotter Uma gets with each of those words, sweat-above-the-lips hot, sweat-on-the-neck hot, sweat-on-the-brow hot, yet she stands perfectly still, that tumbler in her left hand. What Aasha cannot see: the warring currents that move over the darkness of Uma's face. Old loyalties colliding with recent disappointments. The vapor of betrayal, the clammy mist of revenge. Uma's lower lip trembles. Her molars grind like millstones; a sudden grief floods her eyes. *You can fool everyone else,* she thinks, *but you can't fool me.* Her javelin thoughts only ricochet off the elephant skin of Paati's back, but she persists: *You purposely went blind and deaf just so that you didn't have to know anything. And they think I'm the actress. Now you say I'm useless, we're all useless ex-*

cept your precious son. You just wanted whatever you could get out of me, you used me for your own games just like everyone else, every single one of them, every single one, all of you, all of you, all of you . . .

What follows is a dark and furious blur, a thunderstorm seen and heard through a windowpane: the glass of water shattering on the floor, arms everywhere — Uma's brown arm frantic and clumsy as a bird that had flown in through the window and couldn't get out, knocking into things, taking fright, and Paati's short, loose-skinned arms flailing — and gasps (but who gasped first? Paati or Uma? Or did Aasha merely hear herself gasp?), and Paati teetering this way and that like a collapsing high-rise, hands grasping uselessly at the edge of the tub — then, oh thank God thank God, grabbing the water pipe with both hands as she pitches forward. Just in time! Safe after all!

Uma says something then, but her words are so choked that Aasha's still trying to make sense of them when she turns and runs out of the bathroom, her hands clutching her skirt, her lips are pressed tightly together. The corner of her mouth twitches once as she disappears in the direction of the stairs.

Ask your son to bring you your water, then, if he's so wonderful. That's what Uma said. Aasha hears it now, as though Uma tossed the words at her when she passed.

The instant Uma's door slams shut upstairs, Paati's feet slide out from underneath her. Perhaps she was dizzy from the drama of her close shave, or perhaps she thought she could make her way back to the edge of the tub and misjudged the distance. Aasha's considered (but horrified) opinion is that a malevolent ghost pounced on Paati's unexpected moment of weakness and kicked in her knees.

"Ah! Aaah!" Paati flutes, eerily quiet. Hanging on to the water pipe for those few final moments, she looks like a wrinkled Tarzan remembering how to swing from vines.

The sound of her head hitting the pipe travels all the way up it, to where an already traumatized spider on the ceiling decides to scurry into a tiny hole in the plaster. There's blood on the pipe, and on the floor, trickling across the tiles and into the drain. Paati's curled toes uncurl. Her seaweed hair spreads out on the tiles, as nasty and out of place as any clumps of hair on any wet bathroom floor, needing urgently to be hosed down the drain hole, except that among these particular clumps is a head. Aasha cannot see Paati's face, but from the low, clogged-sink gurgle that comes out of her for a full ten seconds, she knows what that face looks like. The eyelids frozen open, the wide cataracted eyes, the loose lips, the dark pink tunnel of throat.

Outside, the rain clouds gather fast and thick. A sudden shadow, typical at this time of the afternoon, engulfs the bathroom, but today it seems anything but typical: the beads of sunlight on the water in the tank, the golden stippling of the floor tiles, the beams that dance up and down the walls, all seem to have been swallowed in a single gulp by something enormous and pitiless.

The bony heap of Paati on the floor isn't moving.

One step, two steps, three steps, and Aasha is standing over that heap. Paati's eyes are open just as wide as Aasha imagined them, but her mouth isn't. It's closed crooked, the lips and jaw askew like a Tupperware with the wrong lid on. All her loose skin hangs limp. The left side of her face lies flat as an appam against the tiles as if there were no bones in it. A patch of hair just above her forehead is matted dark brown, and there, yes, there's the blood streaming down her forehead onto the tiles, not as thin a stream as it looked from all the way down the corridor, a dark little river emptying soundlessly into the drain. There's the blood on the pipe, three fat drops. There's the single flower-shaped splatter on the wall, already thickening. And there, above Aasha's head, is the hole in the plaster where that spider waits, just as terrified as she is.

Lucky Uma, to have escaped in time. She won't have to contemplate this tableau, or dream about it later.

Aasha backs away from Paati, out through the door and to the safety of her wall and, just the way she traveled up the corridor, slides and shuffles all the way back down again, flat against that wall. Like a lizard slithering lightning quick into a crack, she slips once more behind the green settee, and there, in the privacy of her hideout, she shuts her eyes and opens them, shuts and opens them over and over to end this terrible dream. Any minute now, surely, she will open her eyes to find Suresh standing by her bed and shaking her, muttering, "Eh, wake up, stooopid!" But the seconds march on and there is no Suresh, only the dusty back of the green settee. Between this waking dream and the real world to which Aasha aches to return there's a gap that's widening steadily. First just a hairline crack, then a foot wide, now as wide as the monsoon drain outside the Big House. On the far side of the gap Uma still stands behind Paati in a sunlit bathroom, waiting to tap Paati on the shoulder and hand her a tumbler of water.

But on this side there's a small brown heap on the bathroom floor, cobweb shadows dappling the sunlight on its haunches.

The teaspoon alarm rings through the house again before Chellam's footsteps approach. Round the corner she comes, her skirt sopping wet from her impromptu laundry session, her feet dragging more than ever from the weight of all that water. Up, up, up the corridor. Into the bathroom.

There's a long, slow drawing in of breath as Chellam refuses to believe what her eyes are telling her. Her eyes lie to her all the time, after all, and this could be nothing more than a — there could be some other explanation — she should look more closely, she shouldn't panic — and then Chellam screams. It's the loudest sound Chellam has ever made, and for a minute Aasha cannot believe it comes from her. *It's Paati!* she thinks. *Paati woke up and now she's screaming from the fright!* Then she sees Chellam sink to a squat and lean her head against the high wall of the tub.

Footsteps down the stairs. Amma, her caftan streaming like flames behind her, comes running into the bathroom.

"Chellam! O, my God, O Sami O Govinda O Rama Rama Rama, Chellam! I told you, isn't it, not to leave her alone for so long? Didn't I tell you? Now look what has happened! She must have got so tired she fainted and hit her head nicely — oh my God, my God. Did you want this sin on your head, of all things?"

Chellam, as is her habit, says nothing.

AT ONE-THIRTY Dr. Kurian is summoned for the last time to the Big House on Kingfisher Lane. Paati has been towel-dried, laid out on a cot Appa hauled down from the storeroom upstairs and set up in front of the green settee, and covered with a fresh bedsheet. Coated, goateed, bow-tied, tongue-tied, seven grey hairs tufting mournfully from his otherwise-denuded pate, Dr. Kurian whispers his not-quite-questions into the oppressive afternoon air:

"Lot of marks on her legs, hmm."

"Could be she's fallen down before, maybe . . ."

"All these small-small bruises everywhere . . ."

"That's a very big red patch on her back, no . . . Looks like a recent thing. Could be she hit her back also as she fell, not just her head. Yes. Yes?"

The family gathers close around him. Appa in his bestquality courthouse trousers (he's supposed to be righting the wrongful death of ten-year-old Angela Lim; instead, here he is, called away during a courtroom break to witness the aftermath of a death far less sensational). Amma in a caftan whose edges are still wet from the bloodied bathroom floor. Chellam two feet behind Amma. Suresh and Aasha pressed up against the wall by Paati's feet. Uma alone has stayed away: she's upstairs, sitting ramrod-straight on the edge of her neatly made bed. *Dead!* she thinks. *Did she faint from the shock? A heart attack? Doesn't matter. Not my problem.* She shuts her eyes, rubs a hand over her hot face, pictures herself standing in the bathroom. Glass in hand, Paati's leathery old back before her, yes, there she is, and then the moment of — what to call it? Madness? *But when I left her she was fine. She was already gearing up to shout more nonsense.*

Aasha deduces through careful observation of the five other faces downstairs that no one else is wondering where Uma is. Dr. Kurian, avoiding all eyes, would be happier with an even smaller audience; Appa's shaking his head at Paati for her bad timing; Chellam's staring at her feet and rubbing her nose with an index finger; Suresh is studying the cotton wool in Paati's nostrils.

It wasn't Uma's fault, Aasha thinks. *If Uma hadn't been so sad and angry —*

And why was Uma so sad and angry? Whose fault was *that?*

The answer hurts Aasha's chest like too much cold water swallowed at once: *my fault.* She counts her mistakes from start to finish. Finish was just last month. Finish was the sapphire pendant incident. All these mistakes, all her fault; it follows, therefore, that it's her responsibility to set things right.

Amma's frowning and leaning towards Dr. Kurian as if she's about to grab his arm to tell him a secret. She blurts out answers he doesn't seem to want, and his watery eyes bulge slightly as he swallows each sticky glob of words: "Yes, Doctor, could be that. You know how these old people are, always knocking themselves here and there. Yes yes, she fell in the middle of her bath only, you see, she had nothing on, if she hit her back sure it would've made a mark like that on the skin."

Amma never talks so much to any of them, all those curtsying words, such a shameless please-please-thankyou-thankyou behind each one. Aasha wishes she would shut up.

With two fat fingers Dr. Kurian rubs at a spot on his neck just above his bow tie. "But," he says, then stops to clear his throat before starting again, "but you see, the way she fell . . . If she simply got tired and fainted . . . I mean to say, falling forward so very far, to hit her head on that pipe, it's not, you know . . . It's quite an odd angle . . . And the mark on her back . . ."

It occurs to various members of the assembled family that the good doctor will go on like this, muttering and mumbling things no one, least of all he himself, wants to hear, refusing to spare himself any embarrassment or inconvenience, poking and prodding and sniffing about until someone is horribly and irreversibly hurt or something is unexpectedly broken beyond repair. What can they do? How can they shut him up and send him on his way? The problem pirouettes in each of their heads in turn, showing off its skirts, and Appa opens his mouth and draws in his breath to say something—but what? Even as he licks his lips, he doesn't know.

If Dr. Kurian digs up the truth, what will happen to Uma?

Probably she won't be able to go to America. She'll be in so much trouble she'll have to stay here, no scholarship no university no New York. For ever and ever, until she's an old woman, she'll wish she were far away. Isn't wishing just the same as doing? If Uma wants to go away and never come back, isn't she already gone?

The opposite is equally true: if Aasha keeps Uma's secret safe so that she can go to America, Uma will always be thankful. She'll never forget, and who knows, who knows, she might even be so very thankful . . .

Overwhelmed with the possibilities, Aasha fixes Dr. Kurian with her unforgiving eyes, dips her chin, and steps forward to say her opening line:

"Chellamservant *pushed* Paati."

She doesn't turn to look at Chellam as she hisses the *s* of *servant*, nor after, in the perfect silence that ensues. She doesn't need to; she needs no external validation of this moment of triumph, in which, with three steel-bright words, she has (1) punished Chellam (for Leading Us On, for Pretending to Love Us like siblings in hopes of a *salary* and then withdrawing her fakery when we could not pay her price), and (2) saved Uma. Uma! O Uma-alone-upstairs, O dearest darlingest Uma, do you hear your sister through the ceiling and the floorboards? Do you hear how brave she is, how she has finally atoned—or so she believes—for all her past sins, for wanting too much and giving too little, for frantic inventions and fumbling plots? Say it, say it: now you will not fly away to America even though you're free to do so, because at last you see how ardently you're loved, because your sister has risked so very much for your safety, which she has won. Not fairly or squarely, but luckily for you. Everything will be all right now. You and she will make your sins up to each other one by one, plenty of time, you see, all the time in the world. A whole happily-ever-after stretches before the two of you. She strains to hear you think it . . .

. . . but Dr. Kurian, pesky as ever, drowns out your thoughts with further questions:

"Yes baby? You saw her push your Paati?"

"Yes. I saw her."

"Tell me, baby, tell me what you saw."

Aasha swallows and replays the whole scene inside her head. It's stunningly clear now, no longer a blur but a copiously detailed story someone invented for shivers and goosebumps, just like the many fabulations in which Aasha has watched Uma perform better-rehearsed roles on a red-curtained stage. When the scene reaches its end—the fall to end all falls, the cracking the bleeding the goodbye-I'm-going —Aasha starts over from the beginning, making the necessary changes with surgical precision, no sadness, no regret for the moment:

"Paati was standing there in the bathroom and shouting-shouting because Chellam left her there all alone. When Chellam came back—when she came back Paati shouted at her some more, and suddenly Chellam angry and did like this." Aasha lifts her arm and shoves at the air in front of her, pouting as though at an imaginary playground foe. All around her there are stirrings and sniffs, Amma's *tsk-tsk*ing, Appa's headshaking, Chellam's deafening silence, but Aasha must soldier on: "Just to show her anger only. She didn't do it to make Paati fall. At first Paati didn't fall also. She caught the pipe and held on. And then"—now that she's begun, Aasha feels a certain obligation to the details—"and then she said—she said—I think she said, 'Now shout and see lah, shout some more!' Something like that. And then, at the last minute, there was like a—suddenly Paati just fell like that and hit her head, even though Chellam didn't push her again. As if—I mean just like that she fell. And she screamed and started to cry. I mean, *Chellamservant* screamed. And started to cry."

When she's done, she turns to Suresh, for reasons she herself

{159}

doesn't understand. Her final, emphatic *Chellamservant* hangs between them like a lightbulb she's stood on tiptoe to switch on all by herself. Their rule has always been to call Chellam that name only behind their mother's back (and then only when she truly deserves it), for neither one of them has ever had any doubts, shared or private, about what they'd get if Amma found out: mouthslaps, thighpinches, lectures for the public good. But today Amma's stunned, sedated face — a slab of black stone, that face is, a block of nothingness — indicates that Aasha will get away without a mouthslap. That Chellam deserves the slur there is no question, in either of their minds.

Suresh is impressed and gratified by this small revenge Aasha has extracted, yes, but he is also — what? What is it that Aasha reads in his slight frown? A warning? A note of fear clouding his new respect? No: a promise of solidarity. Suresh knows she's lying. But how?

It doesn't matter. It's not important. The only thing that matters is his promise not to tell. *Thank you, Suresh, thank you thank you thank you for keeping our secret.*

You're welcome, says Suresh, his silent reply as clear to Aasha as a news reader's good night.

They have no time for anything more than this now, for already Chellam has turned around and left the room, and Dr. Kurian is patting Aasha's head, sighing, assuring her she's a good girl to tell the truth. Scarcely have the words tumbled off his tongue when he turns to sign the death certificate, laid out on Paati's bedside table, with a hand that shakes to the same rhythm as his wattles. He sighs again and closes his eyes briefly. "I'll write 'accidental death from a fall,'" he says when he opens them. He's old, almost as old as the woman whose death he's come to certify; he's tired; at his age he should (he reasons with himself) be allowed the small mercy of a lie of omission. "After all it's not far from the truth," he says for the benefit of his audience. "I'm sure the girl didn't mean to kill her. These servants, sometimes they let their impatience get out of hand you know? And old people, you know how fragile they are."

No one corroborates or contradicts his hypothesis about what Chellam did or didn't mean. "I'm writing 'accidental death,'" he says again. "You all can do what you want from there."

At five past two, Dr. Kurian shuffles out of the Big House in his shiny shoes, to disappear forever into his lost world in which muttonchop whiskers and pinstriped trousers are still fashionable, decent men dance around difficult questions, and children trail clouds of glory and golden innocence.

When Appa has shut the front door behind Dr. Kurian, he sends Suresh to fetch Chellam back from her room.

"She's her father's problem now," Appa says to Amma's feet while they wait. "He can decide what to do with her. I'll get in touch with the bugger and tell him to come and remove her from our house at once. You all hear me or not?" He looks around the room challengingly, as if one or the other of them might secretly disagree with this course of action.

The only person who voices her objection merely thinks he's being too lenient. "Her father?" Amma says. "We should call the police! She should be handcuffed and thrown into the lockup!"

"Yes," says Appa, "that would be nice, and in the best of all possible worlds that is what would happen. But our only witness is a six-year-old. If we try to build a case on that, Aasha will spend weeks being questioned in court. And even then we might not get what we want. Better to let her family deal with her. I suspect her father's punishments will be as good as anything the lockup can offer."

And so, because Appa is a famous lawyer and must know what he's talking about, and also because Amma is inclined to agree with his estimate of the chastening that awaits Chellam in her village, Aasha is saved the terrible prospect of repeating her lie over and over before an audience.

"I'll send one of my office boys to fetch the bugger from his village," Appa says. "He can use last month's money to come and pick her up, because after what she's done I'm certainly not giving them a penny for the bus fare back."

After a minute or two — for Aasha has to knock on Chellam's door and butt her way blindly through the thick curtain of silence that stands on the other side of it — Chellam drags her feet into the dining room, a breathless Suresh behind her. Silhouetted against the blaze of Suresh's eyes, Chellam peers around the room from under her heavy red eyelids, her hair frizzing around her face in a black halo. Then she shambles towards the center of the room, where she and Appa face each other like sadly mismatched fighters in a ring: she skinny and skittish, he steely, elemental, legs planted firmly two feet apart, right hand on hip.

"So," Appa says quietly, "what have you done, Chellam? Are you proud of yourself? Nothing you do now can fix it, do you know that? Do you know you've left us with no choice?"

As he asks these questions he begins to realize what he wants out of the interrogation: to see her break down and cry, beg for forgiveness, at least tremble a little where she stands.

He's tired and thirsty, and now he has two unavenged, mangled corpses to consider, one tender as a kid goat, one ancient. Why, why must he be mired in all this sordid melodrama? He wants to strangle the world and bend it to his will. He wants to slap Amma and Chellam both, for the stupid games and thoughtless messes into which they drag him. He's been boiling with anger at Chellam for months, for reasons he doesn't give himself time to revisit; now shame blows its dirty breath in his face and sickens him. How monstrous that this walleyed little bitch should wield all this unwitting power over him! She's reduced him to a Hindi-film villain, a Nazi sweating before his serene victims, a petty, vindictive, pitiful creature. For in answer to his battery of questions she simply stares at her toes. His hands itch to grab her arm and twist it behind her back, or spit in her eyes, or pull her hair. He grinds his jaw. He takes a deep breath.

But the heat in his chest will not subside; it's so very much stronger than he, and how strange that at the very moment he feels weakest, his mouth springs open. Out of it pours the most powerful of sounds, a mountain collapsing, a lion's roar. A noise that cannot possibly be coming out of any human mouth, let alone his own, for he is not—has never been—a man who shouts, and yet here it is, this noise. He would think it was someone else but for the fact that he can feel it inside his head, vibrating every tiny bone in his ears, echoing in all the dark passages behind his face.

He sees himself point with his left hand, to some distant horizon beyond the living room, beyond the front door, beyond this universe whose precarious order this stupid, weak-willed girl has disturbed. He sees his family staring at him—no, just at his mouth, as if they, too, are trying to make sense of the amorphous noise washing over them. He yearns to stop, to put out this horrible flame in his throat and go back to his office, but he cannot.

Hearing him, Uma walks to her window, throws it open, and thirstily gulps the damp air that rushes in. *Chellam? Could she really have—* "Maybe so," she says out loud, addressing her conclusion to a sparrow on a high branch of the mango tree. Chellam had her own crosses to

{ 162 }

bear, didn't she? No, Appa might get on his high horse and make like a saint, but Uma wouldn't blame Chellam for letting her frustrations get the better of her, not when she herself, only minutes earlier . . . She laughs mirthlessly and shakes her head at the sparrow. In and out of that bathroom all afternoon, a veritable procession of embittered women, eh? Poor Paati had been a fun-fair target for all their rotten apples. Who else had had a go? *Still, why should I feel sorry for Paati? Why should I pity her when she never pitied me?*

Downstairs, the tempest continues. Appa can make out only a few of his own words here and there, garbled, the inflections all wrong: "Prostitute! Killer!" His tongue stumbles over the same syllables again and again, as if he's only just learning Tamil and hasn't got much further than memorizing handfuls of words from bad film scenes.

But Amma and Chellam, and even Suresh and Aasha — whose Tamil consists largely of words for vegetables and demons and private parts Chellam taught them, or curse words and grumblings they have heard her speak when she can't see them — understand him perfectly well. "Shameless prostitute, don't think we don't know about you! How dare you come into our house and do all this under our roof! One thing after another it's been, sneaking around, spying, spreading your legs for any man that enters the house, but this, this, even I never thought you would *kill!* For one whole year we've housed you and fed you" — no one but Appa himself notes his pointed omission of *paid you* — "and you turn around and do this! How could you! How could you kill a defenseless old lady like that, how could you? What did she ever do to you? Hanh? What?"

In the sudden silence that follows this question, the house throbs to the mad beat of Appa's heart, rattling even the china in the corner cabinet.

The floor hums. A mouse in a kitchen cupboard drops the groundnut it's been gnawing and crouches quaking among the lentils, waiting for the deluge.

Outside, the sparrows and mynah birds hurry home to huddle in their nests.

Uma ponders Appa's question. What did she ever do to you, Uma? What? *I'm just lucky,* she thinks, though she cannot know how lucky she's been, or, more precisely, that her salvation has required much more than luck. Selfless devotion, kamikaze courage, masterly storytelling: of these contributions she knows nothing. *It could've just as easily been my hand that killed her,* she thinks. *And why? What did she ever do to me?*

It's what she didn't do, she replies. *It's what she could've done for me and didn't.* She knows her plea would never stand up in court; it barely stands up to her own scrutiny.

They're still waiting for Chellam to answer downstairs, or to cry, or even just to move, or for Appa to continue. But Appa's outburst is over as abruptly as it began. Now he stands looking out the window at the branches of the mango tree swaying in the pre-downpour wind, his arms folded, his face turned away from all of them. *Good lord, whatever the old lady's faults, did she deserve that horrendous end?* The papery skin of her face bloodstained and imprinted with the floor tile pattern. The hasty dusting off of the storeroom cot so that her slippery, stiffening body could be laid out on it. The doctor jabbing at all those marks, all those mysterious marks, *My God, what has been happening in this house, to the old lady, to all of us?*

"Monday morning," he says, oddly quiet, "I'll send for your father to come and get you. Do you understand me, Chellam?"

When she doesn't reply, he doesn't press her.

One of the children sniffs. The afternoon's first fat drops of rain begin to hammer the metal awnings outside. Chellam blinks at each of them in turn: Appa, Amma, Suresh, Aasha. Her arms fly up and across her chest, as if she's suddenly realized she's naked. Then she turns and, still blinking in all directions like a small animal looking for a hiding place, shuffles away to her room.

For a few long moments no one says a word.

Through the doorway, Aasha can see a pair of stockinged legs dangling between the banister posts, swinging in time to a tune she can't hear. Poor Mr. McDougall's daughter, always a little too hot in those stockings her mother insisted on dressing her in to remind her (and the rest of the world) that she was half white. She's waiting as patiently as she can, but it's not easy when you're wearing itchy stockings. Where is Paati? Mr. McDougall's daughter is all dressed up and ready to welcome her formally into the world of ghosts, but there's no sign of her. No, no sign at all. Aasha holds her breath and waits along with Mr. McDougall's daughter and, it seems, everyone else, until finally Amma speaks.

"What?" she says. A quick puff of a word that startles everyone else, most of all Mr. McDougall's daughter, who rises to her feet and skitters up the stairs. "Are we all going to stand here until the curtains close?"

But real-life stories do not enjoy the mercy of a curtain: there are always epilogues, codas, aftermaths, new stories sprouting from old seeds.

That very night, Amma discovers eight boiled sweeties left in Paati's red Danish Butter Cookies tin on the shelf next to her rattan chair. It's unclear to all present (Amma, Suresh, Aasha) why Paati was saving them, since it's been years since she's distributed boiled sweeties or offered them as rewards. "Here, take, take," Amma says, "I'm going to tell Letchumi to clean up this corner nicely tomorrow. Take two each and give two to Uma." *Of course*, thinks Suresh, *of course you want this corner cleaned up first thing in the morning. Of course you want the tin emptied and thrown out right now.* He remembers Paati's blunt fingers and thick nails struggling to get off the lid of that tin, struggling struggling struggling until one day she could no longer do it and had to ask for help. "I helped you thread the needle first," he'd said at the time, "and then I helped you open the tin, so don't I get two sweeties for two favors?" She'd laughed and called him a sly one and let him take two. Even impervious Suresh, remembering that long-ago transaction, is suddenly not sure he wants a sweetie; when Amma gets the tin open all the colors look sickly to him and he tastes them in his mouth, nasty and sticky and cough-syrup sweet. But reason prevails: he tells himself that he might change his mind later and regret not having taken any. More important, not taking any sweeties won't fix anything now. It's too late.

Amma has miscounted: two each and two for Uma still leaves two extra. At Suresh's suggestion, he and Aasha take three each. Now there's the problem of delivering the remaining two to Uma, who hasn't left her room since this afternoon.

"We better go and give them to her," Aasha says, leaning towards Suresh with a sad, meaningful look. "How can she come out of her room?" If Amma sees Uma's face, she means, if *anyone else* sees that face of Uma's (for she pictures it frozen in the anguish that seized it when their eyes met in the bathroom), won't they guess—

Instead of the well-laid strategy she expects of him, Suresh gives her a blank, open-mouthed stare.

"What you mean? Why should Uma get special service? You want means you go and give them to her lah."

Aasha stares back at him, fiddling with the crinkly wrapping of the boiled sweeties for an eternity. *Why should Uma get special service? Because, Suresh, because. Asking for the sake of asking only, isn't it? You know the answer.*

"Ohhhh," Suresh says suddenly. He covers his mouth like a small boy who's just found out where babies come from, a gesture of innocent discovery so unlike him it makes Aasha back away. "Ohhhh. You mean." His voice has dropped to a whisper.

"I mean what?"

"You mean Uma also saw Amma ah? And now she's scared to look at Amma?"

"What—oh—yah," says Aasha weakly. The truth shoots through her like an eel in black water: Suresh thinks *Amma* pushed Paati, not Uma, and before she can fit the whole of this oversized thought into her head he goes on:

"Never mind what. She saw means she saw lah, so what? If we can face Amma means why can't she? She's bigger, so isn't she supposed to be braver?"

"Don't know. I don't know anything. I'm going to go and give her the sweeties now."

Aasha hurries away and up the stairs, her hot hands melting the sweeties through their wrappers. So she's alone after all; Suresh doesn't understand anything. It all makes sense: of course he thought it was Amma she was protecting, Amma, whose scoldings and slappings and knuckleknockings of Paati they've all had to pretend not to see or hear for years; Amma, whose voice Suresh probably heard echoing in that big, drafty bathroom just minutes before Chellam screamed; Amma, whose breath thrashes about in her throat like a bird in a net whenever she recalls Paati's venomous past. "Your grandmother," Amma said only last week, "acts like a helpless old lady now, but when I first came to this house she was like the devil himself. With a heart of coal and a tongue of fire. Only when she dies I'll have some peace."

And today, Suresh believes, Amma grew impatient and greedy, and snatched at that peace before it was ripe.

Let Suresh think what he must; Aasha cannot, will not, will *never* tell him the truth, however lonely her secret will make her. Because if he doesn't already know, who can say how he might react to the truth?

Outside Uma's room, Aasha finds that she cannot knock. She stands and stands, curls her left foot around her right ankle, her right foot around her left ankle, readies herself to slip the two sweeties under Uma's door and run away when—oh, the feeling of it, like swooshing down a too-steep slide, your stomach turning to cold water—Uma's door opens.

There she stands, lovely Uma, her hair down her back.

"Here," says Aasha, and holds out the sweeties. There is nothing else to say.

Uma plucks them off her palm. "Thank you," she says. She smiles then, a gentle, misty smile, not at Aasha but at the sweeties in her own hand. Such a faint smile, and Aasha's head still swimming from the open door, her vision blurry from the shock of it—yet there's no doubt in her mind that Uma smiled. And said thank you. A great sigh of a thank you. A thank you not just for the sweeties.

Aasha cannot stay here and look at Uma. She's dizzy. Her mouth is dry. She turns on her heels and runs back down the stairs.

That night the sweeties—one red, one yellow—sit on Uma's bedside table as she lies in bed staring out the window at the flickering streetlamp. Paati's leftover sweeties. Aasha did not say so, but Uma recognizes them. That Danish Butter Cookies tin. The way they'd bargain for three sweeties for a favor that deserved two. And Paati's obligatory show of reluctance before she caved in, every time, with a wink and a grin.

At two in the morning, Uma climbs out of bed and flings the sweeties one by one (first the yellow, then the red) out the open window (to be discovered among the chili plants by Mat Din in the morning, and eaten several days afterwards by his goats). Then she gets back in bed and closes her eyes. Her body makes a shallow dent on the pale blue pool of her sleep; her hair fans out around her face. She dreams she is a little girl again, burrowing into Paati's back so that there's space for both of them in the bed. But the bed cracks and falls apart beneath their weight, and Paati is left hanging off the edge of the one remaining board. It takes all Uma's strength and both her arms to keep Paati from plummeting head-first to the floor. *I'm sorry, I'm sorry,* she mumbles, neither awake nor asleep but in some dark gulf in between. And then: *I'm not letting go. I'll keep you safe. Tomorrow we'll have laddoos for tea, okay?*

She rises at seven and begins to sort through the clothes in her cupboard: one pile for packing in her suitcase, one pile for whichever servant Amma chooses to foist them upon.

"Tsk. I don't know *what* I was thinking," Amma says at the breakfast table, with a child's sweep of flat palm against wet cheek. "After *everyone* warned me how difficult it is to find trustworthy servants these days."

"I told you you should've gotten rid of the bloody girl after that first incident itself," Appa replies. "After that mess with my great hero of a brother."

"Don't you think we should inform the police?" Amma says once more. "This type of madwoman will just turn around and do the same thing to someone else if we let her go free."

But Appa's bravado has abated, never to be recovered on this particular subject. The longer his apoplectic rage echoes between his ears (all night it has raged, as he lay, eyes closed, on his pillow, and this morning it continues to rage), the more certain his impression that he has somehow — although there's no denying Chellam's brutish crime — made a fool of himself. That he should've been the bigger person, kept his temper in check, calmly given Chellam a month's notice so that she could go through the motions of looking for another job. Of course she'd never get a job in anyone else's house after this; every bloody Indian family in the country must already know what she's done. Just leave it to the gorgon across the street. But she could look for a factory job, or a cleaner's position in some office building. Something to satisfy her father, because let's face it, all the man will care about is his monthly toddy money, not his daughter's doubtful morals. If she could be seamlessly transplanted from this house to some other job, she'd be safe from — from what?

What will become of her in her father's house?

That's not my problem, Appa tries to tell himself. *I can't bear the whole world's woes on my shoulders.*

Blast the troublesome, contradictory voice that retorts: *Ohoho, weren't you going to fix the whole world's woes? What happened to your big-big dreams, Raju? What kind of socialist hires a drunk tapper's daughter and pays her nothing?*

He tries to defend himself: *But you see I wasn't paying her nothing; the money simply went to her father, who needed it just as badly, if not more, what with those six-seven-eight-however-many children waiting at home. I was only choosing to treat the problem at its source, don't you see, if the head of the household has a little more money doesn't it benefit everyone instead of just—*

Aah, shaddup your mouth, you bastard, says the other voice. It's a real rowdy, this voice, a lorry driver, a mamak-stall loafer with an open-chested shirt and a gold chain. It has none of Appa's refinements. *Who do you think you're fooling? You paid off her father because you're a bloody pondan. A coward. Too scared to stand up for an eighteen-year-old girl. Some revolutionary you would've made.*

So once again he dissuades Amma from her apparent quest for justice (which everyone but Amma knows to be, in truth, a hunger for revenge). "Don't be silly," he says evenly. "You call in the police and the whole thing immediately becomes a front-page scandal. You want your face and your children's faces in the newspaper for everyone to see?"

Amma starts to sob quietly, hiding her nose in the tasseled pallu of her saree.

Perhaps she really is crying.

On Monday Appa sends one of his office boys to Chellam's village, as planned. "Look for Muniandy," he tells the boy. "Short black fellow, curly hair, missing teeth. You'll probably find him in the toddy shop. Tell him we've had to let his daughter go, so he has to come to my house and get her. As soon as he can." He doesn't look up from the papers on his desk.

In court that day Appa stares into Shamsuddin bin Yusof's black eyes and allows something cold to slither from the crown of his head to the end of his tailbone. Yes. A frisson of revulsion: this is how he must begin. He will do his job, bask in the resulting glory, and forget about the rest. The reporters and the crowds will seize upon whatever stale bit of evidence he throws them; the jury and the judge are on someone's secret payroll. They agreed on Shamsuddin's guilt before today, before the trial began, before Shamsuddin was dangled by his feet before them, a rabbit out of some unseen magician's hat. Appa may as well luxuriate in the cleverness of his own tongue. His pleasures are not so different from Uma's: both can throw themselves into a role, secrete abundant hatred for invented villainy, scorn pretend fools. He clears his throat and draws in his breath.

The office boy, after a fruitless two-hour search for Muniandy, leaves a message at the toddy shop before driving back to Ipoh.

"What the bloody hell?" Amma says at home. "If he can't come and get her, let's just put her on the bus. That's how she came here in the first place, isn't it? If her father didn't need to bring her means why does he need to fetch her?"

"Hmm," Appa says from behind his newspaper. "Yes. Technically you're right. But one doesn't want to do anything hasty. One doesn't want to get blamed for any other havoc she wreaks after this. Best to deliver her straight into her father's hands, that way no one can point any fingers at us."

Amma silently ponders the sorts of havoc that Chellam might wreak if released into the wilds on her own: Jumping into the Kinta River? returning to prostitution, so that neighbors and strangers will point and say, Look what happened to that girl after Lawyer Raja-sekharan kicked her out? Yes, perhaps Appa is right. Perhaps this is the only way for them to preserve their blameless status. Whatever happens, they'll be able to say: "Her own father came and took her home."

Not for a second does Appa believe what the grainy female voice on the other end of the phone line claims later the following after-noon: "My husband — my husband's sick, saar, very very sick, cannot come to Ipoh yet, please can you wait a little bit, aiyo, please, saar, I'm asking, we're asking, have some pity? Maybe one week — or — or two — two weeks?" He wonders how far Chellam's mother had to walk to get to the phone booth in which she now stands and stam-mers; how long it took her to scrape the necessary coins together (has she been searching, borrowing, begging for a day and a half, with such difficulty that it will take her another two weeks to scrounge up the round-trip bus fare for her husband plus the one-way ticket for her daughter?); whether it's raining as heavily over her phone booth as it is here in Ipoh (that it is raining he has no doubt: he can hear the rain's muffled hum behind her lie).

He could ask her: Oho, is that so? One whole year your husband has been showing up on the dot for payday at the Big House, and now suddenly he'll be too sick on the first Saturday of the month? Did he break his neck or his head, tell me, what? Instead he says, "I see, I see. Two weeks then. But he must come for sure on the second Saturday of the month. Otherwise I'll have to kick your daughter out onto the streets. Do you understand me?"

"Two weeks!" Amma shrieks that night. "Two weeks we have to feed her and keep her under our roof!"

Amma needn't worry, for Chellam has eaten almost nothing since Paati's death. As for her presence under their roof, perhaps even this is debatable. Certainly her body can be glimpsed on hurried trips to the toilet, but it's a barely inhabited, steadily shrinking body, one foot already in the world of ghosts. Thus begins Chellam's second (and final) self-enforced sequestration since her arrival at the Big House: for the next two weeks she will be spoken for and of and to, but she will not speak herself. Because it's been months since she's spoken to anyone but Paati, almost no one will notice the difference, and those who do will merely wonder idly if this is the same old silence or a new one with a new purpose. It's difficult to say. Perhaps there's a new hopelessness in her eyes. Or fear. Or disgust. Then again, perhaps it's just the old hopelessness. Hopelessnesses are so difficult to tell apart these days, particularly when one has no help from the hopeless.

There's no need for Chellam to speak, anyway, or room for her to get a word in edgewise if she'd wanted to, for Appa's prediction turns out to have been conservative. Thanks in large part to Mrs. Balakrishnan from across the street, all the Indian families in Ipoh and all their relatives and friends — not only all over Malaysia, but also in Singapore, in Australia and New Zealand, in England and America and Canada — have heard the dreadful news within days of Paati's death: Chellam pushed Paati, for whom she was paid to care, with whom she's been rough and mean and impatient from the beginning. Chellam has cold-bloodedly murdered a helpless old woman who trusted her.

"Quietly-quietly she agreed to go, yaar?" Mrs. Balakrishnan says when Amma tells her about Chellam's imminent departure. "Lucky for you. This type of people you never know. Sometime will make trouble only."

"What is there for her to make trouble about?" Amma snaps. "She knows she's in the wrong. A six-year-old child is her witness. Out of the mouths of babes as they say."

As they do indeed say. Amma herself is unsure of the rest of the quotation, and its significance is entirely lost on the less-educated Mrs. Balakrishnan, who adjusts her hair bun, tut-tuts, and coos, "I say, I say, nonono, Vasanthi, please don't take offense yaar, not to say babesshabes or anything like that, I simply talking only. Not bad, what, quietly-quietly she agreeing to go."

"Yaar," says Amma, pushing her teacup away and standing up abruptly, "quiet-quiet-nice-nice, those are the worst types. Quietly-quietly minding their own business, making like good girls, and then stabbing you in the back when you're not looking."

Mrs. Balakrishnan, who has not encountered the metaphor enough to be inured to its violence, is suitably hushed.

On their busy telephones people shake their heads for friends and relatives who can't see them, and remark upon how the incident will scar Aasha forever. Probably going to have nightmares for years, they tell each other. And maybe worse. Who knows what it does to people who witness that type of violence at such a young age.

Uma, too, has heard the details of Chellam's denouncement. Not all at once; no one has sat her down and given her a full account, for she hasn't displayed much interest. The story has floated to her ears in bits and pieces, and always — whether in Vellamma and Letchumi's backyard chatter or in the hushed, behind-one-hand gossip of housewives on the town buses — Aasha stands at the center of it, glowing with courage, wreathed in pity. And if Aasha ratted on Chellam just so she could feel like a heroine? She's only six, Uma reasons. Children are selfish. She, for one, knew that before. If you let them they'll eat you alive. In their sleep. Without even meaning to. *At least Chellam has only two weeks left in this house; then it'll be all over. Whereas if my hand had been the unlucky one and Aasha had been spying on me, it would never have been over, never.*

The neighbors and all their international friends and relatives note how gracious it is of Appa not to press charges, given how easy it would be for him to have Chellam put behind bars, bigshot lawyer that he is, connections in the High Court, judges eating out of his hands. These days, everyone agrees, you just can't trust servants. You pay them and feed them and house them and in the end they murder your old parents or kidnap your baby or steal your wedding jewelry and elope with their goonda boyfriends. No bloody shame. Doing a thing like that in front of a patchai kozhundai, a babe barely out of arms, green, raw, unripe. God knows she's probably done plenty of other things in front of the children as well. What was that story about her and Raju's brother? They dredge up that story, in light of this new evidence of Chellam's depravity. "I mean you would've had to send the girl away anyway, wouldn't you?" Mrs. Anthony from house number 57 says to Amma. "If she's pregnant—you wouldn't want—"

"Yes," Amma hastens to agree, "yes, sooner or later we would've had to get rid of her."

In the bathroom mirror beside the water tank on which Paati hit her head, Aasha studies her face. When people say the words, the spittle collects in the corners of their mouths: patchai kozhundai. An unripe baby. A green baby. A raw baby. Isn't she all of these things? A poor, shivering baby, naked as a peeled banana, with no one to sing her lullabies and blow away her nightmares? But try as she might to see such a creature in the mirror, Aasha feels less like a baby than she ever has. She's all grown up; she has a secret she'll never tell, and no one to answer to but herself. Wasn't she right to do what she did? Didn't she need to make up for all the trouble she'd caused Uma? Even if she told a lie to protect Uma, it was only one lie—less than a whole one, in fact, because Chellam *has* pushed and knocked and pinched Paati before, and pulled her hair.

"But Aasha," says a soft voice, "I've told you my story, so you have to tell me yours. It's only fair. You can't keep your secret for yourself." Mr. McDougall's daughter sits on the closed toilet bowl swinging her legs. Only her coconut-tree hairdo, affixed with a fat pink bow, is visible in the mirror.

"It was nothing," Aasha says to the pink bow. Secretly she's pleased, though not surprised, that Mr. McDougall's daughter is back, although Aasha almost ignored her last appearance. And why not? It's only fair that Aasha, who does all the needing and longing in the seen world, be on the receiving end of need in this other world. That once in a while she should get to breathe easy and relax her shoulders and let someone else burn their hands tugging at an ancient frayed rope. "It wasn't Uma's fault," she goes on. Measured, outwardly confident. "Uma was angry with—with everybody, I think. Or mostly with Paati. She threw the glass to show her temper. It's not a very good thing to do, showing your temper, is it?"

Mr. McDougall's daughter shrugs.

"But still, everything would've been okay, except that—well first of all Uma's hand slipped. I think so. I mean, she threw the glass and then her hand slipped on—on the way back. Or it moved just like that but it wasn't Uma moving it. It flew up like a bird and pushed Paati.

Just the hand, not Uma. And it was only one small push like — like when you suddenly feel too angry and you say *ish!* and you push whatever you see in front of you. You know what I mean, isn't it?" The pink bow doesn't stir, so Aasha elaborates: "Like when Suresh pushes me or I push him. Just one small push, and Paati didn't fall, so everything would still have been okay. It was only *after that* Paati fell. It was a ghost. I couldn't see it, I don't know why I couldn't see it but definitely there was a ghost. A toyol, maybe. It grabbed her knees because that's all it could reach. But Dr. Kurian wouldn't understand all that. If I tried to explain to them everybody would laugh at me only."

"Yah," says Mr. McDougall's daughter, convinced at last. Aasha breathes a sigh of relief that steams up the mirror and briefly obscures her view of the pink bow as the girl goes on: "When you're small nobody cares about what you think, anyway. You have to find your own way to get things done. Lucky for you that you thought of it in time." There's only a faint hint of wistfulness in her voice; mostly she sounds patient, gently generous with her wisdom, and proud, as always, of the stiff little accent that is her father's only legacy to her.

"That's what I also think," says Aasha. "That's what I've been saying to myself."

Yet the indigo-bright certainty of Aasha's conclusions dulls to grey within a week, despite Mr. McDougall's daughter's reassurances. Downstairs, Chellam tosses and sniffles in her bed. As each day passes she ventures less frequently out of her room, as though even her bladder and bowels might be shutting down. Upstairs, Uma hums "Mrs. Robinson" and "The Boxer" and "The Sound of Silence" and goes on with her packing as if nothing happened, as if Aasha still doesn't exist. Perhaps there's no atoning for old sins after all. Perhaps it was already too late.

9

THE FUTILE INCIDENT
OF THE SAPPHIRE PENDANT

July 6, 1980

S IX WEEKS BEFORE Paati dies, Amma hosts the weekly gathering of the Ladies' tea-party circle. She does so against her first instincts, for the household is in disarray. Chellam still harbors the dregs of the fever brought on by the Balakrishnans' nephew's unsoothing soothsaying, which dregs she has generously shared with Paati; whiffs of old-lady urine and Dr. Kurian's dark potions waft through the house on every breeze. But Amma will not live at the mercy of the psychosomatic ailments of lunatics. She will have the Ladies over because it is her turn and the show must go on; because she has nothing, no solace, but appearances, and must therefore fight tooth and nail to preserve them.

So she has Vellamma the washerwoman pull down all the drapes and wash them in hot water; she has Letchumi the sweeper shampoo the rugs and disinfect the floors with Dettol to banish the miasma of Paati's hand-me-down fever. She orders a Black Forest cake from the Ipoh Garden Cake Shop and commissions Lourdesmary to execute a baroque version of the usual tea-party menu: four kinds of noodles, two kinds of fried rice, three jellies (red, orange, blue), pyramids of cottony sandwiches (cucumber, butter-and-watercress, Norwegian sardine) and springy popiah, pigs in blankets, roly-poly pudding, rock buns, rum balls, rumaki. And fruit salad in sherry, stationed on either side of a towering centerpiece custom-made by Flower Power Florists.

A grim determination infects all involved in these preparations; the kitchen, never a hive of whistling gaiety under Lourdesmary's rule, is cold and silent as she chops and kneads and rolls. Suresh spends the weekend speeding up and down Kingfisher Lane alone on his Raleigh bicycle, making occasional trips to the corner shop for sustenance. Aasha tiptoes along the corridors and staircases of the Big House, dry-lipped and goose-bumped. They understand, on variously liminal levels, that this party will be more than an assertion of order over the chaos that has engulfed them in recent months, more even than the usual affirmation of Amma's place in the world. It will be a gauntlet thrown down before all those who have been chipping away, blindly or maliciously or out of sheer boredom, at that place: the busybodying servants, the behind-the-back smirkers and gloaters.

There is one other person before whom Amma wishes to flaunt her feigned equanimity, and that person cannot, try as she might, ignore the brassy glint of Amma's self-righteousness or the rattling of her saber underneath her silk saree. What Uma can or cannot ignore is a great mystery even to Aasha of the ever-peeled eyes, for Uma, unlike Amma, is a master of disguise and dissimulation.

Why, only a month ago, they watched her in a performance so convincing that they were all afraid—yes, Appa himself shifted uneasily in his seat. They'd all wondered if it was Uma who was crying up on that too-bright stage, and not Masha, the second of the Three Sisters, whose name Uma had borrowed for three nights. Aasha alone was brave enough to ask out loud: "Is Uma crying? Is Uma really crying now, not bluffing anymore?" For her trouble, Appa shushed her, Amma pinched her thigh, and Suresh rolled his eyes. And after that point, Aasha knew what the others chose not to acknowledge: that Uma had borrowed Masha's name so as to be able to cry, loudly, in front of everyone.

The play itself is the root of Amma's latest grievance against Uma, the fruit on which her lassitude has been feeding, worm-like, for a month. For at the end of closing night, when Uma and the rest of the cast bowed deeply and gratefully, a boy in a blue shirt and bluer necktie stepped up to the stage with an enormous bouquet of pink roses in his arms, and Uma, in that tight Victorian bodice further tightened to highlight (rather pathetically, Appa considered, slouching with pity in his seat) what little cleavage she had, came forward to the edge of the stage to bend over and take those flowers from him.

At this, someone in the back of the audience whistled shrilly, a long and lewd whistle that attested to the regrettable thoughts everyone else shared with Amma.

Which thoughts she spoke aloud in the car on the way home, and afterwards, for days.

"Everyone knows," she said, trying to catch Uma's eye in the rear-view mirror, "the only reason you're so enthusiastic about this acting-shacting nonsense is that you crave attention. And not just any attention. You want attention from *men.*"

That was Amma's opening gambit in a game Uma refused to join. More accurately, it was, like many opening gambits, merely the latest gesture in a war that had been smoldering for years: it was in the distant era of Uncle Ballroom's regular visits to the Big House that Uma's allegedly insatiable yearnings for male attention had been fatefully and rancorously noted. Whenever Amma caught glimpses of certain clothes or expressions of Uma's these days, the idea of her concupiscence resurrected itself, buzzing and sparking like faulty wiring, shooting words into Amma's mouth and unbearable pictures — scenes of which she could only be ashamed — into her eyes. For a mother to picture her own daughter doing such things! And yet she could not help herself. Now this recent memory of a sleek-haired boy in blue spurred her on. Why couldn't she just ignore the girl, pretend not to notice who gave her flowers when, leave her to persist in her starry-eyed foolishness? According to all the other mothers she knew (with whom she never discussed this problem explicitly), that was by far the most effective cure for what they called Teenage Drama. Ignore it, and all the posing peters out.

But the rope that binds Amma to Uma, burning the hands of both, has a more twisted knot in it than other such ropes do. Amma is not merely jealous of Uma's youth, nor of the inborn wisdom that enables young women these days to float untouched above the mistakes of her own generation. Of course the sight of Uma confronts her mother with memories of her own dangerous naiveté a hundred times a day: but for the better-made clothing and the hands that attest to a liberally servanted household, Uma could be Amma twenty years ago. Stand her at the window just so, remove the effects of years of acting classes, the confidence in her shoulders, the proud tilt of her chin, and there before Amma's eyes is her younger self, gazing from the shutters as Appa's pea-green Morris Minor pulls up the driveway of the Big House for the first time.

Yet what truly torments Amma is that faint, flickering half-smile with which Uma charms men (any men: her own uncle, bus drivers, Mat Din, the roti man on his afternoon rounds); that dip-and-bob with which she gathered Gerald Capel's pink roses from his outstretched arms; the way she says hi—never hello—deep in her throat to the boys who telephone under the pretext of confirming rehearsal times or bus routes. In all of these graces billows something flimsier than an invitation but more substantial than a dream. That Uma, who knows so little about the end goal of her own flirtations, should nevertheless be leaning eagerly towards this goal—that she should be driven so blindly by base instincts—is unbearable to her mother. Unbearably stupid, unbearably off-putting: watching Uma fills her mouth with an actual fishy taste, cold and soft as the flesh of a spoiling cockle.

Only rarely is it also unbearably sad. When was the last time she felt protective of Uma? Not since Uma needed her. Not since Uma was a small child, before she began to read fat books and recite poetry and flaunt her genius. "I'm cleverer than my Amma," she'd announced to the Ladies one day, and though Amma knew then that Paati had fed her this poisonous idea, it had made no difference; Uma was forever addicted to its sweet aftertaste. How can you feel protective of a child who yawns with boredom in your company, who rolls her eyes at you at six and mocks your lifestyle at ten? Your tea parties and jumble sales, she'd say, and for all she had Amma's bones and coloring, how much she looked like her father in those moments! Your charitable endeavors.

If you're so much cleverer than me, Amma can't help thinking now, *we'll see what sort of cards fate hands you. We'll see what fairy-tale life is waiting for you and your men.* The part of her that wants to see Uma slowly destroyed by an endless string of disappointments is not, in truth, so small. *Why should I feel sorry for her when she doesn't feel sorry for me?* It could be the family motto, this question, something to emblazon on their coat of arms, except that not one of them has noticed how often the others ask it.

Of course Amma's tide of distaste has had its brief turnings. Two years ago, when the old Uma began to fade, leaving in her place a distracted, nail-biting hummer with hooded eyes, Amma did feel a twinge. *What happened, Uma? What's wrong?* But she could not bring herself to speak these questions—no, she and Uma would never talk like that, it was inconceivable—and soon they were submerged by rhetorical ones. *I thought you were so strong and happy, I thought you didn't need anybody but your grandmother and your father, now what happened?*

The sharpest twinge of all, an old agony that Amma still struggles to smother, predates Uma's transformation. To quell the guilt that thins her saliva like tears at the memory, Amma must, even now, lie down and close her eyes, and still a certain homemade play performed on a Saturday afternoon in 1978 will not leave her alone. The play had followed a long period—two weeks? three weeks?—during which Appa had come home perhaps twice, and then unseen in the night, leaving in the morning without speaking a word to any of them.

"Can't you shut up?" Amma had said one day when Suresh had made a joke at the tea table after she and the children had sat in silence—the children blowing on their hot drinks, munching their biscuits, arranging their crumbs into neat piles; she staring at the wall behind Uma's head—for twenty minutes. Suresh! The only one who'd been sure enough of his place in the world to speak at all on those long afternoons, and that was what she'd said to him. "I'm sick of your voice," she'd spat into her teacup. "Why don't you tell your jokes to your Appa?" But when she'd looked up, she'd caught Uma's eyes, not Suresh's.

One week later, the children performed their play in the sitting-room. They'd rehearsed every day that week; they'd made the programs, the tickets, everything, all under Uma's expert supervision, for she was already the drama club star. "You have to dress up nicely to come," Aasha had informed them. "Going to a play means must dress up nicely, isn't it?" Grudgingly they'd obliged. Appa had read the newspaper downstairs while Amma got dressed, and when she came downstairs he'd gone up to put on a long-sleeved shirt and tie. She knew he did this to be decent, to save them both the embarrassment of having to enthuse about their dear little ones like normal parents, for it had been weeks since Appa had spent a night at home, and months since they'd had dinner as a family. For them to have to pretend to one another would've been odious; bad enough that they had to sit next to each other on the flowered settee in the sitting room, in special reserved seats Uma had adorned with tissue-paper streamers.

The purpose of the play became painfully clear as it progressed. Its title was *Clara Finds a Family;* it told the simple (though slightly absurd) tale of Little Orphan Clara's search for suitable parents. Having placed a classified advertisement in a local newspaper, Clara sat under a tree in front of the town hall auditioning potential candidates, all based on characters in Uma's favorite books. Aasha played Clara at her own insistence, although many of the lines were so long for her that Suresh had to do a voice-over from behind the curtains (an area known as The Wings for the duration of that afternoon). The first candidate was the Duchess from *Alice in Wonderland* (accompanied by a shriveled Duke all Uma's own), rejected for her predilection for corporal punishment; then Little Nell's grandfather (unacceptable for his history of bad financial decisions); then the bereft Mayor of Casterbridge ("Just because you sold your own family," Clara scolds him, "doesn't mean you can have me"). The next candidates hit closer to home. An aristocratic English couple, distinctly Wodehousian in diction, were curtly informed, "All you know, sir, is your club, and you, ma'am, care only for tea parties and fine hats." Little Lord Fauntleroy's mother fared better — Clara took an immediate shine to her kind eyes — but at the last moment Clara shook her head sadly and said, "No, you're so sad all the time you'll never pay attention to me."

Bolt upright in her seat, feeling Appa shift beside her and cross and recross his legs, Amma hated Uma intensely in that moment, this too-clever daughter of hers who didn't know or didn't care what injuries her rapier inflicted on soft flesh — and then, in a second, as though some precipitating chemical had been added to the beaker, a terrible grief clouded that hatred. She couldn't sit through this play, she couldn't, but she must, or they would all know what she was feeling, she must —

And she did. There was one more pair of candidates, a farmer and his wife. They had no title, no country estate, no great ambitions, but they were simple and kind and good. They had nothing to offer Clara but a straw mattress, a bedtime story every night, and one patched dress that had once belonged to the farmer's wife. "Yes," Clara said — and this line Aasha did not forget or mangle — "yes, of course I'll go home with you!"

The play closed to resounding applause and a standing ovation (if an audience of two can constitute an ovation). There were shoulder-thumps for Suresh and friendly tuggings of Uma's plaits; then everyone sat down together and feasted on a tea party Lourdesmary had been commissioned to prepare for the occasion. But after all the same questions had been asked twice each—How long did it take you to think of all this, Uma? Suresh, how much time did you spend making those programs? Aasha, where did *you* learn to act like that?—they settled back to drink their tea and Milo and think their own thoughts.

Poor things, Amma thought then, *poor things!*

She was entirely correct: the children wrote and performed that play with the sole aim of shaming their parents into better behavior. They'd concluded, after her tea-table savagery, that it was up to them to try to fix all that was wrong in the world; a little initiative might work wonders. "Anyway," said Suresh, always the realistic one, "even if they don't realize what it's about, they'll still have to sit side by side and watch it. Then we'll say, See, we *did* make Appa sit and listen to our jokes! And after that we'll all have tea together. They'll remember it for a while. Appa will feel bad because we put so much work into it and he'll come home nicely for a few days, and that'll make Amma happy. Isn't it?"

Indeed, Appa stayed home the night after the play, but he went into his study and shut the door. And because they'd had all those curry puffs and cakes for tea, no one had dinner.

Uma remembers that afternoon just as clearly as Amma does. On her opening or closing nights onstage, she sees her parents in their front-row family-and-VIP-only seats and is immediately assailed by the image of them all dolled up in their sitting room. For on that day Uma and Aasha and Suresh watched an entirely different play, not just *Clara Finds a Family* from a different angle. This play-outside-a-play starred Amma and Appa, and demanded so much attention from Aasha that the poor child remembered almost none of the lines they'd worked so hard to drill into her. The children watched it from the corner of their eyes, and whenever they had to turn away, their skin burned with such fierce longing that new eyes burst open on their necks and backs, unblinking, begging, *Please like this, please. It's the best we can do. After this we can do no more.* But Appa and Amma could never invest themselves as fully in *Clara Finds a Family* as the children did in that other play: every hohoho, every tinkling laugh, every discomfited drawing in of breath or half second of fidgeting reminded them of the risks of their endeavor. Appa and Amma could fail to grasp their message, or worse yet, could secretly hate both message and messengers.

"Did they laugh?" Suresh asked that night after Amma and Appa had gone to bed.

"Did they cry?" Aasha asked. "Did it make them sad?"

"Ish, I don't know," Uma said, feigning impatience. "Everyone had a good time and now it's over. I don't know who laughed and who cried and who saw what."

But she did know, and these days she has much occasion to resurrect that corner-of-the-eye view of Amma's mercurial feelings that afternoon. First the anger — the way Amma had leaned forward an almost imperceptible inch, then leaned back to sit as still and straight as a telephone pole — and then the sorrow splashed across her face. The trembling chin, the downturned mouth. *You were sorry then,* Uma thinks. *You were sorry you'd been so rotten to us. Have you forgotten? Or did you only decide you had to be even more rotten because we'd made you feel bad?*

There are no answers but Amma's endless provocations, delivered with curled lip and flared nostrils, acidified tenfold since the closing night of *The Three Sisters:*

You know what you looked like when you took that boy's flowers? You think you looked like some fine lady, is it? Is that why you keep looking at the photo? Like a cheap floor dancer you looked. Like a — I won't say it, no need for your brother and sister to hear that word. I know and you know, that's enough.

Any man will do, isn't it? Any man looks at you and you're in heaven. With your own uncle also you were like this, what. We all could see what was coming. Now one pigeon-toed schoolboy looks at you with stars in his eyes and wah, you think you're Sophia Loren.

Suresh wishes Amma would shut up and mind her own business. Aasha wishes the same thing, in less vehement words. Because even though Uma rarely seems to hear Amma — and when she does, only smiles faintly and continues humming to herself — neither Suresh nor Aasha can shake their dread.

No no, Suresh reasons with himself, *we're just jumpy because bad things have been happening, so it seems like more bad things must be coming. It's not really true.* Uma has a shell so hard nothing can crack it, so thick-walled and shiny no one can see anything in it except themselves. It reflects Amma's schoolgirl petulance right back at her and leaves her feeling so foolish that soon, surely, she will surrender.

Then one day Uma does lift her head from her proof-copy photo of the curtain call (Gerald Capel offering up his flowers as if to a goddess, Uma's bosom shining like the promised land above the stage lights). She looks straight at Amma, who has just said, "I suppose if that kind of attention is the only way you have to make yourself feel good, then why not?"

"At least," Uma says, "I have a way to make myself feel good."

That is the day on which Amma announces her intention to host the next tea party.

Every day since then, the infernal tea party has crept closer.

Friday.

Saturday.

Sunday.

Vellamma spreads the Irish linen tablecloth, and a darkness falls over the house like a blanket of smoke. They can hardly breathe.

Amma's in her room doing her makeup when Chellam summons her from the foot of the stairs: "Maddam! Maddam! Paati calling!"

Amma comes out to the doorway of her room and stands there, the stairs making accordion pleats in her long shadow. Leaning on the banister, Chellam repeats her message:

"Paati calling, Maddam." Her voice droops with tears. The skin on her thin calves is dry and white-scaled.

"Ask her to take her medicine. Put some Tiger Balm on a handkerchief and give it to her."

But Chellam says she's already done all those things. Medicine, Tiger Balm, hot coffee. Paati just wants Maddam, that's all.

"Vasanthi! Vasanthi!" Amma can now hear Paati's hoarse shouting. Her voice rises high and then cracks hopelessly on each call, like the battle cry of a geriatric rooster.

Down the stairs a half-made-up Amma glides, her shadow slithering before her, molding itself to each stair. Across the sitting room, through the dining room, down the long corridor, the sleeves of her caftan filling like the sails of some long-ago merchant ship on a doomed voyage. They all feel her pass: Aasha, who stands just behind Chellam; Suresh, who's reading an *Archie* comic in the dining room; Uma, who is in the kitchen stocking up on provisions so that she doesn't have to leave her room during the tea party.

"I'm here," Amma says to Paati very softly. To Chellam she says, "Okay, go now. Go." And Chellam goes, glad to be released, entertaining delicious visions of Paati choking on her coffee that set the lump in her jaw throbbing like a war drum. In the back yard, she picks up a broom and sweeps the cement desultorily. Aasha climbs the stairs and sits on the landing.

"What now?" Amma says to Paati. "What do you want?"

"That stupid girl," Paati says. "I just wanted . . . Aiyo! Amma! Enna? What did I do?" A high whimper trails out from Paati's corner into the children's ears. A metal clatter cuts through that misty sound like thunder.

Chellam drops her broom in the dust.

Aasha hunches her shoulders up to her ears and pulls her neck in like a turtle. Beetle-browed, she begins to count the ancestors in the last row of Paati's wedding photograph. Some are tricky, because they're mostly hidden by the people in the row in front of them. Do they count as halves, then, or quarters?

In her rattan chair, Paati bawls like a small girl lost in a crowd.

Uma shuts three kitchen cabinets one after the other and makes her way back to her room, carrying a small bowl of cold sardine filling, a tin of Jacob's Cream Crackers, two small boxes of chrysanthemum tea, and (in her teeth) a packet of cheese. Out of the corner of her eye, Aasha sees Uma's legs pause on the landing. Slowly, Aasha's eyes travel up those legs, but just as they reach Uma's face it slams shut like one of Tata's old screen doors. A great rush of air as it slams, a bang at the end that makes Aasha jump. A locking and a bolting, and Uma's gone behind that face.

In Paati's corner her eversilver kovalai lies on the floor in a pool of coffee. Paati's wiping her tears with both hands at once, flat palms rasping the skin of her face like sandpaper. In trouble now. Shame shame.

"Chellam!" Amma calls. "Please come in and clean up this mess. Paati has spilled coffee all over the floor. I have to go and get dressed."

Chellam hurries back in to clean up the mess they've made, her Japanese slippers leaving light prints in the backyard dust.

Amma sweeps back up the stairs and into her room.

Suresh slips out to the corner shop.

Aasha climbs the remaining stairs very slowly, reluctantly, arranging both feet neatly side by side on each stair before moving on to the next.

Uma's door is locked, of course.

But Amma's is wide open.

Before her full-length mirror, Amma has slipped out of her caftan and into her silk petticoat. Now she fastens the hooks of her gold-threaded saree blouse from bottom to top: thief, beggar man, poor man, rich man. Always rich man: all her saree blouses have four hooks. She contemplates her reflection and fingers the teeth of her comb. Sunlight glances off her mirror straight into her eyes, half blinding her. She squints, blinks, looks down at the comb in her hands.

Her blue Benares saree waits on the bed; her accessories are laid out on her dressing table. The gold mother-of-pearl peacock pin for her shoulder. The earrings and bracelet of Rangoon diamonds. And on its long, long chain, a thousand facets in its teardrop body, the Burmese sapphire pendant.

The pendant once belonged to Amma's mother, in the days when she attended weddings and other worldly celebrations and had therefore taken pains not to look like a nobody. Just before Amma's wedding, her mother did not, as other mothers did, make an occasion of presenting her with the jewelry that would now be hers until she passed it on to her own eldest daughter. It was Amma's father who unlocked the jewelry safe, not out of any eagerness to give away the riches of his household, but because people would talk if his daughter went to her husband's house with nothing. "Aren't you going to give your daughter any of your jewelry?" he asked his wife, his voice failing to rise at the end of the question. "Take what you want," Amma-chi said. "All that is nothing to me."

Amma took only the sapphire pendant, because she had to take something; her father was waiting. Only one thing: this would pacify him, for all he wanted her to have was a nominal dowry. Too much and he would twitch and seethe. And then her two sisters would have to fight over what was left. She chose the pendant because once, long ago, when bright colors had been enough to delight her for hours — when a deep green bottle or a glass of ruby-red syrup had meant as much to her as this expensive object she now held in her hands — she had loved it. She no longer knew how to love things in that way.

Aasha loves the sapphire pendant with that same pure yearning, like thirst, though Amma does not know it; Aasha has given none but the smallest outward signs of her love. The pendant is like the inside of a snow globe, a whole world unto itself; holding it is like flying, or

swimming, or drowning without fear. A magical drowning, a welcome falling towards an ocean bed of mermaid castles. One day Uma,
lucky Uma, will wear this pendant around her neck before a two-sided
oval mirror in America. Sometimes Aasha wishes the pendant were
destined for her own bridal trousseau. *If only*—but she always stops
herself there, because truly, in her heart of hearts, she wants Uma to
have it.

Aasha leans across Amma's bed and touches the pendant with the
tips of four fingers, though she knows she shouldn't. In the mirror
she sees that Amma is still studying the teeth of her comb. She picks
up the pendant and watches it trap a sunbeam. Bright blades of blue
slice through the room; blue butterflies flicker on the walls and climb
up the white curtains. A single blue butterfly alights on Amma's face,
blue wings draped across her cheek. Amma starts and turns.

For a moment she bites her tongue. A cool wave fills her cheeks
and hands. *Don't,* she thinks. *Just look at her face.* Aasha, stricken but
tempted towards hope by this brief silence, holds her gaze.

Amma knows the games she should play; she's seen other mothers play them; she's played them halfheartedly herself from time to
time when Uma was a very little girl. But now when she remembers
all that—the referring to herself in the third person—*Amma feed Uma
now, okay? Amma coming, Amma going upstairs*—the nursery rhymes
and hangman and paper dolls, the sweaty weight of small children in
her arms—she feels as though she's been swimming underwater for
too long, her lungs stretched till they're transparent, the blood vessels
distorted like pictures on party balloons blown too full. One breath
and she will drown. She remembers, too, the morning she woke up
and reclaimed herself: *I am tired,* she said to herself then, hearing
Aasha whining to be let out of her crib. *I, I, I. Not Amma; Vasanthi.*
She relearned the contours of her name, touching its walls and beams
and doorjambs in wonder, but how insufficient, in the end, that liber-
ation has been! For here is this child grabbing at her life with its sticky
fingers, a child that had crawled out of her only six years ago, transformed in eight difficult hours from an internal parasite to an external
one. That innocent greed on her face, that's always the worst part.

Amma turns her face towards her open window and half chokes
on a lungful of heavy, floral air. Mat Din must be fussing with the
rose bushes. *I'm tired,* she thinks again, and of their own volition these
old words begin to spin, as words sometimes do between brain and

tongue, until they are a cyclone, a blurry, burning, dusty trap. If only, if only she could escape, but instead she shuts her eyes tightly and hears herself say, "Go away and leave me alone, Aasha. I'm tired of you. I'm tired of all of you. Leave me in peace."

Aasha drops the pendant on the mattress, turns around, and leaves. It's that easy.

FOR NINETEEN YEARS the Ladies have circled around Amma, grateful to have been selected for membership in this, the most exclusive of rich-wife circles in Ipoh. The roster has seen few additions since its original drawing up; the Ladies are all married to toplawyers or topdoctors, all coiffed by the same hairdresser, all (except for Amma) genteelly devoted to ikebana, cake decorating, and volunteer work at the Home for Spastic Children. They have never drawn attention to the petering out of Amma's hobbies, or asked her what she does all week between tea parties these days, for though they cannot say exactly how she occupies herself, they nourish suspicions (and sometimes more) of her unhappy home life.

Several times during the course of each Sunday afternoon, Amma is tempted to enlighten them. Without warning, in the middle of someone else's words or during a lull in the chatter, she finds the very muscles of her mouth forcing themselves apart against her will, forming an *Oh* or an *Ah* or an *Eh*, waiting to sneak a by-the-way past her, but she catches them at their tricks every time, and raises her cup to her parted lips, or hastily stuffs into her mouth whatever phrases she has pulled from the air to follow the escaped syllable. Oh — how are your renovations coming, Daisy? Ah — Jasbir, so nice of you to bring us all these jams from your U.K. trip. A close shave every time, and the unspoken confession lingers in her inner ear for the rest of the afternoon: *By the way, Leela, Daisy, Jasbir, Dhanwati, Latifah, Rosie, Padmini, Hema, Shirley, by the way, here's what I did this week. I sat at my dining table watching for my husband's car on the street, for eight hours on Monday, six on Tuesday, eight again on Wednesday, nine on Thursday — what? What's that, you say? No, no, definitely not all that exciting. I don't have any hobbies at all, you see. But my husband does. And it's his extracurricular activities that feed my imagination as I sit at that table every day . . .*

For several years now, the Ladies have been hearing certain entrancing rumors about Appa. In fact, a small faction of the tea-party circle meets Outside, as they put it (which merely means one or the other of their sitting rooms during the week, in addition to the regular Sunday gatherings of the whole group), to discuss these rumors. They have admitted neither the clandestine nature of these meetings nor their purpose out loud to themselves, but each of them deeply, inarticulately, yet reverentially understands both nature and purpose.

Their secret pity for Amma is a rich and oily delicacy; to conceal the unease in their bellies in front of Amma, they flatter her more frantically than ever. They enthuse over her clothes and her figure, her furniture, her china, the skills of her cook. But most of all, they dwell on what they believe to be her greatest comfort and source of pride: her children's genius, which they have charted assiduously for years. They know every milestone and each unreal feat: that Uma had read all of Dickens before she was out of her primary school pinafore; that Suresh beat children twice his age to win the overall gold medal in an international art competition when he was only eight; that little Aasha has memorized all of Uma's stage monologues just from listening at her door. (The discovery of this last achievement must be credited to the Ladies themselves: on her way to the bathroom to powder her nose one Sunday, Mrs. Surgeon Daisy Jeganathan overheard Aasha reciting Ophelia's "O, what a noble mind is here o'erthrown!" soliloquy under her breath on the staircase.) In the past few months they have needed the children's successes more than ever, for Amma's mood has darkened before their eyes. Oh, she hosts the tea parties as regularly as ever and goes through the expected motions, dressing up, putting her cook through her paces. But her veil is wearing out in patches, and she lets things slip: an unnecessary sneer here when someone inquires after her husband, a near snort there at Mrs. Dwivedi's commiserating sighs (*Oh, these toplawyers are so busy, Vasanthi, so overworked, I know*).

What a blessing, what a sweet, ripe blessing it is to the Ladies that Uma's departure for an Ivy League university approaches fast and glorious! They talk of little else these days: everything from the weather (*Just think how much colder it'll be in New York!*) to the local treats served for tea (*None of these Uma'll be able to get in New York, poor thing*) proves an exquisite segue to Uma's full scholarship to Columbia University.

Today the Ladies notice an unusual chill when they walk through the wide front doors of Vasanthi's sitting room. Outside, it's an oven-like afternoon; Mrs. Rangaswamy, who has had to drive herself on account of her chauffeur's stomach flu, has scorched her hands on her steering wheel, and Mrs. Surgeon Daisy Jeganathan's beaded clutch purse is as hot as a live coal from sitting in a patch of sunlight during her ride to Kingfisher Lane. So whatever it is that strikes each of them separately cannot be a chill. Is it a sound, perhaps, a faint hum, a loose blade on one of the ceiling fans? Is it a smell, a cold, harsh smell like Dettol or carbolic soap? Something's amiss in the Big House, and it's tripped even Vasanthi up: when she greets them with her usual bittersweet smile, each one notices a feverish gleam in her eyes. She's applied her lipstick carelessly, given herself a deep crimson mouth a little larger than her own, as if her shaky hands made it impossible to color within the lines. The Ladies' habitual flattery, already sweet on their tongues, melts and trickles down their throats in an instant. But as they stand fingering the tassels of their sarees, Mrs. Dwivedi's late arrival saves the day, and the game begins.

"Had to drop my Rajesh off for his maths tuition class," Mrs. Dwivedi pants, wiping the sweat off her brow with an embroidered cotton handkerchief she's extracted from the crannies of her generous bosom. Her midriff spills out between her peach-colored saree and her saree blouse, like a cream doughnut some impatient child has pricked with a fork. "Sooo long he was taking to get ready, what to do, these children nowadays? Even for tuition class must get all suited and booted. Going to study or to meet girls, I wonder." This exordium has afforded her just enough time to pile her plate high with treats; now the other Ladies follow suit.

"Yes," Datin Latifah offers, "our Hisham also giving us endless headache. Have to cancel our annual Paris trip next year, I think — exam year for him, you know? And he, I tell you, all the time playing the fool, football-crazy, hockey-crazy, anything but school-crazy, hai."

"We parents have no rest," Mrs. Jeyaraj concurs with a sigh. "Everywhere the same story, I tell you, every mother I meet has the same complaints — except you of course, Vasanthi."

"Really," Mrs. Surgeon Daisy Jeganathan says, "you don't know how lucky you are, Vasanthi. Your Uma, without opening her books also can get straight A's. Our children no need to dream of Columbia University also. By now Uma must be packing already, isn't it?"

Amma's mouth is full. She chews and looks around the room, but none can decipher her expression.

"Make sure she takes lots of warm clothes," Mrs. Rangaswamy says. "Even in September New York is like Antarctica already."

"And better you fill up her suitcase with cream crackers and Maggi mee and that type of thing," says Mrs. Chua, "and one or two cases of Brand's Essence of Chicken. She's going into pre-med, isn't it? Where she'll have time to cook? Brand's Essence of Chicken is very good, just open and drink and you get all your nutrition."

"Pre-med, yah, that's right!" Mrs. Bhardwaj says. "I almost forgot, man! It's like a fairy tale only. Pre-med in America, Ivy League some more — where our children can —"

"Actually," says Amma, setting her plate down on her pressed-together knees, "my great daughter thinks she wants to be an actress."

The Ladies twitter. Mrs. Surgeon Daisy Jeganathan throws her head back and grants this joke her late-night, bridge-party laugh, the laugh she generally saves for the tall tales of her husband's tipsy friends.

Upstairs, a door shuts sharply — not a slam, certainly not a slam. Just a decisive closing. Footsteps, firm but not particularly hurried, head down the long corridor above the Ladies' heads. And then a second set of footsteps, less firm and more hurried.

"Oh, didn't you all know?" Amma says in a voice to win an elocution contest. Resonant as a gong, each syllable diamond-hard, a voice that would make Uma's drama instructors proud. "You didn't know all this doctor-doctor farce is just to pacify us? You didn't know about my daughter's flashier plans?"

Upstairs, Uma steps into the bathroom but leaves the door open a crack. Not once since she hid her voice away has she done this; she's always closed the door, even if only to wash her face or brush her teeth. From where she stands, Aasha can barely see her listening face before the mirror.

"My daughter," Amma goes on in the sitting room, "thinks Hollywood is waiting for her with open arms. Because only one thing matters to girls nowadays. I'm sure you all know what that is, no? Well my wonderful Uma is no different. She'll be pursuing the most competitive degree of all. The M.R.S. Her main goal is to meet men, my dears. Here itself she has started; what more in America? Buying her warm clothes is one thing, Padmini. That all you don't worry, her father will buy whatever she needs. But getting her to keep her clothes on is another thing."

The Ladies adjust their hair and look at their watches. Datin Latifah breaks the crimped edge off one of her curry puffs and nibbles it down to a nub.

"Come now, Vasanthi," Mrs. Dwivedi is saying, but Amma will not be deterred; she looks at the Ladies' frightened eyes in their geisha-girl faces and is suddenly more aware than ever of how sick and tired she is of them, and of herself in their company. The exhaustion propels her, makes her sit up straight and speak clearly, fills her with a confidence she has not felt in years.

"Come now?" she says. "You mean to tell me you know my own daughter better than I know her? No, *you* come now, Dhanwati. Already I can barely control the girl. Some St. Michael's boy practically made love to her onstage after her last play. Once she's thousands of miles away what can I do? But it's all right, Ladies, it's all right. Don't feel you have to comfort me and console me. Frankly I couldn't care less. Once they're no longer under my roof it's their business what any of them does. Their father can deal with whatever havoc they play with the great family name."

Because it is only four-thirty, far too early for the Ladies to take their leave of Amma without appearing rude — and because, further, a great quantity of food remains to be consumed, including the spellbinding Black Forest cake from the Ipoh Garden Cake Shop — they mince towards other topics of conversation. Amma has perturbed, astonished, even shocked them, but the cake and the sherry in the fruit salad help them to pretend otherwise. They will have to find other unguents for Amma's wounds; they will have to overhaul their current strategy. And these examinations and investigations will be particularly delicate because they must never be named or addressed explicitly; without raising the issue in their Outside meetings they must, by the time they reconvene at Mrs. Surgeon Daisy Jeganathan's house next Sunday, have devised a new distraction. But for now they help themselves to cake and rum balls, and finger the Irish linen tablecloth in wonder, and remind each other of Miss Chan Sow Lin's Chinese Restaurant–Style Cookery Course at the club next week.

The two pairs of footsteps upstairs, however, cannot so easily forget what has been said downstairs. Quietly but firmly, Uma shuts the bathroom door and continues to study her face in that much-used mirror above the sink. How much introspection this mirror will have to witness in the coming months; how many furiously beating hearts will confront Fact and Rumor in its pristine surface! Uma's face is hot; her hands are cold. A row of tiny, barely visible pimples is beginning to form just below her hairline. *Just heatiness,* Paati would've said in the old days. *Drink some barley water and all your pimples will disappear just like that. Anyway, even with pimples you're beautiful, my Uma child, my kannu.*

But now Paati wraps herself in her own silky web of woes, just like the rest of them. Her blindless, first willful, now literal, protects her. She's abandoned Uma to the mercy of all those who want her to turn blue in this airless house. She doesn't even know what Uma's dreams are, and this is what's hardest for Uma to absorb: that Paati, who once promised her she could be whatever she set her mind on, *doctor lawyer singer painter anything also can, you name it you can do it,* now would not notice if she were married off tomorrow morning to a fat landowner from Mysore. Not that Appa and Amma would ever make such a straightforward move; not for them the poor man's methods of trapping their daughters. They have a façade to maintain; they have to be able to boast (in Appa's case) or shrug off compliments (in Amma's case) about their daughter's acceptance to an Ivy League university. They have to hide the narrow pathways of their minds. And there are other reasons, too, for Appa to ignore the fantastic tales Amma weaves to goad him and occupy herself. Uma knows nothing about Gerald Capel the rose-bearer, save his name; she'd never seen him before closing night of *The Three Sisters,* she has not seen him since, and she's not particularly interested. Oh, he has nice eyes and a strong jaw, but she is leaving in two scant months, escaping this fishbowl town for better things. Boys like Gerald Capel are for the girls who will stay and study practical subjects at local universities and rent double-story semi-detached houses in Kuala Lumpur and come back to Ipoh to visit their parents every other weekend. But *should* Uma, to satisfy a passing fancy or to spite Amma, be seen around town hand in hand with Gerald Capel this week and another boy next week and yet another the week after, what would Appa do? What *could* he do? He would mutter some derisory warning, his face as strained as if each word were a new boil on his tongue. He would avoid her eyes and hurry away to seek solace far from his difficult wife and his daring oldest.

Cowards, all cowards. What are these masked balls her mother hosts in her marble sitting room if not a sickening dance of cowardice? Each woman worse than the next, and her mother the worst of all: she doesn't even like the Ladies.

Uma blows a slow stream of air at her reflection, turns on the tap, and splashes cool water on her face. Outside in the corridor, her sister waits. Uma can hear the small shuffles of Aasha's stationary feet, her sniffs and scratches, her faint and patchy humming. She's trying to hum "El Condor Pasa," but the range is too wide for her, and she slips and stops on the refrain.

For a moment, Uma considers staying in the bathroom just to see how long Aasha will wait before she gives up. She could try out different hairstyles. She could take a nap in the bathtub. When she thinks of Aasha out there, she feels an insurmountable exhaustion, a weakness like thirst. Somewhere deep beneath this exhaustion trickles the old river of tenderness, almost forgotten. But not quite: *Poor Aasha*, Uma thinks, patting her face dry. *Poor thing*. But she won't let pity get the better of her. What a terrifying thing Aasha's selfishness is, a creature that needs no external sustenance: for two years Aasha has coiled her monochrome days around Uma's own like a python, hungered and schemed unencouraged.

In the corridor Aasha hums and stops, hums and stops. The familiar stubbornness creases her brow: she *will* get Uma to look at her, perhaps even to talk to her, she *will*. It's possible, after all—didn't Uma speak to her on the day they went to the library together, before the annual prayers in the Balakrishnans' garden temple? More than speak to her—Uma held her hand and walked with her, and it was almost like the old days. That morning proved that Uma does see her sometimes. And see her she must today; Aasha must make sure Uma sees her and hears her, yes. More than the regular stubbornness impels today's mission. The house holds its breath; that dreaded Something Bad for which she and Suresh have been waiting, towards which everything has been building up for months, is waiting to burst upon them, and its imminence is intimately, though abstractly, connected with the expression on Uma's face. Aasha could cover her eyes with her hands and hope the Something Bad will go away on its own, or she could face it head-on. She's made her choice. She hums all the way up to the highest bit of her song: *Away, I'd rather sail away, like . . .* And stops, and tries again.

In the bathroom, Uma undoes her loose knot of hair and redoes it, low on the nape of her neck. *Little Aasha. You'd use me like everyone else did if I let you, and then you'd grow up to be just like the rest of them. It's partly for your own good I've washed my hands of you.* She opens the bathroom door and pretends not to notice Aasha following her, soft-footed as a cat. But today Aasha is oddly bold: she slips in through the open door of Uma's bedroom before Uma has the chance to close it behind her. Still Uma doesn't meet her eyes. She sits on her impeccably made bed; she picks up *Finnegans Wake.*

Now Aasha's hands are on the bed, flat palms facing down. Now she is drawing her breath in to speak.

"Uma," she says, and already Uma winces at her breathless urgency. "Uma, don't listen to Amma. She's stupid. She doesn't know anything. You're going to be a famous actress and when your picture comes in the papers then she'll —"

Uma turns to her, her right thumb keeping her place in *Finnegans Wake,* her face quizzical. She seems at first to be searching for the words she needs; then, shaking her head, she says, "Can't you leave me in peace, Aasha? Go away and find something else to do, for heaven's sake. Mind your own business."

As if she's waiting for more, for everything Uma wants to say and all she herself can bear to hear, Aasha stands at strict attention, her face growing longer and longer, her lower lip more and more pendulous, before she steps backwards, very slowly, through the open door.

Uma turns back to her book, but her eyes remain on the same line for a long while. *Acting as if you're my guardian angel,* she thinks. *Such altruism. Like I don't know all you want is for me to stay here and be your surrogate mother. Feeling sorry for you never got me anywhere.*

Afterwards, in the commotion that follows Amma's discovery of the missing pendant, no one can confirm Aasha's movements that afternoon. Did she go looking for Suresh at the corner shop, or on the football field on Hornbill Lane? Did she fall asleep in the old velvet armchair in Appa's study, or on the floor behind the green PVC settee? Did she go outside to collect tamarind seeds? It's because none of them know that Appa questions her, and her crude, jumbled story falls apart.

"Yes," she says at first, "I saw the sapphire pendant on Amma's bed after the Ladies left and Amma changed her clothes and went back downstairs. I — I picked it up and looked at it, but then I put it back on the bed."

Then: "N-no, I took it downstairs. Just for a few minutes. I was going to put it back on Amma's bed, but then Dr. Kurian came and — and everyone was running here and there and I forgot. I don't know what happened to it. I left it on the coffee table."

"Want to lie also cannot lie properly," Suresh sneers.

And Appa almost pities her, this fumbling little fibber sitting before him with a cracked and trembling lower lip.

"Of course she took it," he says to Amma later. "She must have left it somewhere or dropped it. It'll turn up somewhere, no need for your hysterics, for God's sake. Already she's so frightened she can't stick to her own story. Ha! If you ask me we should enjoy that kind of innocence while it lasts."

But to pacify Amma, he punishes Aasha, piteously inept liar though she is. Kneeling on the hard marble floor, elbows balanced on the coffee table, she must copy Appa's line twenty-five times: *I will not take things without asking.*

The sapphire pendant never turns up. They cannot blame the servants: none of them were in that afternoon but Chellam, and Chellam, well, Chellam has the perfect alibi.

Amma had found her sprawled, unconscious, in the back yard after the Ladies left that afternoon. Squatting over her, cooing the only two lines he knew of a Malay folk song, was Baldy Wong from next door.

"Chellamservant die already," he said to Amma, rubbing his dripping nose on his knees. "Chellamservant sudah mati."

Chellam wasn't dead, of course. She'd merely fainted. She'd gone out to the yard to empty the Dutch Baby condensed-milk tin Paati was using as a spittoon during her flu. Perhaps she'd had some terrifying vision sparked by the Balakrishnans' nephew's grim prophecy. She'd been seeing shadows and hearing voices since the prayers in their garden temple, jumping out of her Japanese slippers at the slightest sound. Or perhaps she'd simply collapsed from the effort of keeping Paati quiet all afternoon so soon after her own ravaging fever. ("I don't want Paati coughing and gasping and carrying on while the Ladies are here," Amma had warned her. "Please." And *please*, Chellam knew as surely as the children did, meant business.)

So Dr. Kurian had to be summoned, "not for the old lady but for the servant girl this time," Suresh informed his receptionist on the phone, and in that bedlam, full of the slamming of doors and the shouting of orders and the insistent coughing and gasping and carrying on of an old lady outraged at being abandoned, Aasha took the sapphire pendant.

• • •

THE STREETLAMPS shone pale in the dying sunlight when Aasha went to stand before the monsoon drain that day, the pendant heavy in the pocket of her shorts.

A Kickapoo bottle bobbed along past her on the surface of the drainwater. A few feet away, an empty Twisties packet was snagged in a crack.

If the flickering streetlamp stops flickering for five seconds, she told herself, *I won't do it.* It was true, sometimes the lamp did briefly stop flickering, and didn't that prove — she was to tell herself later — that she had been willing to give Uma another chance?

Not just one chance, either, because when the streetlamp flickered on, more spasmodically than ever, she announced, to a ginger cat making its way along the edge of the monsoon drain: "If you get to the culvert without stopping, I won't do it." But the ginger cat, disdainful of ultimatums, stopped to wash its face two yards from the culvert.

Aasha took the pendant out of her pocket. Its blue light beamed all the way up to the main road and all the way down Kingfisher Lane, to the limestone hills and beyond.

The ginger cat paused in mid-lick and stared at her, its paw raised to its mouth.

She shouldn't do it, she mustn't do it, but — *leave me alone,* Uma'd said, just like Amma. No better than Amma. And worse still: *Mind your own business.* She'd been a baby, a stupid, slobbering baby, following people around, hoping for the old days. The old days were *gone.* Uma wouldn't care if she died. If an evil man came roaring down Kingfisher Lane on his motorcycle right now and kidnapped her, and did to her what Shamsuddin bin Yusof had done to Angela Lim, Uma would smile to herself and read her book. And then in September she would go to America and become famous, and one day she would marry a man with blue eyes and a chin dimple and Amma would give her the sapphire pendant. No one would remember Aasha or ever say a word about her. Uma wouldn't care that it was her fault that Aasha had gone out all alone to sit by the monsoon drain at dusk; she would get away scot-free, with her sapphire pendant and her white wedding cake.

They were just the same, Uma and Amma, two dragons, one on this side, the other on that side, snarling and snapping at Aasha. They'd ganged up on her; now they hated her more than they hated each other. They were in — what was that word? — in *cahoots.*

In a flash, Aasha climbed up onto the culvert and flung the pendant into the drain. It swallowed what was left of the daylight as it fell, growing brighter and bluer as the sky darkened. Then it sliced through the deep black drainwater and was gone.

Serves you right, Uma, Aasha forced herself to think. *Now you'll never have it. Serves you right.* But the effort stung the backs of her eyes, and even the ginger cat wasn't convinced. It blinked at her, slow and appraising. She sank onto her haunches and stared at the water. What had she done? She couldn't possibly retrieve the pendant now. It was on its way to Parit Buntar, Bagan Serai, Taiping, Shanghai, Canada, who knew? Who knew where the drain went? There was nothing she could do to fix what she'd done. Now there was no hope of Uma's ever speaking to her again.

At first, though, Uma barely seemed to notice the loss of the pendant, and considered the ensuing pandemonium as though from afar, throwing puzzled glances at Amma and Appa as the one ranted and the other reasoned. To look at Uma, they might have been bad actors in a play she'd been dragged to, or savages of whose rituals she did not approve. She stood in the kitchen doorway and ate cream crackers over a saucer as she watched them. Then Amma paused in the middle of her tantrum, as if she'd run out of words and tears and even strangled animal sounds, or realized, as tantrum throwers sometimes do, that no one could give her what she wanted. She looked up and saw Uma. "Good for you," she said to Appa, "you can be very proud of your children. Your youngest will be a champion thief and your oldest will be a high-class call girl. Such a wonderful example you've set for them with your own achievements."

"Stop it," Appa snapped. "That's enough."

"Why, afraid of the truth, is it? Your oldest daughter is standing there in front of you, why don't you ask her what she —"

But Uma was no longer standing in front of them; she'd dumped her saucer in the kitchen sink (thereby cracking it; the following day Lourdesmary would take it home with her, thanking Amma profusely for the gift) and fled up the stairs. Four pairs of ears heard her shut her door; one pair heard her climb into bed and breathe into her pillow as Appa and Amma resumed their bickering. Late at night, after everyone had come upstairs, Uma got up and opened her window. On the other side of the far wall, Aasha knew what she was doing as certainly as if she were sitting on Uma's bed watching her. She could hear it in Uma's breath and feel it in the wall they shared: Uma was staring at the flickering streetlamp. Counting the days until she could go away and never come back.

In the dark of her room, Aasha fought to keep her face above the black water of the monsoon drain. She was stuck, one sleeve snagged in a crack like that Twisties packet. She gasped and swallowed, spat and gasped; it was a losing battle, for she knew she'd drown. "I'm sorry, Uma," she mouthed into her cupped hands. "I'm sorry. I'll do anything. Just please don't go away forever and forget me."

But all she could do the next day was to follow Uma at a safe distance, as she had done every day for so long. Her eyes were red from her sleepless night. Behind the thin wall of her chest, her heart was pale and tired and almost still. She didn't hum. In the corridors, she didn't sniff or scratch. Her soft-footed shuffling was quick but strangely labored, as if she had a blister on the sole of one foot.

How could she ever make it up to Uma? How could she?

10

THE GOD OF GOSSIP CONQUERS
THE GARDEN TEMPLE

May 4, 1980

THIS YEAR, as always, the Balakrishnans begin the preparations for their annual prayers by appointing a date, on which they settle only after their painstaking consultations of the Tamil calendar culminate in a conference with a sweating, potbellied, ash-vermilion-sandalwood-smeared priest, who licks his lips and runs a thumb down a faded chart, who hmms, who sighs eloquently, who pulls distractedly at the silver hairs on his chest. At the end of the half hour for which Mr. Balakrishnan has paid, the priest offers him a choice of three equally auspicious dates for the busing of Mrs. Balakrishnan's nephew Anand into town and the celebration of Anand's annual trance.

Anand is a holy fool, a starry-eyed savant who cannot quite count to twenty although he is easily twenty-five years old, maybe even thirty. No one really knows or cares. At twelve, he dropped out of school in his small east coast town, after six years of writing his name over and over in exquisitely curled letters on every lined sheet of examination foolscap ever handed to him. He went to work in his father's spice mill, coming home dredged in turmeric and garam masala, sneezing spicy snot all over his mother's kitchen. One morning at the mill he dropped a pair of weighing scales on his foot, fell to the floor, and lay writhing in the spice dust with his head lolling back and only the whites of his eyes showing. He spluttered the name of his dead sister, Amuda; he bawled his family's apologies for pretending she didn't exist anymore; he promised her gold hoops for her ears, a stack of bangles, and a red ribbon for her hair.

The doctors called it an epileptic fit; the family called it a trance.

Anand sucked on the Polar Mint they'd given him and reserved judgment on the incident. "Did you have any pain?" his mother asked him, slapping his cheeks lightly so he'd look at her. "No pain, isn't it? No pain no nothing. That is what I'm telling the doctor. This is not a sickness, it's a gift of the gods." By that afternoon Anand was squatting on the floor of the mill as if the seizure had never happened, scratching his backside and drawing patterns in the golden spice dust with a stick.

But every year after that, Amuda's spirit has returned to him. She foams in his mouth. She dances naked in his head, and he, unable to resist her unspoken directives, strips off his own clothes and mimics her pelvic thrusts and gyrations. She demands trinkets and sweets, and, after the first three years, has made prophecies both glorious and ominous in exchange. She clamps his tongue and throat and balls in her tight fists, and thus thrice throttled, he speaks in her puling five-year-old voice.

Anand's fame soon spread to the extended family. Uncles and aunts, cousins and in-laws made the long express-bus journey to the east coast to make him offerings and await fortune-tellings in return. But Amuda would not possess Anand on request, so these relatives often left disappointed, a dozen bangles or a jumbo pack of Sugus sweets poorer and nothing to show for it.

It was Anand's rich Ipoh uncle, Mr. Balakrishnan, who decided that with God's help, Amuda could be persuaded to make more predictable appearances. After a long and involved discussion with the pot-bellied priest, Mr. Balakrishnan built the garden temple, a gleaming, blue-tiled, no-expenses-spared theater for Anand. An auspicious-day auditorium. The altar shimmers gold as daylight in the dark of night, confusing small birds and insects; before it stands a highly polished coin box for people to leave monetary offerings. In a corner grotto festooned with the flower du jour, a black deity swings his sword above his head in an eternal crescent moon. This is Mathurai Veeran, who feeds on green limes (according to ancestral wisdom) and the blood of field mice (according to Suresh and Aasha, who may at one time have asked Chellam), who howls at the moon and spits yellow stars, who tears at his own skin with his fingernails and grabs at the souls of little children as they pass.

Once the garden temple was complete, Mr. Balakrishnan was accorded (as guaranteed by the potbellied priest) the rare privilege of trances on demand (and by proxy, since it's not Mr. B. who howls for laddoos and does a mean Elvis impersonation in the buff once a year on a date appointed in advance, but his wife's nephew). Anand comes to Ipoh in style, in an air-conditioned express bus from the east coast, followed by a ride to Kingfisher Lane in Mr. Balakrishnan's baby-blue Volkswagen. The uncles and aunts and cousins and in-laws congregate at the Kingfisher Lane house for days before Anand's performance each year, and stay on afterwards; they sleep in the sitting room, on the kitchen floor, in corridors, on stained, sheetless mattresses and coir mats and spare rugs. Mr. and Mrs. Balakrishnan feed them all in the compound, on folding tables spread with newspaper tablecloths and banana-leaf plates. Food, lodging, and fortunes for the bargain price of fifty ringgit per family.

Appa and Amma have always attended the prayers as VIPs, free of charge. In private, though, Appa entertains the children with his reports of the festivities. "One of Balakrishnan's country cousins has been fomenting unrest among the masses," he informed them one year. "Encouraging them to ask why all they get for fifty ringgit is vendikai and kathrikai the man grows in his own garden. I heard Mrs. B. explaining that it's inauspicious to serve meat. Riles up the evil spirits something fierce. Or something to that effect."

"I have my suspicions about their auspicions," Uma had announced, quickly, eagerly. She'd been fourteen then, proud of her wordplay. Her father's daughter. And sure enough, Appa had chortled and slapped her knee. "Not bad, not bad," he'd said, even as Amma had muttered, "*Tsk,* don't simply-simply make fun of people. So they believe in all these prayers and spirits and whatnot, so what if it makes them happy?" But Appa and Uma had high-fived with their eyes, and Suresh had been jealous, as he'd so often been in the old days.

A week before the prayers, the Balakrishnans' relatives begin to arrive in rickety taxis and ramshackle vans, even a few Japanese cars and a single Volvo. (The owners of this last are not among the kitchen-floor/corridor-sleeping number, of course; they're staying with equally rich friends in Ipoh Garden.) In the Balakrishnans' driveway they dis-embark: shuffling grandmothers from Kedah, stylish young wives from Kuala Lumpur, a balding-yet-still-eligible bachelor from Johore Baru (who has come primarily to scout out the extended family's offerings in the potential-wife department, though he hasn't made his true purpose clear to anyone), revved-up and hopeful relatives, gossip-gravid and news-hungry relatives, relatives high with the euphoria of reunion, relatives already jealous of this cousin's new car or that one's son's straight A's, bangles jangling, tongues clucking, hair reeking of jasmine and coconut oil and Ayurvedic hair tonics, relatives swarming in from all over the country and overseas: relatives who immigrated to Australia in the '60s but happen to be in the country this year, relatives who married white people in foreign places and are home on a rare visit to their aging, disappointed parents.

"A star-studded cast as usual," Appa says, rubbing his hands in glee. "I have my suspicions about their auspicions, ohyesIdoindeed." He doesn't remember that the phrase was originally Uma's, and no one has ever reminded him.

The day before the prayers, Mrs. Balakrishnan comes to the Big House to extend the formal invitation, accompanied by Kooky Rooky. It's clear Kooky Rooky isn't ready to leave when Mrs. Balakrishnan is; she takes another Nestlé biscuit from the plate Amma has set out and nibbles on it with her two front teeth, turning it slowly around in both hands like a hamster. She darts Amma a shifty, sidelong glance.

"Well all right then," Mrs. Balakrishnan says. "You can stay as long as you want, Rukumani, but I got work to do. See you on Sunday, Va-santhi."

When Mrs. Balakrishnan has left, Kooky Rooky picks the crumbs from her lips and says, "Such a blessing it is for us to have Anand in the house. God's rare gift, you know?"

"I suppose so, Rukumani, why not, yes," Amma says uncertainly. She knows Kooky Rooky hasn't stayed behind just to extol Anand's virtues.

"In my family also," Kooky Rooky goes on, "we have one cousin with same type of gift. Beeeyootiful temple my Appa built for him in our hometown, you know, Auntie? Gold carvings, marble floors all. Even tourists were coming to see our temple, you know or not, Aun-tie? Vellakaran from England, Australia, Germany, all over the place."

On other occasions Kooky Rooky has told Amma tales of growing up on gruel and daily whippings in a Methodist orphanage in Taiping, of sharing a worm-ridden, earthen-floored hovel in Perlis with her fifteen siblings and her lowly night-soil carrier parents, of being the only daughter of a devout Catholic father, the caretaker of the grounds of St. Anne's Church in Bukit Mertajam. It's these glaring inconsistencies that earned her the evocative sobriquet, courtesy of Suresh, who sits at the table politely eating a Nestlé biscuit of his own, wearing a poker face that betrays nothing of the snort waiting, fully formed, in his nose. And it's these same inconsistencies that will limit people's sympathy for her in the months to come. "For nothing simply making up stories all the time," they'll say. "What for simply-simply lie when you have no reason? Now she knows, isn't it? God is always watching from up there. Today you steal from a beggar, tomorrow a richer man steals from you. Today you tell lies, tomorrow your husband tells you lies." In the privacy of their homes they will repeat these elementary, universal rules to themselves, as a comfort and a reminder.

But this morning the winds of the future do not ruffle Kooky Rooky's feathers. It's the past she's come to investigate, and once the formalities and the *amuse-bouche* fictions are out of the way, she turns her attention to her principal pleasure.

"Eh Auntie," she says, and her rodent's nose twitches and wrinkles and flares as her mouth opens wide for the vowels, "eh Auntie, is it true or not what I heard about your servant girl?"

Amma fidgets in her seat, torn between her reluctance to satisfy Kooky Rooky — whom she has reviled in the past as an untiring digger-up of gossip, a sniffer-out of scandal, and a feaster on other people's misfortunes — and her growing dislike of Chellam, which continues to acquire layers of varying color and density, like a rock formation: on the bottom, her diamond-hard anger at Chellam for stumbling upon secrets she has no right to discover; in the middle, her distaste for the girl's alleged dalliance with Uncle Ballroom; on top, the soft surface of everyday annoyances. It would be well within Amma's rights as lady of the house to complain to the neighbors about these last: the laziness in Chellam's very blood, the slipshod way she does her chores, her seemingly willful failure to remember Paati's daily pre-bath hot coffee. In contrast, the bottom layer, unyielding though it is, must remain hidden, for Amma knows it to be unreasonable and morally suspect: really, she shouldn't blame Chellam for her accidental discoveries (though she does, oh, how she does, and how can she help it? How could any woman withstand such a slap in the face from her own servant?). The middle layer is porous, thirsty, troubling: unappealing as Amma finds the idea of Chellam lifting her skirt for Uncle Ballroom, she's also insatiably curious about the transaction, and eager to hear other people's speculations.

True, she shouldn't encourage Kooky Rooky — look at her sitting there, rapacious, practically drooling — but for how long would Amma be able to hide the truth, anyway? Sooner or later people will find out, whether or not she says anything to Kooky Rooky today, for there has surely been some fishy business between Chellam and that good-for-nothing brother of her husband's. Really, why would a single man — a man itchy in all the wrong places and subject to the daily temptation of an eighteen-year-old maid at his mercy — bolt in the middle of the night and leave no forwarding address after staying for months? "Our upstanding uncle has once again won the top prize in his pet category," Appa said when Uncle Ballroom's sudden flight was discovered. "The Wham-Bam-Thank-You-Ma'am Waltz." In truth, it's been years since Uncle Ballroom did any waltzing at all, let alone won trophies. It's anyone's guess, though unsolicited hints will be provided for all, as to how Uncle Ballroom rewarded Chellam for her special services of extra ironing, laundry on short notice, late-night sandwiches when Uncle Ballroom stumbled in starving through the back door, and who knows what else in that room under the stairs. Two ringgit here five ringgit there he'd paid her, but perhaps he'd left her with a little something more difficult to dispose of as well. She's been looking waterlogged and puffy (at least Amma thinks so); she's been sucking on sour Chinese plums and dried ginger she must've bought with Uncle Ballroom's tips (which happen also to be the only wages her father doesn't know about and therefore doesn't seize for himself on his visits).

Amma sighs. Kooky Rooky leans forward. Suresh drags the plate of biscuits towards himself, and just as visibly as that plate moves, the balance shifts in favor of Kooky Rooky's needs.

"Oh, who knows," Amma says. "Could be true, who knows. Anything could be true, isn't it, Rukumani?"

"Yes," says Kooky Rooky. "Nowadays who knows. Nowadays people doing all type funny-funny thing. Even people from good family can go with servants. Very true."

"Nowadays anything can happen," affirms Amma.

"You think — but if she is — then what will happen, Auntie?"

"That all I don't know. That is her problem. If she doesn't tell us we can't do anything, isn't it? She made her own bed, now she can lie in it."

"But isn't that how she got herself into this mess?" Suresh says, and very quickly, because Amma's already drawing her breath in. "By lying in her bed and inviting other people to lie in it too?"

"Suresh!" says Amma. "Sitting here and listening to ladies' talk, like a pondan! What kind of man sits drinking tea and gossiping with the women, hanh? Get up and go and do your work! You're not a small boy anymore."

If he were a small boy — and how small? ten? eight? Aasha's age? — then would it be okay for him stay and discuss what Chellam's been doing in her (unmade, he would like to point out) bed? Suresh would like to know the answer to this question, but decides it's not worth Amma's wrath-for-visitors.

After he withdraws, Kooky Rooky sighs, leans back, and drags the biscuit plate back towards herself. As she nibbles on her fourth biscuit, her eyebrows rise slowly to her hairline.

"You know or not, Auntie," she says at last, "I think so it will be good if you bring Chellam also to the temple for the prayers. Sometime this type of holy man like Anand can make a person clean and pure again with his blessing. He will say some prayer over her head and she won't do that type of thing again. You agree or not, Auntie?"

Amma knows what motivates this advice: no benevolent desire to see Chellam cured of her alleged concupiscence for the good of all concerned, but an urge to get a closer look at the guilty one, the harlot herself, to study her face and hands and voice and gait for the horripilating evidence of her illicit adventure. *Well,* Amma says to herself, *if they want to look at her, let them look in public instead of coming and sitting in my kitchen in the hope of catching a glimpse.* To Kooky Rooky, she concedes: "Maybe so, maybe so. I'll ask her and see if she wants to come. Who knows whether Anand can help, but no harm trying, it's true."

That is how Kooky Rooky comes to carry a bulky load of gossip back to the Balakrishnans. Today she doesn't even give herself the time to nibble through the five Nestlé biscuits she normally allots herself. Stooped with the weight of her news, she scurries across the street. She kicks her slippers off at the back door and runs straight to Mrs. Balakrishnan, who is pounding onions in a mortar. "Auntie,"

Kooky Rooky says, "it seems the Big House servant girl and Lawyer Uncle's brother were really doing some monkey business. She was eating from his plate, he was massaging her legs. No wonder he running off in the middle of the night like that. I think so something must have happened, isn't it?"

Mrs. Balakrishnan interrupts her pounding, pestle in midair. She wipes a drop of onion-loosened phlegm off the tip of her nose with the back of her hand and says, "*Tsk*, Rukumani, mind your own business once in a while, can or not? What the Big House people do is not for us to worry about. They can do anything and get away with it. Today they make five servant girls pregnant, tomorrow it'll be all hush-hush. That type of filthy-rich people can cover up anything. You'll get yourself into trouble only poking your nose into their lives."

Kooky Rooky, shamefaced, slinks upstairs to find a more willing audience for her discovery, though her prickling ears have caught that word, *pregnant,* and held on to it. Perhaps she can interest one of the fifteen or so bored housewives from Penang and Kuantan and Singapore, currently gathered in a circle around the TV, cracking ground-nut shells with their teeth and fanning themselves with palm-frond fans (if they came prepared) and folded-up pages of the *New Straits Times* and the *Tamil Nesan* (if they did not).

By the end of that week, all the housewives, all their husbands, and most of their children know the details (and possible results) of Chellam's dalliance with the ludicrous, onetime-ballroom-dancer brother of Lawyer Rajasekharan across the street. Each behind the other's back, Mrs. B. and Kooky Rooky have been elaborating on the spare tale (which may be summarized as: Nowadays Anything Can Happen). In front of each other they've been stringing jasmine blossoms and marigolds and limes into garlands for the idols in the temple; they've been stirring milk and ghee in vats over coal fires to produce enough sweetmeats for three hundred guests; they've been laying out banana-leaf plates on the floor in never-ending rows — kitchen to sitting room, sitting room to porch — to feed the children in shifts at every meal while the adults eat at folding tables outside.

Not long after Anand disembarks like a statesman from the Volkswagen to be garlanded immediately by five different women (two marigold garlands, two jasmine, one mixed), he, too, hears about the dirty business between the skinny servant girl across the street and Lawyer Uncle's black-sheep brother. It doesn't take long for him to piece together, before he ever lays eyes on her, the star of the snatches of gossip that flutter around his ears and the snippets that fall at his feet. What he fashions out of them is not a quilt, not a collage, but an unambiguous portrait with an equally unambiguous caption. Chellam is evil incarnate. Chellam is a whore, a dirty girl, an itchy woman. Chellam might be carrying a bastard child in her belly. He's sure he won't like her when he sees her.

He may be five foot ten, the tallest of his many cousins; he may have hair on his chest and even a single silver hair on his head that no one has discovered yet, but Anand has a mind eager for cartoon heroes and villains. Without his clean distinctions he would not be able to function; if someone came to him now (a necessarily hypothetical soul, for no person truly exists who can see or say all this clearly) and said, "Look, this servant girl, she's not all bad; she was kind to those lonely children when they needed her; she took them by the hands their oldest-eldest sister had left dangling and taught them useful tips they'll never forget. And listen, she tried to do a good job with the old lady in the beginning, but who would keep doing a good job when their wages were going towards their father's toddy shop bills, and who wouldn't—" Well, if someone had said all this to Anand, he would've plugged his ears with his pointer fingers and recited his Tamil alphabet at the top of his voice, or buried his face in one of the plump pillows on the king-size bed he's been given in the Balakrishnans' house and covered his head with the other, because he doesn't want or need such complications in his universe, and his delicate constitution is simply not up to them.

For three days, while Mrs. Balakrishnan hand-feeds him extra-sweet neyyi urundai and jelebi and coconut-milk appams with egg in the batter for extra-crispy crusts, Anand feeds his hatred for the unseen servant girl with the extra-sweet gossip his sticking-out ears detect. *Rubber-estate girl,* he thinks, taking entirely too much pride in this contemptuous formulation, for not only is it a hackneyed insult (visit any school playground, Anand; listen to what rich girls call poor girls on the bus; ask anyone to caption a picture of a young woman with coconut-oiled plaits and unfashionable polyester clothes), it's been silently lobbed at Chellam before, by minds much younger than his just across the street. *Tapper's daughter,* Anand adds with some satisfaction. *Doing shameful frontside-backside games with old men.* Because Anand, though celibate by default (who would marry a primary school drop-out who froths at the mouth and strips naked in public once a year on a preappointed date?), once caught a glimpse of a pirated porn film his father was watching while his mother was out visiting relatives, and that blurred, flickering image of frontsides and backsides continues to inform his perception of Things Bad Women Do with Bad Men.

THE ONLY TRUE MIRACLE that occurs on the day of the Balakrishnans' prayers goes unnoticed by Anand's captive audience. In fact, it begins before his performance, at ten in the morning, when Appa is reading his morning paper at the breakfast table, Aasha is reading the purloined comics section in the sitting room, and Amma has just informed Chellam that she is invited to the extravaganza across the street.

"Really, Maddam?" Chellam is saying. "Really I can come?" And her eyes flash, for all week she has smelled the ghee sweets frying at the Balakrishnans', and this morning she saw young girls in bright pavadais rushing about with trays of flowers and bananas and coconuts and betel leaves. Just like a wedding it looks to be, and it's been years since Chellam has attended anything resembling a wedding. Added to the promise of ghee sweets and front-yard feasting under a tent is the peculiar allure of Anand's gifts. Perhaps he will predict her own future, if there's time, if the lines aren't too long and the crowds not too vicious, if they let her near him . . .

"Thank you Maddam thank you," she says. "I bathe and put on my saree and come."

No sooner has she spoken these words than Uma descends the staircase, her hair pinned up, her school bag slung on her shoulder. In the kitchen doorway, she brushes past Amma and Chellam to get herself a glass of water.

"What are you doing, Uma?" Amma smiles almost encouragingly, as if she were asking the question of a child whose crayon drawing she can't interpret.

Uma drinks her water first, the whole glassful in one gulp, then puts the glass in the sink. "I'm going out," she says. She folds her arms and looks at Amma.

"Going out? But Chellam is coming to the temple prayers, and Suresh has gone fishing with Surgeon Jeganathan and his son. Aasha and Paati can't be left alone at home all day."

"You'll only be across the street," Uma says. "You'll see if the house is burning down."

In the sitting room Aasha pouts at Alley Oop's antics. *If the house is burning down.* Uma says it without batting an eyelid, just like that, like she's talking about something she saw on the evening news. Is she imagining it as she stands there with that half-smile of hers? Is she picturing Aasha cornered by the building-high flames, small and scared at an upstairs window? Is she thinking, *Good riddance?*

"It's not a question of fires and landslides and floods," Amma says. "Chellam can check on Paati every half an hour to take her to the toilet, no problem. Paati just sleeps all day anyway. But one doesn't leave a six-year-old child on their own in the house. What if—"

"Then," Uma says, "ask Aasha to come with me. I have to go to the library. My books are already overdue. She's old enough to walk to the bus stop with me."

At this, Amma looks at Appa, who fails to emerge from behind his newspaper. She looks at Uma, who waits, arms still folded, and at Chellam, who has busied herself with peeling the onions for Paati's lunchtime upma in order to stay out of these delicate negotiations. No one will acknowledge the miracle that has just taken place, no one but Aasha, who acknowledges it silently but intensely, in communion with Alley Oop, Dagwood Bumstead, and Brenda Starr. *How many times,* Aasha asks them, *has Uma said* Aasha *since—since she stopped friending me?*

Brenda Starr, reporter extraordinaire, has the honest, unsensationalized answer: *Probably less than three.*

And how many times has she taken me anywhere on the town bus with her?

Alley Oop, caveman that he is, is brutish, merciless, and quick: *None. Zero, kiddo.*

In the kitchen doorway Amma, a little breathless, says, "Well, I suppose . . ."

"I can't be waiting all morning," Uma says. "Aasha! Come then. Put on your shoes."

And that is how the greatest miracle of the year unfolds, hours before Amuda-the-unappeased stakes her scheduled claim over her brother's underused body. No law of nature or history can explain the practiced ease with which Uma takes Aasha's hand as they walk down the long driveway, nor why it feels so natural to Uma, yet tingles the skin of Aasha's neck and arms (those stubborn rashes that never quite surrender!), presses her lips together in a solemn line, and sets her heart a-racing so fast it precedes her down Kingfisher Lane, a small red thing tumbling over itself two feet in front of them, tripping on pebbles and rocks and leaves, each of its dull thuds begging *Please don't step on me please please be careful please.* And here is additional proof of the supernatural forces governing the universe this bountiful morning: though Uma neither sees nor hears Aasha's sparrow-sized heart, her feet just miss it with each step. Just barely.

So spectacular is this scene that it lures even Mr. McDougall's daughter back to the Big House, where she hasn't been seen for months. She shimmies up the tamarind tree to watch the sisters' progression with undisguised raptness. *Hello,* Aasha's tongue says—stealthy, busy as a worm behind her teeth in her closed mouth—*welcome back!* Aasha will not jeopardize the morning's miracle by speaking these words aloud, as fervently as she has hoped for Mr. McDougall's daughter's return; she will not even let Uma see her lips move. Stop it, Uma would say, stop your nonsense, and then the day would be ruined. If choose she must between the glorious good favor of her sister and the rekindled affection of her ghostly friend, Aasha chooses the former. Mr. McDougall's daughter will surely be back; she needs Aasha. To repeat her story to. To see herself in. To be fed crusts and crumbs by.

Even now, despite Aasha's half-snub, her jealous pink mouth whispers: *Lucky Aasha. The only time anyone ever took my hand like that was at the mining pond, and that was only to . . .*

But there Aasha stops listening. She loves Mr. McDougall's daughter's story for its sadness, its drama and color and lessons, but not this morning. She will not brook any comparison of this miraculous excursion with that ill-fated one, and wants no dark thoughts clouding this perfect morning.

Sorry, Aasha whispers inside her mouth. She knows she's already been forgiven.

On down Kingfisher Lane they stride, Uma and Aasha, hand in hand in the here and now. They turn onto the main road and pass the corner shop, with its stacked tins of Nestum and Horlicks, its clear plastic bins of Kandos chocolates and dried Chinese plums. Heat rises from the road in shimmering waves, as in a TV dream. Uma says nothing, nothing at all to distract from the day's soundtrack: sparrows' chirps, Cantonese love songs from someone's distant Rediffusion-tuned radio, the rumblings of lorries and schoolbuses and factory buses. But between Uma's soft, dry palm and Aasha's small, sweaty one is a glass egg growing heavier by the minute with the things they do not say. *Remember when — ? And you let me — And we sat on the swing and — That was what you sang. And this is what I thought the words were. Which made you laugh. And then we went inside and you made us sardine sandwiches on Sunshine bread and drew me a pink rabbit with cartoon eyes and a bow tie. Why do you — ? I wish I didn't have to —* This is how Aasha knows the glass egg is as precious to Uma as it is to her: for fear it will fall and shatter on the hot tar under their feet, she holds Aasha's hand more and more tightly, not letting go even when they get to the bus stop and sit down on its oily, blue-tiled bench to absorb all its disconnected confidences (on one wall alone: *Azmi and Yuhanis forever! Jeya LOVE my dick. Shireen Sexpot brest size SO TOO BIG*) and all the promises of its peeling advertisements.

Even as the number 22 bus jolts and rattles its way across town, farting black smoke that plunges trailing motorcyclists into dangerous coughing fits; even as Aasha watches a lone baby cockroach, still nakedly white, creep from one end of the window ledge to the other; even as they get off in front of the library to find themselves engulfed in a throng of factory girls (all murmuring and giggling and reeking of coconut oil, all skinny, all Indian, because, as Appa has oft explained to all who will listen, the Malays get all the government jobs, the Chinese have their businesses, and the stupid doonggu Indians are left empty-handed to slog in the factories and ditches and rubber estates), Uma clasps Aasha's hand tightly in her own.

On Kingfisher Lane, Anand's trance is in full swing by the time Uma and Aasha are in Children's Fiction, Uma pulling *The Wind in the Willows* off the shelf, handing it to Aasha, saying "Here, take this one," with a flutter of eyelashes some might interpret as impatience or distraction or dust in the eye, but into which Aasha reads a repressed, perhaps bashful, tenderness.

The garden temple is abuzz with delirium. The air is thick with fragrant smoke; behind the altar Mr. Balakrishnan's five different camphor flames crackle and hiss. This afternoon the heat seems to have surpassed all limits in living memory. "Not even a bit of breeze," the old ladies grumble, fanning themselves with cotton handkerchiefs and squinting belligerently at the sky, challenging it to produce the finest shred of raincloud or the faintest darkening over the horizon. Bare midriffs wilt and droop like old tire tubing. Jasmine and marigolds hang limply from greasy knots of hair. But Anand's performance more than annuls the heat's depressive effects on his audience's spirits. After the customary prelude — the buckling of his knees, the rolling back of his eyes in his coconut-heavy head — he's been doling out pieces of his five-year-old sister's mind to deserving parties left and right, not just those who have requested them. "Eh Govindamma," he's advised one aged aunt, "no more beating your poor husband with the broomstick! When he dies next year then you'll be sorry." And to a cousin too smug about his foreign-returned status: "Aiyo yo Kanagaratnam! There's a nice big heart attack coming for you in five years' time! Then will you be so proud of the diploma and the thirty kilos you brought back from Am-ay-rica USA?" And though no one in the crowd is immune to the comedic overtones of these unsolicited prophecies, solemn expectation still pervades the smoky air. Clearly little Amuda's spirit is in an unrestrained mood today. Will there be an incident, a fight, a fainting spell?

A vague line forms in front of Anand as Mrs. Balakrishnan stuffs laddoos and jelebis into his mouth to keep him happy. Mothers and grandmothers, worried uncles responsible for their dead brothers' children, fathers of marriageable daughters, all craning their necks and subtly jostling one another. But as greedily as they covet Amuda's auguries — every year they spend the evening after the trance jealously comparing the length and complexity of her recommendations to each one of them — they are also a little nervous. Which of them will she single out for ridicule? At whom will she spit bad news about which nothing can be done?

Anand rubs his eyes absently as he answers their questions, whining a little as if he needs a nap, and his suggestions are fit for playing doctor or throwing a doll's tea party:

— Boil durian seeds for eight hours while you sleep. When you wake your sores will have disappeared.

— Grind ginger with nellikai and spread the paste in your niece's armpits. She'll never fall ill again.

— Make your son collect his own urine for two weeks, spike it with saffron, and take his morning baths in it before he sits for that entrance exam.

Finally only three people remain in the queue: an old woman whose arthritis has left her lame, Kooky Rooky, and Chellam, who stands off to one side so as not to offend anyone with her presumptuousness. She's not part of the family, after all, or even a true invitee. She may not even be allowed to ask her question. But as Anand studies the old lady from head to toe and tells her to put twenty candlenuts under her pillow, Chellam gathers her courage in meager fistfuls and wonders: What if—

What could her future possibly hold? Once she'd thought: more Big Houses after this one, more fractious old ladies with weak bladders and bowels, more trouble and less money. When she got to be an old lady herself, she'd move into the government old folks' home to eat plain rice porridge and shit in drains until she died.

But then Uncle Ballroom had arrived, and along with his five-ringgit-ten-ringgit he'd also handed out hope. Perhaps she would be able to save up for those spectacles after all, if she was clever and hid this side income from her father, if she got her eyes checked at the government hospital and chose the cheapest frames in the shop. And when Uncle Ballroom had left, pattapattapatta in the middle of the night just like that, and the snarling had begun, and the whispers, and the looks, that tiny seed of hope had sprouted within her and flourished in a most illogical way. For even in the best of possible worlds, what could a pair of cheap spectacles lead to? Still, and though she hasn't broached the subject of the eye checkup with Amma, they have become a symbol of greater things. What if? Don't servant girls get married sometimes? Even the ones whose fathers are too drunk to arrange their marriages with factory boys or road workers? Couldn't she meet someone while out on a Sunday errand, at the corner shop or the market, at the appam stall or the roti canai stall? She's young; she can cook and clean and sew and have babies. There must be some man, poor or ugly or previously married, who would settle for a wife like her. Who would at first merely take pride in rescuing her and then, maybe, grow fond of her.

She waits patiently, already clearing her throat, trimming and smoothing her question in her head. They probably won't let her ask more than one. She knows what they've been saying about her; she's noticed the way the women draw back from her, huddle like chickens in the rain at the sight of her, and pull their pallus close around their shoulders so that no part of them accidentally brushes against her. The children shy away from her too, though they can't stop themselves from staring. And now, to make matters worse, people are getting hungry, their eyes wandering towards the long tables spread with newspaper and banana-leaf plates, their noses raised to sniff the ghee-fed air like dogs. She's an inconvenience — no, worse, she's a curse, because they're probably worried her presence will taint this auspicious day. Maybe she shouldn't take up their time; maybe she doesn't have the right. These people don't need another reason to hate her — but no, never mind. She must ask her question, she *must*. Suddenly she's as sure of what the gods are waiting for as if they'd spoken to her: a small show of courage, a nominal attempt to stand up for herself, and they will all rally around her. Ganesha with his protective trunk, strapping young Murugan, Mathurai Veeran with his gleaming blade raised to scare the snarlers and the whisperers into silence. They will color her future orange and gold; they will send the news of it spiraling out through Anand's mouth.

Kooky Rooky's turn comes first, because a paying boarder ranks marginally higher than a servant girl. Kooky Rooky leans towards Anand, tucks a hank of hair behind her right ear, and squeezes two questions into her one turn: "Tell me, will my mother have good health in the coming year? And when will I bear a son?"

Anand grins and tugs at his earlobe. "Sons all your so-called husband got plenty in his other house," he says. "I don't think he wants any more. Just ask him to share one or two with you. And your mother's dead, don't lie to me, you goat. You lit her funeral pyre yourself five years ago."

A fat, fair woman standing near Kooky Rooky covers her shocked mouth with the pallu of her saree. An unmistakable titter rises from the back of the crowd.

"Okay okay," Mrs. Balakrishnan murmurs, "don't worry, don't worry —" But before she can say more, Kooky Rooky has hurried away, across the garden and through the front door of the house (and then upstairs, where, after a brief cry into her pillow, she calls her husband at his hotel in Penang, only to find him not there).

In the garden temple Mr. Balakrishnan claps his hands and says, "Lunch will be —" And that is when Chellam steps forward, her bare toes curling on the hot cement. In one shaking hand she clenches a shiny twenty-sen coin for the coin box. She searches Anand's face. He licks his thirsty lips and pouts. *I don't like you*, he thinks. *Anyone can see you're a dirty rubber-estate prostitute. And your saree's ugly.* Then, without warning — so quickly Mrs. Balakrishnan gasps to see it — he grabs Chellam's fist, uncurls her tight fingers, and snatches her coin. He squints and scowls and breathes on her, too close, so close she can smell this morning's sweet rice and all the laddoos and jelebis and neyyi urundais fermenting on his breath, and all she wants to do at the sight of his squinting, glinting eyes is to turn around and walk away, back to the Big House, to clean up after Paati's latest accident and re-sign herself to an unchanging future of brown stains on white cotton, of veins that tie themselves in knots from too much scrubbing in too-cold water, of meals made up of other people's leftovers — chicken necks, backbones, bishops' noses, crusty rice and fibrous stems — of narrow beds in dusty rooms when you're lucky, and coir mats on cold floors when you're not, of unexpected tasks on supposed days off, of maddams who think doing nothing will make them happy, of masters who therefore (and with great relief) deem you responsible for their wives' well-being, of their children who condescend to be your friends as long as no one's watching and you remember your place, and un-til such time as they no longer need you. Of, in short, eternal servant-hood. Its doors are wide open behind her; all she has to do is to back carefully out through them into the familiar corridors beyond.

But the gods, who only help those who help themselves, are wait-ing to see what she's made of. She digs in her heels. She lowers her eyelids and whispers her question so softly Anand can hardly hear it:

"When will I marry?"

For three long seconds Anand just breathes, calm and slow and deep, as if he hasn't heard Chellam's question and is still waiting. In the distance Chellam can hear the *slap-slish, slap-slish, slap-slish* of the caterers' wiping down each banana-leaf plate with a wet cloth. The tinkling of wind chimes and anklets. A P. Ramlee refrain from the Malay house down the road, whose inhabitants have drawn their cur-tains against this all-out display of heathen superstition.

> *O O jangan tinggal daku*
> *O dewi O manisku*
>
> (O O please don't leave me
> O goddess, O my sweet one)

She lowers her shoulders, stands tall, prepares to repeat her ques-tion.

Then Anand covers his face and giggles. He rocks back and forth, his mirth gaining momentum, threatening to topple him. He throws his head back and guffaws, a slapstick laugh for outwitted villains and pies in the face. Then he begins his most vulgar dance to date: he grunts and gyrates and thrusts his pelvis at Chellam like a backup dancer in a Tamil film. But where are the lush green paddy fields? The coconut trees? The fat heroine with too much eye makeup and a beauty mark on her chin? Nowhere to be seen. There is only Chellam, chewing on her lower lip, holding back her frightened tears and waiting for little Amuda's answer.

Has little Amuda, too, heard the gossip about her? Have the gods also been savoring the rumors behind her back? For Anand is pointing at her with a crooked finger, and now he pulls at his hair and shrieks, "*You!* You dirty pariah whore, *married,* of all things! What kind of woman gets pregnant first and then looks around for a sucker to marry her? No, your only bridegroom will be four wooden planks and a roaring fire! For you the flames will be as high as my head, no, even higher, like a tree, like a tower, like a mountain! Yes, yes, he's coming for you very soon, that fiery bridegroom, no need to wait too long! Itchy whore that you are, you're impatient for his wedding-night embraces, aren't you? They're coming, they're coming, that mountain of flame will embrace you nicely, you'll see! But better tell your father not to spend too much on the wedding saree!" He picks up a pebble and flings it playfully at her shins. He spits flamboyantly in her face.

Silent, pressing their lips together, the crowd awaits further confirmation of their suspicions. Or (better yet) revelations, or (at the very least) a satisfying resolution. Will Chellam spit back? Will she wail or scream or lunge, and have to be led away?

No, it's Anand who's led away: before he can spatter more front-row spectators with his crotch sweat, Mrs. Balakrishnan grabs his elbow and pulls him across the garden and into the house, shushing him and cooing softly. She will give him a bath and a drink of barley water to cool him down. Then she will tuck him into bed and watch him fall asleep watching the ceiling fan. Mrs. Balakrishnan, barren for the twenty-six years of her marriage, loves having a five-year-old to look after once a year.

WHEN UMA AND AASHA walk through the front door of the Big House, Chellam has gone to bed.

"Pah, pah," Paati is muttering as they walk in, "how thirsty I am, what a hot day it is! Tell the girl to bring me a tumbler of water, I know she's back, call her, call her!"

"Enough of it," Amma says. "Be quiet for a minute. I'll go and see if Chellam—"

Then, as if the still-glowing miracle of the hand-in-hand trip to the library were not enough, Uma speaks. "I'll take Paati the water," she says in a rush. Amma darts her a sharp look and suddenly feels a little faint. The sweet warmth of infinite possibility floods Aasha's hands and feet, and oh, how overwhelming it is, this thought that Uma, the old Uma, might be coming back—cautiously, bit by bit, but nevertheless still coming—to stay. Even the specter of her departure for America has no time to dull this thrill, for already Uma is filling Paati's tumbler in the kitchen, and now she is striding down that long corridor, murmuring, in the measured monotone mothers use for sick toddlers, "Here, Paati. Drink."

Chellam doesn't stir from her bed for three days except for quick trips to the bathroom (during which Amma makes it a point to walk back and forth past the closed bathroom door, ears sharpened, breath held, already dreading the mess and the scandal and the call to the doctor, but she never hears anything, not a peep of pain, and admits to herself that anyway these bathroom visits are too short for the emergency measures she imagines). For now it's all new to them: Chellam's incessant sniffling in bed, the creaking of her bedsprings, the small, animal sounds that rise from her room and through the upstairs floorboards at night. The uneaten trays of food, the shallow, feverish breathing, the rancid-butter smell that wafts out from under her door. "What a wonderful thing," Amma says. "I hire a girl to be in charge of Paati and now I have to keep both of them on top of my head. Running from one to the other, bringing trays for Chellam and tea for Paati. One two hundred years old and the other in the family way or who knows what, both making my life miserable."

And Suresh smirks and whispers to Aasha, "Stupid Chellam. Acts like she's so clever sometimes, like she knows everything there is to know. Now look at her. One no-brains madman tries to frighten her and she locks herself up in her room and shits bricks. That's what these rubber-estate types are like, I tell you. Anything also they'll believe."

For the first day or so, Aasha is too giddy with happy memories and hope to care about Chellam's withdrawal. When Uma sits at the

Formica table reading her library book, Aasha sits opposite her reading hers, which is replete with small wonders: Toad of Toad Hall's cravat, Mr. Mole's underground eyes like embers, the Irish bargewoman who has a bargepole for not touching things with. Although Uma now sits across the table with her face shut tight, turning her pages and never looking up, this book is a golden thread between her and Aasha. They share its delights without speaking: in the privacy of her head, Uma, too, must be thinking about what a dear Toad is even when he's pompous, and how soft Mr. Mole's forehead would be to touch.

At least that is what Aasha believes for two days. Her rise in Uma's esteem is a physical ascent, as real as a journey in a hot air balloon. Each minute, each hour, that balloon expands and rises until, at teatime on the second day, Aasha bobs high above the rest of the household. After fifteen minutes spent rapturously chasing the purple bubbles on the surface of her Ribena — what a delightful game, for each time her tongue is all but curled around the targeted bubble, it rolls away to the other side of the glass! Oh, what a fine, fine day this is, how good life has turned out to be! Aasha's overinflated optimism tries to engage Uma in another game, old but not forgotten.

"Uma," she says, "which do you like better, tea or Ribena?"

It's a game Uma invented long ago, before Aasha could talk. Perhaps she invented it for Suresh. Or perhaps Paati invented it for Uma. For whichever child and by whomever it was invented, the game remained the same until Uma stopped playing it with Aasha. It has only one rule: the tea-drinking player is to pretend they like Ribena better. And one (unstated) objective: to assuage the feelings of inadequacy experienced by the player who has to drink Ribena because they are not old enough for tea. On this exceptional day, Aasha is in fact perfectly happy to drink Ribena, is convinced it's the best drink there is, but she's willing to pretend for the sake of the game, and she's sure Uma will be too.

In the old days, the question Aasha has just asked was Uma's cue to begin begging for the Ribena. Please, she would start out, just one little sip. I like Ribena better, but what to do? Big people have to drink tea. Pleeeease? She would squeeze tears from her eyes; she would fall to the floor; she would resort to such underhanded tactics as distracting Aasha in order to steal a sip of her Ribena.

But today Uma hasn't heard.

"Uma," Aasha says again, "do you like tea better or Ribena better?"

Uma sips her tea. Her eyes flicker, but only to the face of the clock behind Aasha.

Suresh takes a slice of cake from the cake plate and applies himself to crumbling it into a yellow pyramid on his serviette. Not a difficult task, because Lourdesmary took the easy way out this morning: this is cake from the roti man. These bloody Thulkans, Appa has oft pointed out in the past, without batting an eyelid they'll sell us cake as old as their grandmothers. He says it half admiringly, as though he wishes his own ancestors had converted to Islam and thereby laid claim to the famed frugality and business acumen of the Tamil Muslims. Suresh has inherited his admiration: as he draws out a long, oily hair from the center of his cake slice, he thinks, *These Thulkans. Instead of butter they put their hair in their cake. One shot use the same coconut oil for both.* But can he continue to ignore the delicate negotiations going on in front of him? Already Aasha is struggling to raise herself onto her knees, leaning forward across the table, repeating (with a soupçon of a whine behind her voice):

"Uma, tell me. Which is better, Ribena or tea? Tea or Ribena?"

Suresh looks up at Aasha now, his eyes flashing huge and dark, taking up all the space in the dining room, threatening to swallow her whole. Meeting those eyes, Aasha feels as though she's standing on tiptoe, craning her neck to see what lies over the edge. It could be nothing but the black sky. But it could be a return to a past that shimmers vitreous in her memory. To Old Times. Aasha closes her eyes and jumps.

"Uma!" she shouts. "Uma, do you like TEA better or RIBENA better?" The blood rushes to her brain as she dives, and all that air in her face takes her breath away and stands her arm hairs on end. She plunges down through the dining room, spreading her fingers and toes to slow herself, screwing up her face against the sunlight, narrowly avoiding the whirling blades of the ceiling fan. Past Suresh's browful of dismay and Uma's unruffled mien, to land back in her seat just in time to hear Uma say, very softly, "Aasha, please leave me alone."

It's cold and dark in the dining room, and the Ribena bubbles sink to the bottom of the glass like poisoned purple fish. Suresh stuffs a handful of cake crumbs into his mouth, takes a gulp of his Milo, gargles the resulting slurry, and sucks it through his teeth down into his throat.

So Uma has gone back where she came from on the day of the library trip. Whatever took hold of her on that day—a possession as apparent to interested observers as Amuda's borrowing of Anand's body—has released her now.

At least there's always Chellam. Or is there? For almost eight months Chellam's been not quite filling in for Uma: playing similar games in worse English, telling stories about garden pontianaks rather than about Ophelia, introducing them to Tamil cinema's best and brightest. She doesn't smell as nice as Uma—indeed, Suresh and Aasha believe her personal hygiene leaves much to be desired—but she'll do.

Except now she's gone too. She's in her room, but gone. The evening after the ill-fated Ribena game, Aasha opens Chellam's door a crack to see her curled up stiffly in her bed, like a dead cat on the roadside. "Chellam!" she hisses. "Chellam, got Tamil song on the radio." The lump doesn't stir, then or for the remainder of the day. Aasha would've heard it if it had stirred, for she waited on the green PVC settee for a sound or a sign until Amma ordered her to go to bed.

On the fourth day after the prayers, when Chellam gets up and gets dressed and goes about her tasks, she is no longer the same Chellam. She's turned into an echo of Uma. A diluted version, with duller skin, slumpier shoulders, and a pocked face. Nevertheless, the fact remains: eight months ago they had nothing in common but their age, and now they are alike. Their ruinous silence fills the jumbled rooms and labyrinthine corridors of the Big House; their footsteps quiet, their eyes bottomless, they fade like ghosts whenever anyone turns to look at them. Despairing of ever hearing them speak again, Aasha follows one or the other around the house for hours at a time. "*Tsk*, just forget it, Aasha," Suresh begs her. "Action-action only Uma and Chellam, don't want to talk to us means why should we care? Come I'll take you to the corner shop and buy you whatever you want. I got twenty sen left over from today's pocket money. Okay, don't want to go to the corner shop means come and watch *CHiPs*. Your favorite program, what? Oo wah, soooo handsome Erik Estrada is looking today on his motorcycle. No? Come I'll draw you a color picture of Miss Malaysia for your bedroom wall. I'll draw you a map. Russia, China, Brazil, anything you want also can."

None of these bribes lure Aasha. Up the stairs, down the stairs, into the kitchen or the back yard or the garden, she follows Chellam and

Uma in turn. Sometimes when she waits long enough she sees Uma's shadow and Chellam's escape their bodies and together dance wistful waltzes on the walls: a tall young tree shadow with spidery fingers and ravaged nails, and a tiny one, sere as a leaf in a drought, with hands skinned by years of steel wool and blue scrubbing soap. When Aasha tries to join in, though, they turn away from her and flutter, moth-like, up the wall and onto the ceiling, waltzing faster and faster around the chandeliers and fans as she lies on the floor watching them. The seam between ceiling and wall sometimes bends their shins in half when they whirl, unheeding, too close to it. It makes Aasha wince and close her eyes. What she doesn't know is that it's always Uma or Chellam who finds her in the morning, picks her up silently under the arms, and lays her on the nearest settee. Or, on rare occasions, on her bed, if her sleep is deep enough not to be disturbed by the journey up the stairs. For they fear Aasha most when she's awake; when she's asleep they sometimes allow themselves to see — in the fists that refuse to unclench, in the frowns that come and go across her sleeping face and in the tears crusted to her lashes — the waxing sorrow of her need.

Suresh has no time for such pining; he wants to punish some-one — anyone, really — for this untenable situation. Uma's out of his reach; Amma would give him a mouthslap for trying anything too funny with her; Appa's never home; and Suresh has a shred of pity left for Aasha, who has been punished enough for nothing at all. So one morning he gathers his exasperation into a ball and waits behind a corner for Chellam. "Chellam, Chellam, you want a fortune, come *I* tell your fortune," he offers when she passes. She doesn't seem to hear him, but he grabs her hand and peers at it. "Wah wah!" he says. "That bloody fool Anand didn't know what he was talking about, man! It says here you'll be a shitpot carrier, but the best shitpot carrier in all the land. Then you'll be rich and you'll start an international shitpot carrying business." The thick spittle of revenge bubbles in the corners of his mouth. "Satisfied?" he says. But Chellam doesn't laugh or suck her teeth, and in the days that follow she responds to none of his at-tempts to provoke her, not even the old, hissed *Chellamservant!*

TWO WEEKS AFTER the Balakrishnans' prayers, a minor distraction presents itself—no, to be precise, it is a distraction for some, for oth-ers a rhapsody on a terrifying theme, and for Appa an opportunity for rigorous analysis. In a low-cost flat near the Kinta River, one Shamsuddin bin Yusof is arrested for the murder of Angela Lim, a Chinese schoolgirl in Standard Four, and Appa receives a telephone call about the arrest. Just a few inconsistencies, he is told—some busybody or other claims to have seen Shamsuddin in a different part of town on the night of the murder—but otherwise the thing is certain. The police have found the chap's identity card at the scene of the crime. (It's blue, of course, for Shamsuddin is as citizen as citizen could be, a Malay, a Bumiputera, a prince made of Malaysia's own fertile earth, onto which he would gladly spill the blood the national anthem demands of him, though he hasn't yet had a chance, and seems instead—in compensation?—to have spilled the blood of a child with far less reason to feel patriotic.)

"Sick bloody bastard," Appa says that evening. He has come home for dinner tonight, for the first time in weeks. They are eating a fine bawal kuzhambu, courtesy of Lourdesmary. Appa shakes his head and continues, "The girl was ten years old." And even Amma, who for so long has not accorded so much as a nod to Appa's attempts at conversation, shudders expressively as she lays a fish bone on the rim of her plate. Chellam, who is washing Paati's dinner plate in the English kitchen, can just barely piece together Appa's summary of the facts: Angela Lim's body uncovered at the construction site, terrible things done to her beforehand, bite marks, burn marks, a sharp piece of wood in her—

"Please," Amma says then, "Suresh and Aasha are sitting right in front of you."

Suresh and Aasha exhale, one in a rush, the other slowly, but Chellam does not. Death, death everywhere: as long as she doesn't meet Angela Lim's fate, perhaps she should count herself lucky to expire in an accident, or from sudden heart failure, or from unidentified chemicals in her food. Even she, imprisoned and blindfolded by her own terrors, remembers Angela Lim's face on TV when the girl first went missing a week ago. She'd rather go like the two boys who died retching after eating dried peaches three weeks before that.

She prepares herself daily, upon waking and before falling asleep, for Death, however he might choose to dress when he comes for her.

Time's running out for everyone: three more pages of the 1980 Perak Turf Club calendar and Uma will be gone. At night before she falls asleep (on the floor, or on the green PVC settee, or even, occasionally, in her bed), Aasha berates herself for asking the wrong question that afternoon two weeks ago. *Who cares about tea and Ribena? Stupid stupid stupid. I should've asked her a real question. But maybe I can still ask her now. It's just one question. Maybe if I ask her nicely and politely when she's free — when she's not reading or doing something important — she'll answer properly. She won't be so angry then. I'm sure she'll answer. I'm sure of it.*

This is Aasha's straightforward question: Uma, you friend me or you don't friend me?

But when she wakes up (on the green settee or in her bed, but never on the floor) to find the forgiving night gone again, and harsh daylight streaming in through the windows, she never asks.

11

THE FINAL VISIT OF THE
FLEET-FOOTED UNCLE

January 17–March 25, 1980

N o one, least of all Uncle Ballroom himself, expected him to turn up at the Big House ever again after his unceremonious expulsion two years ago. Certainly Appa's relationship with his brother had always been a precarious thing, dependent on Appa's freedom to call Uncle Ballroom a good-for-nothing to his face — and also a useless bastard, a pondan, a pansy, a mooch, a louse, and a go-go boy — and on Uncle Ballroom's willingness to swallow these gibes with a good-natured grin and even a chuckle or two.

Uncle Ballroom's wife had left him in 1970, after they'd been married for five years, and according to Appa the blame fell squarely on Uncle Ballroom's once manly shoulders. "What woman in her right mind would want to stay with a moron like this?" Appa would say pleasantly at the tea table, passing Uncle Ballroom the biscuit plate. "Doing the lobster quadrille and the lindy hop-hoppity-hop for a living, like a bleeding poufter." But these showers of brotherly abuse had never led to all-out war, first because Uncle Ballroom was essentially a peace-loving man, second because he was perceptive enough to notice the affection — an arrogant, warped affection, but affection nevertheless — that underlay Appa's insults, and third because he was willing to withstand a certain amount of defamation in exchange for free food and lodging whenever he fell on hard times. Which he did often enough, disembarking at the gate of the Big House at least once a year from a taxi whose fare he couldn't pay. Appa was resigned to his sponging; Amma complained only behind his back; the children looked forward to his visits, for he looked them in the eye, laughed at their jokes, told them stories, and brought them the varied vestiges of his last hasty moving-out day, odds and ends most adults would never think to give a child: empty tobacco tins, anti–Vietnam War stickers well after the fall of Saigon, shoe trees, dancing figurines that had come unstuck from their trophy pedestals. And then, two years ago, Uncle Ballroom had Crossed a Line and tottered (the children had pictured him on pointe, in a leotard) towards a Slippery Slope, and Appa, sensing the precarious position of his impressionable children and the seedy world awaiting them at the bottom of that Slope, had thrown him out on his ear.

And that, the children had believed, was that. No more teatime tales of San Francisco and New York and Vienna, no more rusty tobacco tins and bent shoe trees.

But on an overcast Saturday afternoon in March, Uncle Ballroom boards an air-conditioned taxi whose fare he will not be able to pay, and orders the driver to head to 79 Kingfisher Lane. "The Big House," he says. "Lawyer Rajasekharan's house. You know it?"

The driver knows it well.

This time, in a marked deviation from his standard procedure before his falling-out with Appa, Uncle Ballroom has given the family no prior notice of his plans. Appa isn't home, and though Amma has some suspicions — thanks to Chellam's bad timing and big mouth — of where he might be, she's sitting at the Formica table, her eyes locked on the reflection of Kingfisher Lane in the glass panel of the wide-open front door. Nothing's happening on the street before Uncle Ballroom's taxi pulls up; nothing ever happens at this hour. In these hours before the downpour, every tired housewife, re-tired husband, aged parent, servant, cat, and illegal backyard chicken retreats into the shadows for a long nap. They lie down where they can, sometimes where they are: on hot and sweaty cotton sheets, on scratchy coir mats, on cool cement, on grass already arching up from the roots for the distant deluge. On and beyond their porches the hibiscus plants and rose bushes droop; even pampered indoor ferns and prized money plants acquire a wilted air that will lift only with the gathering of rainclouds.

Uma is at a rehearsal for *The Three Sisters;* Suresh is at a Boy Scout meeting. Inside the Big House Paati sleeps in her chair, Chellam on the floor at her feet, and Aasha on the green PVC settee. Lourdesmary and Vellamma and Letchumi, their morning tasks done, their bellies full with the rice and sambhar lunch they ate off their special servants' plates, are indulging in a ten-minute, sitting-up doze in three shady spots in the back yard. Mat Din is drooling on a deck chair by the garden shed. Only Amma does not nod off during these dead hours.

What holds her rapt? Is her vision, honed by years of glass-panel peering, so powerful that she can make out the indefatigable ants on Mrs. Manickam's abandoned hibiscus blossoms? Does the sight of those unruly shrubs plunge her back into the old jealousy she felt for Mrs. Manickam when, two years ago, that ringleted lady eloped with her government-clerk lover, thereby becoming the only woman Amma has ever known to put her own happiness before propriety? Or is Amma merely transfixed by the twitches of the dreaming cat on Mrs. Malhotra's front porch, or perversely fascinated by the subconscious workings of Baldy's right hand inside his underpants as he sleeps, in full view of anyone who cares to look, in a woven plastic chair under the margosa tree on the grass verge? Whichever it is, Amma starts when Uncle Ballroom's taxi pulls up at the gate and into her field of vision, as if someone has waved a hand before her eyes. She jumps to her feet, toppling her chair, and inside the house three pairs of eyes jolt open. Paati cries out her standard whos and whats and wheres; Chellam yawns and stretches; Aasha sits up and rubs her eyes on the green PVC settee.

"Don't know, don't know," Chellam says to Paati. "Just someone at the gate. No need to dry your throat out shouting."

Uncle Ballroom is at the open door by the time Amma reaches it. "Oh — it's you," she says to him. Face-to-face they stand, separated only by the spirals and curlicues of the wrought-iron grille. "Did Raju know you were coming?"

"Er — well, no," says Uncle Ballroom. "I'm afraid — I'm afraid I didn't have the opportunity to warn him this time, heh-heh. It was — well, it was a more sudden decision than usual. But —"

"But he —"

"But," persists Uncle Ballroom over whatever Amma's objection might have been, "I assure you I'll stay out of your way. You'll hardly see me. I've got business in town that will occupy all my time. I'll make sure not to step on anyone's toes."

Amma shrugs her shoulders, unlocks the grille with a sigh, beckons Uncle Ballroom to enter. "Well, if Raju —"

"I take it Raju isn't home now?"

"No, he isn't."

"If you prefer, I could call him at his office."

"He's not at his office."

"Oh. Ah. Well —"

"You may as well put your bag upstairs in the guest room while waiting. Your brother" — having restrained herself from referring to Appa as *your great brother,* Amma pauses and licks her lips to mark the effort — "won't be home for some time, I can tell you that. When he comes home you can explain yourself to him."

And so Uncle Ballroom is admitted into his brother's marble-floored, lace-curtained castle, which, within moments of his entry, he finds strangely altered. True, little Aasha, who stands in the shadowed archway eyeing him noncommittally, has grown a great deal, a change upon which Uncle Ballroom feels obliged to remark, being an uncle and all. But it's her manner, not her height, that strikes him more: a quiet vigilance, a silvery subterranean river of distrust. Even if he were inclined to attribute this to two years' worth of growing up and nothing more, other changes hold him back. A sharp new edge to his sister-in-law's voice, a sardonic twist to her face that colors everything she says with irony, an unrelenting tension in the very air. Is the house too quiet? Inexplicably cold for these tropical climes? Too clean? He can't explain it, but there it is, that unease, like the high hum of a distant generator.

And when he goes to greet his mother the surreality of it all stares him in the face: in two years she's turned into a little old lady stuck in a rattan chair, doddering, muttering, cataracted, incontinent, the whole works. At first, when he kneels before her and she takes his hands in hers, he feels nothing but remorse. *You fool, Balu! Did you think time would stand still for you?* But then she fixes him with the clearer of her two milky eyes and nods, as if something in his appearance has either confirmed a suspicion or satisfied her, and he realizes that despite her cataracts she's still the clever old crow she always was. The rattan chair, the weak bladder, the trembling knees, all these might be real and unchangeable in the perceived order of things, but beyond them is a truth few can see. His mother has turned herself into a little old lady at will — but why? Well, it probably suits her at this naturally lazy stage of life, and she's always been one to do whatever suits her. She was tired and bored and all in all quite ready to be waited upon, so she took up residence in that rattan chair. In all likelihood she exerts more power over the household from that throne than she did walking around on her own two feet. Already he sees the evidence of her unchallenged reign: "Vasanthi! Lourdesmary!" she's shouting. "Has Raju been informed? Tell him to come home for dinner tonight, tell him not to eat any of that Chinese rubbish he always has to eat outside. Lourdesmary! Go to the market and buy a live kampung chicken. Buy three catfish. Is catfish still your favorite, Balu? What else shall we cook?"

As surely as it's a throne, the rattan chair is also a retreat. Uncle Ballroom remembers his previous visit, the late nights of blackjack and gin rummy in Raju's study, his mother always winning after pretending the brandy had gone to her head. And then that last rainy night, his mother's see-no-evil-hear-no-evil face, his distressing realization that whatever stand he took would have to be taken alone . . . *Oh, Mother, always so shrewd, so selfish, so weak-willed. So this is how you've absolved yourself of all responsibility, eh?* Well, maybe she's happy this way. This willful blindness must bring her some peace of mind. Through extended and concentrated role-playing, she may even have convinced herself that she really is nothing but a helpless bag of bones. Something in the sudden and excessive rheuminess of her eyes tells him his appearance has dislodged parallel memories from the godforsaken hiding places to which she consigned them two years ago. But before those cloudy drops can spill down the ravines and crevasses of her cheeks, Paati pulls herself together, frowns, and hollers, "Chellam! For God's sake bring us an orange squash or something! Such a hot day, don't you have a grain of sense in your head? Do you have to be told every time?" Homing in on this small irritation, shaking it between her teeth like a dog, Paati thus banishes older, bigger worries: Uncle Ballroom sees that she's completely recovered her composure by badgering this Chellam character, whoever she is. The multiple benefits of playing the crotchety old coot pile up before his eyes as Chellam appears with two glasses of orange squash on a tray.

"Our new girl," Amma says. "Takes care of Mother only. One hundred percent devoted to her. She stays here full time." Yet one hundred percent devotion is not what Uncle Ballroom sees in the hooded eyes of this skinny girl with bad skin: devotion, if it's there at all, is diluted by something else, and when she hands a glass to Paati she's neither gentle nor respectful. "Inthanggai," she says sullenly. Here. Take it. What she doesn't say, but would've said if she'd been alone with Paati: You can stop complaining now, you old fart. Still, he hears the words as clearly as if she's spoken them aloud, and what rises within him is not indignation or a resolve to take this too-big-for-her-Japanese-slippers girl down a peg, but mirth, and more—dare he acknowledge it—a pale current of sympathy. Poor child—how old is she, anyway? She looks exhausted and underfed, and he cannot imagine her life in his brother's troubled household, nor the strain of attending a wizened crone so thoroughly dedicated to her dowager-dragon role.

No, he tells himself. Not this time. He may be a man of integrity, but this time, for once, he is resolved not to be the one who sees too much. He too can feign innocence and short memory; he can wash his hands of other people's causes and mind his own business. He quells the strong whiff of something-rotten-on-Kingfisher-Lane with the assiduous application of Tiger Balm to his temples. "Terrible headache," he says apologetically. "Must be all that traveling." And he returns to his perusal of the New Straits Times, to the winners of the slogan-writing competition sponsored by Chartered Bank on page 3, to the full coverage of the badminton tournament in the sports section, to the recipe for Owl and Angelica Soup with Cordyceps in this week's "Cooking with Chinese Herbs" column.

Just before dinnertime Appa comes home, as if by instinct; he would not normally have returned on a Saturday night.

"So sorry, Brother," Uncle Ballroom says, rising to meet him at the door. "I wish I could've let you know I was on my way, but—at any rate, I'll stay well out of your way this time." And then he repeats, almost verbatim, the promises he made to Amma this afternoon: "You'll hardly see me. I'll be busy in town the whole time. I'll be careful not to step on anyone's toes."

Big man that he is, Appa cannot be seen to deny his brother a roof over his head on account of an old quarrel. He forces his features into some semblance of a smile. "Okay, okay," he says, holding a hand out to Uncle Ballroom. "No problem. Welcome back to the Big House. Hah-hah!"

At dinner Appa is the consummate host, jovial, attentive, expansive.

"Have you heard the one about the three lawyers, Balu, one Malay, one Chinese, one Indian?"

He's delivering the punch line when Uma comes downstairs to take her seat at the table. Uncle Ballroom gives her an unflinching hello and an avuncular smile as Appa goes on, not looking at either of them:

"Wait wait, don't tell me — you're back because of Visit Malaysia Year 1980, aren't you, Balu? You must've seen the ads in New York London Paris wherever you came from? The only time you'll see Indian faces on TV. Local color, what? The Bharatanatyam dancers and the teh tarik sellers and the Thaipusam crowds. The rest of the time we're supposed to shut up and hide our faces."

What d'you think of this kampung chicken, Balu? Not your supermarket rubbish, eh? Let me refill your wine glass. Colleague brought me this stuff straight from France. It's the only wine I've found that goes with Lourdesmary's devil curries.

But despite Appa's best efforts, the somber cloud over the dining table will not lift. Uncle Ballroom manages a smile or two, but these are quickly squelched by the sight of his other dinner companions: Vasanthi as stiff and dry as a lidi broom, Aasha's half-sick, stricken mien, Uma never lifting her eyes from her plate. Even Suresh merely soldiering bravely on through his chicken thigh so as to be released as quickly as possible.

Uncle Ballroom looks again at Uma and finds himself unable to swallow his mouthful of chicken perital. Uma's grown too, but only a couple of inches, and her hair is exactly as it was two years ago, long and wild, dry at the ends. Yet she's changed so much that Uncle Ballroom would have had to look twice to recognize her at a bus stop or in a queue; the girl before him is simply not the same one who cajoled him into giving her dancing lessons two years ago, and gave her grandmother a run for her money at card games, and laughed at the drop of a hat. That easy laugh, that innocent, girlish flirting with father and uncle and driver and grandmother — yes, even grandmother, for Uma had been a charmer then, sparkling, generous with her affections, a lover of the limelight, a tease, an indiscriminate flasher of dimples — has it all evaporated just like that?

Uncle Ballroom takes a sip of water and a deep breath.

"Have you heard Uma's big news?" Appa says. "She's going to the States in September. Columbia University."

Yes, the disappearance of Uma's voice will soon be crowned by her physical vanishing. Every night, Aasha knows, Uma sits up in bed thumbing through the fat letters that have been tumbling one after the other into the letterbox, smudged and grimy from their journey halfway around the world. She plucked each one out before the letterbox lizards had had a chance to curl up on it and bedeck it in beady droppings, and now she puts the whole stack on the pillow beside her and goes through it before bed. As she touches each letter a small part of her temporarily disappears until she turns to the next: the Princeton letter spirits away her right thumb, the one from Cornell steals her left foot under the blanket, the one from Columbia leaves her eye sockets empty.

"Marvelous marvelous," says Uncle Ballroom. "Hearty congratulations."

"She'll be studying medicine. Well, pre-medicine, to be precise. Biology."

"And theater," says Uma. These are the first words she's spoken since they sat down to dinner. Her eyes are looking not at Appa or Uncle Ballroom, but past the latter, at the window behind his head, through which she can see the vast garden bathed in the blue light of the streetlamps.

"Of course! Theater!" Appa says. "I forgot about that. Uma's going to be a thespian-cum-heart-surgeon, I forgot."

"Frankly," Amma says, "I think Uma's first priority is getting out of this cursed house." She can't resist; her opportunities to chip away at Appa's composure are few and far between. Even on the rare occasions when he's home, he's got cotton wool in his ears, but he's taken it out this evening, hasn't he, to impress his brother? *Talks as though we're a nice happy family. As though he only is responsible for Uma's achievements. As though they sat and filled out the applications together. Medicine pre-medicine, oo wah! What's the matter, too scared to admit to your brother that even your precious oldest hates you nowadays?* In case her point wasn't clear the first time, she elaborates: "What Uma wants is escape at all costs and no coming back. Whether she has to sell her soul to Hollywood or Harley Street or run away with the circus is immaterial. Correct or not, Uma?"

"Hmm?" says Uma, smiling mildly around the table, imperturbable.

But Aasha, little barometer that she is, little coal mine canary struggling for air, pushes her plate away and says, "I can't eat any more."

"Not bad, Suresh," Appa says, ignoring all of them (*Does he keep the cotton wool in his pocket?* Amma wonders. *Did he put it back in when we weren't looking?*), "you made quick work of that. Want another piece? Drumstick? Wing? Another thigh?"

"Anything also can," says Suresh.

"I'm not feeling well," Aasha says more loudly. "I don't want any more."

"You haven't eaten anything," Appa says. "At least eat a little bit. Don't waste good food."

Aasha gulps down half her glass of water, holds her breath, and stares at Uma.

Uncle Ballroom watches her watch Uma. She was always Uma's favorite, a sweet kitten for Uma to pamper and powder and show off, and he can tell from Aasha's eyes and the slight downward turn of her mouth that she hasn't forgotten all that. She's become a ghost all right, living in and for the past, sicker with longing than he's ever thought a six-year-old could be. Unaware he's watching her, she trails her index finger through the mound of rice on her plate to make two mini-mountains. She'll pretend to eat, her parents will pretend not to notice, and that, she thinks, will be that.

Alas, her father's not in a compromising mood tonight. "Aasha," Appa says, "stop playing the fool and eat your dinner. Lourdesmary spent my hard-earned money on this chicken. Real kampung chicken. You don't know how spoiled you are. Free-range, fed with proper grain—"

"Oh yes," Amma says before Aasha can say anything (but *would* she have said anything? Her lower lip juts dangerously now; under the table, Suresh kicks her knee to stop her from crying). "Free-range. Since you're in such a showoff mood, why don't you boast to your brother about how you yourself are free-range?" She's sure of one thing: if it's in her power to embarrass Appa at all, it can only be done in front of his brother. She drums her turmeric-stained fingers on her plate as if she's bored, and goes on, "Free to wander all day and night, free to make a special guest appearance to bully your own children when you feel like it, free to show us all you're the big boss in front of visitors, isn't it?"

"Oh, for heaven's sake, must we subject our guest to your hysteria? Must we—"

Appa's diatribe is truncated by a rush of vomit, green, lumpy, frothy, pouring from Aasha's mouth onto her twin rice hills (as Suresh sighs loud and deep), spattering her hair and her frock and her hands, so that as she tries, terrified, to wipe her face with her left hand, she ends up smearing it over cheeks and chin, and it drips in viscous strings from everything. Above the table Suresh sighs more loudly still; under it he kicks her again.

Amma rises and grabs her by one arm. "Chhi!" she spits. "Couldn't you run to the bathroom if you knew you were going to vomit? Okay enough no need to make a bigger mess in front of everybody. Come." As she drags Aasha away she calls out over her shoulder: "Chellam! Chellam! Come please! Aasha made a mess here!"

From somewhere within the labyrinth of corridors comes an answering grunt. *Not quite one hundred percent devoted to Mother,* Uncle Ballroom thinks, if her tasks include emergency vomit-mopping. Perhaps ninety-eight or ninety-nine percent.

But that night in bed, as the branches of the frangipani tree tap his windowpane at the very end of one of the longest, darkest, farthest-flung corridors of the Big House, it's Uma's face, not Aasha's or the poor pockmarked servant girl's, that surfaces unbidden behind Uncle Ballroom's eyelids.

It's not my problem, Uncle Ballroom reasons with himself. *There's nothing I can do.* Yet still he hears Vasanthi's half envious *escape at all costs,* and sees Uma Then and Uma Now, Then and Now, Now and Then, Then and Now . . . He reaches for the tin of Tiger Balm on his bedside table as his head begins to throb with sorrow and helplessness and regret.

Downstairs, stretched out on the settee in his study—where he sleeps when he spends the night at the Big House—Appa, too, ponders Uma's immutable Mona Lisa smile and feels a familiar gnawing at his gut. "That blasted Lourdesmary woman," he murmurs to himself before falling asleep. "Always puts a ton of chili powder in every-thing. It's enough to melt a glass stomach. No wonder the children can't eat her food."

THE NATURE of Uncle Ballroom's business in town is unclear, but on weekdays he leaves the house every morning after breakfast and re-turns well after dinnertime. On the weekends he stays upstairs in his room, watching the frangipani flowers drift down onto the tin roof below the tree. In answer to Appa's questions he has offered only a few derisory clues about an import-export business and a fellow he met in Shoreditch. He remains faithful to his resolution, whistling happy tunes down Kingfisher Lane each morning after a cheery good-bye to all and sundry, humming golden oldies back up the lane in the dark. But the effort is a great strain on his nerves; it seems to him when he sits down to breakfast with the family that they're all afloat on an iceberg. Their movable feast on its red Formica table, the plates and glasses and spoons on their vinyl place mats. The iceberg moans and sighs and carries them all along like a blind slave shouldering a palanquin. The plates and spoons clink incessantly. The water in the glasses threatens to spill with every jolt.

He does everything he can to close his ears to the storm swirl-ing around him, everything short of sticking his fingers in them and singing at the top of his voice, but his very presence has fueled that storm by compelling his brother to play the big man, Lawyer-Saar, Big Spender (out of habit, out of arrogance, out of a vague sense that if he keeps Uncle Ballroom happy with tiger prawns for his nasi lemak and senangin fish curry for his roti canai, they will reach a tacit agree-ment to avoid certain uncomfortable topics of conversation. Never mind that it's Lourdesmary who must bear a burden she doesn't un-derstand. *Tiger prawns?* she wonders as she grinds spices with a batu giling as thick as her waist at six thirty in the morning. *Senangin for roti canai? Too much money can drive people mad, I tell you*).

Uncle Ballroom's keenly aware of two things: Raju's tireless perfor-mance provides Vasanthi with the very best stone on which to sharpen her ax; Vasanthi's got a secret source of venom, a neatly folded paan she keeps inside her cheek and chews on from time to time, tasting its flavor all day, spitting droplets of its red juice in Appa's face whenever she has an opportunity.

"Blue?" she says to Appa one morning, apropos of nothing. "But don't the Chinese like everything red? Good luck and prosperity and all that?"

Appa smiles beatifically around the table and says, "Balu, if you could contrive to be around for dinner one of these nights, I'll ask Lourdesmary to make us a proper old-fashioned mutton curry. Top-quality mutton she gets from the butcher when she tells him it's for us. Only has to say my name and the fellow runs and gets what he's been hiding from everyone else, you know?"

"What about a chauffeur, then?" Amma says. "Shall I tell Mat Din he'll be dividing his time starting next month?"

"Er, I'll see what I can do, yes," Uncle Ballroom says, as though Amma hasn't spoken. Just as he expects, Appa doesn't pressure him into fixing a date for this mutton dinner that will — they both know — never take place.

On Uncle Ballroom's second Sunday at the Big House, Appa comes home from the market with (in one hand) half a dozen live crabs in a basket and (in the other) a fat tilapia breathing its last in its newspaper wrapping. No sooner has he slipped his shoes off at the front door than he booms, "Eh Balu! Look what I found for you! Still a big fan of crabs or not?"

But before Uncle Ballroom can make his way along his dim corridor and down the stairs to prostrate himself before his brother's generosity and thereby mask all lingering odors of unpleasantness, Amma has met Appa at the door.

"Aren't you getting tired of fish?" she says to him.

"What?"

"Didn't you have fish just last night? Maybe steamed with ginger, just the way you like it? I suppose I can ask Lourdesmary to fry this one."

Appa brushes past her, past Aasha, who is standing in the dining room archway, past Suresh, who is standing right behind her, and into the kitchen, where he frees the tilapia from its newspaper and lays it on the draining board. Aasha watches it flip over into the sink with a taily thwack. Glinting scales, writhing tail, bulging eye about to die. In and out, in and out goes that eye, like a red button someone should push to stop the show.

Uncle Ballroom appears in the dining room just in time to see Appa wash his hands and smile broadly at Amma. "Go ahead," he says, "send your wretched little maidservant after me with a tape recorder and a camera, if she has nothing better to do with her time. Or why don't the whole lot of you charter a bus and follow me around all day? It's quite gratifying, I must say, that my dreary daily routine engenders such lively interest. I feel like quite the celebrity. A flim star, just like our dear daughter is going to be someday."

Engenders such lively interest flourishes its gaudy tail in Amma's face until she looks away.

Later that afternoon, through the window above the back landing, Uncle Ballroom sees Suresh corner Chellam in the outdoor kitchen, where she's scrubbing the piss out of Paati's petticoats. "Chellam," Suresh says, gritting his teeth so that Uncle Ballroom can make out his words only by leaning precariously out the window, "why can't you mind your own business?" He pinches her elbow, twisting the loose skin between thumb and forefinger.

"Ai! Ai! You crazy boy!" shrieks Chellam, pulling away and then laughing, screwing up her face at what she thinks is an innocent but silly game.

Again that weak wave of sympathy laps at Uncle Ballroom's steeled spirit; again he wills it still.

But in the end Chellam's father's monthly performance wears Uncle Ballroom's once bitten shyness down.

Uncle Ballroom has been at the Big House for two weeks before the servants' payday rolls around, and a plaintive mewling at the gate interrupts his concentrated consumption of soft-boiled eggs and toast.

"Saar! Maddam!" the voice cries. "Tell my daughter that her brothers and sisters haven't eaten for three days! And one has a fever, but how can we bring him to the doctor with no money? Tell my daughter that, and see if she can live with her conscience! Tell her and see what she says!"

Egg spoon just inches from his mouth, Uncle Ballroom looks around him. Appa, absorbed in the *New Straits Times*, appears to have heard nothing. Suresh and Aasha are smiling enigmatically at each other. Amma may or may not be reading the back of Appa's newspaper (evidence in favor of this hypothesis: her eyes have been on it for the past fifteen minutes; evidence against: it's the sports page).

Uncle Ballroom hazards an interruption. "I think," he says, "there may be someone at the —"

"It's Chellam's delightful old man," Appa says. "Muniandy. Here for his monthly collection."

"He has another six children at home," Amma says. "Can't put food in their mouths without our help."

Appa sighs. He knows how attached Amma is to her version of events; she would like to think of their handouts to Muniandy as charity. It's for this very reason that he now speaks the stripped truth, not in allegiance to any lofty principles of his home. Just to spoil the pleasure Amma derives from floating above everyone else on the white wings of noblesse oblige. Outside, Muniandy continues to caterwaul.

"Actually," Appa says, "it's Chellam who's helping out her family, and not so willingly at that. She refuses to go out and talk to her father, so the only way we've seen to get rid of him is to give him her wages every month."

"Oh," says Uncle Ballroom. And his surprise burbles, unchecked, out through his eggy mouth. "Ah. But—but then, if her wages go to him—does she—I mean, doesn't she—"

"For five days the boy's fever has lasted!" wails Muniandy. "Who knows what's wrong with him? How can people like us afford doctors?"

"Well done, Balu," Appa says. "I'm pleased to see you're capable of at least some elementary mathematics despite all those bright red marks in your report cards. Fifty ringgit for Chellam minus fifty ringgit for her father equals zero ringgit for Chellam, yes. But not quite, you see, because you're forgetting room and board. Three square meals a day and a cushy bed in a room of her own is a fair sight better than what she got from her last employer, who happens to be a good friend of mine. Let alone what she'd be getting at home."

"Hmm, hmm," Uncle Ballroom says. And to himself: *Of course, of course, Raju, her life would be nasty, brutish, and short if not for you.* Then he shovels the rest of his egg down his throat as fast as he can without choking, gulps down his lukewarm tea, and excuses himself from the table. It's a Saturday; he has nowhere to go, but the falling frangipani blossoms outside his window are far less challenging to his conscience than Muniandy's dirge.

But in the afternoon, as he tiptoes down the corridor on a mission to find an unclaimed newspaper, he bumps into Chellam crying into her sleeves. She jumps when she hears him approach; for a moment he does nothing but smile weakly at her tear-stained face. And then something in the way she backs away from him, making room, allowing him to pass untroubled by her petty woes, like the lord and master he is, stops him short. *Good God,* he thinks, *am I that much of a coward? What's happening to me? What the blazes am I so afraid of?* Already he's digging in his pockets, which are not all that heavy with cash. Sure, yes, he should credit what he has to his business capital account so he has something good to report when his would-be partner (the mysterious chap from Shoreditch) next inquires about his money-rolling progress. But if there's not much he can do for anyone else, can't he at least help out this miserable girl? A small act of kindness to someone who needs it so badly — what harm could that possibly do?

"Sorry, sorry," he says as he hands her a five-ringgit note. Earnest, contrite. He has so much to apologize for: not just the thoughtless sins of his brother and sister-in-law, but what he himself was almost willing to become in exchange for his brother's neon-lit hospitality. "I know it's not much, but —"

She looks from the bank note in his hand to his face. Her red-rimmed eyes are slightly out of focus.

"Go on," he urges, "at least buy yourself some biscuits or a magazine."

He's sure she's going to scurry away in that terrified manner the poor have when sojourning in the world of the rich: afraid of being caught turning the wrong doorknob, or polishing the wrong table, or looking as if they might be thinking about stealing. But at the last minute, just as he's about to give up and put the money back in his pocket, she takes it. "ThankyouverymuchMasterthankyou," she says, and to her narrow back he mutters, "Don't mention it." It occurs to him that it's the first time he's meant this figure of speech so literally: he really doesn't want her to mention it, not to the other servants, not to the children, not to their parents, and he doesn't know why, apart from his determination not to be seen minding anything that could in any way be construed as someone else's business. True, he must not repeat past mistakes, but surely no one would care if he chose to condemn himself to destitution through imprudent alms-giving? Has Chellam's servile paranoia infected him? Has the dimness of the corridor lent the transaction a shameful flavor?

Whatever it is, Uncle Ballroom takes to lurking in doorways and around corners to bestow his continued kindnesses upon Chellam, and he notices that her eyes dart like minnows when she receives, just as his do when he gives. He keeps his offerings small: five ringgit and a bag of kacang puteh purchased at the bus station one afternoon, two ringgit and a vadai gone soft in the humid air another. As he earns her trust, she grows more chatty: "Thank you, Master Ballroom," she whispers after he pays her the third or fourth such assignment. "I keeping for buying spectacles."

"Spectacles?" he repeats. "You mean you don't see well?"

"What, Master?"

He pantomimes shortsightedness, peering all around him, drawing the palm of his hand closer and closer to his squinting eyes as if it were a book. "You cannot see? No glasses, cannot see? Kannu —"

Her face lights up. "Yes Master! Cannot see. I want buying spectacles, but my Appa every time coming, every time taking money."

"Ah, yes, I see. Well, save that money, then." He points at the ten-ringgit note still clutched in her fist. "Keep that money to buy your spectacles."

After Uncle Ballroom learns about the unfortunate Spectacles Account, he finds additional ways to fatten its balance. Chellam, he calculates, is only ninety-six percent devoted to his mother, after all. He's revised his original estimate of ninety-eight percent: also subtracting from Paati's percentage are the mysterious, fragile longings of Aasha and her brave-faced brother, who have (quickly, and for purely practical reasons) learned to depend more on Chellam than on their oldest-eldest sister for their education and entertainment; who follow Chellam around at a safe, shy distance; who badger and ferret and weasel their way, when their mother's not looking, into Chellam's routines and her affections. So, figuring that another two or three percent won't matter, he brings her, one Sunday afternoon, a shirt whose collar is stained with the blackest sweat-ring she's ever seen. "Please," he says, "scrub scrub scrub. Take it off. Ten ringgit." And when that shirt is scrubbed, another is missing a button; and when the button's been sewn on, he breaks the zipper of his favorite grey trousers. She doesn't tell anyone about these assignments, of course, doesn't mention it (he never thought she would), and yet a new sense of purpose settles on her skin like a smell. She hums as she brews Paati's morning coffee. She walks briskly up and down the corridors now, with none of the mousy shuffling and slipper-dragging the children have come to expect.

"Chellamservant," Suresh says one day, "why you so action-action now? All the time whistling and singing like a film star? Got boyfriend somewhere, is it?"

She presses the tip of her tongue to a corner of her mouth, shy as an eight-year-old. "No lah," she says. "Where I got boyfriend?"

"Action-action only this Chellam," Suresh tells Aasha behind Chellam's back. "Look at her, walking with her nose in the air. Just a rubber-estate girl but she thinks she's the president of America or something."

At the sight of Suresh mimicking her confident stride, Chellam shrieks with glee, and when Aasha bids her teach them the words of her song, she obliges:

> Darling darling darling,
> I love you love you love you.
> Yennai vittu pogaadhe. (Don't leave me.)

"Darling darling darling," Suresh echoes, "and you trying to tell us you got no boyfriend?"

Encouraged by the disproportionate influence of a little pocket change on Chellam's spirits, Uncle Ballroom sets loftier goals for himself. On his way to the bus stop on the first of March, he spies Chellam's father coming the other way. He's a familiar sight to Uncle Ballroom by now, though they've never met. Today, for the first time since his arrival, Uncle Ballroom has a Saturday engagement in town: an appointment with a loan shark who operates out of a spice mill on Belfield Street. He's in sprightly spirits as he sets out, hopeful about the appointment, proud of the difference he's made in Chellam's life. From a good thirty yards away, he sees that Muniandy's topless except for the stained sweat-rag thrown over his shoulder. The old man's stumbling gait suggests that he's come straight from the toddy shop once again. In front of the Malay house he hitches up his dhoti to his hips and urinates on the grass verge. Uncle Ballroom senses doors shutting and curtains stirring around him, as if some shared radar system has picked up the approach of the pauper, as if every housewife on Kingfisher Lane is worried that one of these days, turned away by Appa, this black scarecrow of a man in his rotting Japanese slippers and his threadbare dhoti will come to sing his liquored lament at her front gate. And sensing this, Uncle Ballroom is at once lifted a whole foot off the lane by his resolution to be a better man than

all these hypocrites, these holier-than-thou brown sahibs and memsa-
hibs behind their lace curtains. He sees no reason why he should not
do better than his handouts to Chellam, why he should not double or
triple his beneficence by attacking the problem at the source, which
may not be so difficult. *Very likely*, he says to himself, *no one's ever tried
to talk to this Muniandy chap man to man. I won't reform him in a single
morning, but I might talk some sense into him.* Thus fortified with missionary zeal, he quickens his step.

At nine in the morning, Muniandy's vision is already fogged over
by a couple of hours' drinking of cheap samsu. This is what he sees,
far up Kingfisher Lane: a blur of white, a bigger blur of white, a blur
of white and grey — no, white and khaki, white and khaki and a red bit
— white, khaki, red, shiny black shoes, and now, finally, a rich man in a
spotless white shirt and pleated pants of the sort he hasn't seen since
his childhood on an Englishman's rubber estate.

"Saar," he says, deciding on the spot to try his luck with this spiffily
rigged-out stranger, "saar, two dollars? Three days I haven't eaten," he
says in Tamil, for he can see enough now to tell that this is no Englishman but a fellow Indian of the worst kind: more English than the
English, probably about to pretend he doesn't speak Tamil.

He's wrong: "Muniandy," the man says in Tamil (an odd, duck-
lame Tamil it is, but still recognizably Tamil), "you know how hard
your daughter works in that house, never to get a cent at the end of
the month? You think she's got no better use for the money than your
drink? If you'd just let her save it for you, Muniandy, she'd do a far
better job than you, and when you really need something for doctors'
bills babies' milk schoolbooks children's shoes whatever you really
need, Muniandy, whatever your six starving children really need, but
not samsu you badava rascal—" He stops here, because Muniandy has
just turned away to hawk loudly and spit onto the grass verge, and he
begins to suspect that only a bribe will open the man's ears to what he
has to say. He reaches into his trouser pocket and pulls out a five-ringgit note. "Here, you want something for yourself, take this. Now leave
your daughter alone and go home like a good man. Just this once."

But Muniandy, far from grabbing the money the way Uncle Ballroom expects him to, steps back. "Oho!" he cries. "Oho! What a great
man you are, saar!" He works another load of saliva into his mouth
and aims it, this time, at those shiny black shoes. He misses; his spittle
hits the dusty ground two inches from Uncle Ballroom's feet. "What a

great man, telling me what I can and can't ask my daughter to do! You rich people think you know everything. Even how to raise our children you'll decide for us."

Faces stir behind curtained windows; whispers float into the slowly heating morning. A child's footsteps skitter away from the front door of the Malay house. "Ee, keling mabuk," the little girl tells her carrot-peeling mother in the kitchen. An Indian drunkard in the street, pissing and spitting and shouting just like they do. "Close the door," her mother clucks. "Close it and lock it and keep quiet. You can't be too careful with those people."

"Let me tell you something," Muniandy continues, for nothing will abate his ire now, neither Uncle Ballroom's restraining hand on his elbow nor his pacific *okayokays*. "Let me tell you what you can do with that money that comes so easily to you. You can take it and use it to buy off some other man, okay, because you can't buy my daughter from me for five dollars. Understand?"

Uncle Ballroom releases Muniandy's elbow and stands there for five full seconds, during which Muniandy clears his throat and begins to work his mouth again, as if preparing to spit once more. What on earth is the man thinking? *No no,* he wants to say, *you've misunderstood, that's not why I'm giving you this money. I'm not trying to pay you off; there's nothing going on between me and your daughter. Sometimes charity really does come without strings attached.* But the shock paralyzes him: greater than the shock of the accusation itself, which Uncle Ballroom brushes aside (who in his right mind would believe a slander so ludicrous?), is the shock of Muniandy's secret lucidity and eloquence, of how straight the man can actually stand, how crisply he can form his words, and how misguided he, Balu, has been in his do-gooding faith that Muniandy would be touched—no, honored—by his man-to-man frankness. And under this shock, a fine, crack-in-the-heart sadness at the assumptions people like Muniandy must make if they are to survive. *Or maybe, in your world, it doesn't come without strings attached. Does it, Muniandy?*

In the end, Uncle Ballroom can bring himself to say none of these things. He shakes his head as if to expel water from his ears. "Fine, then, do what you want," he says, but the cocksure cadence is gone from his voice. "Go to the Big House and do as you wish." As they part ways, Chellam's father expels the spittle he's collected onto Mrs. Malhotra's culvert.

At the bus stop, Uncle Ballroom boards the number 22, on which, at ten o'clock sharp, a fourteen-year-old boy filches Shamsuddin bin Yusof's blue identity card. Had Uncle Ballroom witnessed this sleight of hand, he would've stood up and waved his arms frantically and yelled *Thief, thief,* in English, after trying unsuccessfully to dredge up the Malay word from the depths of his memory. But having got on near the beginning of the route, he has managed to snag the back seat, from where he sees only the bottoms and hips and bellies of those who pile themselves into the bus after the seats have all been filled. As for those who do see the pickpocket's skilled work, they say nothing, for they've been trained, during Uncle Ballroom's long expatriation, to close one eye or both to Fact's grimaces and Rumor's goading; they've learned to sit tight on their hands to avoid action; they've cultivated the patriotic skills of selective blindness, deafness, and muteness.

THE LONGER HE STAYS at the Big House, the more care Uncle Ballroom takes to avoid his brother: Raju is bubbling, threatening to boil over each time his wife fans her fires, and Uncle Ballroom wants nothing to do with the trouble that is surely coming. Already Vasanthi's been trying to sweep him into the imbroglio:

"It's because your brother's here, isn't it, that you're coming home every night like a good boy? Want to show him what a family man you are?" she says to her husband every other morning. Then she turns to Uncle Ballroom: "Why don't you ask him, Balu, what his schedule is like when you're not here? Where he goes and what he does when he doesn't have to come home to put on a grand show for you?"

In response to these instigations, Uncle Ballroom merely smiles wanly and withdraws at the earliest opportunity.

Quietly, unobtrusively, he also tries to insulate Chellam from the ill winds blowing against her, for not only is the children's chumminess as patchy and expedient as it ever was (lush on lonely afternoons, thin as orphanage gruel after each of Amma's inquisitions on the matter of Appa's whereabouts and whatabouts), Appa's been eyeing her unkindly too. "Good work, Vasanthi," he says whenever Amma raises the subject, but it's at Chellam he looks when he speaks, not at his wife. "It's a rare flash of brilliance you've had, sending the girl to shadow me. Why don't you draw up a roster for all the servants and gather the whole coterie for a secret meeting every Monday morning?"

Uncle Ballroom should've known that the ratted-on naturally long to rat on others. That this law applies not only to children caught misbehaving but to grown men made to feel small. Appa might be a rich Lawyer-Saar with a leather-bound vocabulary, but humiliated in front of his too-wise children and his born-loser brother, he growls and paces. He prowls and snaps. He waits to pounce. Who will it be? Lourdesmary, cooking the tenggiri fish the wrong way? Mat Din, trying to cover up a tiny scratch caused by his careless washing of the Volvo? No, Lourdesmary's rubbing chili powder into the tenggiri to fry it just the way Appa likes it; the Volvo's perfect paintwork gleams in the setting sun as Mat Din waters his bougainvillea plants. Appa climbs the stairs, his skin itchy with sweat and rancor, yearning for a cold shower — and there, in the corridor leading to the upstairs bathroom, he sees a tableau that both satisfies and sickens him: Uncle Ballroom, shirt unbuttoned, forcing a red banknote into Chellam's right hand, the two of them stuttering extravagant thank-yous: "Thank you, my dear girl, so sorry to take advantage of you like this." "Thankyou MasterBallroomthankyou."

Appa catches Uncle Ballroom's eye, and Chellam, seeing Uncle Ballroom look past her, turns around to see Appa. Appa says nothing for now; good enough for him that he's caught them in the after-act. (And what a juicy after-act! He never suspected — but then, he tells himself, there's so much one doesn't suspect when one is hardly home.) *Chellam!* he thinks. *How perfect! Maybe now you'll think twice about tattling, eh? Because I've got tales of my own now, don't I?*

It doesn't occur to Chellam that this hurried transaction could look like anything other than what it is: a man rewarding a servant for ironing his shirt. She hides the money behind her back, fearing she's in trouble for doing work for other people behind Amma's back, for stealing time away from Paati's One Hundred Percent.

But Uncle Ballroom's heart sinks. He contemplates packing his bags and leaving that very night, because who knows what his brother's cooking up, or how he will manage to drag the hapless Ballroom Balu and the petrified Chellamservant into the internecine struggles of his household?

So Uncle Ballroom begins to leave the house earlier still, before Lourdesmary even arrives on her bicycle to put the teakettle on and boil the eggs; he returns each night long after everyone's in bed. And it's this unwarranted sneaking and skulking, in the end, that paradoxically lands him in the hot water he knows so well from his previous visit.

Climbing the stairs at two o'clock in the morning on the twenty-fifth of March (having spent four hours on a bench in the bus station, chatting with vagrants to pass the time until it was safe to go home), Uncle Ballroom walks straight into Appa's shadowy form. They stand at the top of the stairs, just outside Uma's room, blinking at each other in the dark for a long while before Appa speaks.

"What were you doing downstairs all this time?" he asks.

"I . . . actually I just got back. I was —"

"Hah! Hoping to catch rats in the dark? Staying up to commune with the undead?"

"I've been out this whole time." Uncle Ballroom's lips and tongue feel suddenly and oddly thick to him, as though he's been drinking all night or sucking on ice. His speech is slow, the words like cotton in his mouth.

"Well, if you don't mind," Appa says, already pushing past his brother, "I'd like to go downstairs and get my glass of water."

Uncle Ballroom moves aside to let him pass.

At the bottom of the staircase, Appa turns around to see Uncle Ballroom still standing there, as he expected. "If you must know," Appa says, "I'm sleeping upstairs in the music room tonight because the air conditioner in my study is giving trouble."

Without a word, Uncle Ballroom goes into the upstairs bathroom. There he waits, running his fingers along the edge of the sink, rubbing at spots on the taps. After a minute or two, he hears Appa come up the stairs, walk briskly up the corridor, and on towards the music room. A door opens and closes. *He really is sleeping in there,* thinks Uncle Ballroom. *But now he reckons I'm here to —* He breathes hard onto the mirror, making a perfect circle of mist the size of his face. Then he brushes his teeth and goes to his room.

When he doesn't appear downstairs the next morning, a hesitant Chellam opens the guest room door a crack to find the bed impeccably made, the almirah door ajar, and the windows flung wide open. A fresh breeze wafts across the room to tingle her bare arms; the cornflower-blue curtains softly billow. The air smells of wet grass and starched cotton. Did Uncle Ballroom squeeze out the window onto the awning and then throw himself onto the frangipani tree or shimmy down the drainpipe? Did he let himself down with a rope of bedsheets filched from the linen closet? Chellam cannot imagine how he left without waking anyone, but:

"Maddam, Master Ballroom gone," she announces downstairs.

They follow her upstairs. Appa opens the dresser drawers in the empty room, peers into the almirah, looks out the window. "No note," he says. "Nothing." He turns to Amma with a tight smile. "Want to know what I think? I think Big Ballroom Balu was just not big enough to face his own music, that's all. I saw a few things I kept to myself, but now I better tell you. He was slipping her money behind our backs as if this house were a cheap brothel — a fellow who couldn't even pay for his taxi when he came. I mean, what do you think he was paying her off for?" When Amma says nothing, he answers his own question: "For the privilege of banging her right under our own roof, that's what. In front of our children."

Amma wants to say something clever about all the things that happen in front of and behind and around the children, and how they must certainly be used to it by now, but her ears and cheeks are burning from the word *banging* — its immediacy, its aptness, the precision with which it evokes the worst aspects of this hypothetical union, thighs banging thighs, chest banging chest, banging, bouncing, slapping — when Appa puts yet another question to her. "I'm sure he tried to buy Chellam's silence," he says, "and then got frightened she'd squeal anyway. But what do you plan to do, dear wife, if the girl's with child? Have her whelp in the garden shed and then hire the child as a shoe polisher when he turns three? I mean, really, what'll you do if she gives birth in this house?"

"Don't be silly," Amma says. "It won't come to that." But already Appa can see the shadow of worry under her eyes. *Well,* he says to himself, *Chellam may or may not be. If she is — well, we'll cross that bridge when we come to it. The problem will take care of itself. At least now I have one less busybody breathing down my neck.*

Miles away, in a seedy boarding house above a massage parlor, Uncle Ballroom watches cobwebs — one, two, three, four — turn with the blades of the ceiling fan above his bed. His one regret is not having the chance to slip Chellam thirty or forty ringgit before leaving. *But never mind,* he tells himself, *at least I did what I could for her. I didn't fail her the way I failed others.*

He doesn't know about Shamsuddin bin Yusof, whose arrest later this week he could have prevented by keeping his eyes peeled on the number 22 bus, or about Angela Lim, over whose rosebud mouth a hard, hairy hand is clamping this very minute at a construction site in Ipoh's Old Town. Gagged and bound and terrified, Angela arches her back to look her attacker in the face. Arrows of recognition shoot from her eyes and ears to shower impotently on the ground around her. *You, you, you!*

He's nothing like Shamsuddin bin Yusof, this boy: he's tall and impressively muscled, he's Chinese, he's unafraid. He's her youngest paternal uncle, who's been extorting cash from his brother for his gang boss, on which payments her hapless father has defaulted one too many times. As he leaves the construction site, he pulls out of his pocket Shamsuddin bin Yusof's blue identity card (which was smoothly passed to him by the gang boss's bus-riding henchman at a lou shi fun stall this morning) and lets it fall from between his thumb and index finger onto the dusty ground.

By the time Angela Lim's muscly uncle is burning his blood-soaked clothes in a big bonfire in Buntong, Angela has only fish-life left to her, as the Malay expression goes — indeed, as the unsuspecting Shamsuddin, who is blithely buying a kati of rambutans at a roadside stall in Kampung Manjoi, might say — not death, not true life, but the twitches and squirms in between.

On Kingfisher Lane, the Big House has begun to whisper, then hiss, then snarl Chellam's name from its many corners. *Dirty Chellam, shameless Chellam!* Across the street, Mrs. Balakrishnan's already brewing hypotheses on her stove along with pacchapairu kanji for tea.

In the days following Uncle Ballroom's departure, Chellam sits quietly inside herself. She naps on the floor beside Paati's rattan chair when Paati dozes off in the afternoons; she buys sour Chinese plums and red ginger from the corner shop and sucks them surreptitiously as she goes about her work. She may as well enjoy these small pleasures: Uncle Ballroom didn't stay long enough to make a real difference to the Spectacles Account, and as Chellam judges by the tenor of the household since he left (now the other servants and the children are hissing and whispering her name too, and she's not oblivious to the quick silences that follow her entrance into a room, or to the needle-sharp looks of the neighbors), no one's going to help her hang on to the little money he did leave her. No one's on her side, and next month her father will turn up, as usual, like a pye-dog sniffing cooked mutton. She figures she has a month to use up her paltry funds on plums and ginger.

Each time Chellam goes to the corner shop to buy them, Mrs. Balakrishnan notes her movements, and Amma verifies the prevailing theory anew with a quick, unseen glance at her purchases.

A craving for sour plums and red ginger can mean only one thing.

"No shame in her," Mrs. Balakrishnan says. And, with a sigh, "We simply can't trust these girls these days. They learn all this from modern films and TV, and they think they can do the same thing."

"In that case," Amma says one afternoon, "hadn't I better take her to see a doctor?"

"Don't bother," Mrs. Balakrishnan says. "This type of people got their own way of taking care of all this. She will find her own medicine. All the time she picks funny-funny leaves and weeds from your garden, isn't it? Now she can pick what she needs."

This prospect temporarily mollifies Amma. Yet contrary to Mrs. B.'s hypothesis, Chellam seems to have lost the foraging habits she had when she first came to the Big House. Though Amma expects to find her stewing leaves and seeds and sticks in a pot any day now, she hardly goes out to the garden anymore.

"She's scared to go outside," Suresh remarked to Aasha. "Remember she told us there was a pontianak spirit in the shed, waiting to drink pregnant women's blood? Now she herself better avoid the shed."

But is Chellam's belly growing or isn't it? It's hard to tell; these rubber-estate women's babies are usually tiny. Even six months pregnant, they barely show under their sarees. No matter. If and when she starts to swell, she'll be sent back to her village before the shame settles on the roof and awnings of the Big House, and there she'll have her bastard child: a tiny ballroom dancer with creases in the back of its neck, tangoing and foxtrotting its way through life with a tin cup held out to passersby.

12

THE UNLUCKY REVELATION OF
CHELLAM NEWSERVANT

December 8, 1979

CHELLAM HAS BEEN at the Big House for almost three months. Into Uma's vacated shoes she has slipped her leaf-narrow feet, and though those shoes are three sizes too big for her, Suresh and Aasha have reconciled themselves to making do. After all, Chellam is better than nothing. Over the past three months, in return for the privilege of Uma's shoes, she has introduced them to many novel wonders. To wit:

— The use of tamarind seeds for backyard games, collected in their pods from under the tree, stripped of their pulp, washed, and dried on a windowsill.

— The little black balls that could be rolled from the paste of sweat and grime that came off their skin when they'd been playing in the sun.

— The white threads of grease that spiraled out of her pores like butter icing from a hundred tiny pastry bags when she squeezed the skin on her nose.

— The singular ability of cats' penises to retreat and hide like turtle heads when poked with lidi sticks.

— The whole bejeweled, mustachioed pantheon of Tamil filmland. Movie gods leer from Chellam's walls in the room under the stairs:

Kamal Haasan and Jayasudha, Sridevi and Rajnikanth, lushly fore-locked and lubricious as lorry drivers. "Oh boy," Appa said when he first caught sight of this glossy shrine (courtesy of *Movieland* and *Tamil Film News*), "I fear our bonny young village lass is waiting for Rajni-kanth to sweep her away on his white stallion. Ah, Chellam, Chel-lam, combing out your long hair in the back yard, gazing into the twilight, how keenly you feel it. 'Even noon is evening to she who waits,' eh?"

"Chellam, you think Rajnikanth is your *lover*, is it?" Suresh de-manded to know. "Your love-love-loverboy? He gonna come and res-cue you on a white horse? Hanh? Rescue you from our house?"

Chellam didn't understand the question, but she sucked her teeth at him, called him a useless boy, and gave him one of her long, grin-ning frowns as he and Appa looked at each other and laughed.

Like an aborigine showing new settlers the tricks of her land, she has shared with Suresh and Aasha glittering scraps of wisdom re-tained from a village childhood beset with unseen dangers:

If you lie on your stomach with your legs in the air, your mother will die.

If you rest your head on your hand at the dining table, you'll have no food next time.

Which time is next time?

Not dinner tonight.

Not lunch tomorrow.

Next time might be months away, but you'll have no food.

A pontianak spirit lives in the garden shed, waiting to drink the blood of pregnant women.

"But Chellam," Suresh says to this, "she better go somewhere else! She'll be thirsty. We don't even know any pregnant women."

"But better you watch out," Chellam insists with some self-satis-faction. "If any pregnant women coming you better faster-faster tell she don't go near the shed. Like that only they found one Malay lady in Kuala Kangsar, you don't know ah? When she going to toilet, you know isn't it the kampung toilet will be so far away outside? That time only the pontianak jump on her and suck all her blood and leave her body like chappai like that, nothing inside. Like the murunggakai when you chew and spit, *puh puh*, like that she was."

They are not to eat in the dark anymore, or hungry ghosts will eat from their plates.

{ 250 }

Aasha likes that idea, though. A circle of ghosts nibbling from her plate, like fish around a sunken bread crust, their ghostly lips and cheeks and maws working busily. She will save the best bits for Mr. McDougall's daughter: the fish roe, the fried-chicken skin, the chicken heart. That is how Aasha will entice her back, for Mr. McDougall's daughter has not been seen since she and Aasha had a certain charged disagreement (which might be interpreted as having been, at least indirectly, Chellam's fault) in the downstairs bathroom. Aasha misses their chats more than she cares to admit to herself.

"What if you like them there, Chellam?" she asks now. "What if you like having the ghosts there?"

"Chhi!" Chellam scolds. "You crazy! You know what happened to one girl in my village? You want to know?"

"What?" they demand, consumed equally by defiance and curiosity.

"Every day the ghost eating her food until she so thin, all the doctor all don't know what to do also. Until he cannot stand cannot walk nothing. Until today she still like that, her mother only must wash her backside, bathe her, feed her."

"Then why when she started to get a bit thin her mother didn't make her eat with the lights on?"

"My village got no light all."

"Then eat outside lah! Eat outside at six o'clock, can what?"

"That all I don't know. You don't try to be too clever. You listen to me and switch on the light properly to eat your dinner."

Chellamservant! they hiss when she thrusts superstitions too audacious or untenable under their noses. Action-action only, making like a real oldest-eldest when she was just a servant girl.

"I'll tell your Amma," she threatens obligingly, to which, in unison, they always answer, "Tell lah!" But she never does.

Although Amma regularly emphasizes that Chellam's Sole Undertaking is to look after Paati, Chellam sometimes cooks, too. "Every day–every day I cannot eat mutton-chicken curry," she says. "After I falling sick, then how?" For even after all these years in service, her digestion rebels against the rich diets of her bigshot bosses, requiring her to forage in their gardens for ingredients for her stewpot: dark leathery leaves, green bananas, banana flowers. She drains the water from rice on the stove and drinks it with a pinch of salt. She boils cempedak seeds and munches on them as if they were apples. She fries rice with mustard seeds and dried chilies and eats it plain, without any curry. On Lourdesmary's days off, she offers her poor man's lunches to the children when Amma isn't watching. "Not bad, this new servant," Appa says when he learns of this. "Two for the price of one. Zookeeper and assistant chef. Nothing like a bargain. Your mother would be quite happy with herself if she knew."

For her intimate knowledge of human secretions and animal genitals, for her wide flashing eyes when she describes the disparate desires of ghosts, for her unlimited stores of arcane information, the children love her. It is a guilty, flickering love, one they will never admit out loud, but love nevertheless, tinged with respect for her witchy aura (the foraging, the plant-plucking, the pot-stirring, the warnings: don't these demand their respect?).

And yet, at times, they hate her, with the primitive hatred of children for creatures weaker than themselves. They hate her coconut hair oil and her hairy armpits and her crushes on fat Tamil actors with moles; they hate her broken English, to which they sometimes stoop in mockery; they hate her T-shirts that came free with Horlicks and Kandos chocolates. They hate all the evidence of her rubber-estate tastes: the shiny polyester blouse she wears to run errands in town, the gaudy flowers she puts in her hair before going out, the chipped, pillar-box-red Cutex on her fingernails. And they hate her dirty habits: the yellow crotch stains on her underwear on the clothesline, the wiry, too-curly black hairs stuck to her soap bar. "Eee," Suresh says when he points these out to Aasha, "you know where these come from or not?" Aasha, though she didn't know before, knows now, suddenly and surely, without needing three guesses. Then one afternoon they catch Chellam stealthily picking her nose with her pillar-box-red nails. "Not red-handed but snot-fingered," whispers Suresh to Aasha, but Chellam doesn't know she's been caught. She wipes her fingers behind the sitting room settee and under the side table before pulling a hairpin from her head and running it under the fingernails to dislodge crescents of dirt that fall onto the white marble floor. "Ee-yer," Suresh whispers, "now just see, she's going to go and mix Paati's rice and paruppu curry with her hands. A real estate-woman she is." And later, a rhapsodic improvisation on Chellam's dubious origins burgeons between Suresh's ears: *Estate-prostate-prostitate-prostitute! Estate prostitute with brothel fingernails!*

But more than any of these, they hate her father, who is a useless, drooling, toddy-drunk porukki bastard; who sits on their culvert and carries on and makes all the neighbors peer through their windows; who is proof of Chellam's dubious origins and the regrettable traits that are In Her Blood.

On Chellam's third payday, her father arrives at the Big House as he did in October and November. Chellam is combing Paati's hair with her mother-of-pearl comb. The lump in the corner of her jaw is already there, throbbing like a tree lizard's green throat, but it's still small, not yet engorged by public humiliations and tragic prophecies.

Outside, her father pops imaginary rice-and-sambar balls into his open mouth and loudly bemoans the plight of his six other children at home. His teats sag like a stray dog's; his grey heels are cracked and calloused.

Trap him in a hole and block off the entrance with a stone, Suresh thinks.

Crush him like an insect, *krik krik krak.*

"What d'you think he smells like?" asks Aasha. "I mean if you stand near him?"

"Catshit," says Suresh. "Clogged drains. Bus station toilets."

"Simply-simply shouting like a — like a —"

"Like a baboon," says Suresh.

Then, from her seat at the Formica table, Amma calls out for the benefit of the whole household: "Oh God, it's him again! Our hero. The great Mr. Muniandy. Suresh, tell Lourdesmary to take him his monthly breakfast. Thirty days a month he has a liquid breakfast, one day he eats bread and jam. No wonder he has Twiggy's figure."

Muniandy gets his once-a-month solid breakfast thanks to two factors: Amma's unflinching knowledge that the watchers-from-windows would cluck and shake their heads at any lapse in the Big House's kindness to poor men and beggar men (*So much money also they can be so stingy! Five cents is as big as a bullock-cart wheel for them!*), and Lourdesmary's conviction that taking a beggar's bread and jam to him is the quickest and simplest of ways to propitiate the Lord. For in September, when Chellam first arrived at the Big House, the limestone caves that could be seen from the front gate had collapsed while Lourdesmary was bicycling to work. Lourdesmary had lived in one of those caves, and when they heaved and crumpled they buried her out-of-work husband, her eight children, and a hundred other squatter families. There were cries from under the rubble for days, but no one was saved. When the *New Straits Times* reporter came to interview her about the incident, Lourdesmary ticked the names of her eight children off on her fingers, one by one, as if they were items on a shopping list.

"Poor bastards," Appa said. "The government only helps those who help themselves. God himself is up there taking bribes."

Lourdesmary skipped one day of work for her family's mass funeral; after that she bicycled to the Big House every morning at six-thirty, as usual. Once a month she takes Muniandy his bread and jam to help herself by bribing God. The plate on which this breakfast is served, along with the tumbler that holds Muniandy's Nescafé, are from an outdoor shelf designated for the servants' plates and cups in 1963, when Letchumi and Vellamma were first hired. The bread and jam are, respectively, two slices from a Paris Bakery sandwich loaf and some Yeo Hiap Seng pineapple jam, both purchased solely for the consumption of the servants and Muniandy. But Lourdesmary believes the offering to be sufficient to stave off crippling bicycle accidents, stomach cancer, blindness, and other ills, and Amma doubts that Mrs. Balakrishnan can tell, through her curtains across the street, that they don't feed Muniandy Sunshine bread.

Chellam's father's breakfast fortifies him for a still more impassioned performance. He wails so mightily that Suresh and Aasha can see the soggy bread bits clinging to his tongue; he pulls his hair and beats his chest.

In Paati's corner, Chellam's hard hands keep themselves busy with Paati's comb.

"Chari, enna?" Appa says when Muniandy's lament has gone on for a good ten minutes (not including breakfast). He stands at the other end of the corridor, waiting to see if Chellam has a plan of action. "Will you go out and talk to him or shall I send him away as usual?"

"No," Chellam says. "I'm not going, Master." Not since her father's first visit to the Big House has she braved a face-to-face meeting with him. She'd known he'd turn up on her first payday; of course Mr. No-Balls Dwivedi would pass on her new employer's address to her father without a moment of hesitation. Appa, at least, made a token attempt to shoo him away on that first day. "Get lost!" he'd shouted from inside the house. "Go away! We don't need your nonsense here." But her father had moaned and carried on and subjected them all to his keening and skirling, and finally her new master had sent her out to deal with her father. "Pathinelu vaisu," her father had said over and over, slapping her mouth each time he confirmed her age: seventeen years old. And still so worthless as to try to keep your wages from her old father. When at last he'd released her shoulder, she'd run in to get the money from Appa. And when her father had left, fifty ringgit richer, she'd run to her room and crossed out the first row of her Spectacles Account with a dry, scratchy pen. Master Gave zero ringgit, nothing, nothing at all; total Things I Bought, also zero. No kacang puteh, no boiled peanuts, no red ginger from the corner shop. Once, twice, thrice she'd crossed the row out, and then, determined to erase all evidence of this fruitless month, she'd gone over her three neat lines in loops and spirals, in lightning zigs and spiky zags, the dried-out nib loudly abrading the paper and finally tearing through it so that a few scratches marked the page underneath.

For the next thirty days she'd consoled herself with a fresh plan: she'd refuse to go to her father when he came back. Nothing doing, she'd say. She didn't think Amma capable of the extremes to which Mrs. Dwivedi, in her pink silk and wrist-to-elbow bangles, had sometimes gone: grabbing Chellam by the hair, yanking her towards the door, screaming that she was not to come back into the house until she'd got rid of her father. This new maddam was too limp and empty and tired to turn herself into such a shrewing, frothing whirligig, and as for Master, Chellam had not, until then, seen him in anything but a good humor.

Chellam had guessed correctly that Amma hadn't the personality for hair-yanking and full-blast cursing, and that Appa preferred almost anything to a scene, but she hadn't considered alternate methods of avoiding a scene, so when — on the first Saturday of November — Appa patted his front shirt pocket and said, evenly, "Well, if you're not going to give him the money, I'll do it myself," a shard of disappointment like a chicken-bone splinter caught in her throat. For a month, she's tried to ignore it every time she swallows. *Master won't do the same thing every month*, she's told herself. *He won't stand for it.*

Now her hands tug Paati's comb through her wispy hair as if it were a mass of tough tangles. Paati's eyebrows arch to meet her hairline, and her head jerks sharply back and forth, as if at any moment it might fall off and roll under the crockery cupboard, where it will shrivel up and turn into Yardley lavender-scented brown dust (all except for the eyes, which will lie like lost marbles under the cupboard, emitting an eerie light after everyone goes to bed at night).

"Well, if you don't want to talk to your father . . . ," says Appa. He pulls a wad of red banknotes out of his shirt pocket. "This month's wages," he says. "Do you want to give it to him yourself, or shall I?"

"I'm not going, Master," says Chellam again, and the teeth of Paati's comb scrape her bone-dry scalp audibly, leaving white tracks.

Three stray hairs float free and catch on the loose strips of rattan on the back of the chair, where they will stay until Paati herself has gone up in flames and returned to hunger, hollow and transparent, for teatime treats. Until Uma's backyard fire singes them, they will retain their substance, weight, and shadow.

"Aiyo, Enna?" Paati fusses. "What are you simply-simply pulling my hair for?"

At the front gate, Appa's voice is like a pair of scissors on smooth cloth, *snip-snip-snip-snip,* a voice he reserves for all the undesirables of this world, the theatrical tramps, the limping armies who offer unwanted parking assistance outside his office, the glib urchins who rush towards his already clean windscreen with wet rags. But Chellam's father isn't picky about delivery. He takes the wad of red notes with both hands and feels its weight course through him like a puff of bhang. *Fifty dollars. More than fifty bottles of samsu.* He's not as slow as he makes himself out to be, and already the effects of the morning's bibulous binge have begun to wear off, leaving him lean and ravenous, ready to kill a goat with his bare hands, father five more sons, swim the length of the Kinta River. He clasps his hands to his forehead and bows his head in prayer like a man before a temple flame. He falls at Appa's feet.

"Chhi! Useless feller!" Appa turns and marches back to the house, his checkered sarong swishing. But the real source of his disgust isn't the knowledge that the wife and six children Muniandy invokes each month see nothing of this money (not a sniff, not a glimpse of the king's fleshy profile), or even a vicarious frustration with Chellam's situation (length of service up to now: three months; payment received: M$0). No, what repulses him is the man's obsequiousness: that's the ultimate insult to these pariahs, he thinks, not to let them kiss your bloody feet. Feeding on pity and debasing themselves as if it were some form of compensation. *For fifty dollars a man like that will kiss your feet, lick your balls, swim through shit, whatever he thinks you want to see. Why can't these people have a little dignity? It's they themselves who perpetuate all the bloody problems — class, caste, you name it, they're the ones clinging to all that nonsense because all they know is begging. The more time you spend with them the more you start to see them as animals because that's what they want. In the end it's better to close your eyes and pretend they don't exist.* Appa shudders and steps into the shower to cleanse himself of his contact with the world's filth, and unseen, Suresh and Aasha shudder and rub Muniandy's latest visit off their arms.

Outside the gate, Muniandy is gathering himself to go, counting the bills, steadying himself on his feet, steeling himself for the short walk to the main road bus stop. But today, much to Suresh's dismay, Amma will drag out his visit and force Suresh to walk all the way down the driveway to look at his face and talk to him.

With a start that topples her chair backwards, Amma shoots up from her seat at the Formica table. "Eh, eh, eh," she says, "I forgot lah, I meant to give the man that bundle in the shed this month. Chellam has enough shirts already, and Mat Din says the trousers are too big for him now. What'll we do with all those clothes? Suresh, go," she continues, her voice rising with the urgency of the moment, "hurry up and get that bundle in the shed and give it to him across the gate."

Suresh feels his bottom sink stubbornly into his seat. "But Amma —" he begins.

"*Tsk,* no ifsandsorbuts," she snaps. "What is all this answering back? For a small thing like this also too shy or what?"

"I don't want to talk to Muniandy."

"Ohoho! You think you are some fine high-class Englishman, is it? You'll catch some disease just by talking to him across the gate? Hanh? Just because the man isn't dressed in bestquality courthouse clothes like your father doesn't mean he's not a human being, okay? Just because he's poor doesn't mean he's a dog. A ten-year-old boy calling a fifty-year-old man by his name! Who ever heard such a thing! *I don't want to talk to Muniandy* it seems. Who do you think —"

"But Amma, I don't think Chellam's father would *want —*"

"Who are you to sit there and decide what people want and what people don't want? Hanh? Oo wah, Mister Lord Mayor of London sitting there and deciding who needs what it seems. Let me tell you something you won't know because you've been a rich man's son all your life: people like that man can't afford to be choosy. People like that will wear gunny sacks if you give them for free. Go and get the bundle — I don't want it sitting there in the shed for the rest of our lives."

Slowly Suresh peels his bottom off the seat. He sighs and pushes his chair back inch by noisy inch.

"*Tsk!* Please, yaar," says Amma, "no need for all this drama. What next, will you wait for the violin music and then start sobbing? Give me a break. Please."

Half standing, half sitting, his hand on the back of his chair, Suresh stops and stares at Amma. His shoulder blades jut farther out than ever.

Suresh is right, in fact, that Chellam's father won't want a big bundle of old clothes — he'll have to walk all the way from the bus station to his village with it — but Amma, in her eagerness for public charity, hasn't thought about that journey.

Every three or four months Amma skims the choicest items off the family's old-clothes pile, stuffs them into plastic bags large and small, and rations them out with her chastened pity. She acquired this proclivity to charity and her voice-for-servants at the same time: together they were one rung on the ladder to Society Wifehood. Each new month her handouts continue to make her feel flush with benevolence, and is this feeling so misplaced? What other household's servants can dress their worm-ridden offspring in Buster Brown and Ladybird clothing? Amma's fantasy is not so far from the truth: on new-clothes day, Vellamma's children and Letchumi's (but not Lourdesmary's, who are turning to dust under the rubble of their cave dwelling) wait by the front door of their respective huts, clapping their hands when they see their mothers approaching, feeling for all the world luckier than princes.

And there have been courthouse shirts for Chellam (who now has enough for a lifetime of gender-bending housework) and trousers for Mat Din. The arrangement has been perfect until quite recently, but Mat Din, alas, has been growing steadily skinnier as prosperity has padded Appa's belly. Amma will not be denied any of her pleasure just because Appa's trousers no longer fit the imploding Mat Din. "Just go and give Chellam's father the bundle," she hisses now, her voice flat and relentless as a dripping tap. Suresh and Aasha will do anything to turn off that voice; only Uma, softly humming her Simon and Garfunkel tunes to block it out, is ever able to resist it. "If you don't want to talk to him, fine, don't talk to him. Just hand him the bundle and come back."

At the front gate, Suresh does her bidding. The bundle is larger than any the other servants have ever received, because pairs and pairs of bestquality courthouse trousers have been accumulating for months, since even Mat Din's belt could no longer hold them up. Besides the trousers, the bundle contains six long-sleeved cotton shirts, the lot wrapped in a worn bedsheet. It smells slightly musty, and on the bedsheet there's a three-toned stain where dirty water has dripped through the shed roof and spread like ink on filter paper. Suresh bites his lower lip and stands with his knees locked and his bare feet turned inwards. In the glass panel of the front door he looks like the picture of the African-child-with-rickets sandwiched inconsolably between the child-with-kwashiorkor and the child-with-goiter in his health science textbook. He's secretly rebelling by not wearing his Japanese slippers. He doesn't need Amma to notice; he doesn't even want her to. *He* knows he isn't following the rules. He might just get hookworm.

"In fact the bedsheet also they can use," Amma says out loud to herself, watching his reflection in the glass panel, which ends a few inches above the ground and therefore doesn't show his bare feet. "It's still good."

But neither Muniandy nor his wife and children will ever use the bedsheet, because they don't own a mattress. They sleep on coir mats on a mud floor in a village whose name Amma can't remember. They'll never use the long-sleeved shirts or the bestquality trousers either. Chellam's father has never worn a long-sleeved shirt in his life; he doesn't work in an air-conditioned office like Appa, and the shirts are far too warm for the seamy toddy shop. To the end of his days he will therefore prefer his sarong and his sweat rag for swabbing his bare chest. But for now he can't tell what's inside the bundle. He takes it from Suresh and says, "Romba thanks, aiyya," as if Suresh is a grown man, a chief minister, the toddy-shop owner to whom he's pledged all his wages for the next five years.

"See?" Amma says inside the house. "I told him, isn't it? Soooo shy he was to just go and give Muniandy the bundle, and look how much pride the man himself has. I *told* him, with this type of people you don't need to feel shy."

Now Chellam's father bounces the bundle in his arms, judging its weight: another bulky encumbrance to lug to the bus station, to maneuver through queues and crowds. He will have to carry it there on his shoulders, and already he's unsteady from the morning's five bottles of samsu. On the bus the other passengers will suck their teeth and glare at him for needing extra space for his bundle. "Romba thanks," he repeats. If Suresh looked up now to meet his eyes, he'd see that they're as unreadable as tinted windows in the daytime. But he doesn't look up. He watches a fat black ant slip into a crack in the cement; then he turns and walks back to the house, his shoulder blades burning from the embarrassment of Chellam's father's following eyes.

"Good, good," says Amma. "Sure enough, isn't it," she repeats as if Suresh could hear her, "he grabbed whatever we could give. Where beggars can be choosers?" Satisfied with the outcome of the transaction, she rewards herself with a prim sip of tea.

In the corner, Chellam twists Paati's thin hair into a walnut-sized knot. "Aiyo! Enna?" Paati cries out again, more loudly this time, though her voice is still morning-phlegmy. She raises a groping hand to her head as if she might find the source of her stinging scalp sticking out from it: a scrap of durian skin, a leftover fish skeleton, a barbed bobby pin? The hand ranges over her head like a spider. Chellam thrusts a kovalai of coffee, Paati's reward for enduring her morning toilet, at her other hand. It knocks against a knuckle with a woody sound; Paati winces and jumps. The teaspoon falls out of the kovalai and onto the floor, and hot coffee splashes onto her saree. Chellam turns on her heels and walks away, the lump in her jaw throbbing green through her skin.

"Aiyo! What sins I must have committed to be left to the mercy of a servant as useless as that girl!" Paati shouts. "How many times I've told her not to leave the spoon in the kovalai! Just stir it, take the spoon out, and give me the kovalai — how hard is that? The whole family has washed their hands of me and entrusted me to this idiot!" Paati bends over in her rattan chair and gropes for the fallen teaspoon, but her arm's too short: her hand clasps and unclasps a full foot above the floor, a goat's mouth in a grassless pasture.

In her slant-ceilinged room under the stairs, Chellam pulls all her clothes out of her cupboard, including the four long-sleeved shirts she's inherited from Appa. She dumps them — a single armful — onto her unmade bed and folds them carefully, for no particular reason, as if she's packing to go somewhere. Then she puts them all back in the cupboard and sits on the edge of her bed, her breathing barely audible above the buzzing of a fly trapped between the window and the mosquito netting. After twenty minutes, she hears Paati shouting and gets up to take her to the bathroom.

That evening, Aasha counts three new marks on Paati: two dark pinch-spots on her right arm and a red welt on her left temple. She files them neatly away under Evidence That Chellam Is Taking Out Her Frustrations on Paati. It's one thing for Amma to inflict mouthslaps and thighpinches and headknocks on Paati; it's another for Chellam to do the same, or worse. She isn't even part of the family. But Aasha can't tell anyone about what she's seen. Not Amma, of course, because Amma would say Oho, so who do you think you are? And so on and so forth, and — and if Amma learns that Aasha notices such things, that she stations herself behind settees and armchairs and watches whoever happens to be around, then the words she uses to indict Chellam — slap, pinch, knock — will hang between them like moths caught in a spiderweb. No, not Amma. And not Suresh: he'd only laugh and tell her she's stoopid. Mind your own business, he'd say. Don't simply-simply go poking your nose here there everywhere, spying on people like a Russian. And not Appa, because he's never home and when he is he doesn't want to talk. Which leaves only Uma, but Uma is not for telling things to. Uma would just get up and walk away when she saw Aasha coming. She'd close her room door and sit humming behind it.

Or would she? What if Aasha could make Uma see that Chellam is secretly a bad person, and no replacement at all for a proper oldest-eldest? What if Aasha's findings are important enough to make Uma sit up and say Hmm, and knit her brow, and listen? Because they are indeed important findings: if they aren't, why does Chellam bully Paati only when she thinks no one's watching or listening?

What Aasha cannot know is that the new red welt owes its existence to Paati's nodding off and banging her head hard on the wall next to her rattan chair, and that Chellam applied liniment to Paati's temple and rubbed it vigorously to minimize the swelling.

Believing, therefore, that she has valuable information that would benefit all concerned (except Chellam), she spends days summoning up her courage. Every time she thinks she might have summoned an adequate supply, it ebbs when she catches sight of Uma. But finally, one afternoon, Uma comes downstairs without a book or a college catalogue, with nothing at all in her hands, and she isn't humming. She goes out to the gate and leans on it, staring down the lane as if she's waiting for someone, except that she isn't. If she has friends at school, they never visit her at home. *Now,* Aasha says to herself. *Now's the moment when I tell her.* At first it seems too much too soon, too huge a truth to impart to Uma just like that, out of the blue, when it's been ages and ages since Uma spoke to her or she spoke to Uma: weeks, months, maybe fifty or sixty months, at any rate not since Suresh got his Standard Five exam results or the Malay girl down the road started school. Maybe she should get Uma to friend her again first, maybe she should—but there's no time for all that, because soon Uma will sigh and go back up to her room, just as abruptly as she came down. So Aasha goes out to the yard and stands at Uma's elbow, and as she expected, Uma doesn't look at her. But she must, she must do it before she loses heart. Quickly, breath held, like swallowing cough medicine.

"Uma," she says, "do you—do you think Chellam is nice?"

Uma turns to look at her, frowning. Aasha's heart turns a somersault, her ears are singing, her breath is hot, and now she remembers that it isn't just speaking they haven't done in ages and ages, but looking at each other, right in the eyes, openly like this. She might explode from the fear and the joy of it. She might burst into tears and not be able to stop.

"What?" Uma says. "What are you talking about?"

"I'm just—I only—do you think Chellam is a good person?"

"Am I a good person?" Uma says. "Are you a good person?"

To this, Aasha can find nothing to say. She keeps her lips together and rolls her tongue around like Baldy Wong, like a deaf-and-dumb idiot, like a cow inconvenienced by the thick, meaty slab inside its own mouth. *Of course you're a good person,* she thinks, with a blazing loyalty that shows only in the twisting of her right leg around her left. *Of course I'm also a good person.* But Uma doesn't want an answer, and knowing this, all Aasha can do is to shake her head, *No no don't be angry, sorry for disturbing you,* and run away to lie on the green PVC settee. After a few minutes she hears Uma come in, shut the front grille behind her, and go up to her room. When she closes her eyes she can hear the *chuff-chuff-chuff* of Uma's feet on the floor as she moves around, the creak of her ceiling fan, her wordless humming, to which Aasha fills in the words:

> *Who will love a little sparrow?*
> *Who's traveled far and cries for rest?*

THE NEXT MORNING, a craving for appams seizes Paati and will not let go.

"Bread and butter, bread and butter every day," she grumbles, "keeping house these days is so easy, I tell you! What-what I used to make every morning for the family's breakfast in my time! Dosais! Idlis! Appams! With extra coconut milk and eggs for the boys! Now all I have to do is mention appams and my son's fashionable painted-and-powdered wife says it's the cook's day off it seems. Hanh, Raju? What do you say to this? God forbid your wife should—"

"Okay, enough of it," Amma says. "Your great son, in case you haven't noticed, is not at home to hear your complaints. I'll send Chellam to the market to buy you some appams. Now just shut up and wait."

Paati waits until the warmth of Amma's breath on her arms has dissipated before whispering to herself, "Look at them, Raju, look at them. You see how they talk to me when you're not here? This is what you get for marrying—" But she's miscalculated the acuity of Amma's ears, for in one smooth movement Amma swings around and gives Paati a mouthslap that echoes all through the house. Suresh hears it in the back yard, where he is racing two snails on the garden wall; Aasha hears it in the dining room. And Mr. McDougall's daughter, who's been sitting in Suresh's chair, dives under the table to shiver and shake unseen. Aasha respects her privacy but drops two margarined crusts of bread so that the poor girl doesn't go hungry.

When Amma appears in search of Chellam, her face is clear and her hands are calm.

Charged with her appam-buying mission, Chellam sallies forth, marketing basket on one arm. She'll have to take a bus, because Mat Din's not here to drive her; Sunday's his day off too. "Oi Chellam!" Suresh calls out to her. "Chellam, going to meet your boyfriend in the market, yah? Combed your hair and put on lipstick blush eye shadow! Walking like a model only!"

Chellam swats at his arm and sucks her teeth, but she's smiling broadly. "Ish!" she says. "Where got makeup? Never comb hair also!"

When she returns, the smile's been wiped off her face, never to reappear in quite the same sunny hue, for she brings with her news that is not for smiling at. News whose reception and dissemination will forever change her place in the Big House.

"Maddam," she says, standing at the back door with her basket of appams (hot-hot, wrapped in newspaper), "I seeing Master outside market with . . . with Chinese woman!" Half triumphant, half terrified, holding on to the doorjamb as if she can't possibly step over the threshold with this news; as if, like someone returning from a funeral, she must cleanse herself in the yard before entering the house.

"What do you mean?" asks Amma. "What are you simply-simply blabbering about?" But Amma's voice is like vinegar. Her heart sends up a great splash of bile as it hurtles down into her stomach. At once she hates Chellam for her gloating, for reporting this as if it were gossip about Kooky Rooky, or the latest episode of a TV show. She's furious and disgusted. She's melting away where she stands, weakening, disappearing. And most of all she's frightened of whatever else Chellam has to say. She doesn't want to hear it, none of it, no, no, she could give the girl two tight slaps to shut her up, but already Chellam has gone on:

"Yah, one Chinese woman, Maddam. I think so she like Master's another wife like that. Because two of them together buying sayur sawi, Chinese cabbage, big piece ginger, one bunch spring onions, big white bawal like this." She holds her hands apart to illustrate the size of the fish, as if this alone leaves no doubt about Appa's salacious intentions. "But Master carrying everything."

And, in a way, the fish does change everything. For Amma has always known there were other women: Lily Rozells, Claudine Koh, Nalini Dorai, all those miniskirted, cigarette-smoking women who gave her mocking sidelong glances at her wedding. Of course, during those long nights when Appa doesn't come home, he's at the club with them, gambling, drinking whiskey, doing other things to prove to each other how open-minded and free-spirited and European they all are. But this, this idyllic domestic scene Chellam has just sketched for them (for now Amma knows, without turning to look, that the children are standing behind her, listening wide-eyed to this account of their Appa's extracurricular activities) — the ginger and spring onions, clearly for steaming the fish, proof that they'd already planned the evening meal — this Amma never imagined. Not even in the depths of her tea-sipping gloom, when she has suspected others of knowing more than she does (why else the specks of pity in their eyes when they look at her? why the falling over each other to pamper her ego?), has she pictured such details. Cabbage. Ginger. Spring onions. Have the Ladies and the neighbors made weekly notes of Appa's secret shopping lists too?

No matter how much Amma wants to fall down on the kitchen floor and weep, she cannot, she will not, cry in front of a servant.

Even if Chellam stopped now, it would be too late. Suresh's and Aasha's grudging affection for her has shifted imperceptibly, for while servant girls may be caught red-handed (and while they themselves, not so very long ago, caught Chellam digging for treasure in her nose, and then — and then — oh, disgusting Chellam with her disgusting habits!), they must never do the catching themselves. Yet Chellam doesn't seem to rein herself in; her skin itches with what she's seen, and her eyes are dry with its heat. "Got childrens also!" she cries, her voice rising. "One girl same size like Aasha like that, some more two small-small boys! All of them calling him Pa!"

Aasha contemplates the girl who is the same size as she is. In what other ways is she like Aasha? Does she like yam chips and sago pudding? Has she read *The Water Babies*? Does she have a blue denim skirt that buttons down the side and a twenty-four-color Staedtler pencil set?

Uma, who's pouring herself a glass of ice water in the kitchen, files away *Pa* instead of *Appa*: a small but crucial variation. To Amma and Suresh and Aasha this is a gratuitous tidbit, Chellam's way of rubbing all their noses in her discovery. *How dare you?* Suresh thinks. *Like a stupid cat bringing a dead mouse in your mouth and expecting us to be proud!* "Chellamservant," he will say to her later that day, "who cares what they call him anyway? You think you so great, is it?"

But Uma watches the two words — Pa, Appa — turn in her head like balls juggled in slow motion in a clear blue sky. She will come back to them again and again in the coming months, at every moment she gets to herself and many moments she doesn't, savoring the secret of her wondering when people carry on other conversations around her. Pa or Appa? Moral, a-moral. Typical, a-typical. Pa, A-pa. Father or un-father, which was he?

"What is this, Chellam," Amma says now, "did you stand there and watch them for two hours?"

Even this between-the-teeth question doesn't deter Chellam. The howling storm in her head won't allow her to see or hear the small signs of danger around her.

"No, Maddam," Chellam says, "I not simply-simply standing there. I going this way, Master coming that way" — she blocks out their steps with her feet, like a dancing teacher — "then suddenly he standing in front of me. Then Master say sorry sorry sorry and quickly-quickly he going away. I no time to say Hello Master also. They going in a blue car, Maddam, nicely shining, I think so must be new."

Now she launches into a full report of the mistress's attire. Brown samfoo. Cheap wooden clogs with red plastic uppers, "you know that type, Maddam, all Chinese women also wearing that type." A single jade bangle around one wrist. No earrings. And she licks her lips to prepare them for the most important morsel of information yet: "She not pretty also, Maddam! Fat-fat like this." Chellam makes a circle of her arms, as if she were holding one of the enormous urns in which the mother-in-law's tongue plant grows by the front door. "Some more not white-white like some Chinese lady. Almost black like . . . like . . ." Here she hesitates, because of course Amma herself is the standard of superlative blackness. *Like you* already buds in her mouth, but as little as she understands the implications of her revelation, Chellam knows enough not to compare Master's real wife to his bluff wife; she knows it is not her place as a servant even to notice Maddam's complexion; and finally, she's reluctant to tell a lie: the mistress is indeed dark for a Chinese lady, but nowhere near as dark as Amma. "Almost black like *me*, Maddam!" she exclaims. These details Suresh and Aasha digest eagerly — they tilt towards Chellam, willing her to paint a still-less-flattering portrait of the mistress — but alas, unpracticed storyteller that she is, Chellam cannot read her audience and does not stop on this high note. "At least if she so young and so pretty, Maddam," she babbles, squandering her advantage, "at least then we can understand, isn't it?"

No, Chellam. They wouldn't be able to understand, not if the mistress were as exquisite as a Mughal empress in a fountained garden, not even if she were as fair as daylight itself. Look, look at Aasha's fierce and unyielding eye; recognize this thing with which you're toying, because you'll come to know it well soon enough. Fire. A ticking bomb. A lit Deepavali sparkler, spitting its sparks closer and closer to your spellbound hands. These are no superficial alliances you're stoking; this is no impartial audience. You're shortsighted in ways no spectacles will ever fix: you're forgetting the thickness and pull of blood. For suggesting that a fair-skinned mistress would be a tolerable thorn in the side of this family, you'll not be forgiven here.

That chill in the air isn't just Uma opening the fridge to get more ice water, but Chellam, oblivious, goes on: "And you know what, Maddam, she got a big hole in her mouth! Tooth come out already or what, I don't know. So *ugly* this woman and still Master following-following her! Maybe she put charm on Master, Maddam. She got one Chinese bomoh giving her black magic."

More deficiencies follow the description of the tooth hole: oily hair, blotchy skin, rough hands with cracked and dirty nails (worn, though Chellam does not know it, from nights of washing dishes in an enormous plastic basin, evenings of scrubbing sooty woks, mornings of plucking the heads off prawns). "Not high class," Chellam says. "Cannot speak English also. Master talking to all of them in Malay, Maddam."

Suresh is assailed by a sudden vision of Appa ruffling the hair of one of his slant-eyed Chindian children. (Later he will tell Aasha: "They probably talk with their mouths full and have sores on their legs. They probably have runny noses and nasty Chinaman manners.") He looks at the *OED* on its high shelf and thinks: *But Appa doesn't speak Malay!* Appa's *proud* of his horrendous grasp of the language. "I've no use for their bloody Bumiputera tongue," he scoffs whenever he gets the chance. "It's good for nothing but fanning their bloody wounded pride. I was tricked into great expectations in my callow youth, but now I'll tell you one thing: we Indians should rue the day the British left this country. No way am I going to adopt their pidgin language just because they tell me to."

Yet out of sight, while his real children sit reading abridged classics in their Buster Brown clothing, Appa goes shopping for fish and spring onions with a woman who can't speak English. Afterwards, he probably lies in her arms and lets her feed him cockles pulled from their shells. The Malay language clearly has other uses than fanning wounded pride, and Amma must be thinking this thought along with Suresh, for now she laughs a laugh like a fine crack in a porcelain bowl and says, "Who needs English when you speak the language of love?"

Because Suresh's heart leaps with jubilation—*Amma got the joke without my having to speak it!*—and relief—*Now she'll just laugh and tell Chellam to shut up, and everything will be all right*—and even a glimmer of clannish solidarity—*It's our joke, Chellam, of course you don't understand, so no need to stand there looking at us like a doonggu*—he wrinkles his nose and laughs back at Amma. But Amma doesn't look at him and laugh some more, as he wants her to: she pirouettes like a dancer to face him and then smacks the grin off his face with her green-veined hand. "What's so funny?" she says. "Don't think you're not going to grow up to be just like your great father." He stands there, grinless, tearless, sharp shoulder blades waiting to blossom into wings and carry him away from this foolishness. He will look down at the layers of dust on top of the kitchen cabinets and the useless cake pans on the fridge, at the tops of everyone else's heads and his own empty shoes on the floor. He'll hoot at them like an owl:

Who, who, whoooo do you think you are?

And with a last wave he will swoop out the door and up, up, up into the blue sky, free of his useless family forever.

Into the bristling silence Chellam persists, in a misguided attempt to soothe him with flattery: "Those childrens not like Suresh and Aasha, talking English like English people only. I think so those childrens cannot talk one word English also."

Stupid Chellam Newservant, thinks Suresh as he rubs at his wounded mouth. *Rubber-estate tattletale. Think you going to get a gold star for attention to detail or what?*

That night Amma waits at the dining table long past her usual bedtime, leaving the front door open though the mosquitoes swarm in in clouds she can see from where she sits. In the glass panel, all she can see are streetlamps and porchlights. At two o'clock she shuts the door and goes up to bed alone.

For three nights after Chellam spots him at the market, Appa doesn't come home.

When finally he does, Amma is ready for him.

Your Chindian clutch, she calls the mistress's children, alighting on the phrase with an immaculate satisfaction. She sits very straight, her teeth unnaturally white, her hair shining in the lamplight, as though she's been burnished from the inside by all her purifying hate. "Tell me," she says, "what else does your marketwoman cook for you? All the Chinaman food you pretend to make fun of in front of us and your more-English-than-the-English friends? Pig-intestine porridge? Bak kut teh? Pork trotters? Hanh?"

"Good one," Appa says. "For how long did your servant girl have to shadow me before she found out something worth reporting? Well, good for you. Zookeeper, assistant chef, *and* private detective in one. I knew you'd be pleased with your bargain."

"As though I need to pay someone to find out these things. I'm sure the rest of the world knows much more than Chellam. If I want more details all I have to do is ask Mrs. Balakrishnan or Mrs. Dwivedi." As she throws this declaration—nothing more than brash speculation—up in the air, Amma watches Appa's face for any clue that she may be right. If indeed everyone knows, does he know that they know? Appa holds her gaze and betrays nothing, no, not a flicker of guilt; he'll not give her a single inch to add to her self-importance.

Of course she's right: Dhanwati Dwivedi's husband is a fellow bigshot lawyer in the deputy prosecutor's chambers. He has followed the flourishing of Appa's romance like a botanist cataloguing a new species. With steadily decreasing guilt, he has sugared the fruits of his study and hand-fed them to his wife: *A Chinese char kuay teow hawker lady! Three children, looking just like him it seems. A terrace house in Greentown. Lies to his wife about traveling for work, actually he's taken that woman on whirlwind holidays all over the place! Singapore, Australia, maybe Europe.* And Mrs. Dwivedi, daintily downing the lot, has bloated with delectation. In three years she gained sixteen pounds trying to keep these secrets. One afternoon a year ago she told all to Mrs. Jasbir Bhardwaj in a single breath. Within two weeks Dhanwati lost all that excess weight, Jasbir whispered the gist of the matter to the elderly Mrs. Justice Rosie Thomas during a five-minute break in their bonsai class, and Rosie single-mouthedly told everyone else. Through their regular Outside meetings, this faction of the teatime circle has formed a definite opinion of the Chinese mistress: gold digger, trap setter, mistress of all that is seen and unseen, gap-toothed, lard-fed, thick-necked, market-bred.

Now it's Appa's (real) family's turn to enhance reportage with imagination. Or with research of their own: Aasha turns to Mr. McDougall's daughter, who was herself half of a bluff family.

"What did *you* call your bluff father?" Aasha asks, frowning, belligerent. In the days since Chellam's revelation, Aasha's fondness for Mr. McDougall's daughter has been clouded by an itch to pinch her. Which would be impossible, since ghosts can't be touched, let alone pinched, but just thinking about it gives Aasha great pleasure. A nice tight pinch, a fat wad of that peachy flesh between thumb and forefinger. She tries to convey the pinching in her voice.

As predicted, Mr. McDougall's daughter turns defensive. "He wasn't my bluff father," she says. "He was my daddy, and that's what I called him."

"But you didn't live here. You didn't live in your so-called daddy's house."

"No, but he bought me these clothes." Mr. McDougall's daughter twirls to show off her ice-blue smocked frock and then holds out her patent-leathered feet one by one.

"But he didn't let you come into the house, isn't it? Don't lie to me. I already know your story."

Aasha has by-hearted every detail of that story: the emerald-green silk cheongsam the girl's mother wore on their last taxi ride to the Big House (because she was much more fashionable, it seems, than Appa's Chinese mistress); the calling and calling at the gate; the mother taking off her shoes and flinging them over the gate (which was higher and blacker than the gate with which Tata was to replace them two years later); Mr. McDougall's real family's amah (also Chinese) coming out to chase them away. The taxi going back where it came from, with Mr. McDougall's mistress sobbing open-mouthed in the back, her bare, blistered feet up on the seat. Only the taxi doesn't reach its destination; suddenly the mistress tells the driver to stop and says, This way, this way. Turn left and right and left again. Stop here.

The taxi driver saying Are you sure, are you sure? And after Mr. McDougall's Chinese mistress takes out all her money and gives it to him, reversing his car and speeding away like a crazy man, hoo! Tires screeching, engine roaring, like a TV car chase.

Then that pond, glittering mirror-bright in the harsh noonday light, it looked as if they might walk on it.

"Och, what a hot day it was!" Mr. McDougall's daughter cries out at the memory. That's how she talks sometimes, like a storybook, peppering her speech with ochs and exclamation marks to prove she's half Scottish.

Usually Aasha appreciates her exotic manners, but today she says, "Action-action only, you think you're the Queen of England or what?"

Mr. McDougall's daughter's face falls, and falls, and falls, until Aasha can barely recognize it: it is no longer the face of an old friend but a long, watery glimmer, already fading, a face for lanterns, candlelight, oil paintings in ornate frames. A dream. A haunting. An unwelcome, unwelcoming stranger. Mr. McDougall's daughter trickles down the bathroom wall and is gone.

"STUPID CHELLAM," Suresh says about a week after Chellam's discovery. "Thinks she's so great." It is three in the afternoon. In the dining room, Amma sits staring into a mug of tea so cold it may as well have been brewed on the morning Chellam came back from the market with her news. Suresh and Aasha are in the yard, melting small plastic objects (toothpaste tube caps, drawer knobs, Chinese pill bottles) with matches to stop up holes in the garden wall that Appa built in 1956. There are too many for them to fill in a single afternoon, but they have braced themselves for weeks of work; they will do what they can today. "Ugly Fairies live in these holes," Suresh tells Aasha. "They look like Chellam's stoopid father. They squat inside there and lick their arms all the way down to their elbows after eating their rice and sambar. And even while eating they're shitting."

Sssrp! Sssrp! The sounds of Amma's slow, deliberate tea sips snake through the open dining room windows and into the children's ears.

"Yuck," Aasha says obligingly. "Chellam and her whole family are *disgusting.*" She stops up a hole with pink strings of melted plastic, blowing on her burning fingers and sucking her breath in noisily as though she were eating a devil curry.

In their dirty, dark hovels in the garden wall, the Ugly Fairies wail and beat their breasts like jilted maidens in Tamil movies. Their writhing traps their matted hair in the hardening plastic; their lungs seize up from the fumes.

"Serves them right," Aasha says.

"Yah, no kidding," says Suresh.

The back yard fills with fumes like a medicine factory's: bone-clean, germ-free, yet somehow dangerous.

"Yabbah! What a stink!" Paati hollers from her rattan chair. "That idiot of a girl, where is she, she's gone and left the stove on. Gas is leaking, gas is leaking!" She blows the bad smell briskly out of her diamond-and-blackhead-studded nose.

Chellam starts awake from her catnap. "Hanh? What?" she says. "What gas?"

"Chhi!" Paati says, choking on the smell, wiping tears from her eyes with her papery palms. "When Raju is away I could die and nobody would notice, I tell you." Her voice quavers with phlegm.

Chellam pulls herself to her feet and shuffles to the kitchen window to see Suresh melting a toothpaste tube lid with unnecessary flourishes, like a roti canai man before a busload of tourists.

"Enna paithium!" Chellam shrieks, and is out the back door like a scalded cat.

Suresh drops his flaming match on the cement to die a slow death.

Amma lifts her head sharply, interrupting a silver teardrop's meandering course down her cheek and sending it flying into her mug, where it hits the surface of her tea with a *plink!* She sees Chellam sprint barefoot across the yard and grab her deviant offspring by their dusty elbows. *Let his children burn themselves,* she thinks. *Serves them right.* And why shouldn't she resent their blatant frivolity in the face of her sorrow, their refusal to bow and hold doors open for that greyly gliding figure in its high-collared robes?

Even as Suresh and Aasha feel Chellam's hard knuckles around their elbows, they're watching Amma, who blinks blankly at them before lowering her eyes to her tea. The gust of her thoughts chills their faces, so recently warm from their match flames; in a moment it has summarily extinguished Suresh's last match.

13

WHAT UNCLE BALLROOM SAW

T WO YEARS BEFORE Uncle Ballroom's final visit, he put in an appearance that started off with pomp and promise and brotherly benevolence, with hugs in the street, fizzy drinks for the children, briyani for dinner, and midnight feasts. But after two months of lushly orchestrated merriment, the visit ended with a single note on an out-of-tune piano. Tinny, unfamiliar, strangely sad. Perhaps even unsettling. Each member of the family was to remember that ending differently, although they would all remember it with equal clarity.

On the afternoon Uncle Ballroom's letter arrived, Aasha was waiting on the green PVC settee for Uma to finish her bucket shower in the downstairs bathroom. Her ears kept track of all Uma's movements through the closed bathroom door: the dips of the big plastic cup into the water basin, the splashes of cool water on hot head and hard tiles, the scrubbing of thick hair with firm fingers, the dropping of the wet soap cake on the floor. The soap would have one flat corner now, with tile marks on it, but there was none of the cursing or tooth-sucking that ensued when Appa or Amma dropped it, just a brief interruption in Uma's humming before she picked up where she left off. She wasn't singing the words, but Aasha knew them all, and filled them in from her seat:

Cecilia, you're breaking my heart
You're shaking my confidence daily . . .

Cecilia was a milk-white girl with dark brown hair and freckles everywhere. She was beautiful, more beautiful than Aasha would ever be, but oh, so cruel: she invited another boy into her bed while her boyfriend washed his face, and then ran away. Aasha suspected that when the lovelorn boyfriend begged her to come home, she would laugh at him, so hard he'd see the pink of her throat.

"Don't you think so, Uma?" Aasha asked when Uma appeared, wrapped in two towels. "If she's not cruel, why doesn't she just come home?"

"Oh, I don't know," said Uma. She unwound the towel around her head and, still standing on the rug outside the bathroom, began to dry her hair. "Maybe the other boy in the song is better. Or maybe she doesn't love this boy. Just because someone loves you, doesn't mean you love them."

This was not, as it would have been to many young children, a revelation to Aasha. "That's true," she said. "Like Mr. Manickam from house number 67 loved Mrs. Manickam, but she didn't love him."

"Yes." They were walking up the stairs now, Aasha in Uma's trailing cloud of scents: Pear's soap, Clairol shampoo, Fab washing powder from her towel.

"That's why," reasoned Aasha, "Mrs. Manickam went with the government clerk in a taxi and never came back."

"Exactly."

"And like Kooky Rooky loves her half husband, but he's half someone else's husband, so he can't love her back the same amount."

"Quite so."

"But they deserve it, don't they?" Aasha stretched out on Uma's bed like a lounging farm boy, arms folded under her head, right ankle balanced on left knee.

"Who deserves what?" Uma was combing her long hair, working out the knots at the end. Droplets of water rode through the air on sunbeams and landed on Aasha's face and legs, cold, hair-raising, goosebump-inducing, but Aasha ignored them to follow her argument through:

"Mr. Manickam and Kooky Rooky. Because Mr. Manickam was just working-working only all the time, and Kooky Rooky tells lies. Who wants to love people like that?"

"Too true," said Uma. "Shall we go and do our homework?"

Aasha had no real homework: seated between Uma and Suresh, she usually had to invent her own, but today, when they went downstairs, Suresh had news for them.

"There was a letter," he said. "From Uncle Ballroom. In New York."

"New York!" Uma and Aasha cried in unison, for the previous year Uncle Ballroom had come from Buenos Aires.

"He says he's coming."

"Of course he's coming," Uma said, for they all knew that Uncle Ballroom wrote only when the unsympathetic winds had emptied his pockets and were blowing him back to the godforsaken strip of land in the South China Sea from which he'd escaped at the age of eighteen with nothing to his name but a pair of dancing shoes and a bespoke suit. But Uma's words tumbled forth a little too fast and too high for the cynic's sour note she'd tried to lend them, and in addition to this discord between content and tone, her brother and sister noticed a puckish twinkle in her right eye, a sudden leaning forward, a quarter smile (the upturn of one mouth corner, just a twitch, a glimmer, a dream). Because a visit from Uncle Ballroom meant fun and games all the way: late nights playing cards in the library, sips of brandy, Sunday roasts, Appa coming home for dinner and staying home on the weekends, rhumba lessons in the music room. And this time they could be uninhibited in their revelry, because Amma, who did nothing but stew in the background and mutter about Uncle Ballroom being a bad influence and Starting Young and what children learned from their elders, was away. She was in Kuala Lumpur at her sister Valli's house, where there would be no race riots and no babies this time, indeed no babies ever again, for Valli was in hospital for a hysterectomy. Valli didn't know anyone else who could take a month off from their life to come to Kuala Lumpur, and so Amma, having a whole fleet of servants to tend to her family's needs in her absence (as they did in her presence), had gone to Valli's rescue.

The children felt Amma's departure on their skin and in their lungs. Now they ate ice cream for lunch and snacks from the roti man for dinner, under Paati's indulgent, milky eye. They watched Indonesian films on TV until midnight and helped Mat Din water the plants. And Suresh rolled out the jokes, loud and hearty, for anyone who happened to be within earshot:

One o'clock, two o'clock, three o'clock ROCK,
Dorairaj tied a RIBBON to his COCK!

"If your Amma were here!" Paati said, wheezing with laughter. And her eyes said: *How delicious it is that she isn't!*

"What's long, hard, and full of seamen? Ho-ho! What you thinking? Such dirty-filthy minds you all got! It's just a submarine!"

This made everyone present shake their heads and groan, all except for Appa, who'd been preoccupied lately, placating them with *hmms* and *ehs* and *sures* when they knew he wasn't listening. "Heh-heh," he chuckled. "Not bad." The skin around his eyes looked thin and dark, like wet newspaper, like something that would shred if he rubbed it. Yet he smiled and rumpled Suresh's hair and gave him a dutiful punch on the shoulder, and Suresh grinned and racked his brain for something even dirtier.

Now that Uncle Ballroom was coming, life would be better still. For all Appa's putdowns and barbs, he could never hide his grudging fondness for his harmless, hapless brother: the minute he read the letter, the children knew, he'd be planning menus, ordering Lourdesmary to reserve whole goats at the market and bring home live chickens to hand-feed for five days.

This time, though, Appa did none of that. "Wonderful, wonderful," he said when Suresh brought him the letter, but he hardly looked at it before setting it down on the coffee table. Then he folded his newspaper, pushed his glasses up to the top of his head, leaned back in his armchair, and closed his eyes. He was besieged by difficulties these days. On one side, the draining gloom of yet another gruesome trial: the Curry Murder. An Indian housewife stood accused, the saree-clad, pottu-emblazoned type who emanated so much good-wifeliness, that she'd managed not only to eviscerate her husband with a fish knife, but subsequently to chop him up, cook him in her largest cast-iron wok — which wok she had brought with her to her husband's house as part of her dowry — and distribute his curried, plastic-bagged remains in dustbins over a twenty-mile radius before her neighbors had noticed anything amiss. The case against her remained flimsy, her word (*Don't know where my husband went. Disappeared just like that. Probably* got *another woman.*) against her neighbors' (*Funny noises came from that house one night. Then for hours got meat-cooking smells, even at one o'clock in the morning.*).

But it was the problem on the other side that was steadily sapping Appa's strength. Murder he could handle; he was accustomed to the grotesque imaginations of the depraved, even managed occasionally to relish them. The souring of his sweet mistress was another matter.

How Appa had come to take a char kuay teow lady as his mistress is a tale so delicate and complicated that to understand it one has to scrutinize their first meeting as if it were an exquisite Mughal miniature: here one must squint to make out the subjects' facial expressions, there to see just how much skin is exposed, and here to determine whether these fingers are really touching or there is a hairsbreadth of air between them.

What we know for certain: he met her on a workday morning in 1973, ten days after a stormy night on which Aasha had been unremarkably and unsatisfyingly conceived and Uma had been taken ill with an inexplicable fever.

Business was slow that morning for the char kuay teow lady. The flames under her wok leaped, danced, burned blue in Appa's glasses, and once, for a brief three seconds, soared as high as her chest, prompting Mr. Dwivedi, who was lunching with Appa on this first occasion, to draw in his breath, and causing Appa to exclaim, "My goodness! Bloody daredevils these Chinese cooks are sometimes!" We know also that while Appa and Mr. Dwivedi ate, the char kuay teow lady sat at an adjacent table to peel prawns for the evening rush, and Mr. Dwivedi, his already jocular mood enhanced by his consumption of two Anchor beers, began to call out friendly greetings and nosy questions in Malay: "Oi, Ah Moi! Why so glum on such a nice day? Oh, Miss! You making good business, isn't it? Otherwise why for you cleaning twenty pounds of prawns?" So by the time she came to clear away their plates and glasses, she felt it would be rude not to exchange a few words with them, and the few words turned into an outpouring of her marital woes and a public denouncement of her no-good husband, who had gone home to China to care for his aging parents and not sent her money or news for more than a month now.

In order to return this touching trust in two white-shirted strangers, Appa told her (by this time she was sitting on the bench opposite them) about his crazy wife—who recently burned a saree in the back yard just because he'd had a late night at the club—and her even crazier parents next door, such impossible cartoon tales that the laughter rose, like a belch after a good meal, from deep within the char kuay teow lady, and Appa noticed that she was not at all ashamed of her crooked teeth, and that he could suddenly smell, my God, yes, his nostrils were coming alive, sighing, swooning, singing, the hairs in them doing a joyous dance, cilia rousing themselves as though from a witch's spell, synapses that had lain idle since whatever mysterious, forgotten childhood injury knocked them out now popping like Chinese New Year firecrackers. And what he smelled was the char kuay teow lady's breath, sharp and salty, like other people's descriptions of the sea. He breathed deeply and looked and looked at her, drinking in the fiery spirit of the wok that cloaked her plump shoulders, her smokiness, her heat.

When her manners and laughter and scent drew Appa back to the stall the following day, and for many consecutive days after that, Mr. Dwivedi began to suspect that something was up: no simple craving for lard and cockles could explain Appa's devotion to this one stall. And after months of worrying his little loose-tooth secret, Mr. Dwivedi shared it with his wife, Dhanwati—hypotheses, observations, conclusions, conjecture, everything. Now the Chinese Mistress was a secret of the nationally sanctioned variety, that is to say, open but not aboveboard. Appa knew that all his colleagues, all their wives, and all their wives' friends knew what car his mistress drove, where she got her hair permed, approximately how much she must weigh, and how crooked her teeth were. The colleagues, their wives, and their wives' friends all knew Appa knew they knew. But none of them ever spoke about the mistress to Appa, nor mentioned her in front of him, and he reciprocated the courtesy.

Only Amma knew nothing of the Chinese Mistress's existence. Her innocence required superhuman feats of discretion, logistics, and cooperation on everyone else's part, but Appa, who should have been grateful for these efforts and for his own sheer luck, was too besotted to consider himself lucky.

Appa had never been one to believe in love before he met his char kuay teow lady; lust he'd believed in wholeheartedly, for he'd felt its pangs and known its effects. The protective fondness he'd once felt for Vasanthi, yes, that he remembered, though he doubted that that sort of thing ever survived uncorroded in any marriage. But falling in love, that was all filmic phantasm, all novelty and sophomoric sentiment.

Except that after their first meeting, Appa could not get the char kuay teow lady out of his head or his nostrils, and not merely because he was lusting after her generous loins. That first night Suresh climbed into his lap at home to see blue flames burning in his glasses, the wildest, hungriest flames he'd ever seen. He reached out to touch Appa's glasses, burned his fingers on them, and put his puzzled palms on Appa's stubbly cheeks. Later, lying awake in bed beside Amma, Appa saw the blue fire leaping in his glasses where he'd set them down on the bedside table. He watched them until, exhausted by their energy, he fell asleep.

Nine months after Appa's first fateful meeting with the char kuay teow lady, Aasha prepared to make her exit into the world, ten days late. She stretched her elbows; Amma gasped. She gave the walls of her dwelling three peremptory kicks; Amma shrieked.

Appa was not at the office when Paati telephoned, an oddity that escaped her indulgent eye. The boy was a lawyer, after all, and not just any lawyer but a Big Name. He might be in court. He might be out researching a case. Who knew? He'd been uncommonly busy of late (of late? Four five months? Five six months? Paati was not as adept at keeping track of time as she had once been, and at the moment Amma, her silk caftan drenched in the waters of her womb, was not as attentive to such minutiae as she would one day be). Just a few months ago, Appa had had to travel all the way to Johore to investigate a case. Such were the burdens of being so brilliant. Paati sighed as she set down the receiver. She shook her head and resolved to see that Lourdesmary fed Appa extra well when he was next home.

Once again a friendly neighbor came to Amma's rescue in her hour of need: not a taxi-driving neighbor this time, but Mr. Balakrishnan, only mildly sozzled at four in the afternoon. Paati sat in his front passenger seat; Amma lay in the back. Uma had been instructed to look after her brother and keep the doors closed. None of them could have imagined where Appa really was that day: on a bench at a stall in Greentown, where the char kuay teow lady had just announced to him, while shelling prawns, that she was expecting his child. In response, Appa stuck his chest out, chuckled, and suggested a string of hybrid names: "How about Ah Meng Arumugam son-of-Rajasekharan? Balasubramaniam Bing Ee? Kok Meng Kanagappa?" His mistress sucked her teeth good-humoredly and swatted his arm. Customers at the other stalls wondered at this informality, but the owners of those stalls, who were by now used to Appa's daily visits, did not.

For four years Appa and his char kuay teow lady had a fairytale romance. When Paati and the rest of the family had believed him to be in Johore, he'd been in a beach chalet on Pangkor Island with his mistress. When Aasha was a year old they went to Australia, Appa inventing yet another demanding out-of-town case for his real family. He sent his lady on shopping trips to Singapore and package tours of Hong Kong. The lovesick state Appa had once dismissed as a Hollywood invention survived two babies, the lovers' long, tiring workdays, and other people's insidious bafflement (what Appa knew other people said about his ladylove had not diminished his adoration). After her sea scent and her inner fire, beyond the unrivaled kick of her chili sauce and the inexplicable plumpness of her prawns, Appa had discovered her wicked sense of humor, different from his only in vocabulary (and perhaps not so different in that respect in her own tongue: Appa and his mistress were forced to speak Malay to each other, a language that displayed neither one's sharp wit to full effect). And after that he'd uncovered what he still thought of, earnestly, boyishly, as her sweetness, a deep, palm-sugar sweetness, the kindness and gentle spirit he had once, for one year, thought Amma had. It brought him a relief he hadn't known he'd longed for; he closed his eyes and settled into it, as his father had settled into the Big House. He felt himself gently embraced, his thirst slaked, his wounds soothed. Other people's love affairs guttered and died out in two or three years, but the Malay language, inside which neither Appa nor his mistress belonged completely, had slowed time for them, so that in her cramped, pink-walled, fluorescent-lit, shrimp-paste-smelling terrace house in Greentown, Appa felt he was unfolding a continuing mystery by candlelight, and had never doubted she felt the same way.

But now something was changing, and Appa didn't know why or how to stop it. Had he been blind to small signs and slow changes, untutored as his eye was from a marriage that had started out stale? No, the perfection he remembered was not imaginary. Was the change his fault? Did she want a bigger house, a new car, was she not as forthright as he'd thought all these years and therefore too shy, or too proud, to ask for these things directly? Had he been expected to read her mind, and failed?

He surprised her with jewelry and flowers on ordinary days. Once, in a reckless move the town talked about for weeks — Lawyer Raja-sekharan's gone mad! What could he have been thinking? — he brought her to the club for drinks and dinner.

"I'm tired" was all she would say when he asked her what was wrong. "It's these children. They eat up all my energy. And the work. Every day, day after day. This isn't what I thought my life would be like when I was a girl."

"You don't have to work, you know," he told her every so often. "You can sit at home and take it easy. I can afford to take care of you."

"Of course," she said. "Of course you can afford it. But my father used to say a person shouldn't trust anything but his own two hands. And this is all I know how to do. Frying noodles. Ha!"

To this insinuation that she did not trust his promises, Appa had no reply.

He wondered if even she knew why, if she could name the reasons for which, before he left her on the evening Suresh brought him Uncle Ballroom's letter from New York, she flew into the sort of rage that brought cases to his desk. A fury that made him think about hiding the knives and pouring the cleaning solutions down the sink, checking their children into a hotel, spending the night across the street in his car to keep watch over her house.

"Everybody knows you'll never marry me," she'd said out of the blue, interrupting Appa's toe-counting game with the older child, a girl of almost four — only months younger than Aasha (who, at home in the Big House, was having her own toes counted by Uma). She was stir-frying leeks on the stove with her back to him. She'd never men-tioned marriage before, never indicated it was a dream or a possibil-ity — anyway, wasn't she still legally married to someone else? Into the silence that had met this statement, she'd gone on: "Those children you sit and play with every day, they'll always be bastards."

"Don't say that," Appa had said lamely, and then, already ashamed that this was all he could think of to offer, "Why don't we go out for a film tomorrow? Take the afternoon off and bring the children with us. You've been working too hard."

In relief — her mother's poisonous mood dispelled by her pa! with a practical solution she could understand! — the girl had begun to clamor and whine coquettishly. "No, no, let's go tonight! Tonight! I say tonight!"

"Aiyo yo," Appa said, smiling and shaking his head at her, "I can't say anything in front of you, hanh? We can't go tonight, Ling, we —"

But the child's air-raid siren of a demand — Promise, Pa! Promise, tomorrow! — had drowned out his excuse. He'd been about to pick her up, sling her over his knees, and wrestle her into silence when her mother had shot across the kitchen like a comet, her face wet with tears, her crooked teeth bared, and before Appa's brain could register her presence in front of him, she had begun to slap the child. Eight times she'd slapped her, as the leeks smoked and burned, sending up fumes that would once have barely ruffled Appa's feathers but now lacerated his sinuses. "What do you expect?" she'd asked with each right-cheek slap, and with each left-cheek slap she'd answered her own question: "You expect to be treated like a princess when you're just a whore's daughter. You expect to be more important than your father's real family. You expect your stupid tears to melt your father's heart. You expect people to make promises to a bastard child."

Appa had watched her, speechless, wishing he understood far less of the Cantonese she'd reverted to in her rage. When she'd sent the howling girl to bed and locked herself in the bathroom, he'd stood staring at the bathroom door for five minutes before putting the eggs destined for the stir-fry back in the fridge, turning off the stove, and leaving.

Now, leaning back in his armchair with his eyes closed, listening to Uncle Ballroom's letter flutter in the fan breeze, Appa was exhausted, broken, afraid.

"Appa, did Suresh tell you? That Uncle Ballroom's coming?" Uma came to ask when, after twenty minutes, Appa still hadn't said a word about Uncle Ballroom's welcome meal. She stood in the archway of the sitting room, frowning and smiling simultaneously at Appa, poor tired Appa, no energy even to loosen his necktie.

"Oh yes, yes. Useless bugger squanders all his money until he has nothing left for a plane ticket and then runs home with his tail between his legs."

"When Lourdesmary comes tomorrow shall I tell her to talk to the butcher? About local mutton for a briyani?"

"Yes, why not?"

"All right then." She retreated, only to return in a few moments with a cold bottle of orange squash and an ice-cube-filled glass. "Appa. Open your eyes and drink something before you fall asleep in that chair."

He opened his eyes and winked at Uma. "Don't you worry about me. But tell Lourdesmary to make sure she sees the whole goat before the butcher skins it. What with all the inventiveness one hears about these days, one wants to make sure one isn't feeding visiting uncles on the butcher's enemies."

"*Tsk!* Appa!" But Appa could tell from the wide smile that broke over her face before she stifled it that she was relieved, even proud, of having pulled a joke out of him. *I'm the only one who can do that without fail,* she was thinking, *and without trying.* Silently he confirmed her assessment: *Yes you are, Uma, yes you are.*

For Uma was his favorite, a fact that no one could change, that Suresh nevertheless resented, and that Aasha celebrated; lovely Uma, whose heart was as beautiful as her face! She deserved to be everyone's favorite, like the heroine of any fairy tale: the woodcutter's youngest and best daughter, the third and last princess, the good queen. *My Uma is worth ten sons,* Appa often said to his friends, and he meant it, though he'd wished for a boy before her birth. Not that he didn't love Suresh; the boy who'd arrived at last, after seven years, was a fine child, clever as a temple monkey, easy to please, difficult to upset. And Aasha, Aasha had promise, though she was a queer little mushroom of a child, always seeing ghosts and drawing odd conclusions. But there was something special about Uma, a hidden incandescence neither of the others had, a rejuvenating energy that made you say *Yes, of course another card game, why not turn on the music, shall we fry up some prawn crackers for a midnight snack?* But also—for there was more to Uma than strangers saw in her quirky teenage smile with its overlapping front teeth—a great strength. He remembered in mosaic detail the play Uma had put her brother and sister up to last year, how she had quietly broken his heart with her bravery. How afterwards, when no miraculous happily-ever-after had ensued in real life, she'd made a point of coming to his study to wish him good night (that low voice, that brief flash of conciliatory dimples) on his increasingly infrequent evenings at the Big House. As if to let him know she forgave him, as if to console *him* for the imperfection of their lives.

Suresh and Aasha recognized Uma's strength too: it was she they ran to when in need, not their mother. Uma's calm smile, Uma's even breathing, that nearly generous—yet faintly quizzical—look she trained on their mother's abundant incompetence. If there was something in this world that could upset Uma, none of them had yet discovered it.

No one—none of the powerful old men Appa knew, no barrister, judge, privy councillor, professor, minister, tycoon—had that kind of strength. Appa loved it, admired it, and almost, sometimes, feared it.

BLAME THE SHORT NOTICE on the various postal services involved: Uncle Ballroom arrived at the Big House a scant week after his letter. Uma, who went out to pay his taxi, got a pick-me-up-and-twirl-me-round hug, though she was taller than Uncle Ballroom now, and had to fold her legs to get her feet off the ground when he tried to lift her.

Uncle Ballroom hadn't changed much since his previous visit, yet he was not the same fellow Appa liked to point out to the children in his old family albums. That trim figure had bloomed into a paunch, saddlebags, and man-dugs whose dropping nipples, like panda eyes, showed through the white cotton shirt he was wearing. His jowls were as soft as overripe bananas, his chin substantial as a dugong's, his thick lips perpetually glistening as if he'd just eaten a bhajia, but he still rigged himself out in the same dapper outfits he wore in those old pictures. The pleated pants four sizes too tight and pulled up to his chest, the red cravat, the shiny oxford wingtips, as if he'd put them on one day in the 1950s and worn them bravely through his ballooning. Partly because of this outfit, partly because of his posh English accent ("Like *royalty*," Aasha said when he wasn't listening, "like people who got *horses*"), the way he ate his rice with a fork, and the cold-weather smell of his clothes, he remained as glamorous to the children as a foreign dignitary on a classroom visit: they all wanted to be noticed, called by name, *chosen*. The minute he walked in the door Aasha was tugging at his trouser legs and Suresh was bombarding him with riddles:

Which Singh owns the swimming pool company?

Kuldip Singh! Ha-ha, Cool Dip, you see!

Which Singh never drinks tea?

Jasbir Singh! Get it, get it? Just Beer Singh!

Even Appa, suddenly faced with such fierce competition for his children's affections, pulled himself together and guffawed appreciatively. "What do you think of our Suresh?" he said. "Can't tell you where he learns all these things."

Uncle Ballroom's suitcase was full, as usual, of peculiar, offhand gifts, a jumbled, wet-wool-smelling free-for-all, each item going to whichever child first pulled it gleefully out. "Oh, that," he said to everything they found. "Yes, I didn't know what else to do with that." But there was one object he'd brought especially for Uma, and this he handed to her, saying, "Watch out, it's breakable. Ha-ha! You'll be getting spoiled now." It was a souvenir egg cup commemorating the moon landing, with 1969 in gold on one side, and on the other the American flag under an image of the *Apollo 11*.

"Wasn't that ten years ago?" said Suresh.

"Eight and a half," said Uncle Ballroom, "but I thought Uma might like it nevertheless, because one day in the not so distant future she's probably going to be an astronaut herself. Eh? With those brains of hers?" He tapped his temple and winked exaggeratedly at Uma.

"Ohoho!" Appa exclaimed. "With *her* brains, she's probably going to be the one designing the spaceship, Balu."

"Appa, *please!* It's not like I'm Albert Einstein or something," said Uma, furrowing her brow playfully, covering her eyes in pretend shame.

"Oh no," Uncle Ballroom said. "Of course not. You're much prettier."

"And more multitalented," Paati chimed in. "Tell me, could Albert Einstein act like Uma? Now itself she could go to Hollywood and become a top actress!"

And so, on this merry note, began what no one knew would be Uncle Ballroom's penultimate visit.

Every night before dinner they ate chicken wings and pakoras in front of the TV. At dinner there was always beer for Appa and Uncle Ballroom, lovely, fizzy gunner for the children, and shandy for Paati, and once, on the first Saturday after Uncle Ballroom's arrival, Uma was allowed a shandy of her own. After Uma had put Aasha to bed, there were games in the library: Monopoly, and blackjack and cheat and trumps, all of which Paati invariably won after a neck-and-neck race with Uma, for Paati, despite her arthritis and her incipient cataracts, was as sharp as a pork seller's cleaver, and as decisive in her victories.

Sometimes she liked to pretend the shandy at dinner had enfeebled her faculties: "Oh my, oh my oh my," she'd say, "this time I'm really done for. Uma's going to trounce me all right." At other times she took a playing-field pleasure in dispiriting her opponents. "You men may as well surrender now itself and leave the game to me and Uma," she'd say, condemning Appa and Uncle Ballroom to oblivion with a flick of her wrist. Then she'd cackle with laughter, take a sip of the sherry Appa poured her while he and Uncle Ballroom worked through his reserve of single-malt scotch, and peer at each of her opponents in turn, shrewd, grey-faced, predatory even in her half-blind state, like an old, balding vulture.

After she'd soundly beaten them all half a dozen times, after they'd gone through half a bottle each of scotch and sherry, and fried a mound of prawn crackers for an emergency snack and eaten them, Paati would announce her bedtime, and Appa would yawn and stretch.

"Getting old, Brother? Turning in earlier and earlier, eh? Next time I come you'll be wearing striped pajamas and drinking hot milk before we tuck you in at seven," Uncle Ballroom said one night.

"Ah, no, I'm just tired," Appa said. He took off his glasses and rubbed his eyes, pulling at that fragile, ripe-plum skin, and Uma knew he was telling the truth. A blue melancholy seeped into her bones then, as surely as the encroaching dawn. A sick feeling, as though they'd all frittered away the night foolishly, and not just the night but so much else, her childhood, all that time, Appa getting old, how could he be old? She swallowed and thought of Uncle Ballroom's image — striped pajamas, hot milk in the nursery — not at all the sort of childhood she'd had, but now she longed for it as desperately as if it had once been hers, that stolid, inert childhood, because if only she could always be that little girl who'd sat on Appa's lap and shuddered and squealed for effect as she ran her palms along his stubbly cheeks, he would not be old. They would all be preserved forever in their safest, happiest states: Uma in her Buster Brown overalls, Appa at thirty, Paati brisk and busy, strong enough to swing Uma around by the arms. Amma as placid as a cow, years away from the slow boil that was her permanent state now.

"All right, Paati," Uma said, her voice so low and hushed that Suresh looked up, startled. "Shall I help you up to bed?" She stood and held out her arm, and creakily, stiffly, Paati rose to her feet and took it.

"Do you know, Balu," said Paati, "what-what Uma does for me? How would I survive without this girl? Everywhere I need to go she takes me. She's my legs and my eyes, I tell you, we all say yen kannu, yen kannu, but my Uma is really literally my eyes."

"I can see that, all right," said Uncle Ballroom. "You're a lucky old woman, Amma."

"Oh, Paati, Paati," said Uma. "When I was small you did everything for me, now I do everything for you. No need to make such a big deal about it."

And together Paati and Uma began their grueling nightly journey up the stairs, Paati lurching from side to side to spare her failing knee, Uma's left shoulder burning under Paati's weight.

"I keep telling the old lady," Appa said as soon as they were out of earshot, "to move downstairs. Lots of spare rooms downstairs, she could easily have one. Then she wouldn't have to kill herself to get upstairs every single night. 'Nonono,' she keeps saying. 'I'm fine. I'm not going to sleep downstairs like a servant.' She's stubborn, you know? Doesn't like to admit she's old. In her mind she's still the dynamo she was in her heyday."

"Yes," Uncle Ballroom said absently. His eyes were riveted to the doorway, as if he still saw his mother and his niece framed in it; his hands were clearing away the bottles and the dirty glasses, stacking the cards.

"Oh, leave all that, for heaven's sake," Appa said. "Letchumi will take care of it in the morning."

Still Uncle Ballroom's hands stacked cards and swept prawn cracker crumbs off the table. "Yes," he murmured, "I'm sure she misses those days in Butterworth. Her life is so—so different now. Not that you don't take splendid care of her, but . . ."

There he trailed off, but Appa wasn't listening anyway; he was rumpling Suresh's hair and hurrying him along to bed. No time for an eight-year-old to be up, he was saying, as if this were the first night Suresh had stayed up with them, as if he'd just realized what time it was.

Uncle Ballroom had much to say about Paati's heyday, but he would never say it, neither to Appa nor to anyone else, for he had carried it within him for thirty years, this knowledge that had taken up less and less space as he'd grown, yet had remained as heavy as it ever was. As a boy he'd staggered under its bulk; now it was a tiny, dense thing, threatening to tear a hole in the front pocket of his shirt.

There he was, ten years old, sent home from school at recess time because of a fever, cycling unsteadily towards his parents' back door, head swimming, hands clammy. And there, leaning against the house, was another bicycle, but it was all part of the day's confusion; his head was too light to wonder at it.

He took off his shoes and stepped through the back door.

He walked through the cool, shadowed kitchen.

And there, by the front window, in a patch of sunlight, were his mother and Mr. Boscombe, one of Tata's bosses at the shipping company. Mr. Boscombe and Mrs. Boscombe had come to tea at their house several times. In his booming, bearded voice, like an actor onstage, Mr. Boscombe had sung the praises of his mother's exotic confections — her vadai and pakoras and murukku, her sago pudding and coconut candy — and Mrs. Boscombe had sat with her knees pressed together, her blue eyes always searching, searching for specks of dust or smears of grime in Balu's mother's kitchen.

They were like a film poster now, Mr. Boscombe and his mother, standing in the sunshine with their arms around each other, laughing like two children who'd just shared a cigarette in the outhouse. They were at that moment when the music swelled and the heroine threw herself against the hero's chest. Then the screen would go black.

Balu padded softly back through the kitchen. Outside in the blinding sunlight he grabbed his bicycle and pedaled, so fast he felt he was turning into vapor. I'm feeling better, he told his teacher at school. My mother said I better come back so I don't miss anything for the test.

All those years growing up in that house with his father and mother and his brother, Uncle Ballroom had never been tempted to tell. Not even to one-up his cocky, know-it-all brother, so unaware of how little he actually knew. It wasn't a choice he made; he'd never thought *I mustn't, because* . . . There had never been a question of telling. It was simply impossible: what would he say? He could not describe what he had seen: the danger, the truly shameful secret, lay behind that, and he did not know the correct words for it. Anything he could say would come out sounding like his own dirty fantasy.

After some years, confessing had come to seem unnecessary. He had thought, when the image of that shining couple in the sunlight continued to visit him after fifteen or twenty years, *Come on, Balu, it could've been much worse. You could've seen them naked. Caught them in the act.* Because that afternoon had whittled his ears to a fine point and turned his eyes feline, and afterwards he had collected all the little clues, all the buttons fallen from his mother's castoff days, that had shown him the scene went on after the screen went black. He could have caught them then, and they might have seen him, and then what? He would have had to share the secret with her. In its dark and airless space they would've had to spend the rest of her life, like two strangers trapped in a lift for sixty years. So he'd counted himself lucky, kept his mouth shut, and tried to forget.

Yet tonight, in the half-light of his brother's wood-paneled study, the secret seemed unbearable, a boulder on his chest, a heat in his head. And a vise tightening behind his eyes: the same sun-blindness that had almost knocked him out on that delirious ride back to school that afternoon.

The boulder wasn't regret, and the heat wasn't anger; it was sorrow he felt, a debilitating sorrow he knew would only grow after tonight. Of all the reasons he might have felt sad, all the ways in which his secret might have reared its head, this was one he'd never seen coming: what he mourned was his mother's cruel decline, the idea that that kajaled, glowing, crimson-mouthed creature by the window could have been reduced to this old lady who could no longer make it up the stairs on her own. All that beauty gone who knows where. *Yes, Balu, you're more than halfway there yourself. You're older now than she was when . . . And what has the point of it all been? What good did your not telling ever do anybody?* If he'd told, perhaps he would've exorcised the dangerous, goosepimpling beauty of that scene by the window. Perhaps his shame and guilt and fear would not have kept him alone all his life, afraid to trust, even now, on the edge of old-manhood, still afraid. What had the secret cheated him out of? Did he even know?

"Is everything all right?" Uncle Ballroom started at the sound of Appa's voice; hadn't Raju gone to bed with the boy? But there he was, leaning in the doorway looking at him, arms folded, suddenly as old and tired as their mother. "Just a little tired?" he went on, without waiting for Uncle Ballroom's answer. "The jetlag, maybe?"

"Hmm, yes, a bit tired," Uncle Ballroom said. "I was thinking, you know, Mother—funny to see her so old—"

"Yes, I suppose it must be a shock each time when you're not living in the same house. Creeps up on me gradually, you see, so I barely notice."

"Yes yes. The thing is, when she was young she was so—things were so different. She had—I mean, she was so beautiful and all that, the talk of the town, you know what I mean?"

"Hmm. Happens to the best of us, you know, Balu, this growing-old business."

"Well, that, yes. But Mother . . . I used to look at her when I was a child, she was like a film star in my head, something that could never grow old. You know, you always think of them the way they looked in your favorite films, Ava Gardner, Rita Hayworth, who imagines them old? Mother was in her own film in my head. Just as glamorous. Heh-heh."

"Yes," Appa said. "I know what you mean."

He could not possibly know. If he had had the same secret, he would never have kept it to himself all these years. Would he? Either way, Uncle Ballroom found he could not go on. "Hmm," he said. Then, with a long sigh: "Anyway, don't let me keep you. You're the one who has to be at the office bright and early tomorrow morning. Better be off to bed, no?"

"Too true, too true." Appa looked at his watch. "Feel free to help yourself to a nightcap. Just switch off the lights when you come upstairs."

And he was gone, leaving Uncle Ballroom in a study that smelled faintly of frying oil. His footsteps on the upstairs floorboards echoed through the house, impossibly loud against the cool silence of this hour.

Uncle Ballroom stood up, pushed his chair in, and was about to switch off the light when Uma appeared at the doorway.

"Oh," she said, "everyone went to bed."

"Indeed," he said. "It's late." He smiled at her.

"Everyone is always so tired nowadays," she said. "I wish we could all be young forever, or whatever age we ourselves choose. What age would you be if you could choose, Uncle?"

"Me?" he said, but he wasn't pondering her question; he couldn't get past the way she'd read his mind. Or had seemed to. It was only a coincidence, but —

"Oh, never mind," she said, and then, with that infectious, lightning bolt of a smile, "Let's do something fun. I feel like — I feel like I want to run all the way to the limestone hills and back just to breathe some fresh air." There was an electric wakefulness in her eyes, but he knew all she'd had was a sip of her grandmother's sherry, and that there was nothing dangerous in her mood.

"Heh-heh-heh, I'm afraid you'd have to do that one on your own," he said. "Ten years ago I might've kept up with you, but look at me now, for heaven's sake! I'd keel over and die if I tried to run to the end of the driveway. Oh, no, my lass, I'm not the man I used to be."

"Come on, Uncle, you used to be a *dancer*."

"Used to, used to, my girl. *Used to* is the operative term."

"Don't you dance anymore?"

"Ah, well—"

"Sometimes? Just for fun?"

"When the occasion arises, I suppose."

"Oh! How come you never show us?"

"Show you, heh-heh, what do you mean, show you? Get up and start waltzing for no reason in the middle of dinner? Make your Paati tango with me in the kitchen?"

"I mean how come *we've* never seen you dance, and we're your own family, and you've won all those trophies and prizes and whatnot and all we ever see is the newspaper clippings! Not fair, isn't it? I think if you have a dancer in the family you should get free performances!"

"Oh, goodness gracious—"

"And free lessons too. I mean, can't you teach me?"

"I suppose I could, and I suspect you'd be a fine dancer, tall and graceful as you are, but look—"

"Teach me, then! You could teach me something now, just a bit, I mean. Come on, you're not sleepy, don't bluff, don't simply-simply start yawning to get out of it! I'm not sleepy either. Just ten minutes, we'll go upstairs to the music room, Appa has all his old records there."

"But everyone's *asleep,* Uma dearest."

"We'll put the music on low and we'll close the door. Nobody can hear anything when the door's closed. Paati and I always go in there so that I can rehearse my lines with her when we don't want Amma to hear, otherwise Amma's always looking for evidence that I joined the drama club just to meet boys. Come on, just ten minutes, and then we'll go to sleep and continue another time."

And so they went upstairs, and among Appa's old records managed to find some tango music, despite all Appa's apparent derision for tangoing (and foxtrotting).

And while they danced Uncle Ballroom laughed and shook his head at the comedy of it all, this walrus of a fellow who hadn't really danced in ten years, trying to teach an almost sixteen-year-old girl, a whole head taller than he, Good Lord, yes, she really was so very tall, this Uma child, and how awkward this was, but how contagious her joy. And so, laughing and shaking his head, he taught her—in fact quite carefully, quite precisely, for Uncle Ballroom was an exacting dancer if nothing else (as evinced by all those trophies): *Slow-slow-quickhold-slow, slow-slow-quickhold-slow, yes, that's right, just let me lead, slow-slow-quickhold-slow, now you're getting the hang of it* . . .

But though Uma had assured her uncle that the music room was soundproof, even the quiet strains of the most mellow number in Appa's generally mellow collection reached Aasha's ears on the other side of the house.

When at first she opened her eyes, she thought Mr. McDougall's little daughter had woken her again.

"Go to sleep," she said, not unkindly. "It's sleeping time now, okay?"

But then she heard faraway music, and voices—two voices—her sister's voice—and sat up. She swung her legs out of bed and waited. There it was again, her sister's voice. She slid off the edge of her bed, dropped onto her feet, and wandered across her room as though in a dream, running her hand along the wall, her small wardrobe, then the door, so as not to bump into things in the dark.

At the end of the corridor there was a faint light on as usual, for when Paati got up to go to the bathroom, which she did four or five times a night these days, cursing her bladder fruitily in the mornings. But the music and the voices were coming from the music room, and beyond this one light, all the corridors in between lay in darkness.

Now Aasha was determined, and nothing, no endless dark corridors, no sleepless spirits waiting to pull her hair or blow into her ears, would stop her. All the way across the house she journeyed, running her hands along walls, and anyone who saw her would've believed her to be drifting aimlessly; maybe she'd meant to go to the bathroom and her sleep-soaked brain had misled her, or maybe she was sleepwalking. But no, this barefoot, tousle-headed walk was in fact entirely purposeful, even if Aasha's rumpled appearance belied her doughty heart.

In the music room Uncle Ballroom was counting faster, one two three four, slow-slow-quickhold-slow, and Uma was laughing and gasping, barely keeping up, for all Uncle Ballroom's lamenting of his flown youth.

"Oh, this is fun," Uma said. "I wish I could dance like this every night."

"Yes, it is fun, isn't it?" said Uncle Ballroom. "I'd forgotten how much fun it was."

"Tell me about New York," she said breathlessly. "Is it — oops, sorry — just like in the films?"

"Oh, goodness, quite."

"But really?"

"New York, my sweet child" — and here he stopped and released her, and pulled out a handkerchief with which to mop his brow, because he really was quite, quite winded now, and moreover this dreadful humidity became less and less bearable each time he returned — "oh what a place it is. What a place."

And then, because Uncle Ballroom loved few things more than telling a good story — and also because he was half drunk with the stirring up of old memories in his feet and head, with the soulful beauty of this dance that had once been his favorite, and with the hungry hero-worship in his niece's bright eyes — he mopped his brow some more, tugged at his shirt collar to let some air in, took a deep breath, and spun his niece the sort of tale she wanted to hear, against the inspiring background of Juan D'Arienzo's orchestra. He told her of the winters that bled you dry, yes, just like in the Simon and Garfunkel song, Uma, heh-heh, and the diner breakfasts, and the hot dog stands, and the leaves in the autumn, the colors no one in Malaysia could imagine. He told her of great universities hundreds of years old where, behind ivy-strangled red brick walls, the cleverest people in the world peered through microscopes and studied their way to Nobel Prizes. He told her of Central Park, of glass skyscrapers and brownstones and fire escapes, of Park Avenue and Fifth Avenue, where the heels of women in furs and diamonds clicked all day long on the pavements.

At the door of the music room Aasha stopped and listened. Not because she was a habitual eavesdropper or tattletale, for her transformation into Aasha the waiter-watcher-listener was still to come. She listened now, with her hand on the doorknob, only because Uncle Ballroom's voice was like a teacher's, a voice you didn't want to interrupt, and if she opened the door he might not finish his story, or he might change the ending just because she was there. Uma wouldn't want that; Aasha didn't want that either.

"It's true," Uncle Ballroom was saying, "anything can happen in America. You can smell it in that cold air. You can see it in the way people walk. They're all expecting it to happen to them, this big anything, because in America you might be a doorman today and tomorrow find yourself rich and famous."

He did the funny accents for her: Brooklyn, Texas, Boston.

Uma doubled over laughing. "Oh, I can't picture all that," she said. "But I'll go there one day and see for myself."

"Of course you will. You could get into one of the top universities, no problem. You must come. Come to New York! I'll take you around and show you the sights. Together we shall ride the subway and the yellow taxicabs."

"Really? Really you'll take me around?"

And Uncle Ballroom didn't hesitate, or admit to Uma that she might have to pay for the taxicabs herself; like a priest blessing the communion offering, he held his palms up to the heavens and said, "But of course, my child, but of course!"

"Soon I can really come, you know? In two-three years' time. I have to finish school first, then I'll apply."

"Two-three years? Just study hard and that'll zip by in the blink of an eye, Uma! That's just around the corner. Before you can say Archbishop of Canterbury we'll be ice-skating together at Rockefeller Center."

Outside the room, Aasha let the doorknob go and stood silent, barely breathing, frowning, pouting. *In the blink of an eye.* In the blink of an eye Uma was going to go away to New York, and Aasha wasn't invited. This adventure excluded her, that much was clear. Aasha had seen pictures of people ice-skating in the wintertime, two by two in fur-trimmed hoods and mittens. It was a special thing for two people, for a man and a lady, like waltzing and weddings and on-the-mouth kisses.

And as if to underscore her deductions, someone put the needle of the record player at the beginning of a number, and fresh music started up.

"Okay okay," Uma said. "One more dance, quickly-quickly, and then we'll go and sleep. Just one more lesson to seal it up nicely in my memory, this way I won't forget before tomorrow night." She'd already grabbed her uncle by the hand and shoulder; they were already poised to begin.

All the way back in the dark Aasha shambled, running her hand along the wall. Inside her head her thoughts spat and sparked, threatening to flare up into a hundred small fires.

IN THE MORNING, Aasha sat frowning over her toast, swinging her legs and humming to herself, intermittently smiling into the distance.

"What are you smiling at, Aasha?" asked Uncle Ballroom after ten minutes of this.

"*Tsk,* don't ask her that," said Suresh. "She's just seeking attention."

"Well, and why shouldn't she be?" replied Uncle Ballroom. "Attention is a perfectly valid thing to seek, especially at four years of age. Do you have a joke to share, Aasha?"

"No," said Aasha.

"Let me see," Uncle Ballroom persisted, patting expressively at his head and face, "did I accidentally leave my funny hat on? Have I got a shaving cream mustache?"

Aasha furrowed her brow still more and looked away.

"Or maybe I've got—"

"You no need to pay attention to me," Aasha said. "I'm playing a game with Mr. McDougall's daughter."

"You see," said Suresh. "I *told* you."

"Hah!" said Appa. "Mr. McDougall's daughter certainly manages to muster up some impressive cheer to be playing breakfast-time games with you after being drowned in a mining pond."

"We're not playing games," said Aasha. "We're making plans."

"Oho! Always wise to—"

But before Appa could finish, Aasha went on: "You think only you all can have plans, is it?"

"Mmm-hmm," said Suresh, making his eyelids droop, pretending to stifle a yawn. "Tell us some more. Tell us all about your plans."

"Why should I tell you about our plans? You don't tell me about your plans, and Appa doesn't tell me about his plans and Amma doesn't tell anybody her plans and Uma—you don't know anything also but Uma's going to go to New York and *marry* Uncle Ballroom without telling anybody."

This did make Suresh sit up and stop yawning, but not for the reasons Aasha had intended it to. No one was reacting the way Aasha had thought they all would. Nothing had worked the way she'd wanted, and now she was the laughingstock of the family, caught with both feet in the middle of a blunder she didn't recognize. What had she said wrong?

"What? What what what?" Uma was saying, but she was laughing so hard her face was almost touching the table, and Appa was laughing too, and slapping both his own knee and Uma's, and Uncle Ballroom was revving up a big engine of a Santa Claus laugh, *hohohohohoHO!*, and Suresh was wiping real tears of laughter from his face now, not fake ones.

"It's true," Aasha said desperately. "She was *dancing* with him in the music room after everybody went to bed."

"That settles it, Balu," said Appa. "You know the laws about dancing with female relatives. You can't be teaching my daughter the two-step if you've no plans to put a ring on a finger."

"Actually it was the tango," said Uncle Ballroom, and then they all burst into laughter again.

"Aasha," said Suresh when he'd recovered sufficiently, "are you daft? People can't marry their *uncles,* stoopid."

And for days afterwards, as Aasha brooded and whispered in dark corners, they all repeated her dramatic announcement to each other, and expanded on it for their own amusement.

But after that comic opening, Appa's week quickly deteriorated. He no longer had the time to play Monopoly and card games after dinner; he excused himself, rushed off to his study while still chewing his last bite, and sometimes left the house during the night. They heard his car disappear down the driveway and expressed their regrets about the hard life of a lawyer while sighing and sucking their teeth over their cards; in the morning they made Lourdesmary bring him extra-strong tea.

The following week, he stopped appearing for dinner entirely. The children were well acquainted with this schedule, of course, but never before had Appa been so absent during one of Uncle Ballroom's visits. "Poor Appa," Uma said. "I'm sure he would rather be sitting here eating black pepper crabs with us. What to do?"

"Aye," said Uncle Ballroom, "but this is the sort of life you'll be condemned to, my girl, when you're a famous scientist or a heart surgeon, rushing around all over the place, eating hot dogs from a cart for your meals."

"Oh," said Uma airily, "I don't think I'll be a scientist. It's all very interesting but my true dream is to act."

"You can do both!" Paati said. "You can be the first one! Whatever you want to be also you can be."

A month into Uncle Ballroom's visit, the Curry Murder trial gained an unexpected momentum that distressed Appa. The defense counsel for the Curry Murderess produced a chimeric alibi, courtesy of a ten-year-old boy who swore the defendant had been in his father's bedroom on the night of the murder, while he himself had been watching *Hawaii Five-O* in the sitting room. As fishy as this young witness and his testimony smelled to Appa, neither he and his faithful team of clerks nor the police could put their finger on anything more damning than the boy's age, his obfuscatory lisp, and his stake in the outcome of the trial. ("She's my Amma," he'd said of the Curry Murderess, in direct contradiction to all existing documents, including, but not limited to, the boy's own birth certificate and a marriage certificate that bound the accused in matrimony to the curried man. "My Appa and I want her to come home and stay with us," he pleaded. "We always wanted her to, but she couldn't because there was a bad man keeping her prisoner. Now he's dead, so now my Appa can marry her and she can come and stay with us.")

That night, Appa's mistress's errant husband got out of a taxi in Greentown at midnight, having traveled home from China on a surprise visit. His suitcase brimmed with rare gifts: dried birds' nests and sharks' fins and abalone for soup, a red silk cheongsam he didn't know would be two sizes too small for his wife now that she'd had two babies; a jade necklace. He noticed a silver Volvo parked a few feet away and marveled at the fortunes of his neighbors. Whistling, he ambled into his house and opened the bedroom door to find his sobbing wife locked in the frantic embrace of a short Indian man. In the sitting room, two terrified children were watching television; none of them were to remember whether it'd been *Hawaii Five-O*. The mistress's husband bellowed, bursting a blood vessel in his eye and waking everyone in their row of terrace houses and the next. He ran to the kitchen, grabbed the cleaver his wife used to chop pig livers for her char kuay teow, and chased Appa out of the house with it. He picked up her wooden clogs and hurled them after Appa's silver Volvo. Up and down the street, lights went on in upstairs windows, and the faces of the neighbors who'd watched the progression of the affair with interest (for these were the days before imported American soap operas would satisfy their desire for sensation) and resentment (for many of these women were much prettier than the mistress, and therefore felt they had more right to a rich benefactor) and disgust (for those who weren't pretty thought it shameful that a married woman should carry on like this behind her husband's back) and jealousy (for, pretty or not, they all wanted to be taken on package tours in Hong Kong and sent on shopping trips to Singapore) hovered behind mosquito netting and curtains.

Speeding past the roaring trade of the suppertime hawker stalls and then over the black, shining waters of the Kinta River, Appa kept a tight grip on the steering wheel, but before him he saw only that menacing steel blade, broad as a loaf of bread, raised high above the cuckolded man's head, and then swinging so dangerously close to his own neck that he'd felt the breeze of its trajectory on his skin and heard its *hwoop* in his ear. Clutching the wheel ever harder, Appa began to cry. His hands shook; his glasses fogged up in the cool night air.

At two-thirty in the morning Appa pulled into the driveway of the Big House, slipped his shoes off at the front door, and crept through the pitch-dark sitting room like a cat.

On the landing, just in front of Paati's wedding photograph, Appa paused to catch his breath. *Hmm hmm,* his sepia-toned ancestors droned unanimously, the ringleted little girl in the front row suddenly as wise as the mamees in the back row with the twenty-sen-coin-sized pottus, *hmm hmm* (as Appa noted that Uma's door was open a crack and her light was still on), *hmm hmm hmm, we're not sure this is such a good idea.*

But too many other noises were ringing in Appa's ears for him to hear his solicitous ancestors. There he stood, the palm of his right hand on Uma's door, feeling weaker and more lonely than he'd ever felt. He'd been publicly humiliated; he'd felt the breeze and heard the *hwoop* of his mortality brandished before his face; he might never again be able to see the woman he loved, who had once loved him back, or their children, who still did. Everything was collapsing around him. What if the sight of her husband reminded her of how much she'd once loved him? What if she went back to him for everything Appa couldn't give her: the respect of her neighbors, and for her children a father who didn't have to sneak and cower and not be seen with them in public, but who would be theirs alone seven days a week, wherever they were?

Uma was awake. He wouldn't tell her what had happened, of course; no need to burden her with twenty years' worth of mistakes. He would talk to her about school, about her latest play, about what they'd had for dinner tonight and how their card games had gone, and just the effort, he knew — just the pretending to be fine for Uma — would pull him out of himself.

He took his glasses off, wiped his tears on his sleeve, and pushed the door open.

Uma jumped when he stepped into the room; she'd been leaning out of her open window, smoking a cigarette she'd inveigled from Uncle Ballroom. (*Oh come on Uncle, this way I can try it in the safety of my own home and not get caught, and then I won't be curious anymore, and I won't have to fall prey to all of New York's temptations.*) She stubbed it out on the windowsill and looked at Appa as he shut the door behind him, wide-eyed, breathing hard. Her skin glowed with sweat from her latest dancing lesson (the cha-cha this time); most of her hair had escaped from her braid and frizzed out in all directions.

"Appa!" she said. And then, drawing in her breath, putting a hand to her mouth as if this were a scene from one of her plays: "What — what's going on?"

He thought he hadn't managed to hide his distress; he thought she'd seen it at once, she with her preternatural senses and her infallible readings of her mother and siblings. His hands were shaking, after all, and he was swallowing hard to choke back his tears.

Doesn't matter, he was going to say. I just came to say good night. Saw your light on, you know.

But she hadn't interpreted his shaking and swallowing correctly, because she began to stammer and defend herself: "I — It's only this one time, Appa, I've never smoked even one cigarette before. I just thought — I don't know what gets into me late at night."

Then he was walking towards her, taking her hands. No no, he was saying — or was that only what he thought he'd said? No no, it's okay my girl, who cares about one bloody cigarette, it's not that —

This he knew he'd said: "Oh, Uma, Uma, I've been such a fool, I've made such a terrible mess of things." He was holding her now, more gently than Uncle Ballroom embraced her during their dancing lessons, and laying his forehead lightly on her shoulder, his tears dripping fast onto the floor, and what could she, not yet sixteen, say to this strangling self-doubt she'd never encountered? It frightened her and broke her heart, and he, sensing her fright, kept his remorse inside his mouth like a hot morsel of food he could not, must not, spit out, even if it burned his tongue and drove him mad with pain.

"Appa, Appa," she said, as she might have comforted Aasha after a bad dream or a fall, but the inadequacy of these words left her helpless; these could be no small or imagined woes that had brought Appa sobbing into her arms, her nonchalant Appa who always turned everything into a joke, who answered Amma's most rhetorical questions with dictionary definitions and clever parryings, who simply refused to play her bitter games by bolting out the front door every time she rolled the dice. Trembling, Uma put her arms around Appa's shoulders and patted the back of his head.

How they traveled, in the short space of three seconds, from the purifying sorrow of that moment to the scene that would forever replay itself in their resistant heads—the tightening of Appa's embrace, his face in her neck, his tears wetting the white cotton of her nightgown, his hands straying a little too far down her back, then withdrawing, as if they'd been burned, to her face, but once more descending to her neck, her shoulders, and then to the comfort of a beating heart behind a warm breast—neither of them would ever be able to say. Not that anyone would ever ask them; they would only seek to retrace the path in between for themselves, and fail.

Should Uma have screamed? Should she have called out quietly but firmly? Why didn't she, when Paati's door was ten steps away across the corridor?

Those questions, too, she could not have answered. What she did was to swallow her thin saliva and close her eyes, certain that nothing would ever be the same. She could not confine her father to the wrath of an unmerciful world, to its red-hot branding irons and its ice-cold whispers, but neither could she bear this, this sorry, weeping mess of a man fondling her breasts and running his hands again and again down the curve of her waist, as if he were describing the female form in a game of charades. And so she did what her mother had done in far less alarming, more publicly defensible circumstances seventeen years ago: she closed her eyes and floated up to the ceiling, and then she kept going, traveling farther than her mother had, out the window, through the clouds of tiny, oblivious insects, into the blue light of the streetlamp and beyond, her white nightgown billowing pale blue in that light. And Appa, in whose chest Uma's limp willingness struck a forgotten chord, felt an obscure, guilty gratitude for that abdication, because anything else would've been so much uglier.

Minutes afterwards, his shock-blasted mind would have forgotten whole swaths of detail. What had she been wearing? What had she said? And always, he would close his eyes in disbelief. Could that really have been him? But he could never escape the olfactory memory he'd retained of that night, for at consequential moments his young sense of smell now caught and held on to every little stimulus: Uma's faintly sweet sweat, and in her hair the hint of cigarette smoke mingled with her shampoo. And there'd been something else he couldn't name, a childlike smell that—though the actual smells of Uma's childhood had never penetrated his hermetic odorless universe—made him remember bathing and putting the toddler Uma to bed. What was it? A kind of soap? A lotion? He didn't know, but it was this smell that was his most devastating punishment, this reminder that what he'd done, he'd done to the child Uma had once been, the child she still was. But why had he done it, and how, and *how*?

That night, a small noise somewhere in the house—water in the pipes? white ants in the foundation? beams swelling with early morning dampness?—brought him back to himself. He pulled his hands away; he looked at his watch. "Goodness, goodness," he said, his voice still thick with tears. "I better go to bed. You better get some sleep too. We both better get some sleep. Tomorrow is a school day." As though he might have stayed if it weren't; as though the thought of having to get up at seven in the morning were the only thing stopping him from further trespasses.

He turned around, walked briskly to the door, opened it, and stepped right into the path of his brother, who'd just come back up the stairs. That night after dinner the family, minus Appa, had played poker, and Uncle Ballroom had lost badly; emptying his pockets of their change, he'd dropped a crucial scrap of paper on the floor of the study (scribbled on that scrap: the date by which he needed to pay this month's interest to his loan shark; the name of a horse someone had told him to put his money on the next race day; the telephone numbers of two more loan sharks). He stood face-to-face with Appa, the piece of paper safe in his trouser pocket.

"Why, hello," he said, smiling amiably, preparing to give Appa a full account of Uma's progress as a dancer, and to recommend that he send her for real lessons, when something in the way Appa stood frozen wiped the smile slowly off his face. He blinked and suddenly saw all that had escaped him at first: Appa's red eyes, his rumpled hair and clothes and face, the open door behind him, Uma standing behind her father in the light. Even before his eyes met hers, he thought *No, no no no, no, Uma,* as if it would be her fault for making him see what he was about to see, for not shielding him somehow, closing her door, hiding behind it, whatever, but no, there she was, hugging herself tightly, her eyes red too, her white nightgown falling off one shoulder, her face, not swollen exactly, but somehow injured.

"What the bloody hell are you doing up at this hour?" said Appa.

And though Uncle Ballroom wanted to be left alone, to go quietly to bed and not face any of this, even, for once, to complain — to say *I'm tired, I'm tired of always being the one to see too much* — he forced himself to stay and explain. "I dropped a piece of paper in the library tonight, you see," he began. He extracted the scrap and waved it theatrically, as though this proof alone would fix everything. "A very important piece of paper, all my information on it, you know, telephone numbers and racing tips and whatnot —"

"Racing tips!" said Appa. "Useless bloody fool, sponging off us for months at a time while you gamble your own money away!" His voice rose and lurched, cracked and banked as if he were drunk, and at all this ruckus just outside her door, Paati stirred in her bed. Looked at her bedside clock. Sighed deeply. *Don't tell me,* she thought. *Balu's nicely dipped into the liquor cabinet and now he's making a scene.*

"Sorry, Brother, sorry, sorry," Uncle Ballroom babbled, and to himself he demanded, *What am I sorry for? Why am I always the one feeling sorry?*

"Sorry!" said Appa. "Of course you're sorry! It's so easy to say sorry and then turn around and do the same thing, isn't it? How many times —?"

Before Appa's eyes Paati's door creaked open, and she stood looking at them, her two sons, fighting like dogs at three o'clock in the morning. Turning his head to see what had made Appa fall silent, Uncle Ballroom saw his mother, a tiny, crumbling thing in the shadows, with sagging breasts and a powdery face. And she saw the unspeakable dismay on his face — not a drunken face, no — and then the panic on Appa's face, that lip-curling rage of the trapped animal, and close behind him, just as Uncle Ballroom had seen her, Uma in the light. Silent, shivering slightly.

All those times Paati had invited a frightened, confused Uma into her bed, all those times she'd promised her granddaughter she would always be there to protect her, all that drained from her face with the blood, and she, too, shivered slightly where she stood. When she spoke, her voice was little more than a hoarse whisper.

"All of you, go to bed," she said. "This is no time for all this tamasha." Then, before anyone could speak to her, ask her anything, or force her to see more than she'd already seen, she retreated and shut her door behind her. She sank slowly onto her bed. She lay down on her side, her thin hips sticking out like a village cow's, and pressed five fingertips into her eyes, though already her cataracts blocked out what little light there was in her room. Outside her door she heard both her sons walk away down the corridor, Raju in front, quick and unapologetic, Balu shuffling wearily. She wasn't sure what had happened, but it was Raju who'd been caught, not Balu, and Uma who had been — what? Rescued? Caught being a willing accomplice? *I don't know, I don't know,* Paati thought. *I'm too old for all this.*

The next morning, Uma rose before anyone else, ate her breakfast standing up in the kitchen, and told Lourdesmary to inform the rest of the family that she'd taken the early bus to school for a prefects' meeting.

At twenty to ten, Appa sat down at the Formica table, forked down his throat the mucilaginous scrambled eggs Lourdesmary had served up at his usual breakfast time of seven-thirty, and hurried off to work.

Uncle Ballroom stayed in bed till noon, then dressed and left the house without a meal.

Paati crept out of her room after he left, took a slow and difficult bucket bath, and limped cautiously down the stairs.

Aasha had surrendered herself to the distracted babysitting services of Lourdesmary and Vellamma and Letchumi, helping Lourdesmary roll out chapattis and Vellamma hang up the washing.

That night, only Suresh cracked jokes at dinner. Aasha sat stiff in her chair, watching Uma's face for the slightest breath or ripple of good humor, shoveling her food so forcefully into her mouth that she gagged twice, and Uma had to chide her. That, in fact, was the only time Uma spoke. Afterwards there were no games. "Getting old, getting old," Paati said when Suresh protested, and Uncle Ballroom cited a nascent cold. Appa wasn't home.

Upstairs in his room Uncle Ballroom waited for the sound of Appa's car on the gravel driveway, and when he heard it, at two-thirty in the morning, he rushed down to meet Appa at the front door. This time Appa had, indeed, been drinking. His breath was heavy with whiskey; his smile was crooked.

"Hah!" he said upon seeing Uncle Ballroom standing at the door in his stockinged feet. "Waited up for me? Want to chaperone me to my room?"

"No," said Uncle Ballroom, "no, of course not —"

"What then? Going out for a walk in the dew in your socks?"

"I — no, Brother, I just — look, I'm not standing here for my own sake, I only — if it's the first time it happened — it's not, I know you love your children, Brother, I know it's not so simple, but there are things one can do, and there's no need to —"

For once, Appa only waited and listened, because he had no clever repartee, because he was tired and sick at heart and drunk, but most of all because, at that moment, he hated his brother and refused to make his finger-pointing any easier. Appa's silence was unyielding and imperious, and faced with it, Uncle Ballroom gabbled and garbled his words — as though, once again, his position were the more awkward — until Appa finally cut him short.

"How dare you?" he said. "How dare you come into my house and accuse me of these sick things your sick mind dreams up?" But already — his defense just begun — he was tempted to sit down in an armchair and say Yes, yes, my God, yes, please do something. Fix what I've done. Erase it. Erase it all and take me back to the beginning, Balu, can you do that? Can you take care of me and chart my fate? Instead, he heard himself say: "I was helping the girl with an essay, that's all. But now I know. Now I know what kind of person you are, what's on your mind. You're the one looking at her like that, dancing lessons it seems, tango it seems, cha-cha-cha, oh sure, and all this time I've closed one eye and let you carry on because I thought you were harmless, you were just playing the glamorous uncle. Now I realize Aasha was the only one who got it right. Out of the mouths of babes and sucklings indeed. Well, enough, Balu. Enough is enough. In the morning you can start packing your bags, and if you have any respect for yourself you'll never come back."

Uncle Ballroom stared unblinking at his brother. Did Raju believe his speech to be true? Some of it? All of it? Uncle Ballroom couldn't tell, and he couldn't decide which would cast the speech in a worse light: for Appa to believe or not believe what he was saying.

Either way, by morning, Appa had slept off his whiskey, but not his manufactured self-righteousness.

"Suresh, Aasha," he said, "you can start saying goodbye to your Uncle Ballroom. His visit's been cut short."

Suresh and Aasha sat speechless, acutely aware that something they didn't understand had just changed all their lives.

"Hah!" Appa said. "Got nothing to say to him? After all this time?"

And Uncle Ballroom could have told him to leave the children out of this, but was not moved to do so after the results of his previous intervention.

"Your Uncle Ballroom," Appa went on, "has crossed a line, that's all. After this it's a slippery slope. After cigarettes, is he going to give her ganja? After the tango and the cha-cha, what do you think he's going to teach her, hanh?"

At this Paati looked up sharply, and Suresh and Aasha, seeing her press her lips together, concluded that there had indeed been some truth in Aasha's fears (*A smaaaaall seed of truth,* conceded Suresh; *I was right,* thought Aasha). They could not know what Paati was really thinking: *Shut up, please shut up, I don't want to hear any of this, I don't want to know what happened between you two, please go away and settle it between yourselves and leave us all out of it.*

Uncle Ballroom, impoverished though he was, had too much dignity to stay on at the Big House. And not just dignity: he was tired and deflated, his leather belt perceptibly looser than it was yesterday morning, his chest softly hissing like a punctured beach ball. *I'm weak,* he thought. *I'm a bloody coward. But I tried, didn't I?* And self-preservation prevailed: *What else am I supposed to do? At least I've got the principles to leave.* That much was true: he didn't prostrate himself before Appa's might, didn't apologize any more than he had, didn't promise to shut up in exchange for free meals and a roof over his head. His bags were already packed; at the front door he said his awkward goodbyes to each member of the family in turn.

Except for Uma, who hadn't come downstairs. But she wasn't where everyone thought she was, behind the closed door of her bedroom; she stood in front of Paati's wedding photograph on the landing, from which spot she had committed to memory every word of Uncle Ballroom's expulsion. Just as he sallied forth down the driveway, she appeared at the doorway in her school pinafore, her hair wet and loose down her back, her feet bare. "Uncle Ballroom's going," he heard Aasha say to her. He looked over his shoulder and waved at her with his free hand. "Study hard, Uma," he said.

Not until he had disappeared from their view did Aasha turn to Uma and ask tremulously, "Why, Uma, why? Why you must study hard?"

"Of course I should study hard," said Uma. "Everybody should."

"It's because you're going to go to New York and live with Uncle Ballroom, isn't it? Isn't that why?"

"No," said Uma, and turned away.

"It is," said Aasha, "it *is,* and that's why Appa *banished* Uncle Ballroom, because it was true he wanted to marry you, and Appa won't let him."

Slowly, Uma turned around and looked at her. "Aasha," she said, and her voice was as soft as Amma's was at dangerous times, "shut up. You're not a baby anymore."

And at that moment, just as the minute hand on the hall clock touched the six, Aasha ceased to be a baby. The dimples in her knees smoothed themselves out. The creases in her thighs sizzled and melted. Her knuckles turned bony. Her forehead flattened.

Uma, too, grew up over the following months. Deprived of her dancing lessons, she taught herself some lessons of her own:

1) Paati was her protector no longer; she was just a selfish old lady who would never do anything to endanger the cushy life she led in her rich son's house, the morning tea, the afternoon coffee, the tea-time treats, the servants and the nice soft bed. Two days after Uncle Ballroom's departure, she'd asked Appa to move her bed to a spare room downstairs, after all those years of refusing when he suggested it. "I think you were right after all," she said. "My bones are not getting any younger. Such a chore for Uma to practically carry me up and down those stairs every day." Uma knew what Paati really feared; Appa knew it too, but each bore the weight of that knowledge separately as, together, they heaved Paati's bed down the stairs.

2) Aasha's adoration came at a price Uma no longer wished to pay. It was the adoration of a newborn for its mother, not love — certainly not what Uma would call love — but a black hole of need. The thought of sharing terrified Aasha; she'd tattled (in her own mind) and lied (in Uma's) to keep Uma for herself. If an equal need ever arose, she would once again do anything, tell any lie, bite and scratch and pull any below-the-belt trick she could think of, to get what she wanted.

But come on, Uma found herself pleading unprompted, *all children make up stories.*

Look at you, she chided herself at once, *you can't stop yourself from taking her side, even at your own expense. That's what's so insidious about them. Children make up stories all right, for whatever reason suits them, or for no reason at all. They're both selfish and capricious. The world is black and white for them:* Appa banished Uncle Ballroom because Uncle Ballroom wanted to marry you *it seems. Simple as that, hanh? Like one plus one equals two.*

Selfishness, capriciousness, reductionism: a treacherous combination indeed. Uma wanted no part of it.

3) There was only one part of the lesson Uma taught herself about Appa that she could put into words: he had lied. In the lowest, most unscrupulous way, to protect himself. She'd always laughed with, for him, when he'd used his clever words against those she, too, had scorned: Amma, her Ladies, the government. But today, in fear, he had taken that cruel wit and thrust it into Uncle Ballroom's belly, and the sight of it — no, the mere sound of it, from where she'd stood on the landing — had knocked the wind out of her.

What had come before those lies she could not verbalize even to herself; it existed only in pictures, in the chill that woke her night after night to lie in the dark and watch the streetlight across the lane. For years now, onstage, she'd been praised for letting her emotions run away with her, and now they ran all right, first at a steady trot, by the end of the week at a canter, working themselves up to a full-blown gallop within a month, though Appa never again entered her bedroom or so much as paused outside her door. And though neither Appa's clothes nor her own had come off that night — though, in fact, Appa's hands had not ventured under the white cotton of Uma's nightgown — Uma had looked up *incest* in the *OED*, that reliable old chum, that stalwart sidekick of Appa's, and then moved on to a thorough investigation of the topic in literature and in history, which investigation she allowed to color her thoughts and steal her dreams.

In the shower she scrubbed and scrubbed herself; at night she locked her door, which had the added advantage of teaching Aasha to fend for herself after nightmares.

But if it was true that all this was typical teenage melodrama, could Uma, of all guilty teenagers, be judged for it? Wouldn't anyone have permitted her these small exaggerations in partial compensation for the far greater crimes — of violation, of willful blindness — that had been committed against her?

Anyone might have, if he'd understood the equation, but the equation was neither obvious nor neat. Uma's descent into an invented hell compensated for nothing, of course; it only churned the regret Appa had already felt that night into a mad froth, forever obviating any retracing of steps or cleaning of slates.

For Appa would only too gladly have erased that night from both their memories, if even the attempt would not have required him to face her, somehow to force his tongue to speak that too-big, too-small word, *sorry.* For months he hoped that one morning Uma would make some shaky overture — a joke, a barb about the neighbors, anything — and he would be able to proceed from there, to work his way towards demonstrating his contrition, if not speak it. But as her silence deepened instead of faded, and he came to realize that she would not so much as acknowledge his own flawed overtures, he settled for denial. He compressed the memory of that night into a knot as tough and wrinkled as a kidney; he did his best to ignore the ensuing tightness in his gut. Eventually, magically, that knot turned itself inside out: he began to believe that he was the one who had been wronged, by a hyperbolic, overreacting teenager who could not forgive; he began to resent and then to despise her childish obstinacy.

In other respects his life did rewind itself and continue from that night when it had stopped short as though a speck of something foreign had found its way into its workings: at the end of two months, his mistress's husband, having burned her curtains and bedclothes, fed her pet finch to a stray cat, put her furniture out for the dustbin men, and, in short, done everything he could to destroy all evidence of her illicit life short of poisoning her two dusky-skinned children, realized that a wife could not be repossessed the way a car could.

All the inexplicable rage she'd flashed at Appa had fizzled out during their separation, leaving behind a hollowness she could not fathom herself. She didn't open her char kuay teow stall for weeks; all day she lay on the floor and wept, refusing to share the new bed her husband had bought for them even when he swore not to touch her.

"This man," her husband finally asked one morning, after they'd eaten Maggi mee in silence at every meal for three weeks, "do you love him?"

"What do you know about love?" she said. "If I said yes, would you let me go back to him?"

That evening he packed his suitcase (so much lighter now, without all those tinned and boxed delicacies) and left quietly.

The next morning the mistress went to find Appa at his office. "Ah yes," Appa said, so as not to put his witnesses in an awkward situation, "one of my clients." But he left with her, and they went to her house, where they sat in her stripped-bare sitting room, on the patch of pale floor where the ottoman had been. He pulled both children into his lap and told them a story about a woman with a magic cooking pot that produced as much chicken curry as she had guests to feed (*except*, thought Appa, *it wasn't really chicken*). By the following week, he'd replaced all the furniture the dustbin men had claimed.

And the week after that, Appa received a telephone call from an anonymous man claiming to have useful information relating to the Curry Murder case. That boy, the man said, the boy who claims he was watching TV while the woman was in bed with his father? Not a chance. He was here, in our flat, terrorizing our children.

This sort of thing Appa had dealt with before, and he knew just how to proceed: an offer of money (not so generous as a layman might think, for they were hard up, these low-cost-flat types, and what they really wanted out of these anonymous phone calls they made after watching too much TV was to be begged, to feel important), a promise of protection from the untruthful boy's thug father, and the man would come forward. He was a relative by marriage of the boy's father, and he and his wife had served, for the past three years, as unpaid babysitters for the boy whenever the Curry Murderess — for a murderess she was, and he was sure of it — came to ride his father's cockhorse on the carpeted floor of their sitting room, on the kitchen counter, or wherever else they did it. On the night of the murder, all of this man's neighbors had been made aware of the boy's presence in their block of flats, because he'd beaten up the man's youngest son and been belted and then caned with the finest of rotans. He'd wailed and screamed and threatened to throw himself off the babysitter's balcony; three people had come running to drag him away from the railing. For a little less money than the star witness himself, each of these people came forward, and Appa soon forgot that this meant his firm would have to ensure the protection of the entire building from the murderess's grief-crazed lover and the useful connections the man would doubtless soon seek out. Appa never remembered: when, months later, three of the neighbors died violent deaths (a man run over by a burger van in the building's car park; a woman slashed, strangled, and dumped at a nearby pig farm; a second man decapitated, skinned like a goat, and hung from a hook in the bicycle shed), only the gossip-hungry public spoke of them — on their tea breaks, at their mamak stalls, at sweltering and shadeless bus stops — as the Lahat Road Flats Murders. Officially they remained three separate cases, each one so bizarre it never came to trial.

In celebration of the murderess's death sentence, Suresh composed a rhyme:

> There was a curry cook,
> Who had a curry pot.
> She found some curry spice
> That tasted nice and hot.
> She bought some curry bags,
> Tah-powed her curried spouse,
> And then she lived alone
> In her little curry house.

And this time Appa did reward him with the sort of response he felt his efforts deserved — the roaring laughter, the thump on the back, the specific praise: "Nice and hot! I like that. Is that a reference to her love life, my boy?"

Suresh surmised that this satisfying reception owed itself to the fact that all Appa's attention and encouragement were being channeled in his direction, having been mysteriously diverted to bypass Uma since the end of Uncle Ballroom's visit. He could not begin to guess the reasons for this change, and did not care to; he only wished to profit from it for as long as it lasted.

Amma, returning from Kuala Lumpur to so many changes, had questions of her own, but no one to ask: not her husband, surely, with whom she hadn't had a real conversation since Aasha's birth; not the mother-in-law who still thought of her as a low-class interloper; not her children, from whose world she'd been excluded for years because she wasn't as clever as their father or as syrupy as their grandmother. But how had her mother-in-law changed so vastly in a single month, from a firecracker with a limp and the beginnings of cataracts into an aged lump, confined to a rattan chair, peering into the shadows, demanding old-folks-home treatment from the servants at all hours of the day? And what had turned her irrepressible, volatile oldest into a sullen teenager in the same span of time? Why had she abandoned her grandmother and her little sister to the care of the servants? Why was she no longer her Appa's girl, and why wasn't Appa more flummoxed by this transformation? They seemed almost to have made a secret agreement to avoid each other, to take turns going up or down the staircase, to find themselves seated across the dinner table from each other as rarely as possible, and, when that could not be prevented, to immerse themselves in a book or a newspaper.

Does it really matter? Amma said to herself after idly pondering these questions for a few days. *How does it change my life? The old lady will continue to be the bane of my existence whether she's walking around making her cutting comments or sitting in her chair shouting for tea. And as for my children, they've always ignored me anyway, so what does it matter if they're ignoring each other into the bargain?* Behind her indifference hovered a ghost of smugness: *What happened, Uma? You always thought your father was some great hero, so now how come you won't even look at him?*

Only Aasha could neither resign herself to the new order of things nor derive any satisfaction from it. Uma had flicked her away like a beetle that had settled on her dress, and it was her own fault. By harping on Uma's plans with Uncle Ballroom, by shouting that secret like a stupid O-mouthed town crier for everyone to hear, Aasha had angered Uma and lost her. Thus began, despite Uma's best efforts to shake her off, Aasha's long years of trailing silently behind an equally silent Uma, longing, hoping for clemency, if not a full pardon, until Chellam arrived to provide an occasional distraction.

14

THE GOLDEN DESCENT OF CHELLAM, THE BRINGER OF SUCCOR

September 8, 1979

I N LATE AUGUST, Amma demands that Appa hire a new servant to look after Paati. In the past few months, Paati's condition has deteriorated so rapidly that some are too stunned to feel sorry for her, and others suspect her of purposely engineering her own senility.

But to what purpose?

"She just wants me to run around at her beck and call," Amma says. "She's realized that if she sits in a chair and acts helpless she can control me the way she has always wanted to. She always thought I was fit only to be her maid, isn't it? A nobody's daughter, after all. Well, now she's finally got her way. Very nicely all of you have dumped the old bat in my lap and washed your hands. What happened to all Uma's love for her wonderful grandmother? Best friends they both were, so faithfully Uma used to tend to her grandmother, but now that it's become a twenty-four-hour job what has happened?" The *t*'s of *twenty-four* ring metallic in Amma's mouth, like the call of some cruel, red-eyed bird with a pointy black tongue: *t-t-t-t.*

It's true: for months Uma has no longer put Paati to bed at night or combed her hair in the morning, and Paati, far from fighting for Uma's favor, has quietly moved into a spare room downstairs. From that room she brays into the darkness whenever the fancy strikes her: for water, for an extra blanket, for the removal of the extra blanket, for no apparent reason. No one else seems bothered by this ruckus, but Amma feels herself shaken by Paati's ferocious will until her teeth chatter and the scruff of her neck smarts from its grip. When she can no longer bear the noise rattling around like hot stones inside her skull, she goes downstairs to throw a blanket at Paati or force water down her throat. And in the morning she has little chance to recover, for, curled crisp as a sun-baked millipede in her rattan chair, Paati clamors for her breakfast, her elevenses, a hot drink to tide her over until the next meal, the teatime treatbowl. The servants grumble at this virtual doubling of their workload, and Amma finds her arsenal of thighpinches and armpinches and mouthslaps to be a progressively deficient defense against the exigencies of daily life with her mother-in-law.

They are eating dinner when Amma registers her formal complaint with Appa, on one of his rare nights at home.

"Are you honestly accusing the old lady of developing chronic arthritis just to spite you?" Appa asks. "Does that not smack just a wee bit of persecution mania?" Then he stuffs a whole chicken gizzard into his mouth to keep down his own theories about Paati's abrupt decline, for in fact he secretly agrees with the basic premise that she's bluffing. At least that she started out bluffing, and has lately convinced herself that she's nothing but a pitiful, chair-ridden old thing who never did anyone any (serious) harm.

"I have to sit here all day in this posh prison," Amma says. "I can't talk your clever talk, I can't use your big-big words, I can't dump your mother and your children in someone else's lap and go off to golf and dining-wining at the club."

There follows a thirty-second silence, broken only by the sound of Aasha's rubbing an index finger against the rasam-wet bottom of her plate. SQUEAK-squeak, SQUEAK-squeak, SQUEAK-squeak.

"Aasha," says Amma. Aasha stops her rubbing.

"But I rather liked that little tune," Appa says. "A fitting musical accompaniment to this family meal. I felt it captured the spirit of the occasion." Noticing Suresh stifle a giggle, he ventures: "I think I have some supporters here."

"We should all join in," Suresh says, grinning broadly. "With our glasses also."

"Of course," Amma says, ignoring Suresh. "Of course you have supporters. Of course all your children agree with whatever you say, because you appear only when it suits you, like a king on a royal visit, but I—"

"I don't want this," Aasha says, pushing her plate away. "I don't want any. I'm full." She peers at the big window across the dining room: pressed against the window, pale as a tree frog's belly, is a child's longing face. "Look," she says, "there she is. My ghost friend. So pretty she is."

"Aasha," says Suresh, rolling his eyes, "stop it. Not now."

No one knows that Amma, too, has been entertaining her own fantasies these days. On trial at the High Court is one Siti Mariam, a pretty Malay housewife from rural Terengganu, twenty-eight years old, a charming beauty mark on her chin in the manner of Malay starlets of the 1960s. Was she coldly calculating (as Appa has taken it upon himself to prove) or simply crazy, off her rocker, bonkers, round every bloody bend in the country (as the defense had it)? One halcyon afternoon, Siti Mariam had cut off her mother-in-law's feet and left her to bleed to death on the loamy soil under her hut-on-stilts. Amma imagined the scene in far richer detail than Appa had: the idyllic Malay kampung, chickens ducks geese goats everywhere, a back yard lush with petai and pandan, children playing five stones in the dirt, adults napping on verandas. Not so idyllic inside Siti Mariam's hut, though. With no trouble at all, Amma's ears conjure up that old lady's curses and carryings-on, oh yes, of course in a different language, in which only a few of the equivalent nouns and adjectives (time, blanket, coffee, cold, hot, water, tea, hungry, thirsty, useless) are known to Amma, but the sounds—the shouting screaming groaning moaning —the sounds of those afternoons she knows too well. And that was probably why the neighbors had paid no heed to the old woman's surely fearful screams on that last afternoon. That was why no children or field-weary men or rice-threshing women had come running. Not because they were used to afternoon butcherings. Oh, you know what goes on in their supposedly peaceful kampungs, people said: rape incest adultery murder, all the dreadful things they can fit in between their five-times-a-day prayers. Nevertheless, Amma told herself, that was not the reason Siti Mariam had been able to carry out her slicing-sawing-dragging with no interruptions: the neighbors had simply heard it all before. The shouting, the screaming, the groaning,

the moaning, the crying wolf and negligence and torture and choking. They'd learned to sleep through it and work through it. That just
goes to show, Amma said to herself, but such glorious action was not
for her; she hadn't the guts. Hers was the realm of impotent thought.

So it is to shut his wife up—at least temporarily, at least on this
particular issue—and to make his own life easier, not to keep mutila-
tion or murder at bay, that Appa agrees to the engagement of a fifth
servant. This new servant will neither mutter about having to wash
the greens when Paati demands to know the time, nor grumble about
having to polish the brass when Paati wants a tumbler of hot tea. She
will have no choice: Paati will be her number one priority. Her main,
if not sole, undertaking.

"Maybe she misunderstood," Appa is to say during those last two
weeks after Chellam had been ordered to pack her bags. "She thought
making the old lady her main undertaking meant being her under-
taker." But by then not even Suresh will be laughing at Appa's witti-
cisms.

One other detail will set the new girl apart from Lourdesmary and
Vellamma and Letchumi and Mat Din: she will be a live-in servant,
for naturally, to take on a twenty-four-hour job, one has to be on the
premises twenty-four hours a day. So this will be her home, Tata's
rambling, lopsided old mansion on Kingfisher Lane, with its dented
and dulled English kitchen, its slamming screen doors, its unused servant's room tucked under the main staircase like an unread newspaper under a businessman's arm, just waiting for her.

After a few weeks of word-of-mouth advertising, it emerges that
the new servant is to be a hand-me-down: Mr. and Mrs. Dwivedi, Appa's colleague and his teatiming wife, have a servant girl they don't
need anymore.

"Nothing wrong with the girl," says Mr. Dwivedi to Appa at the
club on the night they shake on this deal. "The Wife wants to stop
work and stay at home, that's all." Mr. Dwivedi called his wife The
Wife, and his son The Son, even in their presence, as if they were elemental representations of their respective roles. "I'll give you one
piece of advice, if you don't mind, Raju," he goes on. "Don't let the
girl get out of hand. These bloody coolie types these days think they
can make all sorts of demands. TV lah, day off lah, air con lah. The
minute you start giving in they climb on your head." His beerlogged
heart swelled with the passion of his cause: surely someone had to

stand up for their side and stave off the mutiny of the great unwashed. Look at what was happening in other countries, special benefits for Scheduled Castes in India, communism in Vietnam. "I tell you," he says, thumping Appa on the back, "give the bleddi girl thirty-forty a month and a coir mat on the kitchen floor and tell her to shaddup her mouth." As an afterthought he adds: "And dhal curry twice a day, no need for her to be feasting on chicken mutton crabs."

So there's no question, in Appa's and Amma's minds, that the new servant should count herself lucky after her miserable existence at the Dwivedis'. Amma has heard rumors that Mrs. Dwivedi uses her considerable bulk against her servants, beating them with telephone directories, brass lamps, or Nataraja statues when they fail to please. At the Big House the new girl will have her own room, a bed with a real (if musty, dating back to Tata's days) mattress, the leftovers of their own meals, hand-me-down clothing. She will be practically family.

ONE WEEK BEFORE Chellam arrives, the limestone caves collapse, burying Lourdesmary's family. Burying dozens of hunger-shriveled grandmothers. Mothers wrinkled and caustic before their time. Lethargic, beedi-puffing grandfathers. And all their gourd-bellied children and grandchildren. People burn alive first, as their upset cooking fires spread under the rubble. All the way from the main road, bus passengers and hawkers hear their terrible, choked screams. Then there are quiet moans from under the boulders for days, though no one but the disheartened rescue workers hears these. The newspapers and the seven o'clock news buzz and mourn, crackle and sigh. The neighbors murmur: A horrible thing. An unprecedented tragedy. So many people, just like that. But it was illegal, you know, we know, they should've known. They shouldn't have been living in those caves. Under Lourdesmary's black face in the *New Straits Times,* a blacker headline reads: "Survivor of Cave Tragedy: The Government Cannot Replace My Children."

"Poor woman," Appa says when Lourdesmary shows up for work the day after the mass funeral. "Needs the money, what to do?"

On the afternoon Chellam drags her broken suitcase through the front gate, Suresh and Aasha are outside on the culvert, peering at the collapsed caves in the distance.

"Yes I can," Aasha says. "Really I can. I'm not bluffing. I can still hear them."

"Ah, shaddup lah," Suresh says for the fourth time. "They're all dead already by this time. What you think, no food no water, hands legs faces also smashed, and they got the strength to keep shouting for one week?"

"Not shouting," Aasha says. "Just crying a bit. Like — like cats in the nighttime. Like baby cats."

"Yah. Sure. But tell me one thing: how come nobody else has heard these, er, baby cats except you?"

"Nobody else is listening, what."

"Oho. So what else can you hear? Can you hear them singing campfire songs? Fighting with the older ghosts for houses to haunt? Making plans for Deepavali?"

"No. They got no words. They cry like cats only, I told you, isn't it?"

But even as Asha and Suresh wrestle with the aftermath of the cave tragedy, they keep an eye on a quieter tragedy unfolding in their own world: on the ornamental swing, Uma idly riffles the pages of four college catalogues. When these catalogues first arrived, Aasha did not dare to remind anyone that she had told them so, that she had, months ago, warned them all that Uma was planning to leave them. Now she knows that this tragedy is at least as grave as last week's, because everyone can only stand and watch while Uma leaves them; because not only should they have known, all of them, but they *could* have known if they had listened to Aasha; because Aasha herself shouldn't have let things get to this state, this immutable knowledge, *Uma's going away, Uma's going away,* this scene that eviscerates her now though she grants it nothing more than one eye: Uma turning glossy pages of America on the swing. Between them, Suresh and Aasha have a whole eye with which to measure not only the speed and manner of each page-turning and the displayed interest in each brochure (as suggested by the frequency of Uma's blinks), but also distance and depth and perspective: how far away Uma already is, and how much closer to a world composed primarily of these elements:

Red brick.

Green ivy.

Black trees.

White people.

On the other side of the fence, Baldy Wong perches high in the mango tree, swinging his legs and squealing each time he crushes an ant between his fingers. In between ants he pelts Suresh and Aasha with sticks and leaves and unripe mangoes.

"Just ignore him," Suresh says. "He's seeking attention."

Aasha reflects that this was one of the harsh judgments passed on her when, all those months ago, she tried to warn them about Uma's plans.

At ten past three Amma pokes her head out of the back door. "What, no sign of the servant girl yet?" she calls out. "I thought Mrs. Dwivedi said she'd be here in an hour or so when she called at two o'clock?"

But Mrs. Dwivedi, never having ridden a bus in her life, could've had no clear idea of how long the trip would take. She'd been driven past the bus stop a thousand times; she was therefore certain of its existence and its location. "Go straight until the end of the road and turn right," she'd said to Chellam, opening the gate for her. "Tell the bus conductor you want to get off at Taman Pekaka, I think so he'll know. All these bus people must be knowing, what." Then she and her chauffeur had watched Chellam drag her suitcase down the driveway and up the road, she with her hands on her hips, the chauffeur with his chamois in hand, for he had just finished polishing the Mercedes and was about to start on the Alfa Romeo. When Mrs. Dwivedi had no longer felt like standing there tracking Chellam's progress in the punishing heat, she'd come indoors, ordered her cook to make her a tall glass of iced sharbat, and telephoned Amma. "The girl's on her way," she'd said. "Probably it will take her about an hour to reach your place, don't you think so?"

Suresh rolls around on his tongue the sorts of answers his schoolmates might give to Amma's question: *Yah, the servant's here already, I've been keeping her in my pocket only. Yah. She came, but I at once sent her to the corner shop to buy me a toddy and two packs of Marlboros. Yah, wait let me check inside my left ear, okay?* Then, satisfied with just that hint of their flavor, he calls back, "No, no sign of the servant girl."

"Hmm!" muses Amma. "Got lost in town or what." She withdraws once more into the kitchen, and a silence settles over the compound. Even Baldy seems to have been shaken into relative decorum by Amma's brief appearance, for he holds on to the next unripe mango he plucks, looks at it for a few seconds, and seems to decide not to lob it at them after all. He takes a pensive bite of it, puckers his face, and spits the whole mouthful out. As it dribbles down the bark of the tree he takes another bite, and another, and another, spitting out each bite but somehow remaining optimistic that the next one will be better.

"Stoopid idiot," Suresh says. "Look what he's doing, look look. Disgusting doonggu." Secretly, though, he wonders what it would be like to have a memory so short that every new second is full of fresh anticipation.

At four-fifteen, after Suresh and Aasha have floated two twig boats down the monsoon drain, driven one of Mat Din's poles into the earth by the hump to see how far down it would go, and purchased two packets of Chickadees and one of Mamee from the roti man, the gate latch clicks and they look up to see a skinny girl maneuvering a big brown suitcase through the gate. One of the suitcase's wheels scrapes the cement noisily; its skin, pocked, pitted, peeling, and blotchy, matches the girl's. When she's closed the gate behind her, she wipes the sweat off her face with both hands and redoes her loosened knot of hair. Under her arms two dark patches stain the shiny red polyester of her blouse.

For the remaining year and a half of her life, Chellam will retain a crystalline impression of all the conflicting and concerted stimuli that meet her senses in this moment preceding her introduction: the yellow butterfly that bobs across her field of vision, from the guava tree to the tamarind tree, where it's swatted at by a shirtless, bulging-eyed boy perched high in a dark cage of branches; the Milo jingle playing on some neighbor's radio or television; the unshakable feeling that she's being watched (and indeed, at their secret sentry posts behind their lace curtains, the neighbors are separately finding it hard to swallow the idea that Chellam really is old enough to be a live-in maid: Seventeen! Can this chit of a girl really be seventeen?); the pavement-steaming heat; the smells of manure and frying teatime bananas and sun-stirred jasmine; the dust that sticks to her sweaty skin and tickles her throat. She's tired and thirsty; her head throbs in rhythm to a distant crow's caws. She wants nothing more than to lie on a cool cement floor and go to sleep. No coir mat nothing: if they offer her one, she'll say thank you very much and roll off it onto the cool cement when they're not looking. She hopes she'll never have to take a bus again.

In fact, Chellam didn't lose her way navigating the town bus network; the trip simply took longer than Mrs. Dwivedi could've imagined. Chellam had to change buses twice, and the conductor, having asked her three times, with increasingly apparent frustration, which of the three stops in Taman Pekaka she wanted, ejected her at the one farthest from the Big House. From there, she asked hawkers and passersby and, finally, the corner shop man for directions, heaving her suitcase over roadside rocks, ignoring the amatory trills and ululations of long-distance lorry drivers whose groins burned for release.

Her hair knotted and smoothed, she squints around her, one hand shielding her eyes from the white sunlight. What she sees (and hears): two small blurs near a wall in the distance (murmuring to each other); a bigger blur on a low swing (creaking, humming). She takes hold once more of her suitcase (its handle attached only by a twisted tongue of leather) and begins her journey up the driveway, still watching the figure on the swing. The humming grows more audible as she approaches, and gradually her eyes pick out more details: A wild black frizz poised over color pictures in a glossy magazine. Dry skin on exposed knees. Sharp elbows. Long fingers turning pages. And then, just as she passes the swing, the girl's long face lifts, and her eyes find Chellam's with not a moment's hesitation, as if she's been keeping track all this time of Chellam's progress towards the house, and knows — with her ears, her nose, her skin, for she hasn't looked until now — that Chellam is watching her. Under the frank stare of her narrow black eyes, her eyelids are two blue-black half-moons. A half-smile ripples like sunlight on dark water around her wide mouth, so brief Chellam's not sure if she imagined it, though its last dispersed vestiges glint and sparkle in the periphery of her vision. The afternoon sun has burned the gravel so intensely it seems to vibrate under Chellam's feet, and its heat rises through the rubber of her Japanese slippers to scorch her calloused soles. Somewhere an outdoor tap squeals and gushes. Now the girl on the swing, who has not looked away all this while, blinks an answering blink at Chellam and then lowers her gaze once more to the bright pages in her lap.

All the way up the length of her tunnel, from the darkness at its end into the light of promise at its beginning, Chellam has dragged her suitcase for our spectatorial pleasure. Think of our telescoping tale as the opposite of an old-fashioned cartoon close: instead of the pitch black creeping in on Bugs Bunny from all directions, the light expands, and out there, before Chellam, stretches all of life: sight, sympathy (for if that girl smiled at her — and Chellam is almost certain she did — then she might find compassion, if not friendship, here in this house), savings for her savings tin (for perhaps this new boss will, unlike Mr. Dwivedi, have the balls to face her father squarely). Oh, Chellam is not so naïve after seventeen years of hard knocks — of starvation, scabies, ringworm, prostitution, beatings, spittings in the face — to believe in fairy-tale endings or fresh starts, and yet the day is so unremittingly bright, and the Big House such an absurdly happy peacock color, that she can't help but feel something leap in her parched throat, sweeter than mere relief to have arrived at last, larger than new-job nerves.

On the other side of the shimmering wall of dust that separates Chellam from the ornamental swing, Uma smiles — yes, she does smile — and thinks: *So you're the latest putative antidote to the ills of this house. Poor child, how old are you? Not old enough for us, surely.* Then she drops her gaze to the panoramic photograph of the Princeton campus on her lap, but she looks (and turns the page) without seeing, for her thoughts remain with the new servant, and on whether such narrow shoulders will be able to bear all that is in store for them.

And Amma, watching Chellam's progress in the glass panel of the front door, says to herself: *Hmm. Such a small thing. Feel almost sorry for her, actually. Maybe it'll be nice to have her in the house. Maybe she'll be company for Suresh and Aasha, on top of getting the old coot off my back. Maybe she can be their New Oldest Sister, haha. Maybe things will be better for everyone now.*

Chellam's halfway up the driveway. When she focuses her mole eyes on Aasha and Suresh, they lick the Chickadee dust off their fingers and wipe their hands on their clothes, ready to face this stranger and the rest of the afternoon.

"Am-mAA!" shouts Suresh. "The new servant girl is here!"

From his aerie, his mouth full of sour, stringy mango, Baldy Wong screams, "Servant servant servant!" Then he shins down to inspect the newcomer from his side of the fence. He sticks his nose and mouth through a gap and unfurls his tongue like a giraffe, as if he means to touch Chellam with it. Longer and longer it grows, and just as it occurs to Aasha that she might grab it hard between her thumb and index finger and give it a good tug, she feels Amma's breath on her neck. Baldy's tongue has mesmerized them all, and not one of them has heard Amma come through the back door and across the outdoor kitchen on her soundless feet. Her caftan sleeves stir slightly in a brand-new breeze; she's breathing stertorously, as if she's run all the way.

"Suresh, what did you just say?" asks Amma, clipped and clear as a teacher reading Lesson One out loud. *"Servant girl?"*

"Uh-oh, uh-oh," offers Baldy, clutching at the fence. "Uh-oh. Sei lor. You gonna die." He jigs up and down. This is the exciting bit. Don't change the channel now. They'll probably stop for advertisements, though, and he'll have to wait till next week to see what'll happen.

Happily for Baldy, the show goes on: Suresh gets a mouthslap right then. A hard one, quick and flat, Amma's five fingers pressed together to form an unyielding paddle. "Aiyo!" cries Baldy. "Beat him so hard one! Pain, pain, pain!" He clutches his face and sways.

Aasha gets a *tsk* for laughing, but when she looks around to see who issued it (Amma, because she likes to claim one shouldn't laugh at Baldy even when he deserves it? Suresh, who has interpreted the laughter to mean Aasha isn't on his side? The servant girl herself, because she's hot and tired and irritated by both of them? Baldy, who envisioned his melodrama as a serious piece of theater?), she cannot tell, and therefore cannot categorize it as a warning of castigations to follow or a *tsk*ing to be dismissed and forgotten.

From her spot on the ornamental swing, Uma watches them all.

"Angryyyyy, oi!" bellows Baldy.

"Baldy," spits Amma, "behave yourself, for goodness' sake. Go inside and find your ma. All this is not your business, know or not?" Then she says to Aasha and Suresh, "We don't say *servant girl.*" The two words are framed by hot, white silences. "Servant or lawyer or doctor, we are all human beings."

"But—" says Suresh.

"But—" says Aasha, at almost exactly the same time, so that together their two *buts* are a single stammer: *b-b-ut-ut.*

Glumly, Baldy picks his gluey nose and yearns for more slapstick action.

"No ifsandsorbuts," says Amma. *"Servant girl!* Oho, and you are both brilliant sparks, is it? Nuclear scientists? Heart surgeons? High-flying jet-setting diplomats? Who do you think you are?"

The question rises and ripples in the afternoon heat. Parts of it swell and other parts shrink as it climbs higher and higher in the air and settles, shimmering, on the top branch of the tamarind tree.

WHO do you think you are?

Who do you THINK you are?

Who DO you think you are?

Who do you think you are, servant girl, Suresh asks silently, *to stand there like a queen and watch our mother shame us?*

"Suresh," Amma says, "take Chellam Akka's suitcase to her room." Then she turns her back to him pointedly and says to Chellam, "Please come inside and have a drink. *Tsk tsk tsk,* you must be so tired, so hot it is today. Tea coffee sofdrink? What you want?"

ON CHELLAM'S FIRST full day, Mrs. Balakrishnan strolls across the street to wonder aloud about her narrow hips, flat chest, and tiny hands. On her second, Kooky Rooky comes a-calling for the same purpose. "Too-too sorry for her I feel, Auntie," she says to Amma. "I myself was forced to work in other people's houses at that age, you know? Twelve, thirteen years old I was washing bedsheets and big-big pails of clothes with my hands."

"That must've been in a different lifetime from the one in which her father sent her to a boarding school in England," Suresh says after she's left.

Because it simply won't do for Lawyer Rajasekharan and family to be caught employing a child laborer, Amma sits Chellam down at the Formica table for a thorough interrogation. "No birth cettificayte, Maddam," Chellam says over and over. "In my house we got no birth-day-birthday all that." And try as Amma might to intimidate her into a confession with knowing looks and insinuations, Chellam can only say that she is seventeen, give or take a few months.

"Her growth might have been stunted by malnutrition," Amma concludes. When she gives Chellam Appa's like-new-only courthouse shirts, she advises her to pin up the sleeves. "Or you can cut and sew them," Amma says. "Then they won't be forever getting wet and dirty when you do your work, and that way they will last longer also."

Perhaps it is Chellam's youth that arouses some didactic impulse in Amma, or perhaps it's the subtle, childlike quality of her manners and movements: the way she wrinkles her nose to laugh at Suresh's rudest jokes; the way she turns her feet in and fidgets whenever she stands before Amma, shifting her weight from one foot to the other and back again, scratching her calves with her toenails as if invisible flies were bothering her; the way she sticks her tongue out of one corner of her mouth when applying herself to a tricky task. Whatever the reason, Amma brims with this teach-a-man-to-fishing in Chellam's early days. When she catches the girl squinting at the dining room clock from one foot away, she tells her, "Your eyesight is something you must take care of. If you're careful with your money and save up properly, you can go for an eye exam and get spectacles." Amma finds Chellam an empty Quality Street tin to use as a piggy bank. "Here," she says. "Every month put your money in this. Don't simply-simply waste it on magazines and kacang puteh."

Taking the tin firmly in both hands, Chellam runs up to her room and puts it under her bed. She has fifty sen left over from the money Mrs. Dwivedi gave her to take the bus; instead of opening her Spectacles Account with this, she decides to spend it on a long-term investment for more efficient account-keeping. She purchases a pocket-sized notebook from the corner shop, and on the first page she makes two columns, marking one "Master Gave" and the other "Things I Bought" in her beetling Tamil characters. Then she lists the months in a third column, next to the first, one through twelve, deciding one year is good enough to start with. And together (but separately), she and Amma pat themselves on the back: Amma for her invaluable contribution to Chellam's moral education, and Chellam for the good sense apparent in the very preparation of this notebook. She will do good work; she will never grumble back when the old lady grumbles at her; she will be so impressive that they will raise her pay after the first few months.

"How nice for you," the Ladies of the teatime circle say to Amma when they've had the chance to inspect Chellam from a distance. "What a lovely coincidence, the same age as your oldest, you said? She'll be good company for her, then, and another big sister for the two little ones."

But Uma doesn't want company. That evanescent, sunlit smile seems now to Chellam to have been a figment of her imagination: how could this silent girl have even looked at her, this girl who hunched over her books and shut her face — closed shop, chup, lights out, iron grille crashing down like a newsagent's — when she heard Chellam's footsteps around a corner?

Chellam's fading in and Uma's fading out are synchronizing before Aasha's eyes: the color, sound, and smell of Chellam permeate the brightening air as Uma's edges smudge and blur irreversibly. Two weeks after Chellam arrives, Uma starts to fill out her college applications. They're not due for another three months; even accounting for the vagaries of international postage, Uma has no reason to begin them now. No reason, that is, other than her immense excitement at the prospect of escape.

She spreads the forms before her on the Formica table and turns the pages of one casually, as if it were a girls' magazine and she were looking for posters or free samples tucked between the buttery pages. She yawns and rubs the back of her neck; she chews the tip of her ballpoint pen. Softly, softly, just to himself, Paul Simon sings with deceptive tranquility:

> Now the sun is in the west
> Little kids go home to take their rest . . .

From a few feet away, drawing closer with each blank Uma fills in, Aasha watches. Name. Age. Date of birth. P-e-r, per, m-a, ma, n-e-n-t, nent, permanent address. By the time Uma has finished filling this out, her pen making sharp, clean sounds on the paper, Aasha is hovering at her elbow. Almost, but not quite, on tiptoe. P-r-o, pro, s-p-e-c, spec, t-i-v-e, tive, Aasha spells out, rhyming *tive* with *five*. Prospective major. Whatever the meaning of this enigma, Uma now lifts her pen with great deliberation and, like a stonemason carving letters into a pedestal, writes BIOLOGY. The B a pompous doctor stomach, the O's tumbling one after another in disbelief, swelling and shrinking like parts of that question still ringing in Aasha's ears:

whO do you think you are?

who dO you think you are?

Then, excruciatingly slowly, so that the pen's quick chirrups lengthen into thirty-second scrapes, Uma adds AND THEATRE.

Aasha leans in so close her lips almost touch Uma's elbow. In the kitchen, the roar of pakoras dropped into hot oil erupts like applause. But Aasha doesn't feel like clapping, though she knows she should be proud of Uma for showing Appa and Amma and anyone else who's ever poked fun at her acting dreams that she's not so easily dissuaded. And she is showing them, even if they're not looking now: there it is, that word THEATRE, in black ink, plain as the numbers on the face of a clock and practically glowing. Uma's won. Uma's going to do what she pleases and there's nothing anyone can do about it.

Aasha wants to be proud of Uma. She wants to say something small and marble-bright, like *Yay!* or *Keep it up!* or *Our secret!* And she does feel a whisper of pride, a tiny stirring, but it's no match for the great, heaving, howling sorrow that steals her words and sears her tongue. She wanders off and settles face-down on the green PVC settee, and Chellam keeps an eye on her for a full hour before hazarding a bit of unsolicited advice:

"Putting your mouth nose all where people put their backside," she says, pawing at Aasha's shoulder, "get sick only then you know."

"Ish," Aasha says, turning her face just enough to fix Chellam with one eye, "you no need to tell me what to do. You go and do your own work, otherwise I'll tell Amma."

But there is a faint twinkle in that single eye, and the pout that follows this rebuke is almost beseeching, and now Aasha's lolling and rolling on the settee, like a lonely tiger cub itching for a tussle. Chellam understands these signals and knows what's expected of her: "Tell and see!" she says, grinning and tickling Aasha's ribs with five bony fingers. "Tell your Amma and see what I do to you next time!"

And Aasha allows a sad, fey smile to be coaxed out of her, a smile iridescent with tears but unquestionably a smile, for maybe, despite all Chellam's superficial deficiencies, she will pay Aasha the attention Uma used to, and scrub her hair on shampoo days, and teach her songs, even if they are inferior songs in a different language. When Uma goes away to America, Chellam will stay. In this moment, Aasha sees with a psychic's clarity, with a vision unclouded by the tears behind her eyes, that Chellam will be here long after Uma has forgotten who she is. Chellam will always be who she is now, Chellam(servant) of the Big House, even when Uma is someone else, many different someone elses, according to season and time. In summer: an American girl buying hot dogs from a stand. In autumn: a girl out for a walk among gold-colored leaves with her gold-colored dog. In those New York City winters that will bleed her, just like in the song: an ice skater in a fur-trimmed hood and mittens, sitting down to hot chocolate with a boy who wants to marry her. And many years from now: a rich lady rushing around with her hands in the pockets of her trench coat, her head held high because, emptied of old faces, it's lighter than anyone else's.

15

THE GLORIOUS ASCENT OF UMA
THE OLDEST-ELDEST

August 29, 1980

THE NIGHT BEFORE Uma leaves for America is so hot that people wake up drenched in their beds. At dawn the sparrows are neither seen nor heard; Mr. Balakrishnan, who has tossed a handful of rice outside his back door for them as usual, squints up into the bone-white sky and wonders where they could be hiding. By nine o'clock, leaves, flowers, hair, spirits, resolve, and biscuits left on breakfast tables are turning limp. Butter melts. Coconut milk curdles before it can be used for lunchtime curries. Men sit under ceiling fans with their knees wide apart, wiping their backs and bellies with the cotton singlets they've pulled off. Women fan themselves with kitchen towels and newspapers as they tend to their chores.

On the red Formica table in the Big House, the *New Straits Times* flutters untouched under a vase. The sour, inky smell of the front-page headlines (so bold! so black! so sure!) wafts all the way through the house to remind those who might have forgotten that this is a momentous day not only for them but for the nation at large, for this is the victory they have won today: "Death for Sex Killer." And in slightly smaller letters underneath: "Closure at Last for Lim Family." On all the front pages of all the newspapers (rolled up, languishing under paperweights, spread out before husbands too hot to read)

Appa strides efficiently away from the courthouse in his bestquality suit, black as the headlines themselves; his shiny red silk tie; his glasses that reflect the sea of rapacious faces through which he wades. T. K. Rajasekharan, Counsel for the Prosecution. Courtroom genius, master storyteller, legendary wit. Behind him, in the blurry background, two police officers lead an unshaven shrimp of a man in a songkok and a loose baju Melayu away to a dim cell somewhere offstage.

At ten-thirty Mat Din loads Uma's suitcase into the cavernous boot of the Volvo, wondering at the fifteen stamp-shaped stickers of some gap-toothed, wing-eared white boy that emblazon it. He doesn't know that Alfred E. Neuman is running (albeit unofficially) for president; he doesn't know Aasha intended the stickers to help Uma recognize her suitcase in the New York airport pullulating with grey people in trench coats. And he doesn't know, of course, that Uma accepted the stickers merely out of mercy and regret and a sudden, guilty nostalgia, not because she was worried she'd have trouble finding her suitcase.

Mat Din's chauffeuring services will not be required today; Appa has explained to him that they will drive to the airport *as a family.* Much like a family. In a configuration approximating a normal family. Mat Din is not so presumptuous as to entertain these alternate meanings of Appa's words, but Uma, hearing him through her open bedroom window, does.

On her way out to the car Uma walks past Chellam's door, behind which she hears her shallow breath, quick as a dog's panting on this merciless day.

I'm sorry, Chellam, Uma thinks. It's the first apology she's made in two years. And she is sorry: sorry that Chellam had to be the one to do — and to get caught doing — what all of them wanted to do and any of them might have done, had their stars been aligned as inauspiciously as Chellam's were on that afternoon. Hadn't Amma visited her (un)fair share of slaps and pinches and knocks upon Paati? Hadn't she, Uma, herself stood behind Paati, and thought terrible thoughts, and even — yes — acted on them that very afternoon? So Chellam had been the one to deliver the coup de grâce. Still, Uma cannot help but believe — she surprises herself with this irrational thought — that Chellam's act derived its fatal efficacy from all their guilty wishes (and unseen attempts). Like praying for world peace, Uma reflects grimly, only just the opposite. The collective force of their frustrations had animated Chellam that day, quickened her shuffling feet, lifted her arm. She'd only been a puppet.

Uma is sorry, too, about the thousand insectile mouths now relishing Chellam's fate, on Kingfisher Lane and other lanes, in Kuala Lumpur and Sydney and London. *There but for the grace of God . . .* Never mind, she reasons. Maybe Chellam's headed for better things. A factory job. Who knows? Uma, having never considered a factory job herself, doesn't know the requirements, but she can hope.

At eleven o'clock she sits in the back of the Volvo, ensconced between her sister's broken heart and her brother's maddened whistling. Aasha has lost; she's tried everything she could think of to win Uma back, to coax out of her one real smile or one true sentence — not a question pretending to be a sentence — meant solely for her, or one tiny promise, just to write, just to remember, anything. One sign that Uma would be a little bit sorry to leave. But that sign never came. *Promise me you'll never again ask for a promise,* Uma said the night she burned Paati's chair. Even if Aasha had promised, though, it wouldn't have been enough to bring the old Uma back.

Suresh doesn't know about the promise Aasha couldn't make; all he knows is that Aasha is going to wander the corridors of their house like a lost kid goat for the rest of her life, falling asleep on its floors, sitting on the stairs to talk to ghosts, and this vision of her future makes him want to give her a good, hard thighpinch, to box her ears or clamp a hand over her nose and mouth until she's dying for a gulp of air so huge and frantic that she will swallow some sense with it.

Majestic and almost silent, the silver Volvo glides down the driveway. The sun glints off its receding fender, and all down the street the same eyes that will watch Chellam's retreat a week from today, from behind the same window curtains, water and blink. Aasha pulls herself up onto her knees to look out the rear window and sees Paati's ghost, standing just outside the gate, not waving, not angry, not crying, not smiling. Among the objects that show through her transparent, inscrutable body: the distant limestone hills; Mr. Malhotra's Datsun Sunny, parked half on the street and half on the grass verge; Mrs. Manickam's untended hibiscus bushes. Aasha neither waves at Paati nor attempts to alert anyone else to her lukewarm farewell.

As the Volvo passes the Wongs' front gate, Baldy Wong screeches his jubilation into the cloudless sky: "Big House girl gone America! Big House girl gone America!"

"Looklooklook," says Mrs. Balakrishnan, poking her husband's shoulder, "they're going, man, they're going. Style-style only. Acting like soooo many problems they got, crying here crying there. But in the end everything works out tip-top for them, isn't it? When you have money whaaat is the big problem? Today you cry tomorrow you put on your five-hundred-dollar saree and send your daughter to America."

But if Mrs. Balakrishnan accompanied them to the Ipoh airport, the only evidence of a festive mood she'd glean from their journey, their arrival, or their surroundings would be the following:

1) The life-size cardboard ladies advertising Visit Malaysia Year 1980. They are MalayChineseIndian, IbanKadazanDayak, sleek and beaming ladies of every race, namaste-ing and salam-ing the wide world in toothy testimony to the country's legendary Racial Harmony. From the front these ladies seem perfect. Perfectly happy. Perfectly shapely. Perfectly poised. From the side, though, Aasha sees that they are just perfectly flat, and further, that they have no back parts whatsoever.

2) Amma's impressive getup, from the cream-colored crepe silk saree with little indigo flowers cascading down the pallu (only three hundred ringgit, not five hundred, Mrs. B.) to the sapphire studs in her ears and the peacock pin on her shoulder. But the sapphire pendant is missing, and with a little prying Mrs. Balakrishnan would discover that its absence remains a source of suspicion and strife.

3) A large Malay family picnicking on the ragged, notbrown-notgrey carpet, boisterously unaffected by the public sacrifice of one of their own to the gods of closure. Their portions of nasi lemak are generous; their noodles are steaming hot. But Suresh is only one of several people staring at them from a safe distance, and he disguises his disgust better than most. "After eating all those hard-boiled eggs," he whispers to Aasha, "they'll be able to propel themselves to their destination by farting. No need to get on the plane also."

To excuse herself gently from the duty of laughing, Aasha lowers herself into a squat and begins to count the stains on her patch of the carpet.

"Aasha," Amma says, "sit properly. What is this? Behaving like a junglee. No wonder Uma's thanking her lucky stars to be getting away from you. Here itself she already wants to pretend like she doesn't know you."

Now Aasha's given Uma one more reason never to come back.

Aasha stares fixedly at the carpet, and the stains blur and bleed into each other.

"O Mr. Malay man," Suresh mutters under his breath, "with your stinky eggs. Sitting in the airport, stretching out your legs."

Aasha slides one leg slyly out from under her dress and touches the toe of her sandal to the toe of Suresh's shiny airport shoe. A silent, thank-you toe touch, because Suresh is the only one who's trying to help. He looks at Aasha's foot, small and bony in its white sock, and knows quite well what she wants him to think, although she hasn't actually been cheered up by the rhyme. He doesn't compose a second verse. For a few moments Suresh and Aasha sit there looking at their just-touching feet, at Suresh's shiny, polished wingtip with its punched holes curling like cartoon steam, at Aasha's white sandal with its yellow plastic rose. And between the shoes, where their toes meet, a flurry of blue sparks: thank-yous and apologies, confessions and explanations and consolations, of which Aasha's thank-you for Suresh's extemporized egg poem is by far the least important.

The occasion does lack gaiety, despite the efforts of the cardboard ladies and the Malay family, but Mrs. Balakrishnan's envy is understandable: today the Rajasekharan family could, in theory, have a lot to celebrate. Their star's rising and rising; how many families in Malaysia have spawned a winner of scholarships to Ivy League institutions? Even now two teenage Indian boys in open-chested shirts are fighting like goondas on the other side of the lounge, pinning each other to walls, clipping one another on the ears.

"Tsk tsk," Amma says, "just look at our Indian boys. Good for nothing."

"Loitering and playing the fool," agrees Appa.

And this exchange is tantamount to a trumpet fanfare for their own arrival, their indisputable status as a good-for-something family, the great heights to which they have been climbing doggedly since Tata's dockyard worker days. Rising from the morass of tinkers tailors soldiers sailors stinkers drunkards abject failers, their offspring will live out new rhymes for new times: Doctor lawyer engineer, which will be your child's career?

A whole hour remains before the boarding call for Uma's plane.

"How about some pictures?" Appa says into the drowsy murmur of the lounge, jerking his head at Amma though the camera is in Uma's shoulder bag. "Eh? Put that latest-batest-model camera to use?"

And so, because they have to do something with themselves, Uma takes the camera out of her bag, all the while staring at the clock above the Malaysian Airlines System desk. They begin to take pictures:

Pictures of Uma and Amma standing exactly a foot apart.

Pictures of Uma and Appa with their arms folded.

Pictures of Uma, Suresh, and Aasha with their arms at their sides.

Strangers smile fondly and wait for them to finish before walking past them. Nice family saying goodbye. Eldest daughter going overseas in her smart brown suit and matching pumps. Congrachewlations. Wah, so clever one your daughter! They draw close to each other to whisper: "Eh, that one Lawyer Rajasekharan, isn't it?" "Just finished the Angela Lim case, man, yesterday only. If not for him that bastard would have got away."

"Oh boy," says Appa as the camera flash goes off yet again, "here itself we'll use up five rolls of film!" But he doesn't stop Amma from arranging Suresh and Aasha on either side of the Visit Malaysia cardboard ladies for another picture. "Stand straight, Aasha, Suresh," Amma fusses. Her eyes flash in all directions, blinding the onlookers. "What is this, slouching at your age?"

And Suresh and Aasha stand straight, because all this unfamiliar attention has shocked them into submission. Who knew Amma noticed menial sins like slouching and unladylike sitting? In the drab airport lounge she's like a rooster in a small back yard, strutting and preening as she's never done at home. If only the Ladies could see her like this—but no, as soon as the possibility occurs to Suresh, he backs away from it in trepidation. He must be careful what he wishes for; the Big House is not quite big enough for this Amma. He wouldn't be able to hide from her, and then all that attention would give him boils and stomachaches.

As soon as the lady behind the desk turns on her microphone, Amma claps her hands briskly. "My goodness!" she says. "Boarding time already! Put the camera away, Uma, here, don't forget to put it right at the bottom of your bag, otherwise someone will flick it the minute you turn your head."

The boarding announcement booms and screeches in their ears, amplified by all the unnecessary loudspeakers.

"Okay then," Amma says. "Take care, study hard, enough of this drama club nonsense. No fooling around with boys. Just because some useless fellow brings you flowers —"

"No time for long speeches now," Appa says. "Better get on the plane."

"Bye, Uma," says Suresh, rubbing the back of his neck.

Only Aasha says nothing. She scratches her rashes and stares at the plane, hunkered on its heavy haunches on the runway. Poor plane, desperately wishing for some privacy in which to pee. Disdainful of public toilets.

At the very last moment, Amma grabs the stiff scarecrowness of Uma by the shoulders and gives it an arm's-length hug, which gesture makes everyone look away tactfully: Appa pretends to consult his watch; Suresh looks the Visit Malaysia ladies in the eye one after the other, telling each one how nobody's going to be fooled by her fake smile; Aasha goes back to her carpet stains.

Uma walks out to the plane in the sun's breezeless glare. Her knees rub against each other like two starved cats. Aasha lays her hands on the big window, expecting nothing, hoping for little. Maybe Uma has secretly realized she didn't say goodbye to Aasha; maybe she's sorry.

And then, suddenly, so quickly Aasha might have missed it if she'd blinked at the wrong time, Uma turns and waves and smiles right at Aasha, not at her shoes or a spot above her head or a stranger behind them all. That lovely, old-Uma smile they haven't seen in years. Though Aasha forgives everyone else's confusion — at this distance, it's often difficult to know exactly what someone's looking at, so who can blame Amma and Suresh for waving back, or Appa for raising one arm in a stilted salute-cum-wave? — she knows the smile is for her. A tide of understanding washes through her: in that moment she knows where Uma is going and why, and what it means to escape, though as soon as she moves from the window she will find herself searching, once again, for those answers.

As Uma turns away, Aasha peels that smile off the glass and slips it into her pocket.

For what would happen to it if she didn't? It would dry up and fall to the floor, to be swept up by some airport sweeper woman in a uniform. A waste. A travesty.

When she gets home she will crouch in a corner of Uma's empty room to look at the smile in private, but her sweat will have worn away parts of it. Never again will she see it clearly, for of this smile there are no photographs.

At one-thirty they are in the car again, Appa and Amma in front, Suresh, No Uma, and Aasha in the back. Innocent and guilty, knowing and unknowing, hollow and bursting.

Like some oversized, sun-stunned insect on an aimless expedition, the silver Volvo creeps along, full of the heavy smell of hot leather. Suresh and Aasha stare out their respective windows. Sun in their eyes. Long way to go. Hungry thirsty headache stomachache nasty car smell no more oldest. Suresh's palms are slick, and a boil is burgeoning on his tongue, just as he predicted, from all Amma's unwanted attention. "Terrible heat," Amma says every now and then. "As soon as we reach we'll have to have a nice cold drink." Peering into her visor mirror, she peels off her sparkly adhesive pottu and then sticks it back onto the same spot between her eyebrows.

On Kingfisher Lane the sun lies straight ahead, liquid as an egg yolk in the valley between two distant limestone hills, quivering, ready, turning the surrounding foliage to gold. Closer and closer they draw to its beating light, and then, without warning—in the split second when Appa takes his foot off the accelerator for no clear reason—the sun looses itself, slides down into the foothills, and surges out into the street. It brings the water in the monsoon drains to a boil and singes the whiskers of stray cats. It crisps the ants on the asphalt and scorches the grass on the verges. It rolls all the way down the street and finally, against the windscreen of the Volvo, comes to a reluctant rest.

They close their eyes and lean back. "Foof!" Appa sighs. "Hell of a bloody tired." Too tired even for a nice cold drink when they go indoors. In their separate places they lie down—Appa in his study, Amma in her bed upstairs, Suresh sitting up at the dining table, Aasha on the PVC settee. Wherever each one is, they all hear Chellam sniffing and tossing, tossing and rolling to find a single cool spot in her bed.

But that stifling day gives way to a cool, breezy dusk, flickering with mothwings and stars and the gentle regret of the streetlights.

At seven o'clock, Aasha sits on the landing outside Uma's room with *The Wind in the Willows*. Uma never offered to return it for her. Now Aasha will have to keep it for the rest of her life. Perhaps she should bury it in the garden; perhaps she should stuff it into a drawer and pretend it's gone. Pretend she never read it, never had it, never went to the library that day with Uma. If she tries hard enough, she knows, she can force its laminated weight out of her mind, all of it, Toad of Toad Hall, Mole, Water Rat, the Irish Bargewoman, all gone. Failing that, she could, with Suresh's assistance, post it to a charity whose name and address they will find in the phone book. There must be charities that want books. She will tear out the date due slip; she will black out the library stamp with a marker pen.

For now, though, she's too sad to come to a decision. She stands on the landing out of habit, because she has nowhere else to go, and because the gathered guests in Paati's wedding photo have taken it upon themselves to comfort her on this sad night.

Never mind, says a fat lady in a saree with a foot-wide border of gold thread. *Probably—maybe—Uma's thinking of you at this very minute. Don't you think so?*

Just as Aasha's about to nod, a glass-cracking scream shoots through the Balakrishnans' roof and across the violet sky.

The neighbors come out into the street. One unwilling husband is dispatched to the Balakrishnans' house to investigate.

There's smoke in their back yard, snailing out of their back door. But that scream—still vibrating in all their ears—could have been spurred by no burned batch of jelebis, no pot of dhal left to scorch on a forgotten flame.

Amma, her airport makeup smudged, rushes to the gate in her caftan. Chellam shuffles out onto the porch in her Japanese slippers, slow and quiet, pressing her hands to her chest. A little cold. A little afraid that once more Blame will pick its way towards her through the crowds and put its arm around her waist with that eerie, toothless smile, like an old witch who recognizes her without being recognized.

From the window on the landing, Aasha watches.

There are tears and fainting spells, sprinting feet in the street, women rushing about with loose hair. Mrs. Malhotra's grey hair is wet from her evening bath, and her belly trembles under her thin housedress. Mrs. Anthony from house number 27 sinks onto the Balakrishnans' culvert, her batik sarong making a hammock between her stout knees. Even the Malay family from down the street come cautiously out. The mother without her headscarf, her hair a soft bulge under her woolen cap, her lips aflutter as she solicits Allah's mercy under her breath. The father in a cotton singlet. The little girl pale and owlish.

An ambulance arrives, siren blaring, and Mrs. Balakrishnan emerges to sob and bang her head on walls before her stunned audience.

Baldy Wong bursts into song.

In the Big House, Mr. McDougall's daughter steps out of the upstairs bathroom in her patent-leather shoes and walks down the corridor in a perfectly straight line, stately as a bride, hands clasped at her waist, to stand behind Aasha at the window. As the sky darkens, her reflection shows more and more clearly in the glass: her custard-colored skin, her single dimple, her pink ribbons.

"*Now* Kooky Rooky's dead," she says matter-of-factly, though not unkindly. Her clasped hands shake a little; Aasha can tell she's trying to be brave. "This time for sure."

They creep down the stairs to the front door.

There's an odd smell, something burned, yes, but not something on the stove. A thick, sour smell, like insects crisped by a lightbulb, but worse.

Behind the ambulance Mrs. Balakrishnan rocks back and forth as if she is working up the momentum to race down the street. Baldy Wong's mother has emerged to nip and yap worriedly at his shoulders in a low voice that, against her best intentions, carries across the street: "Aiya boy-boy, stop it lah, please lah, people not joking-joking here, you know, you gonna get walloped if you don't watch it. Everybody already so sad and angry and here you with your nonsense! Faster-faster go home. Please. Mummy's good boy."

But Baldy refuses to budge. Cross-eyed and drooling, he belts out his minor-key rendition of a Malay folk song:

> *Rasa sayang, eh, rasa sayang sayang eh*
> *Eh lihat nona jauh*
> *Rasa sayang sayang eh.*
>
> (I've got that loving feeling
> See that woman in the distance
> I've got that loving feeling.)

Amma opens the gate and runs across the street. From the front door Aasha watches her, dry-mouthed, empty-eyed. Only Mr. McDougall's daughter's breath, on Aasha's neck, is moist, for Aasha has no room left in her for grief. Other people's sorrow knocks against her like a spoon seeking a water glass, expecting to draw forth the round, ringing note of a child's innocent sympathy, but finding instead a solid wooden block. Clunk. And then nothing. Humming a tune of her own invention, Aasha strolls out to the gate.

Two men bring a long, blanketed shape out of the Balakrishnans' house on a stretcher, but when they try to load it into the ambulance, Mrs. Balakrishnan blocks their path. She pummels the ambulance windows with her fists; she falls to her knees. She clings to the driver's legs and sobs, and he stands there, bewildered, apologetic, exhausted. Scratching his head, blowing again and again through pursed lips. It's just his job, and he has a cup of masala tea and a new wife both cooling at home.

Mrs. Balakrishnan sees Amma and runs to her, seizing her shoulders, unleashing her demons for this fresh victim. "Aiyo, aiyo, aiyo, I never knew this would happen! Aiyo, aiyo! Who knows how many years of bad luck she has brought onto our house! Why take revenge on us for what her husband did to her? Until I die I'll never forget the sight of her lying there like that! Aiyo, paavam!" She shakes Amma and sinks once more onto her knees, screaming for the solace of her dead mother and her deaf gods. "Aiyo, Amma! Aiyo, saami!"

"Enough, Parvatha," Mr. Balakrishnan barks. Suddenly he's no longer the foolish drunkard rumored to have been beaten, on occasion, by his shrewish wife. "Pull yourself together," he says. "What for all this drama now?"

Mrs. Anthony stands up and grabs Amma's elbow. Aasha sees her thick saliva frothing gleefully at the corners of her mouth, her glasses filmed with cooking oil, but she cannot quite make out her words. Amma's face quakes, her cheeks and brow and jaw on the verge of pulling away from one another like small continents.

"Kooky Rooky burned herself alive," Amma says when she comes home. Almost as matter-of-fact as Mr. McDougall's daughter (who has disappeared, unremarked, into the night). "Poured kerosene on her head and set fire to herself in Mrs. Balakrishnan's kitchen."

The neighbors have all gone home. The splashes of bucket showers drift into the street from the nervous ablutions of people determined to wash off the day's unwholesomeness, Kooky Rooky's restless spirit, the lingering evil luck of what she's done. Not in *their* houses, thank God. A thorough bath and their fortunes should be safe. Too bad for Mrs. B.

Aasha imagines Kooky Rooky with a kerosene tin just like the one Uma used on Paati's chair. Tilting it to pour a little kerosene into one cupped hand and sprinkling this in her loosened hair as though it were holy water. Then hefting the tin with both hands, closing her eyes, emptying its contents onto her shoulders. The kerosene would've gurgled as it poured. Did she light a match or use Mrs. Balakrishnan's stove lighter? Did she change her mind when it was too late? Did she scream a lot, or just once, very loudly?

I'm sure she realized she was damaged goods, Amma will tell Uma in the first of many letters she will write, because now, at last, she's found one motherly duty she can fulfill without having to face her children's supercilious eyes. *After what happened with her so-called husband. Let that be a warning to you when dealing with men.*

Now God himself is up there listening to her lies, Suresh will joke in the note Amma forces him to add at the bottom of that letter. *In our opinion she and God both deserved what they got.* Speaking for Aasha without her permission, for in fact, if asked, she would argue that Kooky Rooky didn't deserve to die writhing in agony on a kitchen floor just because she told a few lies.

Uma will not reply to that letter or any of those that follow it. It will be up to each of them — Appa, Amma, Suresh, Aasha, and Chellam in the red-earthed hell she will inhabit for the last year of her life — to imagine her adventures in America for themselves. With hope and remorse, with longing, with envy, with whatever answers the particular needs of each imaginer.

Appa, never the shrinking violet when it comes to spinning a good story, begins tonight. In his mistress's terrace house in Greentown, he pulls his Chindian children onto his lap and tells them a tale that soars and grips and wrings the breath out of them. He tells them of an aeroplane longer than the entire row of houses on their street; of air stewardesses in batik uniforms; of a foreign land regularly transfixed by such a spell of cold that people eat bacon fat every day and swaddle themselves in wool and feathers. He tells them of a great university hundreds of years old, where Uma, the half-sister they've never met, will study her way to a Nobel Prize. Here on the oily floor of his mistress's kitchen, he finally dares to be proud of Uma. Grants himself the permission to dream for her. Sees New York through her wise, hungry eyes. The autumn leaves, he tells them. The colors. You can't imagine.

If his tale bears certain striking resemblances to the one Uncle Ballroom wove for Uma two and a half years ago, it's because they're brothers, after all, and they've dreamed the same dreams.

He tells his bluff children of Central Park, where Uma will take Sunday afternoon walks; of the beautiful brownstone she will someday own; of how her heels will click up and down the sidewalks of busy streets when she is rich and famous.

And as he speaks his story, it acquires weight and momentum. It breathes. It becomes true. Somewhere in New York, the ghost of Uma Future strides up and down the sidewalks in a stylish trench coat, her heels clicking on the cement. For her, at least, there will be — there already is — a Happily Ever After in which Appa's Chindian children, and his awestruck mistress, and Appa himself, can believe.

In America, he says, his voice low with wonder (for this is the moral of his story, his grand conclusion), anything can happen.

You can go there a nobody, a no-name orphan, and tomorrow find yourself a United States senator.

You can go there starving and crippled, penniless and alone, and tomorrow find yourself a millionaire.

You can go there broken, and tomorrow find yourself whole.

ACKNOWLEDGMENTS

For the chapter on the 1969 riots, I referred to Anthony Reid's article "The Kuala Lumpur Riots and the Malaysian Political System," *Australian Outlook* 23:3, 258–78 (1969).

I also wish to thank:

The MFA Program in Creative Writing and the Hopwood Awards program at the University of Michigan for validation both material and abstract.

My teachers in Michigan and before that for their inspiration and encouragement: Peter Ho Davies, Nicholas Delbanco, Laura Kasischke, Eileen Pollack, Nancy Reisman, and Anne Carson; Jennifer Wenzel, John Dalton, Joanna Scott, Sarah Dunant and Gillian Slovo, Janet Berlo, Hannah Tyson, and Cynthia Thomasz.

My friends and fellow writers at the University of Michigan, especially Uwem Akpan, Jasper Caarls, Ariel Djanikian, Jenni Ferrari-Adler, Joe Kilduff, Taemi Lim, Peter Mayshle, Marissa Perry, Celeste Ng, Phoebe Nobles, and Anne Stameshkin.

Ayesha Pande for loving this book more than I can and untiringly championing its cause.

Anjali Singh for being the most patient, perceptive, engaged editor any writer could hope for.

Mr. Kayes and the members of the Ipoh Talk forum for keeping me connected to my hometown and for their generous answers to my random questions.

My families by blood and by marriage for their love and support.

And most of all, Robert Whelan, for somehow being able to be both my first reader and my best friend.